Ninety Six

A Paninaro Publishing imprint

Social media reception for Ninety

The best fictional story you'll read about the last great youth cult. No matter where you grew up, no matter which clubs you went to, no matter which football team you support; Zico's life is your life. If you know, you know. @Dr_Bass

I identified with Zico almost from the first page. I think we're all a little bit Zico! - @millsy120103

Ninety takes you on a glorious trip of youth culture in the 90's. If you're a fan of terrace fashion, football or recreational drug use and the music that accompanied it during that period, this is a must read. @BazYoung1874

Zico encapsulated everything I felt on my first pill. Even though we're from different generations I connected with him straight away. Fuckin class. @killyrfriends

Football, music, casual clothing. What more could you want. That is until young Stevie journeys through life growing up at the start of THE greatest decade. For most, the extremities may not compare, but we can all relate to Zico in one way or another living through 'Ninety' @LikkleAl

Just finished this cracker of a book. Anyone who experienced the early 90's get it bought. Casuals, raves, nutters and good cunts and a time that changed it all. @gwfitzpatrick

Acknowledgements

To those that bought, begged, stole or borrowed a copy of Ninety. Had you not done so. This book simply would not have existed without your support.

To Pat & Shan Wagner for all the artwork, once again. Without you both, Zico would not have been brought to life in the way that he has been in parts 1&2. Nothing but love for you both x. Also big thanks to Nikki McGowan from Lion Rampant Design for help with the Paninaro Publishing imprint.

Last but most definitely not least, Rachel. Without your love, support and feedback. This novel (in addition to life in general) would not have been the same without you. Love you, PP x

Twitter - @johnnyroc73

Instagram - @johnnyproctor90

Chapter 1

Zico

Dreams can come true, isn't that what those upbeat, reach for the stars happy clapping positive fuckers always say? As much as I can't stand those "it takes more facial muscles to frown than it does to smile" cunts. They do actually have a point. I'm walking talking living proof of that but what they never seem to mention is that by achieving and living out your dreams. Doing so can lead to a ridiculous amount of small print.

On the face of it, to any clubber making their annual pilgrimage to Ibiza, I could only have been looked upon as someone living their best life. With their (at times all too often accurate) stereotypes of me playing to thousands in the most cool and stylish of clubs while all the time having drugs and women thrown at me from north, south, east and fucking west. That's the thing about those tinted spectacled romanticised visions that people can have though. They only see the *good* side of things. They never seem to consider that while I was dropping "Insomnia" on them out there on the dance floor at 5am when they were off their tits. I'd still be awake 12 hours later while they were sleeping away their previous nights excesses down on S'Arenal de San Antonio while soaking up the sun.

On my side of the curtain though? Badly sleep deprived and nursing a sore head that felt like there was a sword fight going off inside it and a strange girl still lying in my bed. Identity unknown. The reason for this was because it wasn't one of your run of the mill British names. After her telling me twice what it was and me left still no further forward and knowing I'd be wasting everyone's time by asking a third time, I sacked it. Her having went into overtime and lying through there in bed and invading my "quiet time" was fucking up my whole equilibrium.

I needed her gone but considering some of what we'd gotten up to since getting back to mines. It would've been pretty poor form from me if I'd woken her from the deep slumber she was in and asked her to vacate the premises. When I'd got up to leave her lying there fast asleep I had that Ice Cube line from "It Was a Good Day" flash through my head. "So deep so deep, put her ass to sleep." I'd been actually feeling pretty fucking chuffed with myself there and then as I dealt with that particular thought at the time but that had been hours ago by then.

I sat through in the living room putting the finishing touches to a shamefully poor attempt at a joint while pondering just how I was going to get rid of her. Apart from the all too real and undeniable fact that I was working later on. There was the matter of the big box of white labels that had been lying outside the front door of the villa when we'd arrived back from Playa den Bossa that needed addressed.

You're left in absolutely no doubt that you've kicked the arse out of Space when you get back home after the postie has been because those San Antonio postmen aren't exactly what you'd call pro fucking active.

I know getting a pile of exclusive and yet to be released records for free is something that should eternally be considered a privilege but when you've been up for near on 36 hours and have a mindset that would generally come with the order for the removal of all sharp objects from reach. Sometimes things aren't all that black and white. Add to all of that, a woman in your bed that, to your own self loathing, you knew you shouldn't have brought back and now need to get shot. Stack up all of those factors and you may well find that you're not so much in the mood to sift through, what appears at that moment to be, an endless amount of vinyl.

That's decent enough if you're the type who has the whole luxury of choice. Prerogatives and all that. Only, your options are severely reduced in that respect when you're opening for your DJ hero, Carl Cox in around 10 hours time on the decks at the legendary Amnesia. There could well have been a couple of diamonds in amongst the predictable dirt inside that box of white labels. The kind of big tune that would have the ability to make a clubbers night when dropped at the right moment.

With the prospect of "Coxy" actually around to hear me play, I especially wanted to bring out a few surprise tunes that hardly anyone (if at all) in the room would've known even existed. From talking to others inside the industry I'd already heard that Carl Cox was absolutely golden with the other deejays he'd play with wherever he was. A proper godfather of the scene and supportive to all the younger deejays on their way up in the business.

Since last week when my manager Lee had informed me that Erick Morillo had dropped out of his Amnesia appearance and that he'd bagged me the spot to fill in on the night before Cox. I'd tried not to let it affect me but in all honesty, the thought of playing on the same bill as who I looked on as House Music royalty made me nauseous.

Here I was though, hours away from it and I could not have been so poorly prepared had I tried. Any chance of sleep before heading up to the club had been and gone. Precious snoozing time had been substituted for time in bed with *insert name* then, after we were done and she'd passed out. I'd elected to pass on sleeping in favour of sitting watching Only Fools and Horses episodes and smoking Moroccan Double Zero while simultaneously sweating out the same amount as I took in of water inside the searing heat of the living room.

I glanced upwards and laughed at the irony of the fact that there was an industrial sized fan attached to the ceiling, that didn't work. It had stopped working the first week I had moved in and due to the partying lifestyle that I'd embarked on since arriving on the island. I'd never gotten round to fixing it. Well, gotten round to calling *someone* to come and fix it. Given the fact that I can't even wire a plug it was probably best for all concerned that I didn't fuck about with electrics. Proper smacks of "Brit dies abroad in freak electrical accident" newspaper headlines, that.

It had been a bit of an intense introduction to my latest instalment of the summer season in Ibiza. I had only arrived two weeks before and by then still hadn't even emptied out my suitcase. From the afternoon I arrived it had been a worrying and carnage filled amalgamation of work and partying. The predictable too much drugs, regrettable sex and not enough sleep. Kind of like any other visitor to the island I suppose but the key difference being that those bastards get to go home again after a couple of weeks to get their heads and shit together. I mean, I walked into the wrong room in Manumission last week and saw a man sucking his own cock whilst a dwarf sat in the corner playing FIFA Ninety Five on the Playstation. That's what I was up against.

It would take the average person the whole fortnight of their holiday to try and shift that image from their minds alone. There I was though. Two weeks in and already of a broken state of mind and I, understandably, was already fearing for what version of Steven Duncan that would be returning back to Scotland at the end of the residency. With the best part of a couple of months still scheduled, the only real certainty was that things would get a lot fucking worse before they got better.

I was about halfway through the "Jolly Boys Outing" Christmas special episode when I heard some muffled noises coming from the bedroom. I'd specifically chosen the extended episode to assist me in the next level procrastinating that I was performing at. The aim? I simply wanted to avoid listening to the promos I'd been sent. To listen to them would be to plan my set for the night and I was hours away from expending such energy. That could all wait. Well, actually it couldn't fucking wait. Without doubt the most important set in my six years of behind the decks. What it might mean for my career? It was a night that needed to be taken seriously by myself, that, despite the slowly setting in psychosis, I had still managed to grasp and recognise the gravity of it all.

I made peace with myself over the fact that I was evidently in no frame of mind to be picking out some bangers amongst all of that vinyl and *then* finding out a way to merge them alongside some of the other tracks I'd been playing over the previous few weeks. I promised myself that I'd be in a better frame "in a while" so swerved all of it in favour of watching the regulars of The Nags Head jumping on a clapped out bus and going on a bender to Margate. All of my plans proved academic the second I heard the bedroom door opening down the hall.

Turning around, I watched as she walked towards me. Sleepy smile on her face and apparently wearing one of the t shirts that I'd been given by Pepe at Space after my set on the terrace the previous night. Cheeky hoor, it's only cute when a girl wears a guys t shirt the next morning *after* it has become one of his old ones and a piece of clothing that she's found randomly lying around. When she has gone to the trouble of actually taking a t shirt out of its fucking wrapper and removing the tags then that kind of takes the edge off things in my opinion.

As she got closer to me though it became clearly obvious that the t shirt thing was a mere side issue compared to her hair. She looked like the fucking singer from The Cure. She even had some smudged make up on from the night before which, coincidentally, complimented the Robert Smith barnet to an absolute tee. I'd already been filled with deep regret over bringing her back to the villa with me and in that moment, seeing what was walking towards me, I truly hated myself.

'Hola, sexee' she said in a deliciously alluring Spanish accent that completely betrayed the appearance of the girl that was in front of me. All I had in me was an in no way convincing half smile back in her direction. I'd obviously been wanting her out of my bed for hours by then but in achieving that it would've then placed me in the position of having to talk to her. Something I wasn't ready for. Is anyone really ready for that next day awkward conversation with the person that they hardly know yet have spent hours having sex with though?

She sat down beside me on the sofa while on the TV, Rodney Trotter was being huckled by the police after hitting one of them with a fitba. I reckon the copper went down a bit too easy to be fair to the boy, Trotter. I don't even need to add the fact that had "Wodders" actually *meant* to hit the police officer with the ball then the cunt should've been playing for Brazil.

I had one eye on him getting escorted away and one on her as she joined me. Without any kind of warning she moved in for a cuddle. One that I was in no way ready for. As she moved in on me I, while in a sitting position, recoiled back away from her until I had nowhere further to go. Fucking hell, talk about setting your stall out with someone. Her smile dropped like a tonne of bricks. It was a complete overreaction on my part admittedly but I had that whole Robert Smith stuff in my head and to give me a wee bit of credit, she *did* look fucking horrendous. 'Oh, you be this way with me now?' she asked with a hurt look on her face. 'You were happy to hug after you get your dick sucked huh?'

That one line from her gave me way too many things to think about all at once. I had the flashback of her, there on her knees in front of me last night through in the bedroom which, as nice a thought it was it, wasn't the most important thing to take away from what she said. Instead I had to focus on the fact that, sat beside me, she was now using the fact that she'd given me oral as a stick to beat me with the next morning. My head couldn't deal with any kind of confrontation. Not then.

'No, no' (It would've been an ideal time to have known her name to throw it in for reasons of sincerity) 'You get me wrong' I said with what felt like a concerned look on my face as I tried to stop her rage by stroking her arm as I spoke to her. 'I feel absolutely ruined right now, I've barely slept for 2 days and my mind body and soul are absent, even the thought of a hug right now gives me the fear' I felt that with what I was saying being technically true it was able to give me more credibility as I spoke to her. She didn't need to know what was really in my mind and the dark turns it had started to take.

To kiss or hug her was the equivalent of snogging and cuddling with a goth. Not in this life, amigo. She didn't look too impressed although, I'm not quite sure how much of me she was actually understanding. Just because someone can speak English as a second language that doesn't always (as in, ever) mean that they can understand Scots. I'm rattling off some spiel about how I needed to sleep for a week never mind playing the biggest set of my DJ career ahead of my fucking hero while she's sat there with a look on her face that's saying 'calm down, mate, I only wanted a hug, don't need to hear your life story eh?'

When I paused for a second to catch a breath, she took her chance. 'Baby, I understand. You need to live better or you break down. You don't worry a thing, I look after you, I be the best girlfriend for you.' As twisted as I was feeling I was still pretty sure that she'd just sat there and referred to herself as my girlfriend. Under any other circumstances that would have been met head on but I couldn't face it. Instead, I opted to completely and conveniently ignore it. I just wanted her away and out of my own private maximum occupancy of one cocoon that I wanted to hide out in until my performance later on at Amnesia. From the moment that I'd heard her coming out of the bedroom that had been my one and only goal. Be a hermit.

'So what's your plans for today?' I asked her in that smalltalk way your hairdresser will ask you if you're going on holidays anywhere this summer or how you ask a taxi driver if he's been busy. 'I just relax all day, chill, then get ready for tonight.' She said this exactly at the same time she appeared to make herself more comfy on the sofa by pulling her feet up to her side. 'Better not get yourself comfy, darling as you'll be out of here within the hour,' I thought to myself. 'Oh where are you off to tonight?' I asked. 'Amnesia to see you play, silly man' she laughed back at me.

'You put me on VIP of course' She added. I nodded back to her while already making the decision to actually *not* have her name down on VIP. Leave it off said list and then ride out whatever fallout would come as a result. If there was one thing that I knew was a certainty it was that with me being here for a few months in the Balearics. She wasn't going to be the first or last person that I was going to end up pissing off. It's kind of what I do. I get up, I piss someone off, I go to sleep again. It's simple.

It is of course a lot more achievable to do when you're dealing with complete lunatics like she appeared to be. There was undoubtably some "missing scenes" from the night before. Sex had definitely taken place and over a prolonged period of the morning but even so. Where did she get the girlfriend stuff from? That it hadn't come from me, the only fact that I knew.

'I've got so much to do before now and my set tonight' I said in one of those "well, you might be doing fuck all today but I've got lots" kind of ways. It didn't seem to register with her in the way that I'd intended as she gingerly stretched over to the table to pick up the lighter and ashtray with half a joint sat in it. 'Awwww poor baby, my heart bleeds for you that you need to play to thousands in the club and get paid lots of pesetas for it' she giggled as she sparked up the J.

We sat and had a brief chat about the night before. What Space had been like and some of what went on over the night and morning. Through talking together a lot of the missing scenes began to return to me. The two of us had started speaking in the VIP area while Sasha and Digweed were playing. What had got my attention from her wasn't her looks or the predictable sycophantic patter I'd occasionally hear from strangers after I'd played a set.

It was that she'd once stayed not far from me when at university that had stuck out. I was taken in by the novelty of it to begin with.

I mean, you should always expect the unexpected in an Ibizan nightclub but even so. Finding yourself sat in Space out of your tits with some Spanish It girl who's talking to you about Anstruther fish and chips was still quite utterly bizarre. Of course, as the morning had went on and the two of us became a lot more wrecked. Me, fuelled by my own sense of sexual selfishness was eventually asking her if she wanted to come back with me to San Antonio.

The rest, as they say, was history.

Just as she appeared to be settling down for the afternoon with no apparent looks of going anywhere. I hit her with the bombshell. 'So would you like to have a shower or anything before you go?' She seemed confused by this. I'm not sure why this was as I felt that despite my lack of motor skills. I'd been short yet polite and very clear without any nastiness to go with it. I was effectively saying that it was time to leave, she'd left me with no real choice.

'Baby? Amnesia isn't for a long time yet. There is no need for shower yet, silly man' she giggled while confirming that what I'd said had went right over that fucking birds nest of a head of hers.

Worse still, unless I had misheard her I was sure that she was saying that she was intending on hanging around for the whole day. 'No, I *know* Amnesia isn't for a while yet, what with me being on the bill and all' I tried to joke before I explained to her in more basic terms that I wanted her to go.

'I was meaning that if you wanted to have a shower before you left here and went back home. You're from San Antonio too aren't you?' I asked half hoping that this piece of information that I was sure I knew from the night before hadn't been just made up pish and that in fact while in this part of the island she wasn't left high and dry. That as a reality would've made it a lot more harder to get rid of her.

'I have a lot to do before tonight's set, I'd love to sit chilling with you but I've got too much on,' I said, hoping that this would be understood.

'Like what?' She replied looking none too happy with the penny that had finally dropped.

I managed to fight off the initial reaction to tell her that it was none of her fucking business. Hadn't even known her for a day and in my book that does not earn one the right to give it the "like what's" and definitely not in the tone that she'd put it across to me. Sounding like some nagging wife when trying to catch out her husband over why he got back late from the pub. Full on Gestapo mode, likes.

Whilst I was able to bite my lip so to speak with regards to the way she'd spoken to me That didn't mean that I was able to keep my sarcasm under a tight leash. 'Well you know how when you'll go to Space or Amnesia and there'll be deejays up there playing music to dance to?' I was pretty much being rhetorical anyway so didn't bother waiting for a response. 'And for these deejays to work their magic they have to actually plan their set, which tracks they're going to play, when they'll play them and in which order?' 'And unless I haven't mentioned it a thousand times in the past 12 hours, I'm warming up for CARL FUCKING COX tonight and by this point I haven't a scoobie what I'm playing, I've got a shit load of new vinyl to listen through before I can even plan things for tonight.'

'I still do not see why you cannot do this and me still be here, I won't get in your way' she said all puppy dog eyes and trying to put on a cute face but one that had me with that fucking "Love Cats" song running through my head. She'd have actually had a point had her and I been some kind of an item. Doing every day stuff in each others' company. We weren't one though, even if this lunatic goth woman had seemingly deludedly taken on this impression.

She didn't take my hints nor my outright blatancy and I began to question if it was a cultural thing or in fact she knew fine well what I was getting at and was deliberately being a bit of a brat with me. 'Look, how much clearer do I need to make this?' my patience starting to crack. 'Tonight is the biggest night of my life, literally THE biggest. I'm nowhere near ready for it because of my activities the past 3 nights. I need some space and peace to prepare, por favor.'

She didn't appear pleased. She reached over for the lighter to relight the joint that had went out long ago after the solitary toke that she'd taken when she'd come through and joined me on the sofa. Taking a long toke of it she looked straight at me, blowing the smoke in my face before screaming 'LIAR, LIESSS.'

Fuck, that was the best part. I was telling her the fucking truth. Ok, I hadn't added the part about me having a friendly face come round with some of Escobar's finest once she'd left. That was very much deliberate from me. I've seen these girls that are always at the big nights. If she got wind that there was Coke being dropped off then she'd have never fucking left, at least until after all the Ching was finished anyway.

The powder itself was needed much more than for the standard recreational use by me. It was the exact reason why I hadn't panicked too much over the fact I was leaving my Amnesia set until later in the afternoon. A couple of lines up my conk and I'd breeze my way through those white labels that had taken on the importance of not looking at in the way as if the box had been fucking Medusa.

I couldn't exactly have guaranteed what quality of tunes I'd have picked out by the end mind you. I'll fully admit that listening to and choosing tracks when you're high can sometimes bite you on the behind. Let's face it, things generally appear to better when you're high. This is fact. That schoolboy error I committed years back when I decided to have a couple of pipes of Hash in the train toilets on the way to Glasgow to get some new vinyl at 23rd Precinct.

By the time I'd got through to the Weeg I was fucking wrecked and after I got the obligatory pile of vinyl to listen through inside the shop handed to me I'd spent almost £200 on records. Everything just sounded amazing, one track after the other. By the time I got home and listened through them again on my own decks I then found out that I'd spent a good £100 on absolute shite that would never see the light of day.

Never the less, this was not really all going to go down through choice on my part. In my own ideal world I'd have had days to prepare for the set. Ironically the kind of preparation that I *would* go through back when I started out and would be gearing up for a low key night in front of a few hundred people. In a complete apples to naranjas move I'm playing in front of thousands, one of them being someone I looked up to in the scene and with hours left didn't even know which song I was starting with.

'YOU HAVE ANOTHER GIRL COMING ROUND BASTAAAD' She went completely radge, throwing the lighter against the wall. It must've made impact in an unfortunately specific angled way because I saw the pokey bit from inside the lighter detaching from the rest of it.

The mind does its own thing at times like that I suppose but while I should've been more concerned by the fact that this Spanish girl was, by the looks of things, kicking right off. My thought process was one of that it was going to take ages to find that pokey bit from the lighter again.

'What?' My reaction was one of more disbelief than anything else. This didn't even make sense. The way she was reacting and why she was reacting the way she was. Pragmatically I wasn't ruling out drugs. You meet a lot of weird and (not so) wonderful people in Ibiza but like it or fucking lump it, drugs are always there. If you're unlucky enough to spend part of your night and then the next day when the comedown has set in. You'll see the full gamut of that person. Sometimes you'll wish you hadn't and I fully understand that there might be others out there who will say the same thing and have me in mind.

'You got what you wanted from me, I LET YOU PUT YOUR DICK IN MY ASS.' - 'Fucking hell, I'd forgotten about the anal stuff,' I thought to myself. 'You fucking deejays, you think you are Jesus fucking Christ.'

I definitely didn't need to justify anything to her but yet her insinuation that I was going to be shagging within the hour showed me that she hadn't truly grasped what a complete shell of a man she was sharing a living room with. I don't think I would've even had a wank in me and yet she's got me down as getting the old sword out again for the day with some other lucky lady. En guard ya cunts.

'Well while I'm flattered that you have the impression that I have girls lined up around the corner all taking a ticket like they're at the butchers I'm actually ..' I was done with diplomacy. 'Look, I hinted earlier on over the fact that I needed you to leave, normally someone else picks up on that fact. You haven't though and now I'm actually *telling* you that you need to go, and fuck your shower.'

She made to say something but for whatever reason, thought better of it. Instead she chose to get up off the sofa and storm back through to the bedroom. My instinct was to grab the joint from the ashtray and spark it up. Of course though, no fucking lighter. Well, two pieces of lighter in and around the living room but as predicted, from my seating point I could only make out the main body of it lying on the ceramic tiled floor.

Reluctantly, I got up from the sofa and walked through to the kitchen to get a light from the cooker. While up there I could hear the racket that was going on through in the bedroom. She'd elected to turn to her native tongue to release some of the rage that was evidently needing to get itself out. You know how the Spaniards talk about a hundred miles an hour, especially when they're annoyed about something? Well that was her. She was obviously taking me for a mug though thinking that I didn't recognise some of the words.

'Hate to break it to you sweetheart but I know what Puta means' I couldn't resist shouting down the hall to her. I'd learned that particular insult during my previous Ibiza stint the year before when, innocently, I was walking along the street wearing a Barca top and some boy in a passing car leant out the window and shouted it at me as it passed by.

'Vete a la mierda' she shouted back at me with us still separated by the closed door.

Now that one, I didn't know but made a mental note to find out. Always trying to pick up extra bits of the lingo where I can. Oh aye, a big advocate of trying to make friends when in another country and there's no better way than showing your willingness to talk their language. They lap that stuff up.

It felt pretty surreal, the two of us arguing in this fashion no holds barred. It definitely had the air of an argument between a couple who knew each other well, stayed together likes. Not between two people who barely knew the square route of fuck all about each other.

The (assumed) insults were coming thick and fast from the bedroom but she was going way too fast for me to understand her. I let her get on with it. Intermittently shouting a random insult back at her. In no doubt that while I wasn't able to understand her she was most likely suffering the same affliction on her side. All the time we'd spent at Space together I'd been speaking in the accent that I normally adopt when I'm away from Scotland.

When you're Scottish and travel abroad you soon get sick of having to repeat almost every single thing that comes out your mouth and eventually you find yourself talking slightly different to how you normally do. You barely even know you're doing it yourself. That measured way of speaking had been kicked to the side in the heat of the moment as I unleashed my inner Scot on her. 'You no ready yet? Time you fucking bolted, darling' I shouted through to her. I had decided she had five more minutes to come back out or I was going in there to get her. They were minutes that I wouldn't need.

She came back out a changed woman, literally. Roberto Smith was now gone and she'd transformed back into the tidy looking girl that I'd been so drawn to when we'd started talking back at Space.

Watching her walk back down the hall in that short flowery dress and those high heels, giving it the whole proper sexy strut. I was given a reminder *why* she was actually there in my house in the first place. Weirdly, she was walking towards me with a warm friendly smile on her face. Almost as if those crazy ten minutes between us hadn't even happened.

I stood there trying to work out what the fuck was going on. I was ready for her coming back out tooled up and ready for a fight to the death and instead she comes out with a killer smile and heels to match. 'I let you do your important things, baby. You must prepare for tonight.' She said as she walked into the kitchen where I was still standing, once again relighting the joint from the cooker.

Not one single word from her about what had gone on before with her spitting the dummy. I stood there leaning back against the kitchen bunker nodding my head in agreement with her while I tried to weigh up the situation. 'I'll see you out' I added as I motioned for her to move with me. There was so much that my instincts were telling me to say. Proper devil and angel on the shoulder stuff.

Half of me wanted to give her a piece of my mind over her coming into my house and acting the way she had. The other side to me wanted to say some completely fabricated pish about how it had been a good night and we should do it again some time. Wisely I kept my mouth shut on the short walk to the front door. You always do feel the need to say something though but there really is no better strategy than keeping your fucking mouth shut.

Once she stepped over the threshold she wheeled round unexpectedly and launched herself into a hug that wasn't so much one way and more ninety nine percent from her and a token percent from me. She obviously sensed this and broke off from it as quickly as she'd began. Sometimes words aren't needed. I could tell by the sheepish look on her coupon that she knew she'd fucked up with that whole psycho killer qu'est-ce performance. Little did she know it was academic. I already wanted rid of her *before* she showed her nutter properties so it was hardly a dealbreaker when she turned out to be that way. More a pain in the arse than anything else.

'So I see you tonight' she said all matter of fact as she readjusted the positioning of her handbag over her shoulder. The mad thing was that I wasn't even surprised by that. The past hour I'd seen her refer to herself as my girlfriend, break my fucking Clipper, accuse me of shagging another girl in addition to calling me more names than I could even comprehend. 'Fuck it,' I thought to myself. If she's as mental as that then I'm not going to reach her. There's fucking doctors out there that couldn't fix her, I imagined, so there was no point in me complicating things as far as my own day went, was there?

'Yeah I'll leave your name on the door for the guest list' I replied which produced a big smile from her and for a second I thought she was going to hug me again. 'Bueno, babee' she beamed. 'Amnesia is going to love you, I love you.' I skilfully and diplomatically dealt with this madness with a playful 'No you don't senora you just love the VIP now get your sexy booty out of here and let me get to work.'

Fuck knows why I do this shit sometimes, mainly because my head, in that moment, couldn't deal with the reality of having to live through an awkward couple of minutes with some girl that (hopefully) I'd never see again in my puff. Instead though I'm happy to joke around with her in the way that a couple would do and definitely two people that will be seeing each other again would carry on.

Anyway, she skipped away, on top of the world oblivious to the fact that when she turned up at Amnesia later on she would be getting hit with the whole "your name's not down you're not coming in" embarrassing stuff and in that moment as I watched her depart, that was the most important thing to me. That she was on her way. All of the rest involving her and that insane notion that her and moi were a couple was just noise as far as I was concerned.

I had a quick look at my watch, a rough guesstimate gave me around five hours before I'd have to start getting ready and myself up to the club. That in itself sounded like plenty of time and all aligned with my earlier thoughts of getting rid of, fuck, I wish I'd learned her name, and it all clicking into place. As much time as I appeared to have. I knew that the reality of the situation was that the walls were closing in. I wasn't going near that pile of records until I was more alert and for that to happen I was going to need the assistance of the most unpredictable, transient and reprobate of a drug dealer.

I grabbed my Motorola and hit the obligatory speed dial number one. He answered after a couple of rings, like he'd been sitting on his phone waiting on the call coming.

'Alright, Zeec. What's good?'

'Well not very fucking much, mate. You're going to change that though when you get here' I had no time for any kind of smalltalk. I felt a bit shitty, actually. Didn't even ask him how he was on his side. Just launched myself right into the whole "sell me drugs" line of conversation from second one.

'What's been going on?' He asked.

'I'll tell you about it when you get here' I repeated. 'What were you up to last night anyway? Never clocked you at any point inside Space.' I asked him while it had entered my mind. He just gave me a laugh that suggested there was more to it when he replied that he'd ended up going to Manumission before adding 'details to follow, mate. Give me half an hour, what is it you want? Ching?' With him being out on the street. The final part was hushed right down to the point I could barely hear it. 'Aye, Ching, and as much of it as you've got on you' I confirmed. He laughed back before hanging up. I wasn't joking.

Chapter 2

Eva

I was in the middle of painting my toenails as I lay out in the mid morning sun when I heard the roar of the engine from the car coming up the drive. I'd already assumed that it was his Audi due to how secluded our hacienda was. There were no salesman, charity seekers or wrong turners that ever came close. Absolutely nada. If you were coming up the drive to our homestead then as far as my husband was concerned. You better have had a bloody good reason for doing so. It was the ultimate in a paradox, the hacienda. Unquestionably the lap of luxury we were living in but my god did it get lonely at times. I wanted for nothing, Luciana and Camila our two maids saw to that.

The only "jobs" that I had was lying on the sun lounger reading and generally making myself the presentable young trophy wife that I'd long since realised he saw me as. There was also the little care packages from my mum back home containing stacks of video tapes with Coronation Street on them. It felt plain weird though actually sitting watching them during the day time however. All I did when I lived in Moss Side was moan about the rain and it felt just hypocritical to be sat indoors watching a U.K soap opera when it was over thirty degrees outside.

It had taken me a while to get used to my new surroundings. New country, language, food and obscenely warmer climate. Laughably, I'm living in the house and grounds of my dreams, money without question no object. Any designer clothes I want, I get. I don't need to lift a finger and I'll have any meal that I ask for served up at my request. All of that was more than I could possibly have imagined but it still hadn't been enough to prevent me from being homesick to start off with.

It's crazy to think that I was homesick considering if I was to reverse things. I'd be walking in the pissing rain to my job in that coffee shop, maybe take a little look in Topshop on the way home to see if I could pick out something to wear for the weekend for going out raving with the girls then back home once again in the pissing rain to make lasagne for one for myself.

It was just a little cut off out there and would've been good to have had a few friends around now and again. Some company, any company. We all need that and I'd admit. Considering I was in a foreign country miles from Britain. That was a case of magnified times a thousand.

Yeah, of course it got lonely, with what occupation my husband had and the hours and days it would keep him away for at a time. We had our bigger picture planned though. It wasn't always going to be like that. We were only there *through* work and the plan had been for an early retirement and us moving back closer to something that the two of us could call home.

I didn't know what his hurry was but he was racing up the long drive so fast he was kicking up dust behind the car from the gravel of the driveway. It unsettled me enough for to get myself up from the sun lounger and walk over to the balcony on the other side of the pool to greet my darling hubby who, as far as I had been led to believe, was gone for the day and not due home until evening.

The car skidded to a stop but before he'd even got out I could see through the windscreen and the look on his face that something wasn't right. Actually from what was looking back up at me. Things appeared to be a long way from fine and dandy.

'Eva, darling I'll explain later but we need to leave and we need to leave NOW. Grab whatever you need, clothes, possessions. Whatever you cannot possibly live without but isn't bigger than a suitcase then now's your chance. I'll get the passports from the safe.' He was in my favourite Hugo Boss suit of his but yet looked a mess. Despite the obvious heat factor he'd never been one for showing it, even in a suit. Yet there in front of me he was sweating more than someone who had pulled a hamstring slap bang in the middle of the Pamplona bull run.

His tie, which was never ever in the state of short of an exemplary Windsor Knot was loosened off with the top shirt button undone.

He said this while running from the car and up the front side stairs to join me. Despite the fact that he obviously was looking for me to have been triggered by this point. I was stood there frozen in the way that someone probably would be had they been rudely taken out of their own personal bubble. Stood there still holding the bottle of nail polish. All I could muster was a pathetic 'Wh w what? Passports? Wh wh why?' He looked like he'd seen a ghost. Actually, it was one of those moments where you see your partner with a look on their face that despite, how long you've been together, you've never seen *that* face across them. He looked almost scared and that alone scared me by association.

'Well, come on, chop chop, this isn't a drill' he said as he ran past me into living room. Evidently he wasn't in any mood to stop and chat. Sensing the urgency that he was displaying I managed to give myself a shake and ran after him to try and get some backstory over the fact that my husband had just appeared out of the blue acting very strangely and talking about us leaving our home as soon as possible. It wasn't exactly normal behaviour by any means from a husband and I don't think that there would've been a woman on this planet who would not have had a list of questions as long as your arm to ask about it all.

I followed him into the study, he didn't seem aware of this. This confirmed when I spoke out while he had his back to me as he attempted to open the safe. It looked like he wasn't making a good job of the safe due to the reckless speed he was trying to unlock it.

'What the hell is going on here? You appear unexpectedly and give me minutes of a warning for to get ready and leave? It takes me around ten minutes to put those bloody contact lenses in alone, you know what I'm like with them.' He about jumped out his skin at the sound of my voice behind him, so preoccupied he was with getting the safe open.

'Darling what are you still doing here? You should be about packed by now. Why aren't you listening to me here? We need to leave, not this evening, not tomorrow or next week. We need to go NOW so please do me a favour here and go ... and .... get .... packed ... comprende?' The patronising prick stood there talking back as he finally got the door to the safe open, fishing out a serious amount of American

Dollars in addition to what looked like half a dozen passports. There was a lot more than was needed by us that's all I knew.

I'd never been inside the safe. It hadn't been something that, despite being married to each other, had never been considered my business and I had been happy enough with that arrangement. Obviously I assumed that there would've been money in there but the wad of passports took me surprise. 'At least he's not got a gun in there,' I laughed to myself. That was about a second before he then brought out the handgun from inside. I think he was so far into his own state of survival mode at that point that he never registered what must've been my visible shock upon seeing it.

He put it down on the desk beside the other items like he was putting down the remote for the tv and walked up to me. He took his hands and gently placed them on both of my cheeks and for a second managed to stop and breathe and stared deep into my eyes as if he was looking into my soul.

'Eva, do you trust me?' - 'Of course I do' I replied, starting to fight back tears over how scared he was making me. 'Then trust me when I say that it is of great importance that we get out of here' - 'b b bbbut why? What've you done? Where are we going? Are we coming back here?' I was full of questions that I'd already assumed he wasn't going to answer.

That was proved when he brushed past me out of the study, shoving the money, passports and gun into a leather Dior bag before running upstairs to the bedroom to grab some clothes. Offering me yet another reminder as he frantically made his way to the bottom of the stairs that I needed to be doing the same.

I rushed after him, following up the stairs behind while constantly looking for answers from him that he either didn't want to give me or, like he had insinuated, he didn't have the time. The circus that was soon taking place upstairs in our master bedroom looked every inch the scene that you would imagine accompanying the scenario where a couple have to get packed in an extreme hurry.

Clothes were being thrown all over the place to the point that within minutes it looked like our home had been burgled. Clothes, shoes and random possessions were scattered all over the floor and bed. While trying to find my most favourite pair of Louboutins. I turned round to see what he was doing and I was instantly drawn to the checked Burberry polo shirt that was spinning round and around up above. Apparently caught on our bedroom ceiling fan. It pretty much summed up the state of affairs inside the room.

I heard the zip going around on the suitcase. Followed by a 'right, time to go, vamos.' He stood there looking down at me tapping on his watch. 'Yeah some hope of that,' I thought to myself.j I barely had half a dozen items inside my own case. 'I NEED MORE TIME' I barked barked back at him. The stress and worry of everything finally beginning to take over. 'Have you been listening to a single fucking word I've said to you since I got here? WE DON'T HAVE ANY MORE TIME' He snapped back. Whatever that was left of his patience now having seemingly expired.

I felt a little wounded by his tone but knew no good would come out of it if I argued back. I met him with silence. I'm not sure if it was through feeling bad at how he'd spoken to me or simply through the panic he was in but he attempted to help me by indiscriminately grabbing some of my clothes and cramming them into my suitcase. As is normally the case when men are trying to help. He only made things worse. I immediately saw a Versace dress crumpled up in there, one that I'd not had on in over a year and therefore not exactly something I'd be wearing anytime soon, wherever we were heading. 'I can't find my Louboutins' I said out loud more in frustration than intended for him.

'Forget them, I'll get you another pair.' He said in what sounded like an attempt at a compromise. While I appreciated his apparent sentiment. With the greatest of respect, he didn't have a clue what he was talking about. 'You can't just get me another pair, they're the same ones that Princess Diana wore at the Taj Mahal. You can't buy them now, it wasn't even a case of being *able* to even buy when they were available. Telling me that you're going to get me another pair you'd be as well adding that you'll have Lord Lucan gift wrap them for me' I informed him while continuing the search.

'Well, Eva. How do I sugar coat the next thing that leaves my mouth? Actually, screw it, there's no sugar coating anything here. Shoes?

Darling what good will your fucking shoes be if you're six feet under the ground?' He said, in doing so completely securing my attention.

He'd never looked more serious in all the time we'd been together. Due to the sheer surprise of him arriving in the way that he had minutes before and how quickly things had escalated since then. I'd had a hard time attaining any kind of controlled and measured thinking. Only a few minutes before I'd seen my husband take a handgun from out of our safe while acting erratically yet moments later I'm freaking out over not finding a pair of shoes.

It took his last comment however for it all to click into place for me and if what he was hinting at actually was what I was taking out of it then yes. In the scheme of things the shoes now were not as important as I may have initially thought. Now I "got" why he looked so worried. It was unquestionably a work thing and whilst he'd protected me from most of what went on when he was "at the office." I wasn't stupid either.

The less I knew the better he'd always told me. My role was to just enjoy the fruits of my husbands labours. Unashamedly I did.

'Shit, are things that bad?' I asked, frozen to the spot. I'd hoped that he'd only said the comment about being six feet under as an attempt to get me to move myself but I knew he wouldn't joke about something like that. The look on his face doubled down on that he was indeed deadly serious, deadly. 'I'm afraid so. God only knows who's on their way here right now, the police or worse. I promise I'll explain but I'm sorry Eva, you've had your chance. Times up, we're leaving.'

Grabbing hold of his suitcase with one hand and my arm with the other he started rushing towards the door. 'WAIT' I screamed as I instinctively dug my heels in and played dead like a toddler does, becoming a five hundred tonne weight. 'My picture,' I insisted. Just as I was being more or less dragged out of the bedroom I seen it out the corner of my eye. The framed photo of me, my two brothers and mum. Christmas Seventy Eight and the only picture that I had of us all together. We'd all looked so happy in it, crowded round mum all showing our love for the presents she'd gotten us.

I honestly don't know how she managed it. I'm losing pairs of Louboutins while she had to work two, sometimes three jobs at times to provide for us. I'd have been heartbroken had I forgotten it and truth be told. I probably would've done so had it not caught my attention at that last second. He let go just enough for me to escape his grip and dash over to scoop up the frame from the table. I understood the gravity of things though and was instantly following behind him again as he rushed down the stairs.

Considering the incessant rush he'd been in since he'd arrived. It was my impression that the first thing he was going to do was to run right out the door to the car. Instead, he dropped the suitcase and produced a bag of Coke from the inside pocket of his suit jacket and proceeded to rack up a series of liberally sized lines on the kitchen table.

'I don't know about you but I could go a couple of lines, darling. The next hour or two is going to need some clear heads' he said enthusiastically. The fucking hypocrite?! I've not got time to look for my shoes but he's got time to play with to rack up enough Cocaine to feed the five thousand. That was when I knew things truly had went south. I knew he liked the occasional line. I can only imagine the staff discount that he would have had made available to him. As a rule however, he never usually took it in the homestead.

I barely ever touched the stuff myself but neither was I a stranger to the drug. The night we met each other for the first time we must've polished off an eight ball between us. That wasn't behaviour that we carried over into our marriage however. My raving days were prematurely ended the moment I moved to the other side of the world to a country that wasn't exactly famed for its House Music scene. And even then, who would go out with me to a rave even if there was one?

Since this evidently was an exceptional circumstance. I decided to join him. He seemed to understand and offered no resistance when I asked him to pass me the Peso note that he was using as he set about the small pile in front of him. Within the space of five minutes we'd managed to polish off all the powder that he had tipped onto the table.

Additionally, within that time I also had a mini break down and while consoling me, our bodies tight against each other, we almost ended up having sex right there on the table.

Despite that mad five minutes we were out of there and tearing down the drive even faster than when the Audi came down in the other direction the fifteen minutes or so earlier. I'm not sure if it was meant to be unspoken or whether it was my own logic that registered but as we pulled away from the hacienda I was left seriously doubting if I'd ever see the place again.

I sat in the passengers seat with my glare fixed on him, receiving the occasional look back as he kept his eyes on the road for the main part. 'Don't' he said while negotiating the car round a tight mountainous bend at what I felt was way too fast and dangerous for the car to handle. 'Don't what?' I asked, admittedly already knowing "what" but wanting him to say it himself. 'You fucking well know what' he laughed, genuinely, back at me. 'I'll tell you why we're in this position as soon as we're on the plane and settled. Just let me get us in the air and out of this madhouse of a city first, ok?' He asserted, frustration covering his face at the tractor that was holding us up.

'Ok, can you at least tell me where we're going?' I asked, feeling that even being handed that specific information might help me cope with things. Given the circumstances, just being able to know what our next move was going to be would've been assistance to my mental state. 'That's going to be for the airport to decide when we get there. First flight to Europe that we can get ourselves booked on.' - 'Well that's narrowed things down then,' I replied sarcastically which was met with some sarcasm of his own.

'Well you can narrow it down further by scratching off Istanbul, Kiev, Bilbao, Casablanca and Belfast off your shortlist as well' he kept his eyes on the road during all of this. He'd driven like a maniac since we'd left but to his credit we'd always been nothing less than safe and were now starting to see signs for El Dorado international airport ahead on the road.

'So why not those five cities then?' I asked, of course, we had more pressing issues there and then but I was genuinely intrigued why we couldn't visit those specific cities that he'd listed.

'Some unpleasantness, I can't go back.' He diplomatically replied with a straight face.

'And now you can add Bogotá to the list then Peter, can't you?' I replied, a lot less diplomatically.

Chapter 3

Lee

Well as far as a masterclass in making a royal cunt of things goes then it was mission accomplished for that fahking liability of a client of mines. I'll be surprised if he's not the talk of the island by this point today with last nights performance. Don't know why I even bother with him sometimes. What is it with the Jocks though! I've never met a single one of them that wasn't daft as a brush and Stevie, aka DJ Selecao, was no different. In fact, I'd say that in the four years of managing him I'd noticed that he'd seemed to get worse by the year. The future is going to be "interesting" for him if this trend is going to continue.

I started looking after him, and at times that really should be taken in *every* sense of the word, after we'd struck up conversation in Newcastle during a Rezerection event. I'd watched his set from the side of the stage that night. Myself only there due to one of my own clients being on the bill. What struck me was how young he appeared behind the decks. There was barely anything to him. I mean, bleeding African rock groups should've been putting together a benefit gig for the boy. I hadn't heard of him and due to my line of work. I'd always prided myself in knowing all of the up and coming deejays that are getting ready to force their way into the bigger nights across the country.

He'd crept in under my radar but I certainly knew his name by the time his last record had been spun. So did the crowd. The set that he had played, the choice of songs a perfect mix of some old and mostly current that had done the business enough to have them eating out of the palm of his hand by the time he was finished.

I had bumped into him by chance outside the main entrance. He was leaning against the wall smoking the longest joint you've ever seen a single person smoking. I actually noticed it before I saw who it was attached to, you know? I was on my way out to the car to grab my phone charger but stopped and instead walked over to him. 'DJ Selacow, pleased to meet you' I stretched my arm out for a handshake. 'Lee Isaac, Ragamuffin Agency' - 'It's Selecao, pal' he replied while shaking my hand. It's Portuguese for "selection." - 'Sell-ass-eeow, Brazilian fitba thing, likes. Anyway, it's definitely not the way *you're* saying it though. The c is silent, ken, mate?' He corrected me.

Regardless, he didn't seem too concerned with me getting his name wrong however as he stood there taking a toke on the family sized reefer in his hand. I could tell it probably wasn't the first time he'd have had to correct someone over his name and, considering he was a Scottish DJ who had chosen a Portuguese name to go under, it wouldn't be his last time either.

'Ok, I stand corrected, mate' I laughed back. 'I really enjoyed your set tonight, haven't seen you down here before at any events, do you do many nights in England?' I asked with already an eye on possibly securing him as a client. Obviously, I had no idea as to his personality at this point and how much hard work he was going to be and that, at times, our relationship would end up mirroring one of father and son. I was simply basing my instincts purely on the actual performance I'd seen him put in behind the ones and twos.

'Just really the North of England as well as, obviously, Scotland. Ibiza too recently,' he replied as he made to pass the joint to me. By this point, still longer than any average doobie you'll see someone puffing on. 'No you're ok, you don't look like you've got much left of it so you're better hanging onto it' I joked which had him laughing at my dryness. We continued chatting outside, instantly hitting it off. I shared a little about myself and the agency. Who I managed, which clubs and promoters I helped supply acts to across England and beyond. Of course, it didn't exactly harm things that while we stood there chatting I was repeatedly interrupted by deejays, producers and general faces in the scene who would be coming and going. All saying hello. That, leading to introductions between DJ Selecao and them.

I asked him to tell me a bit about himself. He'd stubbed the joint out by then. It was probably still at the half way point when he did it but credit where due to the young man. He'd had a bleedin good crack at it. He'd told me how he'd gotten into the Acid House scene a few years before. It was quite the story. I couldn't help but admire his tenacity over the fact that he'd made all of this happen through his own sheer hard work and determination. No mentors or muses while coming from a small town that was hardly considered a hotbed of House Music.

I liked him straight away. The scene was already choc full of geezers who were already in their own bubble. Believing their own hype, assisted by their old friend Charlie. I get it that Stevie was still young at the time but I got the impression that his attitude was one of someone who genuinely appreciated what a privileged position they were in. Doing something that they loved and getting paid for it.

When he told me that his first set of Technics had been given to him via a Colombian cartel though. That was the moment where I knew that I wanted him on team Ragamuffin. He could've been taking the piss of course but it was the most obscurely random story for a person to come out with that, of course, I unquestionably took it as true. That fact about him alone I could've seen becoming a piece of mythology or folklore inside the industry as he became more famous. Publications like Mixmag and DJ Mag would have a field day over it.

I could hear from the shouts of the MC from back inside the venue that my client, Bass Generator was now up. Telling Stevie that I needed to go back in I left him, once again, to spark up the never ending joint. Departing with a business card placed firmly in his hand and a request that he called me to talk about the opportunities that I had open for him.

Call me that week he did and with that our four year adventure began. Taking us up to that summer and yet again another long and mentally taxing run on the Balearic island of Eivissa. Mentally taxing for me because of having to look after rascals like Selecao and DJ Scratchmaster (who incidentally I've never seen scratch a single time during a set) who were there for extended stays due to the residencies that I'd arranged for them over in Playa den Bossa and Ibiza Town at Space and Pacha. I suppose it's no different to a rock band manager, looking after club deejays. The ultimate aim generally being keeping them out of trouble and making sure they're up on stage at the time they're meant to be. It all depends on who the rock star or deejay you're looking after though, I suppose?

On an island like that with all its ways and means of temptations, especially to a young Jock and Geordie barely in their twenties. Keeping characters like them out of trouble is something that is easier to say than it is to do, geezer. Give the two of them their due though. Despite the capers, and of which there has been many, that I'd had to mop up for them. Like all legendary hard living rock bands. Once I get them up on stage, they deliver. Quite a reputation the two of them have built up on the circuit the past couple of years. Through their raw talent and my negotiating skills they'd managed to push themselves onto some impressive bills during recent times.

Like I said though. Even by his own standards, Stevie's appearance at Amnesia truly was a tutorial of epic proportions when it came to losing friends and alienating people on the island of Ibiza. I'd seen the warning signs the night before at Space. I wasn't even meant to be there in any capacity but thought I'd show my face as I was in town having dinner with a friend. I'd missed Stevie's set out on the terrace. A residency that I'd managed to bag him months before the summer season began. I wasn't interested in the set as such, what I *was* interested in much more though was the man's after dark habits once his set was over for another day.

I'd pulled off a bit of a coup earlier in the week. Getting him an extra gig by managing to sneak him onto the Carl Cox bill that Amnesia were putting on. I barely knew how I'd managed it myself. When I'd been put on notice that Morillo had pulled out I literally stopped what I was doing, which incidentally was sitting watching my eight year old daughter's school play back home in Kent. She was right at her part where she got to say her lines while I was sat there on the phone to Paco the manager over in Amnesia. I'll never forget the look on my wife Lucy's face as I stood up to exit the assembly hall right when I should've been beaming with pride as a father over their kid's performance.

I knew I was already chancing my luck by putting in the call but nothing ventured nothing gained ain't it, mate. Let's start with the fact that with the best will in the world and all of the love I have for the guy. Stevie is not Erick Morillo. He shouldn't feel bad about that fact because their careers could not have even been put up for comparison. DJ Selecao was in the process, if he didn't end up blowing it, of being

on the way up and gaining followers as he did so. Constant bookings
and in essence, on his merry way to joining the higher bracket of
deejays. That's when it would all go stratospheric for the fella. He
wasn't close to there yet though, that shit takes time. The idea of
replacing Morillo on the bill with Stevie seemed outlandish but fuck it
yeah? Shy kids don't get any sweets, you know?

'Ah Lee, how are you my friend, bueno?' He answered. 'We haven't
spoken in a while, are you here right now in San Antonio?' - 'Muy
bueno, senor' I laughed back while estimating how long it was socially
acceptable before I broke ranks and blatantly let him know why I was
calling.

I didn't take long, I didn't have to. 'Sooooo, Lee, would there be any
coincidence that we're speaking for the first time since all the
residences across the island were negotiated and announced and
within half an hour of Erick Morillo announcing that he can't appear
on Tuesday night?'

'Well, Paco my hombre, if you're asking that question then it would
appear pretty fahking obvious what the answer is.' I said cutting to the
chase. 'I've got a ready made replacement to slot right in and he's free
that night from his Space residency.' I could tell that he was mentally
trying to work out who played where and on what night but not even
fahking rain man could remember all of the permutations. I put it to an
end. 'DJ Selecao'

'Your Scottish boy?' He seemed surprised yet, with the emphasis on
"boy," still managed to sneak in a slight dig over the fact that I was
suggesting someone as young as Stevie to replace a House Music
legend like Morillo. 'Don't be fooled by his young age amigo' I replied
confidently knowing that this part of the conversation was my turn.
'The boy has some skills, I literally signed him on the spot after
hearing his set, had already signed him mentally in my head after half
an hour of the same fahking performance. He's already got a bit of a
following building up steam. Is over here for three months, already
has a presence on the island and I can give you my own personal
guarantee that whilst some of your clubbers won't have heard of him
before Tuesday night

they will, without question, know who he is by the end of it. Come on, where's that anythink goes Ibiza spirit the scene is known for?' I pressed him.

There was a pause on Paco's end while, as far as I was concerned I'd said my piece and had now chosen to fall silent.

'You know, Lee? Any other night I would have agreed to you but even before your call today I've had David Guetta, Todd Terry, Sasha and Judge Jules all offered to me. All of them also on the island and available at short notice. Obviously, you will admit that they are all more, how should I put it, more bookable than your client?' He had me. I couldn't disagree and didn't bother in doing so. 'No worries, comprende, mate. Just remember my boys name because by next summer it'll be you that will be coming to me looking for him. Obviously Space have got there first by booking him this year but yeah let's see what next summer brings. We'll catch up sometime over the season though, dinner or something?'

I inserted the Space part especially just to give him something to think about. Knowing Paco, if he thought that Pepe over at Space had the jump on him over something, he'd be pissed right off. Despite the mind games that I couldn't help but play I left the conversation with everything all good with future plans for a social evening. It was never bad for business to be on good terms with all of those responsible for oiling the cogs of the Ibiza nightlife and I was on first name terms with pretty much anyone that I needed to be with over there. It was around six hours later when I was getting myself prepared for the early flight out the Balearics the next morning when I had Paco calling me back.

'Is Selecao still available for Tuesday? He asked with a hopeful tone to his voice.

Advantage Lee! I teased the fucker by telling him that he must've had a serious amount of fall throughs to be darkening my door after knocking me back initially. I kept at it right up until the moment he interrupted and let me know that there had been a concrete offer from Darren Emerson's management. That's when I stopped fahking about with him and and talked terms. Beautifully, had he even entertained my earlier request he'd have found that so desperate I was for the opportunity of Stevie getting to play on that particular bill. I was willing to give him an unusually low price (kind of what we call in the business as a loss leader) but with roles now reversed. All previous bets and terms were now off the table.

By the time we were through I had this loveable lunatic from Scotland with a heart of gold slotted in right fahking before the three deck fahking wizard himself, Coxy. It was one of those moments where I couldn't have given a toss about the percentage that I'd make out if it. Looking at Stevie getting to play that particular night it was like the equivalent of Joe Pesci's "Tommy" in Goodfellas when he was being "made." Recognition from your peers that you're "good enough" to be accepted as one of them. DJ Selecao going on before one of dance music's biggest names was literally recognition of being, good enough.

I couldn't have been prouder had it been my own flesh and blood.

And yet there he was, biggest night of his life and all. Making an absolute fahking twat of himself and in a plethora of ways. By the time I arrived I found him prior to his set inside Carl Cox's dressing room, completely out of his tree. I'd known Coxy for years so immediately seeing the look on his face as he sat there listening to Stevie. I could see that it was a look more of humouring him than anything else.

'Well if you've not got any records by The Cure on you then surely some cunt *will* inside here' he sat, still oblivious to my entrance, looking manically at Carl. Why the fahk was he asking Carl Cox if he had any Cure songs? That in itself could only ever be considered a bad sign as far as a window into my clients state of mind. I quickly interrupted the conversation, putting distance between what was, for me, incredibly the top two billing deejays on the night. Captured together in that moment they certainly didn't fahking look like it.

I expertly managed to combine saying a quick hello to Coxy while physically lifting Stevie up from off the chair by linking an arm with his. Not saying a single word to him, keeping eye contact with his peer sat opposite him. Cox looking a combination of bemusement over what was taking place before his eyes and relief that it appeared to be coming towards an end. I had plenty to say to Stevie but wanted to remain professional and keep it in house between the pair of us. Just about managing to resist the strong urge to go completely nuts at him there and then.

'He got the bags wrong, Lee. I mean, he labelled them wrong the dyslexic fuck' he said, sat there back in his own small room that Amnesia had provided him with. This was his attempt at offering some form of an explanation to me after I'd torn into him once we were alone. Eyes rolling in the back of his head and trying to find the weed that he assured me he'd left sitting on the table before he'd decided to go and look for Carl Cox to inexplicably seek a loan of a record by The Cure.

It was either through intoxication or simply just bad attitude but he didn't seem too concerned by the anger and incredulity that I was showing him. He did at least try to offer an explanation to me which I guess was something at least. Not that I got much sense out of him. I'd never seen him like this before. Full of drugs? Absolutely. Let's face facts, in my line of work I'm never not going to see someone on drugs in some capacity or other. It's just how the scene was, is and forever will be. He appeared different from whatever "normal" I could ever say I'd ever witnessed though and no mistake. After initially being chatty (without making too much in the way of sense) he eventually began to clam up. It looked like he was in a complete trance, proper hypnotist stylee, rudeboy.

With time for him going up on the decks fast approaching, I was soon betraying everything I'd ever stood for as a DJ manager. Sending out a messenger to pick up a couple of grams of marching powder to try and claw back the situation. It's pretty much the last thing I would ever advocate any of my clients do. I'd seen a lot of close friends and acquaintances mess their life up through lack of moderation when it came to narcotics. Through those experiences I'd been left not so much anti drugs but very much someone who neither looked at them as one of life's great answers either.

Soon we'd banged enough sniff into Stevie to get him up on stage as planned but it was far from ideal. A lot like his set. He was fahking up all over the place. Lifted the wrong needle up from the two records that were simultaneously playing within the first ten minutes of him even being up there. A while after that he actually left the decks altogether to have a shouting match with one particular clubber who had been incessantly shouting for a specific track to be played. In the second hour of his set there was the case of him getting so much into the tune that he was playing, I'm sure it was an oldie from the start of the nineties, Cubic 22 but don't quote me on that, that he forgot all about bringing in the next track which led to complete silence inside the club once it had ended. It was an unmitigated disaster all round.

The irony of it all was that by the time he'd spun his obligatory "ironic Ibiza record" that he always ended with while he played on the island. The previous nights offering being the most unexpected "Love song" by Simple Minds. I'd assumed that song hadn't been his first choice given the fact that he was so desperate to find a Cure song. Stopping my digress though, despite all of his uncharacteristic mistakes that he'd made. Stevie received a near on football stadium like roar of approval as he exited the deejay booth, waving to everyone with a size of smile you really would've needed to have seen to believe, making way for the man they'd all really came to see, Carl Cox.

It was the roar of approval that I knew he'd get when I'd booked him for the gig yet paradoxically, not in the way I had envisaged. Ecstasy is a hell of a drug. He may have fooled most of the near on five thousand crowd inside there but as far as I was concerned. He wouldn't have fooled those that mattered. That was not restricted to while on the decks either, regrettably. Being on the roll of self sabotage that he was on. He didn't stop for the night with his nonsense after the set had finished.

He was barely inside the VIP area ten minutes after his performance had finished when he ended up having this massive row with some Spanish girl. I was sat across the other side of the room with Paco and some of his investors while also keeping one eye on Stevie. She looked different as in hair style but I was sure that she was the same girl I'd seen him with the night before at Space. He had been sat talking to her the whole time that I was in there.

I'd managed to grab a quick chat with him when he'd went to the bathroom. I knew he was enjoying what was effectively his free time so I kept it crystal clear. 'You've got a big fahking night ahead of you tomorrow, Stevie, don't fahk it up. Get yourself some proper rest between now and Amnesia. Space will still be here in a few nights time, mate' I said earnestly, feeling like I was Alex Ferguson or some cahnt.

'I fucking hope it's still going to be here in a couple of nights time, either that or you're going to have to find me a new gig,' he replied in that usual sharp as a tack way way of his before adding. 'Nah it's cool, Lee I'm going to be heading soon, you don't need to remind me about tomorrow.' It was almost reassuring, the sincere way he had delivered those words to me.

Fast forward approximately twenty four hours and that small exchange of words was shown to be a complete waste of everyones breath. I'd actually taken my eye off him for a few minutes as Paco's wife was beginning to tell me about this little known seafood restaurant in Ibiza Town when we were rudely interrupted by.

'You fuckin bastad, you fuckin rrrrrrratta' I wheeled round to see the girl from Space trying to lunge at Stevie who was standing back at distance while others held tightly onto her. She looked like she was completely losing her mind at him. The anger on her face was a sight to behold. 'I'm a fucking rat aye? That so, darling? Well who's the fucking thief then? You stole money from my flat ya wee tea leaf' he turned to no one in particular and with no sense of decorum shouted 'right off my bedside table. She's lucky I'm no a grass by the way because otherwise the Guardia Civil would be putting her up for the night.'

I hadn't a clue what had blown up between them because initially they were just chatting as far as I could see. Blow up it had though and after saying a rushed and embarrassed goodbye to everyone at our table. I got up to go over and fix whatever was going on before whatever slim chances of Stevie reappearing at Amnesia disappeared for good. Before I'd even got to the two of them security had already began the process of marching her out, leaving Stevie standing there with his motors still evidently running.

'She took my fucking Space performance money, Lee. Not fucking on ma man is it? Not on at all, proper bad craic' He pleaded in my direction, now aware of my appearance on the scene. As far as I was concerned, damage limitation was the name of the game so I simply agreed with him, telling him exactly what he needed to hear in an attempt at calming him down. Who the hell knew what ups and downs he must've had over the night, emotionally as well as in a pharmaceutical sense. His head must've been fried.

Whether he liked it or not I'd already decided that after what had just happened. It would be the end of the night for him and it would now be a case of getting that across to him. He *is* sensible though, can be smart when he wants to be and give him his credit, he seemed to know that it had been a night that would be best not extended.

Zico came quietly, something Carl Cox could not have ever been accused of. The sounds of fast techno on three decks playing the two of us out as we left to catch a taxi back to Stevie's villa that I'd ever so generously arranged for him. What Stevie didn't know as we left Amnesia was that his night really *was* about to be coming to a much earlier end than he'd most likely anticipated. Sure, once in the taxi I was going to be offering to buy him a drink at one of the backstreet bars I knew of in San An but what he didn't know was that when we would decide on having our "one for the road" I would be having, through some assistance from a friendly face behind the bar at Isabella's, some crushed up Diazapam launched right into his bottle of San Miguel.

I had them prescribed to me back in England by the quack for my chronic back pain but I was sure he'd have approved over my reasons for sharing a couple of them with someone that needed removed from the outside world for the night. There was obviously a moral and ethical side to what I was doing which, pervertedly, allowed me to sleep a lot easier that night having earlier drugged someone.

I was comfortable with it all, safe in the knowledge that what I was doing was *for* him rather than to him. I wasn't going to lose any sleep over him not losing any sleep, put it that way. After we'd finished our drinks it was a case of enforcing military precision timing to get us back to his to drop him off. I told the cab driver to wait a moment until I actually saw him reach his front door, open it and it closing behind him. I couldn't have cared less if the Valium kicked in as soon as he closed the door and that he'd slept on the floor all night.

He couldn't cause himself or anyone else any trouble for at least a while and that, for me, was key. I had still to really assess what damage he'd done over the night, the possible things that I didn't even know about for instance. One step at a time though and like how a good football manager builds a team out of a good defence. By getting him indoors and out of everyones way for at least twelve to twenty four hours, that was my form of defence. 'I'll launch my counter attack tomorrow,' I thought to myself as the taxi drove off.

Chapter 4

Zico

You know that feeling when you first wake in the morning? Those first few incoherent moments? The waking assumption where, for at least a couple of seconds or two, you are blissfully unaware of all the shit that you're in. I'm a big fan of them. Of course they only last that couple of seconds before the real world starts to encroach. Allowing you to come face to face with whatever it was that you did the night before.

Moi personally had an awful fucking lot to face up to but I hadn't exactly been in much of a hurry to do so. When I woke it must've taken me a good couple of minutes if not more to even come to and recognise my surroundings. Which was me lying on the sofa in the living room with my head hanging off the side of it. Hanging so far off it my forehead was almost touching the floor. For some reason, when I realised the way I was lying, something my nana used to tell me when I was a kid popped into my head - 'If you lay like that all the blood will rush to your head.'

If that truly was the case then it was going to take until fuck knows time for it to find its way back again. Actually what *was* the time was what I found myself starting to think once I'd started to deal with reality. My phone was in my pocket of the shorts I was still wearing from the night before. Fuck, last night, just looking at what I was wearing gave me unpleasant flashbacks. It was going to be a day filled with apologies but also with a hint of me saying my piece to certain people. Namely the people responsible for the early part of the night going completely tits up. Well, when I say "people" I mean only one person in particular. 'I'll deal with him though,' I thought to myself as I reached for the phone.

I pulled it out but found the screen dead. Fairs fair. It had seemed like weeks ago since I'd last charged it. I thought that a quick flick around some channels on Spanish TV would at least find me a news channel with the time stamped in one corner but I couldn't get any joy there either. The video recorder was flashing all zeros on the LCD screen on the front so that wasn't much more of a help.

I couldn't even remember falling asleep as no way would I have slept on that sofa, in the position that I'd woken in. 'Thank fuck I have the day off,' I reflected to myself while I remembered what day it was. Fuck was I groggy though. Felt like I'd been blasted with an elephant tranquilliser gun. With all of the memories from Amnesia flooding back to me thick and fast. I had already taken the conscious decision to take a day off from the rest of society. I'd gather enough provisions from the local supermarket. Enough for a prolonged stay indoors and the rest of the world could do whatever the fuck it wanted as far as I cared.

I needed to at least know the time though before I started to get my own house in order. It felt hot so I guessed that it must've been at least around ten in the morning or so. Struggling to even stand up before falling down again. I got myself up again and slowly made my way over to the front door and out onto the veranda which overlooked a series of shops and bars all lined up facing each other in a arcade kind of format. My first impression was that it was too hot, far warmer than what mid morning would've normally been. Looking down I shouted to this, evident, English guy. Bronzed tan and wearing nothing but a pair of Union Jack shorts and flip flops. 'Scuse me pal, do you know the time?' I shouted down to him from above.

He wheeled around, so did his wife and little boy who was holding onto his mums hand as he stood with an ice cream, more of it dripping onto the pavement than was going into his mouth. 'Just coming up for four o clock, mate' he helpfully shouted back up to me. I kind of wanted to laugh at the fact he'd sounded like a rubbish local radio DJ with his choice of wording but was more impacted by the fact that he had said it was four o clock in the afternoon. 'You sure?' I asked.

It was almost like I didn't want to believe that I'd slept for so long. How had I slept so long? He just laughed back up at me. I could see the way that the situation was probably being viewed by him. I must've just looked like any other British kid up to no good abroad on their holidays. Staying up all night and then sleep all day. 'Absolutely, mate. We're all going back to the hotel for a siesta, we've been to the beach all day' he laughed. I could see them carrying their wet towels and the kid's lilo right enough.

How had I slept as long as four o fucking clock? I mean, I knew that I was heading for a major crash and burn but even so there was really no explaining sleeping for so long. 'I must've needed it' I reasoned with myself even though I couldn't help but feel that I'd been cheated out of part of my day off. I shrugged it away as I sat back down on the sofa again after returning back to the inside of the villa. Whether I wanted to or not I really had to start facing up to some of what had went down the night before. Well, *all* of what went down really. There was plenty to revisit that was for sure.

The funny thing is that it had all been going swimmingly as well. As planned, I had my man pop round to the villa and help get my arse into gear while I got into *his* gear. The Ching sorted me out like a wee sweetie. Fucking fired my way through the box of white labels in no time. I had my set for the night put together within a couple of hours. The both of us went through the best part of three grams while I listened my way through all of the new vinyl that had been sent to me. By the time I'd put it together I felt invincible. It was hard to believe that I'd not slept for a couple of days because there I was, opening for Carl Cox in a matter of hours and was feeling pretty fucking good about it too.

The irony was there for all to see when it came down to the fact that I was happy enough for my partner in crime to hang around. He'd planned to go up to Amnesia since it was such a special night so I was cool enough for him to tag along with me. In doing so allowing him to walk through the main entrance with me on arrival. It was only when we got there to the club that it all went sideways. Ok, downhill and no mistake.

My friend and also the worlds worst drug dealer. Honestly? If there was like those Fifa international team rankings but for drug dealers he would be the equivalent of Burkina Faso or someplace radge like that. Through simply wanting to do right by me, and on my biggest of nights, done me the complete contradiction of a favour.

'So, how are you feeling? Bricking it mate?' He asked, stupid grin on his face while we took a seat at the bar.

Why do cunts ask questions like that at such times, especially with a stupid smile on their face and think that they're being anything other than annoying? Back at the villa when I was flying on the Ching there wasn't anything close to nerves but once I'd arrived at Amnesia? Aye, different story. Not that I was letting on to him though of course. 'Nah, you know me eh, once I'm behind the decks it doesn't matter where I'm playing. Could do with a wee refresher though, my head's feeling more spacey than Kevin right now.' I said, palming away his words like Dino fucking Zoff. A big smile appeared on his face. 'Aye well I've got you covered muchacho, have no worries about that.' He fished into his pocket and, discreetly, brought out a small wrap and forced it into my hand in the fake handshake style that looks nowhere near as subtle as the two people doing it ever think it is.

'Primo, my friend. Pree-fucking-ee-me-um' he said with a self satisfied smile. 'Mate, I'm under no illusions just how important tonight is, you don't need to tell me and *that* is why you will always remember the night that you opened for Carl Cox as the night that you had the best Charlie in the fucking world. Forget about everything you've ever stuck up your hooter up until tonight because this is the realness.'

I had a few thoughts over this. The first one being that I'd have assumed that years from now when I recalled the night where I went in front of my hero on the decks, that in itself would be more than enough to be fondly looking back on the night. Not because I'd had a good line of Ching or because I'd tried Dandelion and Burdock for the first time! I appreciated his thoughtfulness, regardless. That though wasn't enough to save him from me sharing with him the second thought that I'd had.

'So, what you're effectively saying is that all the other times you've been selling me low grade shite then?' I done well to keep a straight face as I delivered the words. - 'No no no no no, it's not like that at all. Zico. King hell? How long have we known each other? When I was saying that this stuff was' …. That must've been the moment that he realised. Stopping talking altogether, he just stared at me carefully for a second as if he was trying to figure me out. Eventually he started laughing, me along with him.'

I could've done with wiring right into it there and then but knew I'd have all the privacy I needed in the changing room that I'd been told I had waiting on me. The fact that I'd turned up with fuck all but a record box as far as possessions went pretty much invalidated any requirement of mines *for* a dressing room but hey, if they were offering me a bit of private space that I could get up to no good inside then who was I to stop them. The actual night itself inside the main room had already gotten underway. I hadn't seen how many people were inside, or who was playing to them but the vibration of the music, which practically travelled all over the inside of the building, was difficult to ignore.

It was around an hour or so before I was due to play so, agreeing to catch each other after my appearance, I made my way to the changing room, leaving him still sitting at the bar. Almost skipped my way to that room. Apparently a gram of the best Cocaine in the world in my pocket and off to get myself prepared for the biggest night of my life.

It was only when I really started to think about it all, the gravity of what was happening to me. That was when I started to get excited. A nervous kind of excitement. The good kind. It felt like there was a fucking butterfly sanctuary located inside my stomach. It's probably just some footballers cliche of course like 'I'm over the moon' and 'We're sick as parrots' but you often heard football players before a big cup final saying comments like 'if you're not nervous before a big match like this then you shouldn't be a professional footballer.'

That was how I was beginning to feel now that it was around sixty minutes until "kick off." I'd deejayed so many times I could probably have done it blindfolded but of course, there had been some gigs where those type of nerves would appear. The first time of playing, crossing the border to England and playing there. When you finally got yourself on a bill that had other deejays playing that you already knew of and had read about in Mixmag and DJ Mag for years before. The first time of playing Space? I had those nerves for fucking weeks leading up to that first set out there on the terrace. A place I'd danced as a clubber until sun up and beyond so many times.

And here we were again. I'd never played at Amnesia but had been to my fair share of parties inside there. The knowledge that I was going to be up there playing inside that huge fucking room was enough to blow what was left of my mind after those carnage filled first few weeks in Ibiza. The whole Carl Cox situation though was too much. I kept having this idea that my set was going to be like some kind of job interview. There would surely be a lot of important people in attendance who, depending on my "interview technique," would be hopefully looking to hire me.

A lot of that came from Lee though. I can't even imagine what I'd be like if somehow I was able to bag DJ gigs across the world and not have him around nipping the absolute fuck out of my head by, admittedly, helping keep me on the straight and narrow. As much as he could, of course. He was just one man after all. With that, he couldn't ever have been expected to be around me all the time and the nature of the business that we're in pretty much dictates a certain type of lifestyle will follow for most.

Lee had always been drumming into me about how hard you had to work in the industry because there was always another thousand hungry others out there just dying to take your place. He's a good lad though and there was absolutely no way that I'd have found myself out there on the Space terrace three times a week for the summer without the work of his hand. One of the things he looked down on though, proper parenting stuff likes, was any of his staff taking any gear before or during their set. Each to a man, every single one of us generally, as far as I'd seen, had stuck to that golden rule. That night at Amnesia was an exception to the rule. After the night was over I'd already committed myself to twenty four hours of R&R but for that one night. The Ching was of paramount importance. There is always an exception to the rule, always.

By pure chance I was just getting to my room when Cox was arriving outside his along with a couple of other guys carrying his record boxes. I absolutely loved the fact that he needed boxes, plural. The amount of tracks that he always managed to squeeze into a set, two boxes of records seemed almost appropriate. Both standing there outside our respective doors. We locked eyes and while knowing that there was a very high risk that I would open my mouth to speak and no words come out through sheer nerves over me being stood beside him. I said 'fuck it' and just went for it. 'Carl, honoured to meet you and be on the same bill, DJ Selecao' With a big smile I offered out my hand to him. 'Good to meet you, mate.'

He replied, meeting me with a big toothy smile. Almost breaking my hand with the enthusiastic handshake he pulled me into. Totally crazy, I'm up soon, opening for this guy and he's almost breaking my right hand! Anyone else I'd have called them everything under the sun until they'd let go of my hand but well, this was Carl fucking Cox. I even started to visualise what it would be like to DJ with only one hand up there in front of everyone as he stood there tightly holding onto it.

'I've heard some good things about you from the right people. Stevie? Isn't it?'

FUCK OFF! 'No way did he know my first name,' I thought to myself. - 'A a a aye, Stevie' I said with my nerves starting to show, still blown away that he knew my name. 'Listen, mate, give me ten to get a few things organised in there and come through for a chat before you go on if you have time.' He said as he started to walk through the door into his room. 'I'll give you a knock in a while, aye' I agreed as I made to enter my own room. 'I've got a few things to fix out in there and then I'll come through' I confirmed. The two of us then walked into our rooms. Both doors closing in a way that sounded like two badly matched beats on a set of Technics.

The only thing I needed to "fix" inside there was myself. It had been quite a few hours now since I'd torn into that Ching back at the villa when I was getting my set prepared. By that point though I'd been left with that spacey after effect. There was still the not too small matter of me having not slept for over two days and that I was only managing to keep myself one step ahead through my intermittent narcotic consumption. In my mind I only had to stay one step ahead of this scary as fuck prospect of a deadly crash and burn just enough until the end of the night. Then I was removing myself from things for a while. I wouldn't have been left with any other choice than to put up the white flag of surrender by then, regardless. I'm not the fucking Terminator.

The wrap of Coke was out of my pocket and on the table within five seconds of my record box hitting the ground. Before opening it up and tipping some out onto the small mirror that I'd found hanging on the wall nearest to me. I took a moment to pause, to try and breathe for a moment and take all of it in. How I could not have dared imagine up a scenario that would involve me being separated by a wall, as performers, from Carl Cox while both inside one of the most famous nightclubs in the world. Playing to thousands of party people who would have flocked from all over the island for the night. Back when I got my Technics for the first time it would've taken an obscene amount of cheese before bedtime to magic up such a night that I would be part of.

My period of reflection didn't last that long. In no time I had knocked up a couple of generously sized lines, polished them off and found myself next door sat inside in his dressing room. Weirdly the two lines I'd taken had not provided the immediate impact that I had anticipated. It hadn't felt at all like the hit you'd get from doing a line or two. By rights I shouldn't have even needed to use his door. I should've been able to just just burst through the joining wall like the Incredible Hulk instead of gingerly walking from one room into another.

I put it down to the fact that this Ching had been put across to me as something special. A different beast when it came to that white powder that the South American's were so intent on getting up our hooters. It *did* make me feel good, I'm not going to deny that. Gave me a nice wee pleasant buzz likes and despite how surreal this all was with me sat down to have a one to one blether with Carl Cox. I wasn't fazed one single bit.

'You looking forward to getting out and up there, mate? Can I get you a drink?' He asked me as I took the seat he'd offered me upon entering the room. 'Aye, I'll have a water please' I replied 'As for looking forward to going on? It's a bit of a headfuck right now that I'm opening for you in Amnesia, can't quite get my head around it. I mean, I'm sat here right now with you and it's all a bit surreal if I'm being honest' I said in a jokey way that had him laughing but remove the tone of voice that I'd said it in. Strip down the words though and I wouldn't have been able to deny that they were ones that I was serious about, every single one of them.

'This is your time, fella. Take advantage of it. You got yourself to here and it's now down to what you do with the opportunity. I've been hearing your name mentioned recently so you're on the grid now. Believe me, you wouldn't be opening for me tonight at a place like this if you hadn't earned the right.' Cox said encouragingly like he was fucking Yoda. 'Aye b b but, Erick Morillo? It was meant to be him opening for you tonight. Going from having Morillo support you to me is like a fitba player who was promised Bayern Munich for his testimonial game getting Huddersfield fucking Town' I replied, once again laughing but speaking truths.

'Forget Erick Morillo, Stevie. I'm good friends with Erick and I know for a fact that he'd be thrilled that a young DJ on the come up was getting a chance to fill his boots in the booth. It's all about taking the chances when they come along in life. Look at how Oasis got signed? Turning up to a gig they weren't even scheduled to play at and threatening to burn down the place if they didn't get to perform? I've got a lot of time for such entrepreneurial spirit' he hammered home his point while laughing out loud. I assumed over the image of Liam & Noel Gallagher standing inside King Tuts with petrol cans in their hands.

'Well when you put it like that, mate' I agreed - 'You've got to make things happen for yourself, doesn't matter what game you're in' he responded while not even looking at me. He had seemingly taken another thought on as we'd been speaking and was now in the midst of delving into one of his boxes of records.

As he continued his search inside the box I sat there remarking to myself about how not only was he one of the best if not THE best deejays in the world, he was also a pretty fucking top notch life coach into the bargain.

Gave me a nice wee booster before my set anyway. Talking of boosters though I couldn't help but notice that the Charlie hadn't actually came to anything. I'm not sure if he was taking the piss by giving me it and talking it up as something from another planet only for it to be the opposite or not. Would've been a strange thing to do to a pal though when you knew it was a big night and they actually *needed* the Coke in a professional capacity.

The thing though was that whilst I wasn't flying and talking Carl's ear off at a hundred miles an hour and subjecting him to the most irrelevant and random of nonsense that came out of my mouth. I felt relaxed, really warm with a peaceful buzz. If it was Cocaine then it wasn't like any that I'd ever had before, it couldn't have been, it wasn't like Ching at all.

I'd noticed that, unlike a line of Coke, this stuff seemed to be more of a slow builder, none of your immediate Cocaine hit. Due to speaking to "Coxy" I'd not noticed it so much but with us having a break in the conversation I'd been given the chance to clock what was now going on. Despite how good it felt I had a slight bit of anxiety about the fact that it wasn't exactly what I'd been planning in terms of a booster for getting myself up for my ninety minute set. Also, there was the question over how long was this going to get stronger for?

He returned back to the conversation as we rattled through the subjects quick fire. Favourite tunes of the summer that we'd been playing. What dates we had scheduled from now until the end of the year which, had this been converted into a game of top trumps he would have fucking annihilated me on. Anecdotes shared over our appearances at clubs. It was a great experience and whether it had been intended or not, I was learning a lot from him. They say never meet your heroes but this was nothing like that. This stuff I'd snorted though, whatever the fuck it was, was definitely coming on stronger and stronger and was now starting to become a problem.

It was difficult to describe but it was almost like I was becoming a little detached from things, the conversation, myself, from the room in general, actually. He was in the middle of telling me a story from the Love Parade in Berlin when my phone started ringing. It was my excuse for a pal and dealer. I really wanted to answer it and ask him what he had given to me, it sure as fuck wasn't Coke. I felt it wouldn't exactly have been appropriate to answer it when the king was sat there holding court.

You could've landed up in the Tower of London for less. Carl, the gentleman, said for me to answer it if I needed to. I actually had the mind to take him up on his offer but managed to pluck some sense out of somewhere. Realising that even if I answered the call I had no way of being able to ask the one question I had for him without Carl Cox knowing that I'd been taking something before speaking to him and going on stage.

Obviously, at the time, I had held no inclination for the fact that quite possibly Carl was doing just fine all by himself over noticing how wrecked I was as I sat there talking to him while my whole descent had taken place. The longer we talked the more I felt I was being removed from the room and all of what was inside it. Here's the thing and I know this is going to sound more mental than a pissed off Honey Badger but it felt like I could actually see myself sat there holding the conversation. Out my mind sat there but yet still managing to hold the conversation. Yet, I'm there watching myself hold it and have no ability to guide what I was going to do or say. I could see the, by now, concerned look on Cox's face which didn't really indicate that I was saying anything what you'd have described as conventional.

The phone went again soon after. Same caller as before. This was all starting to go horribly wrong. Two calls within two minutes and, understandably, Coxy was now assuming that this was some kind of emergency and saying how it really was no problem for me to answer it. That in itself fine but I wasn't even sure if I had a conversation in me. I had this mad image flash through my head where that if I'd reached to pick up the phone, my fingers were going to go right through it like a ghost.

'Go on, answer it' he pushed me. It was hard to tell due to how distorted my mind was feeling but I was starting to get the impression that I was now beginning to annoy him with the change in my behaviour and that I was in danger of becoming an unwanted guest. Almost feeling like I was doing something against my will by now, I picked up. Pressing the green answer button on the keypad and putting it to my ear.

'Ummmm Zico?' He said. In that hesitant way that a kid will do when they know they've got to tell a parent something heavy and are not looking forward to the reaction it's going to provoke. 'Aye, what's going on' I replied, well in my mind that's what I'd said but considering it was met with a 'FUCK, I'm too late, you've already taken it, haven't you?' as a reply from him,. Possibly I hadn't answered the phone as textbook as I'd believed.

'That stuff I gave you earlier on? You've, ehhh, fired into it, aye?' It was either just me and my mental state or else it was well difficult to hear him due to how loud the music was. Sounded like he was standing in the main room while trying to have a phone call but even he was not as radge as that, as unhinged as he was? 'Well, aye and on that very same subject, we need to talk after my set. I'm no happy, mate.' I must've managed to put it across in some authoritarian of ways because it was met with an apology over something I hadn't even got close to being explicit about it. 'I'm really sorry, Zico. I lifted the wrong fucking wraps before coming out. Thought I'd lifted the primo Ching, specially chosen for tonight for the both of us. Not for sale stuff likes, only for the people with a need to sniff clearance eh?'

'So what happened then?' I interrupted, sick of his rambling. 'I fucking lifted the Ketamine instead by accident. Only twigged when I had a couple of lines myself.' I felt like I was playing one of those games you'd play as a kid on road trips where you had to say a sentence but not use a certain word in it or you would lose. Fucking Mallet's Mallet type of deal. No way did I want Carl Cox to know what a car crash my night had become. At the very least (and understandably) he would've possibly been left feeling a little disrespected with regards to how I was appearing to be treating my opportunity to open for him. My apparent answer to that being to get completely spangled on Ketamine before I even got myself behind the decks.

'So what now then?' I asked - 'Well that's the thing, mate. Everything I've brought up with me tonight I thought was Ching and I now find is Ket. My night is ruined, you know how much I hate that shit, fucking horrible drug.' Came the reply from him, clearly misjudging the question that he'd been asked. I couldn't believe what I was fucking hearing. I'm about to blow the biggest chance in my career because of him being such a shit drug dealer and all he's concerned about is how his night out has been ruined due to lack of drugs. 'I meant me for fucks sake, what now for me?' I barked back, patience expired. Carl Cox had began to take some clothes out of a big Adidas holdall while I was on the phone but wheeled round at that moment through the raised voice.

'Well, I'm not sure what you can do other than try and get some actual Sniff into you double fucking quick, you're on in half an hour are you not?' I wasn't really liking his cavalier attitude to all of this. Stating the fucking obvious while offering nothing in the way of help or showing any kind of willingness to make up for his whole fuck up in the first place. 'That's your job though is it not, you know, to help me when it comes to that, no?' I snapped at him but due to all that was going on with the Ketamine, the venom I needed to accompany my words was lacking. 'Aye, normally eh but not when I'm up here. You obviously know that I'm not exactly the best of friends with the Scousers that run the operation up here, plus, bit of a principle thing here when it comes to me buying from them, bit embarrassing if I was to do that would it not be?'

'And you think that performing out of your nut in front of over five thousand people on Ketamine that your fucking moron of a friend has given you by accident *won't* be embarrassing?' I'd decided to do away with the whole charade in trying to keep it all from the daddy of House Music sat beside me. I was completely gone by that point anyway, there was no way that he wasn't going to have noticed. The way we just connected straight away when speaking but then how it had all changed. I thought that if I at least let some of my frustrations out in the phone call he would be more likely to believe that I wasn't purposely in the state that he saw before him.

All along I'd treated this night as a chance to "level up." To give myself a chance to move into the next bracket of deejays and push my name up that one notch higher on a poster and flyer. It was my "job interview" and I'd effectively turned up for it out of my fucking tits. I felt it important that Carl Cox at least knew that none of this had been done by design.

It was met with silence on the other end of the phone. 'Ok, thanks for fuck all then' I said before ending the call. By this point, Coxy was back sitting down, munching on an apple. I started to try and speak to him again but even in my state I could tell that the vibe had now been ruined. I could see that I probably should've been getting on and making my final plans before heading to the DJ booth. Of course though, instead of actually doing that I proceeded to sit and talk complete bollocks until Lee unexpectedly appeared and in a matter of seconds had whisked me away and out of the room.

I'd been sat there, to give it the best description I can give, feeling like I was one of the people in the photograph in Back to the Future that were fading away. Asking Carl if he had any songs by The Cure in his record box that he could loan me for going on. Preferably, Love Cats. He had no Cure. I'd had the, what I felt was the best idea I'd ever had, idea to sneak in a song by them into my set due to my whole Robert Smith experience earlier on in the day. Whether the Amnesia clubbers were going to be down with that, I didn't care. I'd started thinking about what had happened when she turned up outside the club. I pitied the security team who would have the misfortune to deal with her.

I was back in my own room before I even realised Lee had overseen the transition. I tried to explain myself to him but wasn't doing a very good job of it. The man was not happy with me though. It didn't take a straight and sober man to see that. He stood and read the riot act to me, he shouldn't have bothered, I'd had Ketamine for fucks sake. That's what made it all the more surprising when I was in the process of grabbing my record box, having been alerted to the fact that I was up in ten minutes through a friendly knock on the door from some Spanish girl who worked for the club, when Lee burst back through the door again with a gram of Ching (actual Cocaine as opposed to pretendy Cocaine that isn't fucking Cocaine at all and is in fact a substance used to knock out horses) for me.

'You know this goes against all of my rules Stevie but tonight is a case of needs fahking must. Right now you're minutes away from going into that booth and you look like you couldn't tell me your middle fahking name right now, pal' he tossed the little baggie on the table for me to get torn into. I obliged.

The first record of my set was already playing by the time I was able to get my head around the battle of wills that was going on inside my head between the Ketamine and the Cocaine. It was just as well because I was soon requiring a state of togetherness to get myself to mix in Armand van Helden's "Sugar is Sweeter' CJ Bolland remix. That's when I knew that everything was going to be absolutely golden. The flawless way I'd taken Todd Terry's "Jumpin," which I'd shamelessly chosen for the first track due to it already being a massive tune on the island and a guaranteed way to get the crowd onside. Replacing it with the van Helden track gave me the confidence boost that I sorely needed at that exact time.

Possibly it was too much of a booster. Well, either that or the Coke was now the undoubted all fearing ruler of my mind body and soul because I managed to go from such a calm and skilful piece of mixing to the exact opposite.

Committing the cardinal sin of picking up the wrong needle after I'd eventually mixed out Sugar is Sweeter. Doing so, plunging the arena into silence. The crowd actually fucking cheered at it?! I even heard an air horn go off somewhere amongst the thousands down there on the floor. Realising what I'd done I slammed the needle back down onto the vinyl without any particular discrimination to fill the room with a beat once again.

I regained my composure once more, looking down on the thousands of party goers, the colour, the sea of dancing and unpredictable shapes. From what I could see they were lapping it up. It was an unbelievable sight. I'd never played to anything close to that amount of people and it was hard not to stand there and take it all in. I got myself together after the initial mistake and was fine from then on. Right up until the next time I found myself going off the rails again. Until then I'd done exactly what I'd came to do. Hit the crowd with the finest electronic music at my disposal. Some crowd pleasers, some of my own personal favourite tunes alongside a few of those twelve inches that I barely knew myself but had sounded good when high back at the villa.

It was this fucking Dutch guy who caused it all really. For pretty much the whole of the first hour of my set he'd stood there, not dancing but shouting at me. Why he fucking thought that I'd be able to hear whatever it was that he was shouting I really didn't know but it was obvious that he was shouting towards me. I would see him every time

I looked up from the decks and cast an eye across the crowd. After a while I'd finally had enough of it. If anything my curiosity had been piqued.

I'd dug out a blast from the past with Beltram's "Mentasm" which I'd just mixed in so with a few minutes to spare I took the chance and moved to the front of the booth to see if I could hear him. Standing there in a Planet Hollywood beat your wife up style muscle vest with what looked like a cycling cap on his head. Emblazoned with what appeared loads of sponsors on it. I looked at him cupping an ear? This drawing me to the attention of everyone else down there at the same time as well as him.

It was a waste of time though, of course it was. The level of volume coming out of the speakers had relegated this Planet Hollywood cunt to a bit part role in a silent movie. Unfortunately for me, without any subtitles. No matter though because obviously on a night where all eyes were on me for that ninety minutes. I initially went back to the decks to kill the music so that I could return towards him and hear what he'd been desperately trying to tell me all set. Once again, the sound of silence brought on an initial cheer from the crowd. A chunk of them still appearing to be dancing even though there was no beats to dance along with. After the cheer, things kind of died down.

Once again cupping my ears in his direction. It was his chance. I'm not even sure why the fuck I had become so fixated on him anyway. I'd been used to performing in all kinds of places. Some where the crowd was detached from you while others they could practically be up your arse while you played. I think it was his complete dedication towards getting my attention that had *got* my attention.

'PLAY KYM SIMMS' He shouted at the top of his voice. I heard a ripple of laughter. Aye, with good cause.

I'd become obsessed over why he had been shouting at me. Literally stopped my fucking set just so I could find out. Thousands of people all brought to a standstill in their night through my intrigue and for what? So that some clueless cunt can request a song and not even a song relevant to me, ever. No disrespect to Kym Simms in any shape or form because I fully recognise that there's a lot who do like her but if you've ever heard even just one of my sets then you're going to know that you will be left waiting an awful long fucking time before you hear her. If you can't see that then maybe it's a case of you being too blind to see it. Thank you, I'm here all week.

I mean, asking a DJ to play a tune other than if you're at a wedding or a twenty first birthday party is a big no no. Trust me, we've got it covered. It's kind of our job. Fair enough though, I understand that sometimes people will not be aware of this or actually, more likely, ARE but still think they'll chance their luck anyway. If they do though it's always a good policy if they come up with a song that the DJ actually likes themselves. Come at me with a Kym Simms request and it's going to be treated with the disdain that it deserves. Exactly like I did stood there in Amnesia when I laughed right back at him. This response bringing a lot louder laughter from some of the crowd who were close enough to hear what had been going on.

He didn't take too kindly to what he must've felt had been a slice of public humiliation and within seconds I'd found a plastic cup of beer coming flying up towards me from his direction. Splattering the front of my red Scotland away shirt from the eighty two World Cup campaign with watered down San Miguel.

'BAAASSSSTTTAAAAAARRDDDD' I shouted down at him. In what was a knee jerk reaction while the mist came down that was the same colour as my fitba top. I reached over to the table next to the decks and grabbed a plastic cup full of Sprite and with no thought for any kind of planning, launched it back in his direction. Did it hit him? Did it fuck. All fantasies that I was entertaining where his Planet Hollywood vest was going to be covered in Sprite were dashed when I, in fact, watched my cup go straight into the face of some innocent girl to the side of him. 'Thank fuck it was only plastic' was the very first thought I had before coming to terms with the fact that this still was not an ideal situation. It could not have looked good from any angle.

You know? I still managed to get away with it though through a little bit of luck and some extreme quick thinking on my side. Despite hitting the girl it appeared that everyone around this lad were already giving him a hard time due to the fact he'd thrown the beer at me. I could see him being jostled around and security on their way to grab (save?) him. Whilst this was going on I went into damage limitation mode. Getting security down to the girl and her friends and bringing them up to the booth to dance inside there for the rest of the set.

I soon regretted it when I found myself sharing the space along with six over exuberant party girls from Rochdale. There wasn't much time left of the shift anyway so I knew I'd get through it relatively unscathed. I actually got so distracted over having them in there that before the end of the shift I still managed to find time to squeeze in one last indiscretion. Leaving one of the later records in the set to completely play itself out without mixing another one in as a replacement. Me, instead, choosing to be stood talking there to a couple of the girls while having a cigarette while the room was, again, plunged into silence.

Once again, I got away with it but that really wasn't the point. If I was willing to be objective then looking back, my set was a fucking mess. I was the happiest man in a room that was rammed with "happy people" when my last record had been and gone and I was finding myself handing over to the great man himself. Due to the amount of Ching I'd put into myself since last seeing Coxy I must've looked like a man transformed to him.

He complimented me on my performance, said he'd been listening to half of it from the side. That alone struck fear into me considering he'd have heard the whole unfortunate Kym Simms episode take place. I apologised to him over it and tried to reason over the fact that I'd had to put up with this cunt shouting at me all set. He was absolutely brand new over it. Telling me that we're all only human and all have our breaking points. It really put me at ease to hear him say that. He was more interested in the ID's of some of the white labels I'd played than me launching missiles at the crowd.

I joked with him that I'd only listened to them for the first time hours earlier and didn't even know the names myself but if he wanted to give me his number I'd call him with them. As he broke with his digits it dawned on me that despite all the Ketamine craziness earlier on in the night. The damage appeared to have been repaired, well with Carl Cox at any rate. Not for the first time over the night he flashed me that big trademark smile of his as he passed me the record that I had finished off with while his first record of the night was already starting to put the crowd under his spell.

'You know, I've never seen anyone end their set with Blitzkreig Bop before' he said with one eye on me and the other on putting his second track of the night down onto the SL's. 'Aye well you've never had me on your bill before either, mate' I tried to joke but was left fearing that it had come out like some Coke fuelled arrogance. He gave me one last handshake and side hug before telling me that it was now his time in the office and that I was to give him a call. The girls from Rochdale were still there dancing away in the booth as I left. I did think to go and tell them that it was now time for them to go back downstairs to the dance floor again but it really did look like more hassle than it was worth. Instead I decided, quite easily, that they were Carl Cox's problem from then on.

I'll readily admit that looking back the next day and seeing me there in VIP after my set. At that moment in time I don't think I had a care in the world. I'd faced some adversity across the night before and during my set but had pulled it off. Probably the worst set I'd ever done in my entire career but the way the crowd were cheering at the end was all that I had been interested in. Obviously I wasn't budgeting for the fact that they might've been cheering because Carl Cox, and the actual DJ they'd came to see that night, was about to take to the decks. Cocaine doesn't read the blueprint of things. It obviously looks worse in the morning though when you're not looking at it through intoxicated prescription spectacles? Exactly like the pair that I'd been wearing the night before.

At the time though after the set I felt triumphant. Sitting having a few drinks while chatting to some new and some old faces from the island. Signing a few autographs for a group of Irish girls which, despite the rocket fuel that was flowing through me, left me embarrassed over their request. Lee had been sat across the room sitting drinking with some of the people who ran Amnesia. I knew I had a bollocking over what had gone on over the night in the post from Lee but I was also aware of the fact that he was a sound enough guy and wouldn't go over it in public with me. I wouldn't have to worry about the inevitable lecture any time soon, I reassured myself.

I was sat beside a couple of guys from XL Recordings discussing some of their back catalogue when I clocked her walking in. I knew that it was something I'd have to deal with at some point. I just didn't expect that it would be so soon. Coincidentally though, I'd been unexpectedly sprung with a very good reason to speak to her after she'd left the villa earlier on in the day. She walked into VIP looking a woman on a mission and it didn't take a genius to work out who her intended target was. The moment we locked eyes it was all over, while paradoxically just about to begin.

'Excuse me, lads. I'll catch up with you later on' I made my excuses with the boys from XL and got up. Making sure that this potential car crash of a conversation was going to remain as private as it possibly could. I had entertained trying to lie to her again and put her inability to get inside under my guest pass down to some boob from the Amnesia staff but those thoughts were academic the moment that I inexplicably asked 'how did you get in?'

'Pfffffffft you think I need you to get myself into Ibiza clubs?' She was fuming, likes. I was cool as a cucumber on my side. Definitely the mixture of the Coke and the self deluded idea that I'd just blown Amnesia away on my debut there. I didn't feel like I could be touched and she was just going to be a speed bump on what was otherwise the tippest of top nights. 'You don't seem too pleased right now though? You ok, hun?'

I knew full well that me talking in a calm, cool and friendly manner would only wind her up more. Which, I suppose thinking back probably wasn't the best idea. 'You, you are fucking problem' She started prodding my chest with her finger. She really was out of her mind as a girl and best swerved if you ask me but, and there's always a fucking but. I actually needed to speak to her while the opportunity had been presented to me.

When Pablo fucking Escobar came round with the Ching later on in the afternoon to me and we'd sat having a few lines while I put my set together. Once I'd got myself ready to head up to Amnesia I went to grab my money so I could square up with him for the Ching. No money there though? I had gotten into a wee habit of shoving all of my money on the bedside table when I would go to bed. Apart from a few notes and some coinage, nada. My pay from Space wasn't there. Didn't take Kojak to work out who fucking took it as well. Obviously I couldn't go to the police about it. Didn't quite fancy going to them and telling all about my night and morning. I didn't even know her name for one thing.

I was doing my dish though when I discovered the missing money. Gave her the benefit of the doubt to begin with though and had a good look around the house just in case I'd taken it out when I was wrecked and had put it somewhere else. You know when you start looking in areas of your house that you didn't even know existed though that it's time to call off the search. So aye, the idea that she was giving me attitude there and then, considering she'd actually stolen from me hours earlier, was almost impressive in terms of a show of cojones from her.

'You a fucking liar' she continued while I stood there with a daft grin on my face. I could feel it stretching my face. She looked funny when she got angry. Fuck knows what it's going to be like for her kids in the future when she's trying to give them a hard time. 'Me? What have I done?' I pleaded my innocence to her like a dirty bastard of an Argentinian centre half who has just been pulled up by the referee for the assault that has just taken place on the opposing teams number nine.

'You did not put me on the guest list, you lied that you would' - 'Look, I'm sorry, I just forgot when I arrived here. It was all a bit hectic, lots of stuff was going on. I didn't lie to you,' I lied. This seemed to calm her a little. I barely knew her but already had begun to see that, emotionally wise, she was up and down more times than Dundee FC from the Premier League. Of course, I can't really say that I was helping her mental state by one moment calming her down and the next bringing up the subject of the fact that she'd stolen my wages from Space.

She went absolutely radge at this accusation. Lunged at me and everything like she was going to give me a slap. I could see what she was doing, caught over what she'd done she was going with the public overreaction to double down over what she'd done in pinching my pesetas. I wasn't expecting to see them again and was prepared to put it down to a life lesson to not be so trusting with random girls you don't even know the name of but even so. There was no way I was letting her away with it without me having a few words on the subject.

This "accusation" seemed to be too much for her though and she just plain flipped, people having to get in the way of her and moi until security arrived on the scene to cart her off. She didn't go quietly though. 'YOU SELESOW ARE A SHIT LOVER WITH TINY PENIS … EVERYONE, DJ SELESOW HAS A PENIS SO SMALL YOU CAN'T EVEN SEE IT. IT, IT IT'S LIKE A WALNUT WHIP.' She continued this rant as she was led away out of the place. My first instinct in terms of a reaction was to ask her how she even knew what one of those was. 'How do you know what a fucking Walnut Whip is?' I shouted right as she was removed from the room before it occurred to me that she'd obviously stayed in Scotland for a while.

Sitting there late that afternoon recalling all of this. I cringed at the mental image of, while she shouted her way out of the room. I had thought it a good idea to take my zip down, put my hands inside my shorts and stick my pinkie out of the fly. Definitely seemed a good idea at the time even though I was, for the first time, dropping my coolness and sinking down to her level. It was probably more a coping mechanism than anything else. When an embarrassingly loud woman is creating a scene where the size of your penis is taking centre piece then it doesn't matter who you are. Whether she's lying or not. You're going to have to find your coping mechanism to get you through the moment.

That was around about when Lee appeared on the scene. I swear that cunt is like Batman. When I find myself in the worst kinds of trouble he just appears from nowhere. I don't even need to phone or shine any symbol up into the sky to get him to come rescue things, he just always seems to know. He was pretty understanding when I was telling him about what had happened with *insert name* and was good enough to make sure I got home alright. We went for a couple of beers before I crashed for the night. After what had been a rollercoaster of a day it was actually decent to just sit with him and have a wee blether together over a beer. No industry people that you need to be "on" with, no ear splitting house music which renders conversation a challenge at the best of times, no distractions at all.

Most of the night seemed a little vague from that point on. I remembered being back in another taxi after the bar but zilch from then on. Anyway, I obviously made it home, if not to my bed. I'd fucked it and missed the day time part of my day off completely and was now heading into evening which, the early part at least, was going to be spent making some apology phone calls to certain individuals.

The first call I'd be making though would be to that fucking dealer of mines after last nights capers. One mistakingly passed wrap to me may have caused fuck knows what untold damage to my reputation and indeed, future. Something told me that I was only able to remember elements of the story of the whole night and that there was still some unwanted revelations to come.

'If that fucker Si thinks that he's getting away with that Ketamine stunt then he must be still stuck in a K hole somewhere himself.' I thought as I got up to get the phone charger so that I could at least charge enough battery to take care of the apologies that I was going to have to make to get me out of my own K (related) hole.

Chapter 5

Si

The worst thing about Ibiza, without question, is the Scousers. Not the lack of tins of Irn Bru or a decent bit of bacon. Not the smell of sewage or even those club 18-30 cunts (The reps OR holiday makers) that roam San Antonio. It's those scallies from Liverpool. They act like they run the fucking place. The truth is though, they kind of do. This was something I found out early doors on arriving. I'd decided that with Zico being out for three months I'd follow him out to Spain and from there? The plan was really nothing beyond making it up as I'd went along.

We've been through a lot Zico and I over the years and I'd felt that it would've been a case of failing him as a friend if I didn't go out to Ibiza and support him at what was the most exciting time in his life. Who knows what he'd be getting up to when over there and aye, I admit. I wanted a piece of it too. Fuck being back home and getting phone calls from him everyday telling me all the mad parties that he'd been to, the birds that he was riding night from night and (obviously) all the chemicals that he was getting wired into.

Nah, fuck that, likes. Ok, it was maybe a bit excessive of me to hand my notice in at work to enable me to follow Zico following his dreams but what's done is done. I hadn't actually wanted to quit my job at Wilson's but I guess it was a case of brinksmanship that went too far after I'd asked my boss if I could have three months off. Unpaid, likes.

From the moment Stevie had told me that he'd bagged a residency at the world famous Space I was made up for the cunt. One of those moments where something really big is happening to someone super close to you. Someone that you love and would go into battle for. I HAD to be there with him. This was decided early on and for me, it was really a case of how I would make it happen. I toyed with the idea of going to the doctor and hitting him with some tall tale about me being depressed. Don't want to go to work, can't face getting out of bed. Feel I need to recharge my batteries and so on.

I was going to say that I had the chance to go and get some extended sun and relaxation in Spain and felt that it would benefit me health wise. Thought it would work but I didn't want tarred with the mental brush. It's scandalous really though that a man isn't able to open up about stuff like that. Cunts at work talking about you behind your back. Promotions scuppered because they have you down as someone with mental health problems. I decided against going down that road and instead went for full honesty, well, ish.

I told my gaffer, Davy Bannon, that I'd had some personal stuff going on in my life that needed attending to. Things that I wouldn't be able to fully concentrate on my job until I'd had some time away to tend to things and in him, as my gaffer, I was seeking some compassion. In fairness all of that wasn't lies as such. The only thing I could have ever been accused of was being deliberately vague. Playing the personal reasons card wasn't exactly a smart move because I knew that would've only prompted more questions back in my direction but it was the only thing I could think of.

It didn't go well. I wouldn't answer the questions that I was being asked about my personal circumstances. I could hardly answer that I wanted the whole summer off so I could party from San Antonio to Playa den Bossa only to return back to work a completely broken man in need of *another* three months recovery. I had to have meetings with HR and everything. It was a fucking drain on my resources as a human dealing with those sanctimonious pricks I can assure you.

In the end I forced the issue by walking in one Monday morning and handing in my notice. I'd said to Bannon that I was sorry it had come to it as I'd really enjoyed working there. I admit, by handing in my notice in a way that clearly showed that I wasn't actually wanting to. I had entertained some fantasy that it would all work out and I'd end up getting the time off. Didn't fucking work out that way. Bannon snatched the resignation letter from me like a crack fiend would take a freshly packed pipe. Called my bluff and that was that. I was out the door.

'You were in with the bricks here, Simon. I hope you don't go on to regret leaving, son.' I'll always remember him saying when I was leaving his office that day.

Getting a job when I got back from Ibiza wouldn't have presented too much of a problem, I'd felt. That in itself wasn't much of a concern for me although deep down I had the fear that once it started to enter the last few weeks before coming home, that's when it would start to gnaw away at me. And it went without really saying. If the Ibiza experience was going to be anything remotely close to what I'd envisaged then the last thing my head would've been able to handle as we reached the final furlong before facing reality and coming home. It would be worrying about looking for a new job.

All of that was so far away at that point though it wasn't even worth a seconds worth of my consideration. The bigger challenge for me was how I was going to live over there for so long and keep myself subsidised. Fuck, all the other times I'd been over on holiday was for either one or two weeks and I'd always spent the equivalent of the deficit of Zambia. One year I had to get my mum to transfer money into my bank account because I'd ran out after less than a week on what was a two week stay. I'd already accepted that I'd have to do something when I was out there to earn a crust and keep myself topped up in pesetas for all of the night time activities that I was actually there on the island for.

Bit of PR for a club or working in a bar, that kind of deal or something to that effect. I thought even through Zico's connections he'd get me something fixed up. Apparently my suggestion that I could carry his records into the club for a job wasn't a winner with him. He was well chuffed at the news that I was joining him out there though. Three months to get up to fuck knows what capers. A long way from the days in fields in the middle of nowhere in Scotland. Fucking SPACE and Zeec playing at it?! Proper pinch yourself stuff, like.

I say "capers" but in the weeks before us flying out, Stevie was trying to play it straight. Telling me how it was his big chance and that if he played things right it could do good for his career. Because of this he wasn't intending on going too radge when he was over there. Wasn't going to be staying up all night, some nights just staying in completely and all of that. Who was he trying to fucking kid eh? I thought it admirable that he even appeared to actually believe what he was saying. He was fooling no cunt though, especially me.

He took Ibiza by force that first week, so hard that after a couple of days I let him get on with it as even I couldn't keep up. That third night when he was off through to Ibiza Town that's when I got speaking to Ivan in The Bucanero. You know those occasions where you meet a complete stranger but yet within minutes the two of you are on such good terms that it almost feels like you've been friends for years? That was what it was like when we got talking. I was there on my own but I guess he'd heard me speaking to the waitress because out of the blue he asked me the question that certain people from Scotland cringe when confronted with.

'Sooooo you Celtic or Rangers, friend?' He asked from the table behind me. Myself at first, not even realising that he was actually speaking to me.

There's not many things that I hate in life, I've always felt that it was a waste of emotion to take yourself in that direction. Some things deserve that status though. Paedophiles, terrorists, shop keepers who don't say thank you after you've thanked them once the transaction has taken place. Being asked if you support Celtic or Rangers however is one of those things. The fact that because you're Scottish, someone has already assumed that you support either or of those teams is a little patronising, even if the person asking is only doing so out of ignorance more than anything else.

'Neither' I replied back while turning around to clock who had spoken. 'Dundee United' I added. In what was obviously my own private joke I asked him back 'Sooooo Real or Barca?' He smiled, back a sheepish kind of smile before spilling. 'Barca.' I, half a dozen beers in and feeling like the holiday bug had bitten me big time and full of the joys, exploded with glee.

'HA so you know full fucking well who Dundee United are then, amigo' I said, smiling at the guy. - 'Ahhh you were lucky in eighty seven' he laughed. 'I guess we were just lucky when we beat you twice in the sixties as well then, aye?' I ribbed him. He joined me at my table and we must've sat and talked fitba alone for the next hour. Like I said, we connected with each other very early doors. I'm not exactly in the habit of sitting talking to strange men in pubs either by the way but I guess. Put a Dundee United and a

Barcelona fan together and they're going to have something to talk about from the very start, even if only one of them actually *wants* to talk about it.

We soon got onto other topics and during the conversation. He asked me how long my holiday was for. Me replying that I was actually out for three months filling in the blanks while my mate was working as a DJ.

'So you have job when here, Simon? yes?' - He asked like it was already a formality. 'Well aye, that's the plan anyway. Haven't started looking for one mind you. Those first couple of nights on the island almost finished me before I got started. That's why I'm having a quiet one tonight just here in the bay while my friend is out clubbing.'

'Can you drive, Simon?' He bluntly asked. 'Ummm aye of course, pal' I replied, his face lighting up. 'Then you do not even have to search for job, I have one for you. Mostly day time work, not many hours but good pesetas, brother. My delivery driver just left and I need a new one. I have people coming tomorrow about the job but if you want it then it is yours.'

Fucking hell, how easy was that to get a job around here? Almost as easy to get some drugs, which incidentally, took me all of seventeen and a half minutes after dumping my suitcase in Stevie's villa.

I asked if I could speak to him the next day about it but that yeah I was interested in the job. Nice wee driving gig eh? No having to deal with pissed up holiday makers at night time on the street or picking up glasses in some pub sounded like just the ticket to me. As always though, things were never as they seemed. I went home that night thinking I'd bagged a decent wee delivery driving job. Could've been fucking anything for all I knew. Car parts, caged animals, fucking fresh off the pan paella to some hungry holiday maker for all I knew. That was the point though, I never fucking think and it was only the next day that through speaking to Ivan on the phone that I saw that things were a bit suss about it all. What he was offering for what looked like it would amount to only two to four hours work a day seemed overly generous.

I still took it, likes. Started the same day and carried out a delivery for him to a secluded house outside of San Antonio. An absolutely stunning place that you wouldn't have known was there were you not actually looking for it. I didn't know what was in the small jiffy bag that I was transporting as it was sealed and any tampering on my part would have been obvious to the recipient. Something else that was obvious though was that this was a drug run that I was on. The reaction at the villa on my arrival was like when you see the crowds waiting at the airport for a country who have returned home with the World Cup. There was around six people, a mix of men and women, all standing around outside in the gardens of the house jumping up and down and pointing at me as I slowly pulled up in the car.

Some guy, in his forties dressed in a Hawaiian shirt that was undone exposing his massive gut, came rushing over, not even giving me a chance to get my seat belt off and get out of the car. 'Cheers, mate' he said in a Mancunian accent. 'We were almost about to run out, scary stuff' he laughed away to himself as he passed a wad of notes into the open window to me. 'Oh and something for yourself for getting here so quick' he winked as he slipped me some pesetas. 'Very kind of you, squire' I smiled back as I passed him the jiffy bag.

He quickly opened it up, checked the contents and smiled back at me. 'And with that our transaction is now at a close' he saluted me, taking his hand away from his head and motioning his arms in a kind of 'you can go now' gesture. Fucking Cokeheads eh. The absolute worst cunts. I should know, I regularly *am* that same cunt. He reached his hand in to give me a handshake before I left, wishing me a good day before adding that thanks to myself. Him and everyone else certainly would be.

Upon getting back to the cafe that Ivan had asked me to take the money back to. I found him sat there reading some sports paper called Marca, a cup of coffee on the table along with a danish pastry of some Spanish variety. The first thing that struck me wasn't that I knew he was connected to the drug game and that I was about to tell him that I knew what I was delivering and that I wanted to know more about what I was getting myself involved in. Instead all I could think about was the fact that he looked just like that James Richardson who does the Football Italia with his newspaper sat in a cafe and that. I wasn't sure if Ivan was about to tell me a little bit more about his narcotics operation or give me the run down on who Real Madrid's transfer targets were during the pre season.

To give the man his due, after my full transparency and admitting to him that I was in no way a stranger to drugs/the whole scene in general and that it was obvious what I'd delivered for him. Told him that I wasn't exactly against the idea of working for him but had also wanted to know more about it. After all of that, he gave me a bit of background. His family, the Camachos had been the major drug suppliers across Ibiza for over a decade. Then the English arrived.

What began with just your usual party people descending there for two weeks eventually led to some holiday makers seeing potential business opportunities with apparent easy money to be made. This led to some friction across Ibiza as the English that had decided to set up shop same up against the Camacho family and their associates. This provoked a turf war that had rumbled on for a couple of years which had seen a constant battle for supremacy between the Camachos and the O'Halloran family from Liverpool. Apparently it hadn't been anything too heavy but there had been casualties on both sides with some poor cunts on the receiving end of some brutal medieval type stuff. No deaths though. Then the Scousers introduced guns to proceedings and as you can imagine. That altered the whole dynamic.

Ivan admitted that the family were more or less muscled out by the Liverpudlians and all of their men stationed on the island. He told me that he still moved a lot of product under the radar of the Scouse boys. Had lots of loyal customers who wouldn't go elsewhere for their narcotic needs and that it was now a case of doing business discreetly but how business was booming.

I probably should have walked out the cafe and left him to it. Fucking drugs? I'd come to Ibiza to take them not transport the things around for other people to take. The Scousers side of things? It seemed a little dangerous. Guns and everything. It was definitely something to be swerved. Especially with the luxury of having multiple red flags already being raised before me agreeing to take the job.

Instead, I was back the next day for more. Off in that Volkswagen Golf to a collection of varied destinations. A hotel, golf course, marina. It spiralled from there inside that first week and a half. It had truly been an eye opener. A lucrative one at that. I'd probably earned more in my first two days of delivering than some poor PR sap out on the streets would've done in a week. Then again, there was a pretty good reason for that. The British PR folk over in Ibiza don't normally find themselves given a couple of broken arms and marched to the top of a hotel with threats to throw them off the top of it like what happened to wee Juanjo the other night when he got caught punting gear near the West End of town.

Luckily I'd not had any contact with any of these lads from the O'Halloran family but from the stories that I'd been getting fed to me, shit was certainly a bit real out there on the street. I guessed that it was possibly only a matter of time before I *did* come across them in some shape or form. Not something that I was relishing too much as a prospect but neither was it like I was some daft kid who didn't know or appreciate the risks that I was taking either. If it was a case of the ends justifying the means then the money I was pulling in, which not only guaranteed that I'd be able to live quite comfortably while out there but that if it continued I'd be going back to Scotland with some paper in my pocket, then aye. The ends justified everything.

That day after the night (and morning) of Amnesia though I, ironically, felt that there were more troublesome elements of my life than trying to avoid Liverpudlian gangsters that I needed to steer clear of and that came through my best mate in this life, Steven Duncan. I'd made a right royal cunt out of things the night before by handing Zico the wrong wrap which near enough fucked his night (life?) up. For all I know I DID fuck it up for him. I wasn't exactly feeling too clever myself due to going through the exact same situation in taking one drug that was about from Ibiza to Australia away in distance to the drug I thought I was taking.

The last I actually seen of him was at the start of the night. Never caught up with him after that. We briefly spoke on the phone before his set was due to start and it didn't sound like that he was in too good of a nick. Aye, well you wouldn't be after taking a couple of lines of Ketamine up your beak when you thought it was Ching though. He wasn't too chuffed with my honest mistake. Effectively hanging up on me when I'd told him that he was on his own from there on in. It wasn't like I could go and buy gear from the Scousers who were doing bits across the place on the night though, was it?

For my sins, I ended up getting fired into the Ket over the course of the night which aye, I should've never fucking done but what's that thing Jesus always said about he who is without sin? Aye well there's not too many of those cunts around Ibiza who are able to lob stones at you. I ended up not going to bed until the afternoon the next day which meant I was waking up well into the evening.

Finding six missed calls from Zico waiting for me. Something told me that this wasn't a case of him needing me to run over with some sniff or weed. I knew it was connected to the Ketamine I'd given him. I also knew what the cunt is like when he's on his high horse about something. I didn't even know what his issue was. Most of those deejays are out of their tits when they're up there on the decks anyway so it wasn't like he would've stuck out.

'Not with this head I've got on me at present' I said to myself as I put the phone back down again onto my table, making a commitment to myself that however many times he was going to call, he would be getting hit with the 'hey how ya doin, sorry you can't get through' for the rest of the night.

Chapter 6

Zico

Something really fucking strange happened at Space. In what had been an otherwise standard warm up set for the night ahead. I found myself, for a few minutes, going back to back on the decks with a member of Johan Cryuff's Barcelona. Too mad likes. I was just minding my own business, playing to what was the usual half empty terrace with anyone who was serious about making a right good fist of Space, still many hours away from turning up. I was feeling recharged and hadn't seen anyone since *the* night of Amnesia and had taken some much needed time out to get myself together again. In a good way, that whole fuck up of a night had been a blessing in disguise. It had been the slap about the dish that I had so desperately needed. I'd started to think that I was fucking invincible, on it, partying night after night. That whole fucking Ketamine business showed me though that I was quite the opposite of invincible.

I had turned up at Space with no other intention than getting my set out the way and then I was heading back to San Antonio for an early night. Lee had managed to squeeze in a booking for me at a festival in The Netherlands between my slots at Space so wisely, I decided I'd keep things low key for the night due to the knowledge of me leaving early the next again day for Amsterdam. The good thing about my terrace residency was that with the place half empty I got the chance to test out some new tunes, see what they sounded like in a club coming out of giant speakers like Space boasted. Don't get me wrong, obviously I'd be wanting to be inside the discoteca playing to bigger crowds but all in good time. Rome wasn't built in a day. It just burned inside one, eh?

I was up on the decks when I noticed Pepe walking through the place with these two youngish looking guys. Both around the same age as myself. They looked Spanish, possibly even South American. I could see that Pepe was leading them in the direction of the booth. Him, waving at me to get my attention. 'Stevie, this is Giovanni and

Ronaldo, my guests for tonight' I reached over to shake both their hands with big smiles exchanged between them and I.

I couldn't help but think that I recognised one of them. The young guy with the big teeth. Even I knew it was mad but he looked totally like the Brazilian kid who played with PSV Eindhoven. Fuck, he even had the same name as him. The other guy, Giovanni? Nah, I'd never seen him before in my life. The both of them though didn't exactly look like your regulars that you'd see inside Space with their sports leisure clobber that they were dressed in but technically, considering they were walking around with Pepe they might as well have set the dress code given how pally the owner was with them.

'When they heard your name they wanted to meet you' Pepe informed me with a look on his face that honestly reminded me of a kid on Christmas Day. I mean, I hadn't known Pepe long, didn't really know him at all apart from a few words back and forth when I'd been appearing at the club but there was no doubt, as understated and humble as he was. He *was* Mr Space.

'What? Stevie?' I asked, taking leave of my senses for a moment. He looked back at me with a look of exasperation. 'Nada, tu tonto, Selecao.' A big smile appearing on Giovanni's face at this which prompted him to start speaking to me. Pointing towards his mate while repeating the Selecao part. The rest of it I hadn't a fucking clue what he was banging on about. Already sensing this, Pepe set about translating almost before the words had escaped his guests mouth.

'What Giovanni is saying is that both himself and Ronaldo are actually from the real Selecao, they play for Brazil.' - 'Wait a fucking minute' I twigged. 'This fucking WAS Ronaldo.' Ever the professional I raised my hand to indicate that I needed a second before proceeding to mix in the Tori Amos remix of "Professional Widow" that I had lined up to go. Once done I was able to go back and make some attempt of conversation with the two (I assumed) Portuguese speakers and Pepe who favoured a mix of Spanish and broken English.

Straight away it looked like the van Helden track I'd dropped had met the approval of the two Brazilians. The two of them bobbing their head to the beat which I found surreal and comical in equal measures. 'If you are Scottish, Stevie why do you choose the name 'DJ Selecao?' Pepe asked me on behalf of Ronaldo. By this point he was verging on speaking to me more inside that one single exchange than he had in the entire time since I'd started at the club. To be fair to him. Due to the early time of my slot he generally wasn't around the club until I was done for the night. I'd only really see him on the occasions when I would decide to stick around for the night and morning.

'Well, people back home call me Zico so it came from there' I said, providing him with the short version while keeping in mind that he was then going to have to repeat it back to the other two. Once again this brought big smiles from his guests. Ronaldo, moving towards me with his hand out to shake it again which I more than happily reciprocated. 'Zico, ow melor' he beamed, or it sounded like that anyway. I didn't get a translation from Pepe on that given the fact he was already standing listening to Giovanni speak into his ear, out of range of Ronaldo.

I had the passing thought about Si and how he was missing out on all of this. Then again if the fanny couldn't be arsed answering his phone? I'd called him half a dozen times the day before. I admit, the initial first few were motivated purely through me seeking some kind of retribution from Amnesia and "Ketgate." Once a few hours had passed and I'd managed to clear up some of the regretful behaviour from the night before and had calmed down. I'd tried him again a couple of times to see what he was up to and if he wanted to come over. The next couple of attempts later again was purely me wanting him to bring some Hash to me, whether he wanted to do the mates thing with me or not.

'Giovanni thinks this is brilliant' Pepe beamed, visibly happy that his guests were happy. - 'So why do you have two Brazilian football players inside your club then?' I asked, a pretty pertinent question I thought. I'd never had any celebrities up at the decks before but I'd have to be honest and say that if there ever was to be any up there beside me I'd have imagined it as some D list celebrity from a British soap or something like that. Not two top level football players who, technically, should be a million fucking miles away from the complete madhouse that is Space, Ibiza.

'They are enjoying the island of Ibiza before starting training for the new season. I am BIG Barca fan so it has been my pleasure to offer them my beach house to live in when here.' I never even took a second to ponder what he'd said and before I'd known it had pointed towards Ronaldo and asked in amazement 'When did you sign with Barcelona?' Not that he'd have been able to understand what I'd said anyway. For a moment the most important thing for me was that despite being a self confessed fitba anorak. The best young player in the world had signed for Barcelona and it had went completely under my radar, which pretty much highlighted how life had been for me since I'd arrived in Ibiza.

It was as if I'd completely detached myself from all of life normal realities after swapping Scotland for Spain. Euro Ninety Six was almost ready to start and I didn't even fucking know what squad Scotland had picked for the upcoming games against Holland, England and Switzerland. I almost felt disgusted with myself that I didn't know of such a major signing in world fitba like Ronaldo to Barca.

'They both sign for the team this year' Pepe told me with the greatest of pleasure before putting an arm around the two of them and pulling them both tight towards him and shouting 'we win La Liga this year, Atletico only have it on one year loan.' It was quite cute actually, to see how excited he was to have the two players there with him. That's what fitba can do to someone though. Over the years I can only imagine the great and good who have been inside his club. Film stars, musicians and all of that and I'd bet that he hadn't been fazed by them yet stick two players of the team he supports inside there and he turns all excited fanboy.

Things led to another with the three of them and before long Ronaldo was in the DJ booth beside me. Speaking purely from the perspective as a DJ, this felt conflicting. Don't get me wrong, I was happy to extend a warm welcome and roll out the red carpet for any guests of the guy who was effectively paying my wages when in Ibiza but when you're a DJ it's a bit of a personal thing too. Do we try and tell you how to do your job or actually try and step in and do it for you? We'll do our thing and you do yours and aye, that also means no fucking requests.

Fair enough, if you're going back to back with another DJ then it's all good as you can generally trust them to know what they're doing when up there in front of everyone. It was fair to assume that the newly acquired Barca Brazilian wonder kid would not be in possession of mixing skills, which he obviously wasn't.

Stupidly, my main concern had been that the crowd in there would have mistaken his mixing for mines and that they'd be going away at the end of the night thinking how shit I'd been. I hadn't really sussed out that while I'd been having the "conversation" with the Brazilians that most of the crowd in there had already realised that there was famous fitba players amongst them so when it came to Ronaldo going back to back behind the decks with me. It was hardly incofuckingnito.

It was only once he was in there beside me that I took moment to pause and noticed that all eyes were not exclusively fixed on me but my DJ partner. I'm sure some of those big name deejays (the ones with an ego bigger than all of the Balearic Islands combined) who were the headliners across the island over the season would've been put out by this and the attention not being showered on them but personally, I loved it. Once I'd gotten past the fact that actually no, the crowd would most definitely not be leaving the club later talking about how shite "my" mixing had been, I really got into it.

As for Ronaldo? That buck toothed smile was so big I reckon it could've been seen from San Antonio. The lad was having the time of his life beside me. Did he have a clue what he was doing? Did he fuck. Fair enough, stick me on a football pitch beside some hard bastard defenders like a Bergomi, Hierro or Baresi and I'm pretty sure I wouldn't know how to negotiate my way around them so really, why would've or should've the boy from Brazil known his way around a pair of SL's? He wasn't giving a flying fuck in any case. Happier than a pig in shite so he was. With this all being a bit spur of the moment I completely sacked off any idea of actually trying to show him how to beat match.

His mixing sounded like some poor cunt trying to play bongo drums while also falling down a flight of stairs. That though, kind of was the whole point. It wouldn't have been too good a look for moi if some fitba player who hadn't been near a set of decks in his puff had been able to get up there and come across as Todd fucking Terry, would it? The worse that he was the better this all then would look.

Unless I had grossly read the room wrong. This was most definitely a case of everyone knowing the DJ was unskilled but *because* of who he was this was one of those times where everyone lapped it up regardless.

It was too radge though watching him whipping up the crowd with his arms as another badly mixed in tune was dropped. All I'd really shown him was where the crossfader was on the mixer, displaying to him what would happen if he was to move it from one side across to the other. This he got straight away before proceeding to go back and forward from record to record. Much like the effect you'd have expected if you had let your three year old nephew loose on the decks in your bedroom.

It was a complete mess but it was beautiful. I was handing him the records as despite the unexpected turn the set had taken. I remained determined that the tracks I'd picked out earlier on in the day would be stuck to. I did however come up with an inspired choice for the very last one of the set that hadn't initially been planned. Watching both my fellow DJ and Giovanni down there who was having a wee dance to himself feeding off each other it came to me in a flash. First of all I had to go looking for it because I wasn't even sure I had it inside my record box. Having only played it once before but fortunately inside the couple of weeks that I'd been there in Ibiza. I wanted to surprise the both of them with my choice so making sure that Ronaldo didn't get a chance to clock what was written in the centre label of the record, I slapped it onto the deck I was stood over.

There wasn't a fucking chance I was ever going to be able to mix it into a house tune so with the end of the set fast approaching I reached over towards the SL that he was standing over and purposely switched the deck off. Allowing the Dave Angel track that was playing to start slowing down. This, giving off the effect as if the batteries on your Walkman had started to die in the middle of the song that you were listening to.

Ronaldo looked at me with an inquisitive look on his coupon. Almost as if he knew that I had done it deliberately but couldn't work out why. He didn't have long to wait before the record on his turntable had stopped playing altogether. The crowd, which had gotten a lot bigger from the moment Ronaldo had taken up sticks alongside me, mistakingly taking this for the end of the set and starting to cheer and whistle. That's when I pulled the crossfader back across in my direction just as the piano started to kick in on the track that I'd lined up to close things off with.

The smile on both players faces was one of the single most satisfying moments I'd ever experienced as a DJ right there when they both began to recognise the unmistakable intro for "Mas que Nada."

'This is for you and Giovanni, amigo.' I smiled, giving him a hug right at the same time as a fucking big KLM passenger jet came flying over our heads, to the cheers that the crowd on the terrace would generally greet an overhead airplane with. He reciprocated back with a hug that felt like I'd scored the winner in the Champions League final as a teammate of his. I looked over his shoulder towards Giovanni and Pepe. Giovanni dancing away while singing his heart out. He knew the lyrics at least which was a whole lot more than I could ever have claimed.

Surreal, it was, but once the tune had finished. Ronaldo and myself exited the decks to rapturous applause. I had a mini moment of being a little pissed off because I'd had the sense that all of the cheers and adulation were aimed in his direction rather than the one who had, largely, had them dancing for the past couple of hours. It was only a few seconds and it had passed again because, despite that slight twang of jealousy, I got it. This was not what could have ever been described as a normal set on a normal night. Despite how many years I (hopefully) had ahead of me in the game. Even then, I knew that I wouldn't be playing again back to back with a guy, for all I knew, who was going to go on to become the very best player in the world.

I had planned to head straight back to the villa after my set was done because of the early afternoon flight to Schipol but I really couldn't turn down the invite of going through to VIP with the other three of them for a "chat." I had so many questions that I wanted to ask them. Turned out that Giovanni had come from Santos while Ronaldo had made his way from Eindhoven so aye, despite me having never heard of him. The boy Giovanni obviously had a bit of talent. Then again, if Barcelona want you then you're not exactly going to be a mug with a ball at your feet, are you? From the questions that I was asking them via Pepe. They were able to see that I knew a bit about the sport.

They seemed impressed by this. It appeared that they had no idea that people from a country like Scotland would have had so much knowledge about their own domestic game back in Brazil. I thought about being a fanny and asking them what they knew about Scottish fitba but already knew that my "joke" would not have come across too well in translation so left it.

Then again, I couldn't resist having a little play around with them by telling them that Maradona was better than Pele and that half of Pele's goals that he claimed over the years were scored in his back garden while having a kick around with his kids. Technically I wasn't actually joking at all but had said it in a way that had at least suggested that I had. 'Ohhhhh ohhhhh' Giovanni said waving a finger back and forth at me smiling while Ronaldo screamed out 'sacrilegio' at me. Something I didn't need any assistance from Pepe on.

I departed a while later with hugs and handshakes exchanged along with promises that if I was ever playing in Barcelona that coincided when there was a Barcelona match on I was to come to the Nou Camp as their guest and I'd return the favor later that night wherever I was playing. I'd normally have said that there wasn't exactly much chance of me ever playing in the city of Barcelona but who really knew? When I travelled across to Playa den Bossa earlier that evening I wouldn't have thought that I was going to playing back to back with a striker for FC Barcelona at Space!

I left them to it. Pepe had been talking about this five star restaurant he was going to be taking them to for dinner so it had looked like they were going to be making moves of their own. I think that it was some seafood place so aye good luck to them with that. Not for me likes. As a young boy (and on more than one occasion) I'd peed in the Mediterranean when abroad on holiday. That's all I'm saying about seafood.

Afterwards while I was hanging around for a couple of beers before heading back. Sandro, one of the staff at Space, came up to me to hand me my fee for the night. The money inside the customary white envelope that it would always be presented to you in. I really didn't know why they bothered. The envelope (minus the money) would always be left in a crumpled up ball before I'd even left the club.

'Your fee for tonight, Stevie and also your fee from last appearance' he said, handing two envelopes to me. This created some confusion. Why would he be giving me money for an appearance that I'd already been paid for and then subsequently had stolen from me? The easy option would have been to just smile, thank him and take the money that was being offered to me. The easy option, however, is not something that I have been renowned for taking. Ask around.

Completely risking having one of the envelopes being withdrawn I couldn't help but ask him why I was being paid for the previous night. This caused him a bit of amusement. Laughing while telling me that it had been my own request that the club hold onto my fee the last time I had been there. Apparently I had told Sandro that if I had held onto the money I was going to end up making a beast of myself and that maybe it would be a good idea if I didn't have it on my person. I was actually admiring the maturity that I had shown in that moment even if I couldn't actually remember it.

She hadn't stolen the money after all. Oops.

I had a cab called for me and was soon on my way on the twenty or so miles stretch back up to San Antonio. I was actually pretty fucking proud of myself for the discipline that I'd shown the previous couple of days. Didn't venture out the whole day before on my day off. Just chilled there in the villa and had let every cunt else get on with their own stuff. Even the next day, I actually went down to the beach for a walk and a swim. Oh aye, Mr healthy and clean living, me. I wasn't about to start sucking my own dick yet though. I was off to Amsterdam for a gig on the outskirts of the city. I'd only been to Amsterdam twice in my life and both times had been less than straightforward. A city that will fucking skin you alive if you've got enough money and are weak willed enough to let it.

I'd never been there as a DJ however and was excited / intrigued to see how different a visit it would be for that reason with me being there in a professional capacity. First time I visited, the place blew my mind. Aye, obviously it's a complete cliche by this point and has been for decades but for fucks sake. You try and not lose your shit when you visit a city for the first time that you can legally buy the strongest grass known to man and walk about perusing some really tidy as fuck girls behind glass windows that, if you're that way inclined, you can quite literally get your Nat King from. Too mad!

Not that it would've ever been an option for moi, likes. I was there with Lisa at the time for one thing. It wasn't much long after we got back home from that weekend break, few weeks or so, before her and I split up. It was quite sad the way that it all worked out between us. An absolute diamond of a girl and someone who stuck by me through some really difficult times and for that, it's not something that I would be ever likely to forget. Maybe we just met too young, her and I but once I'd started to DJ that's when the problems started to follow.

With me traveling around quite a bit she wasn't always in a position to go with me which equalled the two of us inevitably not spending as much time together in the way serious couples need to. Especially weekends and as young as I still am it's pretty obvious if a couple aren't getting to spend the weekends with each other then that alone is going to lead to problems.

There was also the jealousy aspect of things to take into account. She'd been to enough events to clock how some behaved around the deejays and how, at times, they would be the centre of attention. Specifically, girls. I'd seen it myself so got what Lisa was worried about but this was at odds with the undeniable fact that I had not in any shape or form cheated on her in my life. Fuck, I looked upon her, and treated her accordingly like she was the centre of my world. Had I had opportunities for one night stands while traveling around? Of course I had. Had I acted on them? Absolutely fucking not. You just don't do that to someone who you claim to be as "your world" and if you do then evidently they're not the person that you're telling yourself that they are.

Still, even the fact that she got jealous of it all when I had given her nothing to suspect me over was something that grated a little with me.

I didn't like it. Almost had the opposite effect on me in the sense of that if I'm going to be receiving grief over something that I hadn't done then fuck it. May as well actually DO what I was being suspected of. Not that I did though even if I could've done time and time again.

When we split there was no real animosity between us. More a case of realism and acceptance that it wasn't going to work between us anymore. My first real break up. Shit, she was my first actual girlfriend. We made a vow to each other that we'd stay friends. This in itself would've been preferred considering the close proximity that we were located. Really though, how many couples actually say that and how many actually do stick to it?

We were just one of those statistics I guess. The actual facts of it all was that despite living within ten minutes of each other I'd seen her something like twice from when our relationship had come to an end. Once in Paul's corner shop and the other when I was walking my auntie and uncles dog for them. Both times felt just weird. Don't get me wrong. It was all friendly and civil likes, asking each other what we'd been up to lately, the usual stuff. Felt a little, I don't know? False? Maybe not the word. Definitely a feeling of standing speaking to someone but knowing that you've seen a lot more to that person than you're seeing and hearing right there in front of you.

Once I was back from Space I cracked open a bottle of Sol for myself and settled down to see what el Spanish TV had for me. Striking gold with the repeat of the Spain - Peru match from Seville earlier on in the evening. The Spaniards looked pretty tasty in the three nil hiding that they gave the tins of Red Stripe in what was apparently their last friendly before the real business of the European Championships got underway. Tasty or not you just knew that they were never going to win it. They never do when it comes to tournaments though. Sitting in a pretty fucking big glass house lobbing the stones when I say that as a Scot, I have to admit.

As for us and the tournament being staged down the road in England. It was a case of pragmatism. Well it was for me anyway. I couldn't really comment on the rest of Scotland and how or if they were being whipped up by the tabloids back home but as far as I felt. We wouldn't get out of the group stages with England and Holland being the obvious favourites to progress. If though, we were to get some kind of result against the English at Wembley then that in itself would be the equivalent of bringing the trophy back to Scotland with us.

From the moment we were drawn out of the hat alongside them I knew that right there was an opened and closed case of that particular day being either heaven or hell for me and my fellow countrymen. One thing that was completely taken as fact was that regardless of being in Scotland, Ibiza or Timbukfuckingtu. When the day of that match against them rolled around it was going to be an enormously stressful and emotional day, whatever the outcome. Fitba can do that to you when you're invested too much into it though, can't it? Scotland versus England was one of those matches where you almost don't want to play it for fear of how bad it is going to feel if your team loses.

With a mind to all that I had to do the next day before I left for the airport. I sensibly took myself off to bed with around twenty minutes left of the Spain game. It wasn't lost on me that there I was in bed before the point that the clubs in both San Antonio and den Bossa had even really got going. Amsterdam being Amsterdam, it was pretty much assumed that whatever the city delivered for me it would be the antithesis of my pipe, slippers and early sleep the night before.

Chapter 7

Peter

A table sir? I was asked by a kerb side waiter for what felt like the hundredth time on my stroll down Las Ramblas as I headed down the street in the direction of the beach. The stench of desperation from the young and immaculately turned out Spaniard was palpable. He had the look of someone who had been turned down so many times inside the one shift that his soul and spirit had almost been destroyed. I allowed myself a passing moment of sympathy for him before remembering that I didn't exactly have my own problems to seek myself.

I'd given Eva my credit card for the morning to go and stock up on some clothes while I went for a walk along Barceloneta Beach to try and clear my head. Take a moment to inhale and exhale and assess just how monumentally fucked things were and the most important thing of all. What the next move was going to be because the only thing that *was* for certain was that we couldn't stay there in Barcelona. Despite what I'd told Eva. That I was getting us on the first plane out of Bogotá to Europe wherever the destination. This conveniently being a flight to Barcelona. The actual facts to it all however. That Barcelona was, at the time we did our moonlight flit, the absolute last place I wanted to be in. Yet in the most crudest of irony, the one single place that I needed to get myself to.

I just needed some time on my own to work it all out. I'd made thinking on my feet an art form throughout my life but sometimes you just need to pull back from everyone and everything to find your way again. Fuck, was I mentally and physically drained though. From the moment I'd walked into Mik's apartment and found him there. Throat slashed with his tongue sticking out of the open wound. I had been acting on adrenaline all the way up until that point walking along a beach in Catalunya.

Despite my occupation and the fact that murders were a daily occurrence in some way or other. I'd never actually seen a dead body in my life until that moment. It was horrific. If thinking about a dead body I would've always had the hackneyed image of someone lying in a coffin at the funeral, peaceful. There was no peace to be found inside the villa that day in the heart of the vibrant Zona Rosa district of the city. Only an image that would haunt me for the whole of that long distance flight out of South America. Why had my long time friend and business partner been murdered in such a brutal and sadistic of ways? That, I actually didn't know but when you're in the line of business like Mikael and I. Sometimes it's best not to stick around and find out the why.

As I left his place, only after having thrown up all of my breakfast right to the side of him. I knew I had two choices. To get the hell outta dodge and work things out remotely or stay there in Bogotá and roll the dice over what may or may not have been a fate every bit as grotesque as what Mik had been handed. Knowing just what a dangerous game we played day in day out through our choice of work and specifically the area of the world that we chose to carry it out in. There was always the potential that some nasty scenarios could present themselves in our direction.

We'd made a connection with the Ramirez brothers, Eddy and German in the late eighties. With the political focus being mainly on both the Medellin and Cali cartels it left the brothers to get up to all sorts of business which in part, came with some assistance from Mikael and myself. A partnership that had proved lucrative for all concerned but the moment I found my mutilated friend there in his chair it had appeared that our contract had officially been terminated.

Barcelona was unavoidable as far as the initial destination when I'd decided to flee town. Given the fact that it was a city that had concrete links to the Bogotá Cartel it should've been a city that I had headed in the opposite direction of. Along with Naples it was the main entry point, through its ports, for any shipment heading from Colombia to Europe. The Ramirez brothers also had various "legitimate" businesses in the city as a cover for them operating in Europe. Working in tandem with the Italians who were coining it in from just allowing the product to enter the Moll D'Adossat port.

With the reach that the mafia had in Barcelona and by that extension, the Colombians. It wasn't exactly a stretch to suggest that through their connections at El Prat airport. Eddy and German already knew where I'd ran to. I took some small comfort over the fact that I never really had any other choice. Going on the run and with no idea what would follow as a result. I needed to ensure that I would have the funds required to facilitate Eva and I going off the grid.

That's where Sal Sanchis came in. Sanchis, a lawyer as bent as a five fucking bob note and in my personal predicament, the *exact* person that you need. A man with the capabilities of, for the right price, making sure that a clients ill gotten gains remained safe and sound away from law enforcement's prying eyes. Half the time I didn't even know which country my money was even being stored such was his frequency for, as I'd termed, "fucking about." Something that he had always countered as "being smart." Not that it really mattered. I never at any point needed to lay my hands on it for any reason. It was nothing other than a rainy day fund. I always knew that one day it wasn't going to be so much of a rainy spell but a typhoon crossed with an electrical storm and I wanted to make sure I would be ready for it when it eventually came.

Why would I trust someone who I would, and to his face, describe as bent as a five bob note? Well when you swim with sharks as I'd been doing for over a decade in one way or another. You needed to sharpen your teeth and develop a sense of smelling blood. Years back when we'd first started doing business when I was still based in Europe. We took care of the whole trust issue over handing over substantial amounts of money to shifty lawyers. 'Why should I trust you with my money?' I bluntly asked him in what was the equivalent of an audition that day sat in his office in the Les Courts area of Barcelona. This, he seemed to find amusing even though it was without doubt a pertinent question.

'Well unless I've been misled, Peter. You were sent here to see me by Hakan Yilmaz, yes?' It almost felt like he was talking down to me. The tone he spoke in alongside him going with the whole asking a question that we already both knew to be fact. I allowed him to continue. 'So if you are someone that does business in the same world as Meester Yilmaz then it would not be so good a business move for me if your money was to go missing.'

I wasn't prepared for that. I expected something along the lines of some confident and slick response that was designed to put me at ease with the thought of handing over hundreds of thousands of pounds to what was effectively a stranger. Instead, he showed a vulnerability that suggested that while the man clearly enjoyed the lifestyle and the riches it brought him. He wasn't someone who had forgotten the type of clientele that he was working for. My old mate Hakan was a fucking pussycat as well. That was the comical thing. Of course, he had his links with some serious people back in Istanbul. Sometimes, that's all you need though. Links and connections.

Picking up on what Sal was getting at I played along with him. 'Well I'm not going to disagree there, I'm not sure how much money you have of Hakan's that you're safekeeping but I'm assuming that if you ever do steal it then you're going to have enough money to fly to the moon to escape what would be heading your way. Even then, Yilmaz would probably kidnap some NASA scientist's kids and make him build a rocket for him to follow you in.' We both laughed at this despite the clear undertones of a threat that was contained in what I'd said. Being a big believer in first impressions truly shaping what someone is going to think of you. I continued with the same line of conversation.

'Jokes about space travel aside. You'll obviously be aware that Hakan already has a contingency plan in place should his money go missing or he finds himself arrested and you being responsible?' It was completely made up on the spot but I guess must've sounded plausible to him because his face dropped for a second before pragmatically agreeing that he would've been surprised if there wasn't any measures put into place by his Turkish client. 'And it goes without saying that I'll be deploying such a tactic myself just to make sure that nobody does anything stupid.' I paused for a second for effect giving him a chance to jump in but he remained silent. 'But nobody is going to do anything stupid Senor Sanchis, will they?' It was funny how quickly a conversation could turn on its head because it was undeniable that it was me who was then doing the talking down out of the pair of us.

'No no no no Peter, your money be safer than in, what is the place? Fort Knox? No DEA, no Interpol, no, nobody will be able to get your money' he said almost sounding like he was trying to defend accusations to the contrary. 'Good man, Sal' I'd said with a smile trying to put the poor guy at ease. 'Just you do what you're getting paid to and you're going to make a lot of money. I very much plan on making the type of money that would make your eyes water so it would be in your very best interests to keep onside with me as we move forward.'

From the day of that first meeting I knew my money was going to be safe as houses with the likeable but undeniably slippery Catalunyan. I'd decided against calling ahead while Eva and I were waiting to board our flight. Not knowing what plans had potentially been put into action with regards to yours truly. I thought it smart not to broadcast to anyone in advance where I was headed. Literally from the moment that Eva planted a kiss on my cheek and went off in search of the boutiques I was on the phone to him.

'Surprise' I said like I was at some aunties surprise birthday party and she'd just walked in to find the whole family all crammed into her living room. 'Peter, como esta?' He replied, very much indeed caught off guard. 'Me, Salomon? Me? Well allow me to be blunt. Remember the day that I always knew had a chance of coming and you said never would? Well it's here. The end times and I need you to take care of moving my money. Now obviously you're not going to convert all of those millions in Apple, Saab and Bayer into cash overnight but I want you to set the ball rolling on it all. Whatever you've got planned for the next couple of hours then I'm afraid you're going to have to shelf it. Get all the paperwork together that you need me to sign because I'm getting the hell out of here again by tonight and can't guarantee that I'm going to be able to revisit, for at least a while.'

'Bu b b bbbbbut, Senor Duncan' - 'No fucking buts, Sal, this is serious stuff here. Just get what you need to arrange arranged and meet me at Kuba's in ninety minutes, oh and remember to bring that yellow padded envelope that's in your safe for me,' I asserted. With him always having entertained the impression that I was someone looked upon as a dangerous client, never more so when I started bringing him much larger deposits through my work with the boys from Bogotá. Sometimes it was advantageous to have that hold of fear hanging over someone. Never more so than then.

I'd strategically chosen Kuba's as the meeting point. I'd wanted a chance to see him approach from a distance to make sure he wasn't being followed or that there was any hint of a set up. Apart from Sal it was simple common sense to choose a venue that would allow me the chance to scope it out from a distance. Telling myself that if I spied anything remotely like Colombian sicarios or mafia in or around the scene I would then need to think of an alternative plan of action.

The beach right next to the small strip was the perfect place for me to hang around on, blending in with all the holiday makers and residents of the city enjoying the sea and sand. Even though within myself I sensed that I was being overly paranoid it was still something I was more than happy to go along with. Nothing really could have been ruled out when it came to the situation I'd been placed in and due to that it would've been dangerously moronic not to plan for all eventualities.

Kuba's was the ideal location and place for it to all go down. Well, that and also the fact that the small cafe, owned by Manuel Terrosso, a Barca player from the fifties, served up the best Catalan Sausage Bocadillos in the whole of the city. How I could even think about food at that point was beyond me but over the years I'd found it quite literally impossible to visit the city of Barcelona without visiting Manuel to have one.

With time on my hands before meeting Sal I decided that a walk along Barceloneta and away from the waiters, street vendors, artists and pickpockets would provide a little piece of calm to try and weigh up what options I now had. I'd left as much of the story out as I could when I eventually gave my wife the explanation that she had more than deserved. There was no way that I was going to be sharing with her what had happened to Mikael. Some things are simply best left unsaid. What is it they say again, ignorance is bliss? Trust me, no good could ever have come out of me sharing with her that my close friend of many years had been fitted up with a Colombian neck tie and that there was a high chance that there was one with mines and, knowing how Eddy and German operated, quite possibly her name on one too.

Chapter 8

Zico

'Mate, you're actually doing my fucking nut in now with all of this. Just fucking drop it or this bong is getting cracked over your skull.' The sound of a man, who had reached the end of his tether, broke the otherwise relative silence of the room.

I was sitting in The Doors coffee shop making the most of the spare hour I had to kill before catching my train from Centraal Station back to Schipol for the Ibiza flight. Obviously with a spare hour to play with in the city of Amsterdam there are many options open to you. I could've spent it taking a casual walk around Anne Frank's house. Marvelled at the visual delights on show at the Van Gough. Fuck, I could've easily squeezed in a threesome with two hookers if I'd had the incline as well as well as the funds and stamina. When it all comes down to it though. I simply cannot say no to Cannabis Sativa.

I decided on The Doors as I'd deemed it near enough to the train station as to provide me with a chance of zero distractions as far as me, stoned, getting on the train to make the flight back. I was completely hanging after my appearance the night before at the Hup House festival. Being there on my own and not knowing anyone I'd done a bit of socialising with some of the other deejays that were playing the same stage that I'd been booked to play on.

I'd ended up having a really good laugh with these lads from Sweden that were on before me. I'd only met them for the first time when we did the handover as I took command of the decks from them. I'd complimented their set (this, absolute bollocks considering I'd arrived so late to the site I was already flapping that I was even going to make my own appearance on time never mind the luxury of listening to theirs.) What they didn't know though eh? My compliment producing big smiles from the both of them who had been playing back to back.

Once I'd finished my set, which had been in the most surreal of settings inside a disused prison, I was surprised to still see the two Swedes hanging around backstage. It was only then that we began chatting over a couple of beers. Proper infectious fuckers the pair of them, likes. Lucas and Hugo. Apparently they were pretty big in the Netherlands. Unlike the rest of the acts on my stage I'd at least vaguely heard of them through a couple of tracks that they'd produced that had made their way to the U.K. I'd even played one of them, "Rock the Discoteka" over the summer of ninety four. The one that had used the old Roland 808 on with the Hispanic guy speaking on the lyrics. I never knew who the artist behind the tune was though. In my defence a white label with a number thirty seven & DSTB scribbled onto it with a felt pen doesn't exactly give you much clues, Clouseau.

Didn't know that the people behind it were absolute party maniacs though. Obviously I'm no doctor but within half an hour of being in their company I was fucking positive that they both had one of those conditions that has A's and D's in them with quite possibly an "H" or two thrown on for good measure. They'd been knocking back the Ching at an impressive rate which didn't exactly help their hyperactive sides. In one of those rare moments in life I immediately turned them down when they had pushed the mirror, that was still covered in white powder, over in my direction.

'That'll have to come in a while. I'm waiting on my rice table coming, lads' I said, actually feeling pretty fucking pleased with myself over what was heading my way. Already on its twenty minute drive as I had been informed by one of the festival staff upon me leaving the stage.

'Rice table? What the hell is a rice table?' Hugo said with this daft grin looking to his side at Lucas. 'Oh you'll see soon enough' I laughed back at them while in all serious knowing that it would've probably taken me longer to try and describe what a rice table was than it would for the actual fucking thing to arrive there at the prison ready for consumption.

It was too fucking mad but the day before I'd flown out to play at Hup House. Lee had called me to ask what I wanted in my "rider" for when I was there at the festival. Rider? Who did the organisers think I was, the fucking Rolling Stones?! 'Fuck it,' I accepted. I won't take the piss too much because at the back of your mind you're always aware that if you play the game correctly you'll likely to be invited back to play again. Come the cunt with the organisers and you won't. Still though, I thought I'd at least chance my luck so when asked the question I told Lee that for drinks I wanted them to sort out some tins of Red Bull and bottles of Corona. A very humble request if you ask me. Which, I felt, paved the way for me asking for something a little bit more obscure and niche when it came to edibles.

I didn't give them a list as long as John Holmes' penis. No bowlful of red M&M requests. All I asked them for was some Indonesian food. Well, a specific dish from an extensive list of one restaurant in the whole of Amsterdam, Doe-Joe. I'd visited there before with Lisa. Fucking tiny place. Could've only had about half a dozen tables inside it. I'd been hitting the skunk hard that day at The Old Church so my recollections of how we ended up inside are a bit hazy but I recalled Lisa pretty much deciding for us that we were going to go inside for a meal, only to find the door locked to the public. There must've been a spare table though because, once the front door had been unlocked for us, we were ushered in.

Skipping to the end. There had barely been a day go by that I hadn't thought of that meal. Couldn't tell you what Lisa had been wearing or what the two of us spoke about while in there but the fucking food? What the Amsterdammers called a "Rijsttafel." I'd be lying if I said that the first thing that had entered my head when informed that I was off to Amsterdam had been something along the lines of me never having deejayed there before. It had been 'AMSTERDAM? I'LL GET ONE OF THOSE FUCKING RICE TABLE THINGYS' before any other thought.

I was still sat with the two Swedes when this festival worker appeared on the scene carrying two take away bags with an accomplice following him with another two in their hand. Both of them dumping the four bags on the table in front of me. 'Your food, sir' he said with a nod. Catching my eye before him and his mate disappeared as quickly as they'd appeared.

'Your food' Lucas said, eying up the bags sat there, putting the emphasis most definitely on the "your."

'Oh aye, my friend' I replied, not taking my eyes off the bags in front of me as I set about emptying them of their contents. First, laying the massive bowl of rice out in front of me. Then embarking on arranging the near forty small dishes full of all kinds of Indonesian delicacies on the table. I say "near forty" due to the fact I'd stopped counting them by the time I got to thirty due to the very real prospect of my food getting cold had I continued my count. 'It's a shame you two have just hoovered up a couple of grams inside the past half hour boys because this shit is really quite something' I said, breaking my silence as I picked up the most succulent looking piece of lamb satay and dipping it into the small bowl of peanut sauce that had been provided.

They both kind of evaluated my words before instinctively screwing their faces up and shrugging their shoulders in a "we're still on top" fashion. I'd never really thought things through with regards to the rice table. I suppose it's one thing to order the house special while sat inside the confines of the restaurant who have cooked it. A meal that comprises of many different parts across multiple dishes ranking from medium to mentalist hot. Another thing, completely, to take this same meal and think it possible to then eat it backstage at a pop up festival situated inside an ex penitentiary without attracting any attention.

Cunts kept coming over for a wee nose. Some even taking liberties by asking if they could have a taste from "that bowl there" and something from the one "over there." Never got a minutes fucking peace, likes. Hugo and Lucas could tell that I was getting pissed off about it all, sat there laughing their tits off over my annoyance. Once I'd eaten enough I left the rest for the assortment of vultures who had been milling around us. Jokingly (not jokingly) saying that I hoped it would choke them.

It was round about that time when the night took its turn. Fed for the night, the next time the mirror was pushed my way I wasn't going to be sending it back so quickly in the direction of the Scandinavians. Up up and away and so it was then a case of gentlemen start your engines. I'd actually behaved myself for the most part since I'd arrived at Schipol. Had remained the consummate professional upon finding myself in a city that is perennially full of temptation. My main motivation of keeping a straight line had admittedly been that I was shit scared of getting further into Lee's bad books so soon after the unpleasantness of Amnesia.

Once I'd played my set though? Well that was my own time then wasn't it? My personal life time to do as I pleased. As long as I was back in Ibiza in time for my next appearance at Space then who would really care what I got myself up to? Once I'd accepted the gifts from the Colombian gods, well, Swedish I suppose. The blue touch paper hadn't been so much as lit and more a case of doused in petrol, put inside a microwave along with a pre lit zippo and a rocket launcher then taken to said microwave.

When talk turned to leaving the prison and looking at getting back to the city centre. The pair of them indicated that the night really was just starting and that they already had a club they were going to be hitting and asked if I was up for going along with them. While I'd had every intention of just heading back to the hotel, via the nearest coffee shop and having myself a nice chilled night. The couple of lines I'd had, alongside the suspicion that a night with the two Stockholm lads would be one not to be slept on, was enough to see me altering what plans I'd tentatively made with myself.

Within the hour we found ourselves in the questionably titled "Twisted Nipple."

'What you mean you've never been to The Twisted Nipple?' Hugo had said to me while still backstage. 'Can you believe he's never been to The Nipple, Lucas?' He continued without giving me any chance to reply back. Lucas giggled back at him before looking at me. 'You've been to Amsterdam before, yes?' I nodded back. 'And you've never been to The Twisted Nipple?' - 'Aye ok then, lads,' I thought to myself. I've not been to The Twisted fucking Nipple, ALRIGHT! Instead I settled with a final 'no.' - 'Well that's going to change tonight, Zico' Hugo said. 'You won't find a better club in the whole of the Netherlands never mind Amsterdam, we go every time we're in town.' Lucas added. - 'Actually on that same subject shouldn't we be getting on our way?' Hugo, looking a little impatient, cut in as Lucas was set to continue.

That was enough to snap his mate out of whatever monologue he had appeared to be about to deliver my way. This being the catalyst for the three of us to escape the prison and on route to the city centre through the medium of a spacious Mercedes with a driver more than happy to turn a blind eye to the antics going on behind him in the back. Henk, I had a wee blether with towards the end of the journey. Funny looking guy likes, not a million miles away from Ronnie Corbet with the glasses and that. Feyenoord fan as well. I told him that it must've been a tough gig being a taxi driver in Amsterdam supporting their eternally and bitter hated rivals from Rotterdam. He laughed at the irony of it while admitting that I wasn't exactly wide of the mark with that assumption.

Once we got ourselves inside the club that was situated just off the Leidseplein District I could see that this wasn't in any way what I'd been expecting. As a DJ I'd often been accused of seeing with my ears before my actual eyes. Something as nonsensical as it may have sounded. It actually made sense. My very first impression when walking through the reception after Hugo and Lucas stopping for a few words with the security who appeared to all know each other, wasn't the beautiful rustic decor which gave off the feel of possibly being hundreds of years old. That in itself didn't exactly come close to looking like any of the dark and dingy clubs I'd ever visited or played at.

Most of them I'd had to wipe my fucking feet after leaving as opposed to this, almost, private gentleman's club vibe. The kind you'd see barristers and brain surgeons cutting about in having a glass of port and a wee game of backgammon in. It wasn't any of that though but the music that was playing. Instead of the standard techno and trance that was common place in most of the clubs and festivals in The Netherlands there was more of a slow garage style vibe to the place. That in itself didn't exactly present a problem. Not what I or the two Swedes ever played ourselves but not exactly offensive to the ears either.

If anything, hitting a club that *isn't* playing a bit of techno or trance pretty much guarantees that at least it wasn't going to be full of sweaty fucked up teenagers. It wasn't just the music itself that had caught my attention but the actual volume of it. Aye, I could hear it but considering I was practically inside the club by then. The volume sounded like it was sitting at the level much like "playing records upstairs while your parents are downstairs" as a teenager. Once I'd began to take in my actual surroundings however it was pretty evident that this was not the kind of establishment that you'd be finding spaced out teenagers patronising, regardless of music policy.

This, clearly, was not anywhere remotely close to what I had imagined the "club" to be when we'd all agreed to hit the city centre when we left the festival.

One thing that the two Swedes had said had been the truth though. They *were* well known faces inside there. From the big scary special forces looking cunts on the outside to the woman on reception right through to the shifty looking Turkish boy who took the coats. They all reacted like their long lost sons had arrived after being chained to a radiator somewhere in the Middle East for a twenty stretch.

I don't think Charles and Diana could've walked in there and received a warmer welcome. The pair of them, who must've easily done a gram between them in the Merc on the short journey back, were absolutely lapping the attention up. Both were sound as a peseta. I'd taken to them at a drop of a hat but it's moments like that where you just capture things and see them for what they are. By that I mean the old Charlie, likes. How much it can turn people into complete and utter fannies. You can see how some disappear up their own derrières though. The pair of them fucking strutted through that reception area like they actually believed they were Kings of Siam through the combination of all the Ching attacking their membranes and the sycophants who were aiding and abetting that feeling.

'Ahhh Hugo, Lucas, so good to see you my old friends' This guy in an expensive looking suit said with an outstretched arm towards them. After their pleasantries had been exchanged, the attention was briefly turned to me. 'We have a guest with us tonight, can we sign him in?' Hugo said to the suit while putting his arm around my shoulder as if for extra validation that I wasn't just some silly cunt who had wandered in behind them from the street by accident. The three of them instantly laughed at this while, clueless about pretty much most of what was going on other than the fact that there wasn't a house club in the world that had cunts in suits greeting you as you walked in like that, stayed silent, not getting the joke.

I thought it was a fair enough question from Hugo, likes. I've had to have members sign me into the United social club in Dundee on occasion so to have to be signed into some strange and mysterious backstreet club in Amsterdam. It didn't exactly sound like a stretch to the imagination. At that, the guy in the suit, sporting one of those slick European pony tails, led the three of us from reception towards these big ten foot wooden doors. I could've sworn I'd seen the fucking things inside Edinburgh Castle that time the school took me on a field trip. Opening both of them at the same time in a way that left me unable to decide whether he'd been purposely dramatic with that or if it had just appeared that way. He ushered us in.

'Gentleman, welcome to The Twisted Nipple. Please enjoy our unrivalled and world renowned hospitality, wide range of beverages, and if inclined, party favours and of course ..... the girls.'

I'd just about managed to piece things together a few seconds before he'd wrapped up his speech. As he spoke I'd been looking around the room to see what the surroundings was and first up. It wasn't a club at all. It wasn't even close to what you would class as a nightclub. There was no DJ for one thing. This, possibly being just as well considering there wasn't a dance floor either. Apart from a few generously spaced out sets of tables and chairs. The only real focal point of the room was the sprawling bar which almost stretched from one side of the room to the other. It was at the bar where the girls were all sat.

That was when I realised what kind of a venue that they had brought me to.

Hugo and Lucas wasted no time in getting acquainted with the waiting girls. Their eyes had been fixed on us from the second the chap in the suit had brought us through into the room. Well, I say Hugo and Lucas got acquainted with them. Technically it was just Hugo while Lucas, clearly knowing where he was going, simply walked past the waiting women without so much of a hello before disappearing through a door and into a side room.

'Petra, Baby how are you?' Hugo said before giving her a hug. With her facing towards me she flashed a quick smile my way as Hugo held onto her. Already I was wondering if she was smiling because she was just being friendly or if it was part of some potential business pitch. The second I clocked onto the fact that this was obviously some knocking shop, a classy one I'll give it that, I was on my toes.

'I'm good, lover boy, missed you lots, baby' She replied back once she'd been freed and able to look at him. Distracted by them I hadn't noticed that one of the women had left her place at the bar to come get me. 'Would you like a drink, young man?' She asked while pretty much deciding that I "did." Taking hold of my arm and gently leading me towards two free seats at the bar. She must've been at least ten years older than me but really attractive. It was almost intimidating how elegant and beautiful she was but with the additional maturity and self assurance to match.

Didn't matter a fuck how much in awe of her I was there and then. I wouldn't be having sex with her, or any of her colleagues for that matter. Had the Swedes actually told me what kind of a club we were going to I'd have parted ways with them for the night and went and had a couple of joints, a quarter pounder with cheese and a wank. Enough activities to ensure that I'd be fresh for my flight the next day. Too late once you're in there though isn't it because it goes without saying that you can't be rude to a bunch of high class hookers you've only just met moments before, can you?

While Hugo, once again with that big bag of Ching that he was getting fired into, sat talking with this Dutch Surinamese girl called Petra. I sat making small talk with, Lara. What do you do for a living, that type of stuff. I didn't really think that I needed to ask her what she did so left it. As we all sat talking, the side door that Lucas has disappeared through began to open and fuck me, I wasn't expecting what came back through it.

Lucas was standing there in what looked like some official mint green and white Twisted Nipple silky house robe, untied at the waist. Cock and balls hanging out for anyone who cared to look in his direction. He had the manic look about him which gave the game away over the fact he'd just had some kind of chemical injection into him seconds before. Either he'd completely forgotten to tie the robe when he'd gotten out of his clothes and into it or the man simply didn't give a fuck.

'Jesus, Lucas, tie your fucking robe, man' I said making a joke of shielding my eyes. This producing laughter from the girls sat around me. Hugo sat there shaking his head. 'I cannot take him anywhere' he added, laughing. Meanwhile Lucas just stood there looking back at everyone while making absolutely no fucking attempt whatsoever to actually close the robe and spare everyone the sight of his meat and two veg. 'What?' He asked, arms outstretched with a bemused look on his coupon which only served to open the robe even wider.

I had to get up for a minute and go over to him and tie it up for the cunt before bringing the two of us back to the bar. Leaving him with a couple of girls to take care of things. I'd done my portion and honestly, I'd seen more than I'd wanted or needed to see. It was explained to me that any members would get out of their clothing and into one of the complimentary robes before they got down to business in one of the private side rooms.

Fair enough from Lucas, likes. I mean, from what I gathered. You slip into that robe then you're pretty much making your intentions known. To be cutting about with your cock and balls hanging out while giving not one single fuck about it certainly does add the feel of rubber stamping things. Maybe around five minutes after Lucas had appeared. Hugo then, although much more efficiently than his partner, made the side room trip to then appear back in the exact same robe. That's when they both disappeared. Hugo with the girl named Petra and Lucas with two of the girls from the bar. Which then left me on my Jack.

'Would you like to go and get changed too, Stevie?' Lara asked while confirming that we'd now reached the point that I was hoping to avoid if at all possible. I can be too polite at times, not wanting to be rude and turning down a hooker because I didn't want to offend them. That would be classic me, peak me, actually. Shagging a prostitute just because I didn't want to appear rude. Now I'm not one who likes to follow many rules in life but up there along with the whole not eating yellow snow, feeding the lions and pressing big red buttons on trains. Having sex with a prossie is definitely up there.

When I shook my head to her suggestion that I get out of my clothes she seemed a little disappointed. 'I'm just having a drink while waiting on my friends' I added which seemed to upgrade her disappointment to annoyance. 'Then our conversation is over,' she said, all miffed as she stood up and walked away from me. 'Wait, you mean that you were only speaking to me because you thought that I was going to pay to fuck you?' I said, sarcastically only to immediately regret it. Either she hadn't understood me or had chosen to not react. Instead, she kept on walking which was probably for the best.

See the hassle you get when you don't ride a random hooker to prevent causing a scene? Don't know why I even bother, likes! I eventually got speaking to another girl, this pretty blonde in a short dress, stockings and heels, who had either seen what had went on between Lara and I and simply wanted a bit of company or had decided that she was going to have a crack at me to see if she could squeeze out a different outcome. 'Not in this life, darling,' I thought to myself as we got speaking.

She was actually really sound though, interesting girl. Not only did her uncle play alongside Marco van Basten for Ajax but, very fucking randomly, she also knew tonnes about Evel Knievel. Two facts that were as eclectically random as they brilliant. How many times could you possibly say that you had been talking to a prostitute who had a less than seven degrees of separation connection to Marco van Basten and was an expert on America's most famous daredevil?

'Did you know that by the end of nineteen seventy five Knievel had suffered from four hundred and thirty three broken bones?' She asked while I spoke about him at Wembley the day when he was trying to jump all the buses. 'Nope, I did not but if that ever comes up in a pub quiz then I'm going to be absolutely sorted, babe' I replied, completely absorbed in the conversation. 'Pub quiz?' She seemed confused by this. 'It doesn't matter, it's just a thing we have in Scotland to stop people from glassing each other for a few hours of drinking.' Once again she seemed confused by this but I had the feeling that no matter what I did and however I explained something it would only lead to her needing to ask further follow up questions.

I was trying not to picture what was going on outside of the room with Hugo and Lucas. My guess had been that once they'd disappeared they'd have ended up in their own rooms but this was Swedes we were talking about here. That's where half the fucking porn comes from does it not? Aye they're definitely not shy in Sweden, likes.

I was actually getting to the stage where I was just going to say fuck the pair of them and head home for the night when, around ten minutes apart, the two of them rejoined the room again with perma smiles that could not be wiped from their coupons. They weren't fucking chuffed when they learned that I'd spent my time sitting around talking to the girls but not fucking them.

'Are you gay or something?' Hugo teased. 'Nah, mate, I just like to know that when I go to bed at night my dick won't have fallen off by the next morning.' It was out my mouth before I knew it. One of those "did I just think that or say it" moments. 'No offence, girls' I quickly stammered but it was no good. What was said could not be walked back.

'Oh so you don't think that we're clean' Another one of the girls, one that I'd never spoken to was right off her seat and in my face. This redhead with Crystal Tips type curls said, jabbing her finger into me. I could tell that Hugo and Lucas couldn't decide whether to be horrified that their guest was making a scene or laugh over how helpless I must've looked with this woman going completely elite level radge at me.

'We are not some fucking red light window girl who themselves, incidentally, are cleaner than any prostitute in whole of world' She definitely had some kind of Eastern European accent but I couldn't nail it. During the heated debate I had to catch a hold of myself because I was about take her into a room and have sex with her just so I could save face over the whole them having a disease comment. Thank fuck I elected to go down the "I'll get my coat" route.

The Swedes, having gotten what they'd came for followed suit. That was probably where it would've been better if separate ways had been agreed but that would've been way too such sensible measures to take. Instead, we went on to a "club" club. Then some pubs, then a casino when we couldn't get any pubs to serve us due to them closing. The night ending in us all going back to a "friend of a friends" party inside their penthouse in the docklands. A brutally punishing night all round and one that, technically, was still going when I left late morning to go and check out of my hotel. I was glad to get out while the going was good because the place was full of casualties from over the morning. It was like Vietnam in there with how many men down there was.

It was in that coffee shop working my way through a scarily strong joint of White Widow though that my much needed peace and tranquility was broken by the raised voice.

'Just fucking drop it or this bong is getting cracked over your skull.'

I'd already clocked that him and his mate had been having a bit of a disagreement. It had actually been quite amusing for a while and, in a people watching sense, I was filling my boots with the pair of them. They sounded like they were from the Glasgow area as there was definitely a Weeg accent to the two of them.

The amusing part was down to the fact that they were so wrecked, so confused that they had descended into a conversation where each individual were talking about an entirely different thing yet for a period, at least. The conversation still made sense, individually. Throw in the fact that one of them was talking about a Chinese meal and the other a Chinese prostitute and you had all the makings of some comedy gold laced with violent undertones.

Through sitting alone with my own thoughts it wasn't hard for to overhear what they were saying to each other sat at the table next to me. Going by all accounts they'd had quite night before and day after in the more seedy part of town. An American had been fucked. So had a Czech, and a Russian. It was like sitting next to the fucking United Nations.

Then, I guess, aided by the bongs that they were smoking the confusion began to set in.

'Tell you what, lad. After all we've been up to I really fancy a Chinese next' one of them said to the other. His compadre's, sat next to him, face lit up. 'Fuck aye, now you're talking.'

The main issue here however was that Shagger number 1 was meaning for them to go for a Chinese meal after them "working up an appetite" during their afternoons work. This while his accomplice had taken this to mean that they should go back down to the Red Light District and look for a prostitute of the Asian kind. It would take them all of 5 comical minutes before their individual pennies dropped and they eventually realised what they were independently meaning and until that point arrived. Every time one of them opened their mouths it only led to their confusion spiralling further and further out of control.

Shagger 1. 'I could probably go fifty fifty though so, you wanting to share one with me?'

Shagger 2. 'Fuck off man get your own, I'm not having one WITH you I'm wanting one all to myself'

Shagger 1. 'Come on you've shared one with me before'

Shagger 2. 'Have I fuck shared one with you before'

Shagger 1. 'Aye you fucking have , plenty of times'

Shagger 2. 'When ? You're needing to lay off the Jack Herrer, it's frying your brain, man'

Shagger 1. 'You're well out of order here by the way. Fucking standard suggestion and you're losing the plot at me'

Shagger 2. 'Standard suggestion?!?!?!'

One was, in his mind, quite rightly thinking that it wasn't exactly asking much of of a mate to share a, traditionally large, meal with another while the other one was outraged and not really into the thought of having to tag team a prostitute with his wing man.

I sat there enjoying the show and left it as long as I possibly could until it reached the point where I was certain that violence was then going to play a part. Eventually, not exactly of sound mind myself, I slowly got up from my table and stepped in like some boxing referee giving out a lecture. First of all saying to Shagger 1. 'You're talking about going for something to eat correct?' which was met with a look of disdain from him. In his mind what else could he have been speaking about? I then turned to Shagger 2 and confirmed that HE was indeed speaking about going to the Red Light District to look for a Chinese girl to have sex with.

'We good now, boys?' I said ribbing them as I sat down to finish my spliff and hot chocolate. Fucking radgeys, the pair of them. We got talking for a wee spell while the three of us were sat there. They were from Paisley. Billy and Craig. Decent lads, like. They'd told me how the night before had been their first night since arriving but that they still had another three nights left. The city was going to systematically take them apart, day by day. Nothing surer. That's what Amsterdam does to you though.

I was glad that I was escaping it, actually. Especially after the night I'd just spent with those two Swedish lunatics. Another night like that in a row with them would've probably put me in a fucking box. Maniacs, the pair of them.

I was soon on my early evening Iberia flight back to the Balearics. Taking the chance to grab my first real bit of sleep since arriving in the low lands, exactly as I was leaving it.

Chapter 9

Si

It all seemed to be a fairly straightforward drop. Just another one of those "take this package from address A to destination B" tasks for Ivan. As it always was. And the beat goes on. I suppose everything is straightforward until you've got a shotgun pointed at your face though. I was obviously heading towards a more affluent area of San Antonio as I drove towards its outskirts. The houses kept getting bigger and the cars more expensive as I followed the directions given to me by Ivan.

When I reached the address. Initially, I'd thought that I'd got the wrong house as it appeared to be in darkness until, just as I pulled to a stop. I noticed one small light on in a room around the back. Generally I'd found that most of my deliveries were met with eager recipients on the other side. A lot of times I'd arrive in the middle of a party, full flow.

I was very popular in that respect when everyone knew that "the man" had arrived. With their order placed, the anticipation on my arrival must've been top of their list. No different from calling an Indian for your tea, I suppose. I'd prided myself on getting there before the fast food industry standard delivery time of "thirty to forty five minutes" though.

This time around however there was definitely no party going on unless everyone was rocking some army issue night vision goggles which would've been unlikely. Even for Ibiza. With no one seemingly waiting impatiently around the grounds of the house for me getting there. I was left with no choice other than to get out the car and walk up to the front door of the place. I couldn't hear anything inside, no music, voices, S.F.A. Even as I knocked on the door I'd already convinced myself that I must've had the wrong house. When the door slowly opened and I was standing face to face with a man already holding a shotgun up at me head height. I definitely knew I was at the wrong door. That was the pisser though. I was at the *exact* door that I was meant to be at.

My very first thought was that whoever I was dealing with was one paranoid fucker who had been hitting the chemicals a little bit much over recent times. For all I knew, this was generally his reaction when someone was on his property until he knew who they were. I couldn't imagine that he'd get his papers and milk delivered every morning too easily if so. Way too many complications for any kid just trying to earn their first crust. When I heard the Scouse accent though. That's when I realised that there may have been other motives for this whole "delivery."

'In you come, la' he, big hook nose and Ian Rush style tache with a roman crop haircut, demanded. Faced with those gun barrels pointed at me. I felt that I didn't exactly have much of a choice as I did as told and stepped into the house.

'Kemon, this way' he ordered, now behind me. Prodding and pushing my back with the end of his weapon as we made our way into what was a dimly lit but very stylish looking open planned area with a dining room and massive kitchen.

Who the fuck even needs six ovens? I can't believe that even went through my head when I walked into the room but you can never control that brain of yours can you? Fuck, I wish you could.

One time when I was shagging this girl after I'd played at The Metro a few years before. I'd thought I was going to come embarrassingly prematurely. Like, after a minute embarrassingly prematurely. Scrambling for something to put into my mind that would be the opposite of exciting and sexy. I'm not sure where it came from but I ended up with George Graham's Arsenal in my head and their fucking boring one nil victories. Their fans even had a song to accompany the fact that they won so many times by that scoreline. How ridiculously organised they were at the back. Tell you what though. It done the trick. One second I was ready to explode. The next I'm thinking of Tony Adams and Steve Bould standing there, confident as fuck with their arms in the air waiting on the linesman's flag to go up. Which it always would.

Problem is that from then on, anytime I'd found myself in fear of climaxing too early. My train of thought would always take me to those two defenders every fucking time. A truly terrible affliction I can assure you.

Once I got myself over how obscene the amount of ovens that the kitchen boasted I was able to fully focus on the fact that there were a couple of bulky looking guys sat on a sofa watching me being escorted in. The one with the shotgun dragged a chair over from the dining area while one of the boys on the sofa told me to take a seat. Looking like he was taking things from there, he motioned with his hand for the shotgun to be lowered.

'There's no need for all of that stuff is there, mate' He said with a condescending smile at me. Safe in the knowledge that they'd be getting no trouble out of me.

The two of them sat there with some kind of Superman style laser glare at me the whole time. Even when the one who had been doing the talking reached forward to the table to pick up his bottle of Budweiser he never once took his eyes off me.

I was fucking bricking it. The combination of the shotgun and the fact that these lads were obviously from the city of Scousepool all added up to that this was all heading in a direction that I wasn't going to be much a fan of.

'Do you know who we are?' He asked. I felt it would've been stupid of me to do anything other than to plead ignorance. Obviously these fellas were associates of if not part of the O'Halloran family. It wasn't so long ago some of Ivan's soldiers ended up in hospital at the hands of these cunts so I had already defaulted to survival mode. Should survival have even been on the cards that was. I shook my head without saying a word in return. He seemed neither up nor down at this news. 'Well that isn't really important right now. What *is* important is that we know who you are, Simon.' With threats of shotguns and fuck knows what else they were capable of I didn't think it any more possible for them to have my attention but you had to hand it to him. One drop of my name and my state of alert was heightened once more.

'That's right, la. We do our due diligence and it's only because you're clearly some clueless cunt of a Brit who doesn't yet know what he's really involved in that you've not had a couple of big holes put through your chest by this point in proceedings.' I wasn't sure whether to be relieved over the fact that he seemed to be saying that I was cool but I couldn't help but shake the feeling of that "by this point" that he'd left menacingly hanging there. I thought I'd spied a chance for me to try and curry some favour with them, fucking idiot that I am. Sat there with some hardened criminals from gangland who were operating at a level that I would never understand and I'm thinking that I can talk them around.

'Aye pal, that's about the size of' I tried to offer in agreement - 'Did I say you could fucking talk?' I was cut off again as quickly as I'd started. He was visibly unimpressed at this social faux pas of mines. 'Scanner, give the little prick a slap.' He said, visibly unimpressed by my impudence. I wasn't even afforded the chance to process this before I felt the handle side of the shotgun crack the side of my face. So hard that it knocked me off the side of the chair sending me crashing to the ground. My head, missing the side of the coffee table by inches. Fucking hell, I'm not sure where this lad Scanner went to school or what dictionary he'd read as a youth but in what world does a "slap" equate to having what was effectively a block of wood smacked off someones face?

'Jesus Christ, Brian. What kind of fucking dig do you call that, la? I said to give the boy a slap, not knock his head clean off his shoulders, fucking hell!' I heard one of them say along with the group laughing.

Dazed, I remained on the ground until I felt two hands grabbing my arm and pulling me back up to my feet and shoved back onto the chair again. 'Someone get the lad a glass of water' the other guy sat on the sofa said, speaking for the first time since I'd sat down. When Scanner, who if he wasn't smacking you around the face with firearms was running to get you a glass of water, returned with the H20. The guy who had been sat talking to me asked for it to be handed to him. In one free flowing move, taking the pint glass from his lackey and throwing its contents right into my face. As demeaning as his actions were I was just glad it was just the contents rather than the glass alongside it.

'Shall we try this again? I talk, you listen, understand?' I nodded, thinking it wise to follow these instructions to the absolute letter of the law. 'Before I was rudely interrupted I was in the middle of giving you reasons why you hadn't had a couple of bullets put into you on principle of working for the Camachos but, that arrangement can always be amended if you're not happy with it? He continued.

Given the fact that this was the highest level of how rhetorical a question could be I didn't even bother shaking my head at that and let him continue. 'Actually, where are our manners?' he asked like he'd just remembered something important. 'We never introduced ourselves to you' I wanted to tell him that when someone has been marched into a room by shotgun, introductions aren't as important but sensibly kept schtump. 'I'm Danny O'Halloran and this is my brother Carl.' I'm not quite sure what my facial reaction to the names must've been but I guessed it had to be something visible to them because the two of them instantly started chuckling away. 'Since you're one of the Camacho runners, we want you to do some "running" for us,' Carl said, leaning forward in his chair.

Do something for them? I reckoned in that moment I'd have been willing to do most things (within reason) for them if it meant avoiding taking a couple of bullets. Something which I felt was always a threat and possibility for any single minute that I sat inside that plush villa alongside them. I wouldn't do any gay stuff, or anything to do with me going near snakes. Both those things alongside not having to build any Airfix models due to being really fucking shite at them but aye, anything else to keep me above ground, I'd have complied with.

'As much as Senor Camacho thinks that he's in the middle of a war over control of this island, he really isn't.' Danny O'Halloran said, taking over once again. I couldn't decide whether there was some level of supremacy that Danny held over his brother or not but that was definitely a moot point for someone sitting in my position. 'If we actually were at war with him and his family the stupid dago cunt wouldn't even be able to lay a glove on us. Proper America versus Switzerland type stuff, la.' I nodded my head in recognition while continuing to keep my trap shut. 'Attempts to reach out and broker peace with him hasn't gone too well by this point, people have ended up hurt, unnecessarily ... "your people" and it's only going to increase if he doesn't get the message.'

What was blowing my mind the most was the calm and composed rational way that he was putting all of this across to me. Almost reasonable had it not been for the fact that I was only sat there listening to it through being held hostage. 'We've got the bigger manpower, weapons, police and political assistance and thirty years experience in running a crime family in one of Englands most hardest and violent cities. Do you honestly think that just anyone can come over to another country and take over an operation like this? By the looks, yer boss hasn't quite figured this out for himself but we're done waiting on that fucking lightbulb going on. We've wasted enough time and energy on the soft cunt already and we're done fucking about now. It's time for him to know his place.'

He reached over on to the table and picked up what I had, when sat down half an hour before, assumed to be a flyer for one of the clubs or bars in the area. He passed it over the table towards me. Hesitantly I took it from out of his hand and had a closer look at it for the first time. My first thought was that I'd never heard of any club called Bambino's. The words splashed across the front of it in an attractive rainbow coloured font. The reason I'd never heard of such a club on the island was mainly down to the fact that it wasn't a flyer for a nightclub that I was holding in my hand at all but one for what looked like a kids nursery. Alongside a few pictures of some pretty looking Spanish women in matching yellow t shirts being hugged by an assortment of kids there was the address and telephone number of the nursery.

On the flyer was a message scribbled in black marker pen over it.

CALL ME - 0034-7684-335623

Ivan had never shared much of his private life with me during the times that we'd found ourselves chatting but sitting there looking down at the kindergarten flyer it didn't exactly take the brains of a rocket scientist to come to the conclusion that the O'Halloran's knew more on that subject than myself.

'Give this to Ivan Camacho as soon as you get back to town, without any delay. Trust me on this, he's going to be as angry with you about not seeing it as soon as possible as we'll be if we find out that you sat on yer arse.' Danny said while his brother sat there nodding along in approval.

'It'll be the first thing I do when I get back' I assured him. Sensing that it was ok for me to now speak. - 'Good lad,' Danny said while giving me a playful slap to my cheek having stood up and walked over to me only a few seconds earlier. 'As long as yer boss man plays the fucking game, you and I shouldn't be seeing each other again but Simon? You'll know that if he doesn't, then the next time we're in each other's company. Things won't be so cordially civilised' he added while not waiting around for any answer from me. Correctly taking it that I understood things in the crystal clear manner that he had intended.

I wasn't much for turning around to see where he was going but his footsteps on the marble floor told me that he was moving further across the room. 'He can go now' I heard that rough Scouse accent announce before then, the opening of a door.

'What about the product?' Scanner, the lad with the shotgun shouted back across the room to Danny before then turning towards Carl as to get some double validation from the two brothers. 'He can keep it, Brian' I heard Danny O'Halloran reply before the sound of a door closing again. 'That's right, mate. Tell yer gaffer that his gear is so sub standard compared to ours that we wouldn't even jack off someone to sell on as we don't even want our name associated with that shite. Got our reputation to keep up, aven't we?' Carl added.

Inside, I breathed a sigh of relief over this. I wasn't particularly looking forward to the prospect of being the messenger of the flyer for the nursery to Ivan. Messengers tend to get shot at times. Had they not then there wouldn't have ever been a need for that whole "don't shoot the messenger" saying that you'll hear cunts coming out with whenever they've got the job of delivering some shitey news. Having to also say that the couple of thousand pounds worth of blow I'd had in my possession had been confiscated was something that I really would not have relished sharing with a drug lord right after he'd (I assume) just been told in a round about way that someone was threatening to kidnap their kids. Or worse.

Carl picked up the small parcel that I'd entered the house at gunpoint holding from back off the table and threw it over to me. Despite not being in any way prepared for this I still managed to catch it with one hand saving it from hitting the floor. 'Check out Neville Southall there' he laughed, closely followed by Scanner to the side of me. I even managed to find the funny side of the comment and let out a small laugh which was probably more to do with the relief that things now looked a lot more promising for me than they had when I had arrived at the property.

Carl O'Halloran then also stood up from the sofa. Looked over towards his goon and once more with a straight face said 'See the young man out, Brian' before walking past me, flashing me a wink and patting me on the head as he walked towards the same direction as his brother had previously. I looked to the side to see the boy Scanner raising the shotgun. Specifically lifting the end of it in a way that indicated for me to get back up onto my feet again. 'Time you were gone, la' he said as he manoeuvred himself behind me once again while he "saw me to the door."

We walked back down the hall towards the front door in silence. What really more was there that left needed said? Especially now that I was fully aware that when it came down to it. This was the monkey I was with as opposed to his organ grinders of bosses. Reaching the front door I felt the double barrelled end pressing into my back once more.

'Open it yourself' I heard him say to me. That was most definitely something I was more than willing, as well as capable, to do. Soon finding myself walking back out into the humid night air again towards the motor. When I reached the drivers side door of the car I chanced a quick look back at the door of the villa which confirmed what I'd already thought. Scanner still stood there watching me. Seeing me turn around he waved back in a mock campy way. Just as I opened the door to the Golf he wanted to squeeze in one last word.

'Ay, Jock' I turned round but kept on getting into the car. 'Just so you know, la. If it comes to it, it'll be me that'll be the one that gets you' as he finished speaking he pulled the shotgun up to his eye level and pointed the thing at me, pretending to pull the trigger. Bet he had a fucking hard on right there and then, saucy cunt. Emboldened by the fact that now that I had an errand of sorts to run for his bosses. I knew that he wasn't going to be pulling any fucking trigger. For the time being, anyway. With this added confidence I just gave the boy a thumbs up and a 'sound, mate.' Instantly then jumping into the drivers seat of the Golf and getting myself turned and back in the direction of San Antonio Bay before anyone changed their minds.

My first guess for where Ivan would be at was the restaurant he co-owned, El Tonto Cangura. 'Let's get this over and done with,' I thought to myself as, still shaken by what had just happened. I opened up the GTI on the quiet motorway on the journey back in towards civilisation.

Chapter 10

Gilberto

The pager, to my extreme disgust, went off while I was relaxing at Adolpho's, enjoying a few bottles of Club Colombias watching the Copa Libertadores match from Medellin. Adolpho's was traditionally a bar that was "Millonarios friendly" and the locals sitting inside that night were in good spirits having just seen Enzo Francescoli put his second away from the penalty spot to send River Plate three goals up away to our hated rivals Nacional. Not only were they a match on the pitch for our team but there was also the cartel side to things. Nacional being owned by Pablo Escobar at one point when he was alive and an association that the team or its fans will ever be allowed to forget.

"NACIONAL, DONDE ESTA TU PATRON - NACIONAL DONDE ESTA TU PATRON" The bar all chanted together asking the team up on the television where their sugar daddy was now. Dead, that's where and there could not have been a single person in the country who would've been surprised when the news broke three years before that the search block and DEA had finally caught up with the fat piece of shit.

With there still being half an hour left of the second half the potential for this to become a hell of a lot more embarrassing for Nacional was there for anyone with a football brain to see. When I looked down and saw the message travelling across the screen from Jefe telling me that the bosses wanted me at the house. I knew immediately that I wouldn't be seeing any more of the second half. Fuck, had I been out on the pitch playing in the game and was given word that my pay masters needed me I'd have had to leave the pitch immediately, never mind the minor inconvenience I'd been handed in having to leave the raucous bar.

It doesn't matter what you're in the middle of. When Eddy and German Ramirez call. You answer. It really is that simple.

I arrived within the hour and was personally met inside the grounds of the sprawling compound that was one of the fortress like properties Eddy Ramirez owned and could be regularly found at.

'Ah, Gilberto gracias for getting here so fast. German and Eddy need to see you as a matter of urgency. Jorge is already inside, he just arrived before you. I'll escort you to them, follow me' he said. All before I was even properly out of the car.

Knowing better than to ask any questions to Jefe under such circumstances. I nodded my head in understanding and followed closely behind the man who was my immediate boss and effectively, the intermediary between myself and both Ramirez brothers. We walked through the maze like building in silence until reaching the study where Carlos and Tino, two of Eddy's most trusted security detail, stood guard outside.

Both men I have a lot of time for and would've normally stopped for an exchange of words but, and in what was completely out of character, the two guards stood ashen faced without any eye contact between myself and Jefe as we walked past them and into the room. I walked in to find Eddy pacing the floor of his study. German was sat on a leather sofa nursing a glass of his trademark Scottish whisky while Jorge, without doubt my closest friend and ally in the cartel, sat in silence on another sofa looking back at me with a face that, despite how familiar we were to each other, I couldn't read.

Eddy wheeled round when he heard the door open as the two of us entered.

'Ahhhhh La Cobra, bueno bueno. You got here. And there I was betting German that you would be at Adolpho's with too much cerveza inside you.' Despite his warm welcome that he had appeared to extend to me on my arrival I could tell that all was not well in both brothers' garden. I wouldn't have been standing there before them otherwise.

Smiling, he invited me to take a seat beside Jorge. Jorge Lozano otherwise known to all as "El Jugador" through his known love of gambling. Soccer, horses, cockroaches. If you could bet on it Jorge would be right there waving a thick stack of pesos in the air. We'd been through wars together Jorge and I and to the Bogotá Cartel. He was the Lennon to my McCartney. As sicarios to the Ramirez brothers we were only ever handed, what was classed as, the most high risk of assignments. Politicians, journalists, figures in the media. With Jorge clearly getting the same message sent to his pager it appeared that there was some urgent work that needed attending to.

'Gilberto, Jorge we have someone that we need you to find for us' German said before taking a sip of whisky. 'Of course, Don German' both Jorge and I said in a way that could've almost suggested that it had been a carefully planned routine that we'd rehearsed earlier. Eddy who had yet to take a seat since I'd entered, walked across to the oak desk at the other side of the room. Returning with two brown envelopes. Tossing one to Jorge and then throwing one my way.

German then spoke up, telling us to take a look inside. Despite the large size of the envelope. The contents amounted to nothing other than a passport, a couple of photographs of a man and woman and no more than six sheets of paper containing our vital information stapled together. The man definitely fitted the look of an assignment I'd had time and time again. The photo looked like it had been taken through a telescopic lens from distance but the picture itself showed a slick looking tanned man in a suit. It was a face that I recognised. It was the gringo from Europe and whatever he had done he must've really fucked up because it was not only him that we were being tasked with finding but his wife also.

You couldn't see as much of her in the other picture as you could of him but what I did, I liked. It would almost seem like a crime to have to hunt and kill such a hot looking chihuahua. She looked far younger than he did but then again. Can you ever be sure what age most adult women are with all the make up that they wear? In Bogotá at times you didn't know if a sixteen year old was a twenty seven or if a fifty year old was thirty two. It screws my head up, brother.

It wasn't unusual for to be handed an information pack like this when it came to being issued with a target. Primarily to avoid detection should any phones be tapped. When discussing a hit we'd always refer to our assignment as a "little girl" rather than say their actual name. With the Americans having been in the country for years it had felt like a forever since any of us hadn't had those DEA hijo de putas snooping around in the background.

When they first arrived they were only interested in Escobar. He was like their rock and roll drug lord. This suited both the Cali Cartel along with their Bogotá counterparts. It let us all just keep on in the business of making lots and lots of money, free from any interruption from law enforcement. I'm not quite sure if anyone really thought things through when it came to *when* Escobar was caught though. Did everyone think that the Yankees would all just go back home again? America would still need their Cocaine and it was our duty to make sure that we did our part to make sure that the flow continued.

What wasn't standard however was to find a passport enclosed along with the intelligence relating to the little girl. I couldn't help but raise an eyebrow at the brothers when I pulled it out from inside the envelope.

'Si, Gilberto, we need Jorge and you to travel out of the country' German confirmed with almost a glimpse of surprise written on his own face to match what Jorge and I most likely were showing back in his direction. As he spoke I had already began looking through the passport until finding my picture in there alongside the name "Paco Herrera." I stifled a laugh over the realisation that in a bizarre quirk of fate I'd been awarded the same name as one of my teachers when I was a kid. The same teacher who had told me that I wouldn't make it in the world and that if I was lucky I would get a job washing dishes for some tapas bar. The irony of me taking on his name while being paid more for one job than he would've been rewarded for a full year at Santa Ines was not lost on me.

'Who did you get?' I asked Jorge as if we'd both been part of a Copa Mundial sweepstake and I had enquired which international team he'd drawn out.

'Juan Pablo Munoz, apparently' he replied non plussed putting the envelope and all its contents down on to the table before diverting his attention back towards Eddy and German. I took my cue to do the same. 'We're sending you to Europe' German said, as if it was an everyday instruction. Europe? The furthest I'd ever been out of

Colombia was north to Mexico two years before for that favour Eddy cashed in with the Sinaloa Cartel. Yet there was German. Sat there with his dyed black hair in a striped Sergio Tachini polo shirt which was about three sizes too small for him, swigging a whisky glass in his chair like a boss. Which, I suppose he was, in every way you wanted to name. Sat there telling us we were going to Europe like he was sending us out to "Bandito's" to pick up some tacos for dinner.

'We understand that you may have some questions. We have never asked you to travel to another continent before and there are many additional risks to that but we assure you. The rewards will be great.' Eddy, at last from one of them, introduced some empathy over springing this on us. When I'd received the page that took me away from the match I'd already assumed that there was a job that my services were required over but I'd imagined something local where, depending on the circumstances, I may have been able to take care of in time to get back to Adolpho's for the Copa Libertadores round up on ESPN.

'Do we need to have injections to travel to Europe?' I took Eddy up on his offer as soon as the man had stopped speaking. 'What about French girls? Are they as hairy as people say?' Jorge chipped in laughing. German, obviously more relaxed through the alcohol, looked like he was ready to laugh along with Jorge but seemed to think twice of it which I guessed was to avoid winding up his more stressed out looking bigger brother.

'I meant questions about the assignment, not that I was a living breathing rough guide to Europe you fuckers.' Eddy definitely wasn't seeing the funny side to anything inside the room. 'Ok, Don Eddy,' I said in a tone that showed the intention of talking more on his terms. 'Why Europe?'

'They skipped town. When Picky came back to us with nothing, the trail was cold only then for a contact at El Dorado to pass on word that the two of them had checked in on a flight to Barcelona, Spain.'

'Barca! Nou Camp, Ronaldo, Figo, Stoichkov!' Jorge, ill advisedly cut in. Unable to contain his excitement over heading to the city of the world famous F.C. Barcelona. A team so many of us had supported as kids.

'No, not fucking futbol, Jorge. Tracking down two thieving fucking ratas and, all going like clockwork, murdering them in a way where they die a long and painful death, fuck Ronaldo and Pep bloody Guardiola!' I couldn't work out if he was more exasperated than annoyed but whichever it was out of the two. It was not an emotion that would have been wise to provoke from Eddy Ramirez.

All I knew for certain was that if Picky Mendoza had not been able to find the two of them inside Colombia then they most definitely weren't there. I'd known Picky since we'd been kids and in some quirk of fate, despite all those hundreds of days we spent in class studying for a brighter future, we both ended up working for the same "company."

I've never known someone so paranoid in my life. Even as kids he used to talk about how there were police spying on everyone from deep inside Guativita Lake when we used to go and play down there. Whether he was full of conspiracy theories or not there was no better person in the country at finding those types of people who had went out of their way not to be found. I'd always joked with him that if he tried he'd be able to find my papa who went out for a cerveza one day when I was six and never came back again.

'You fly tomorrow morning and will be in Barcelona by evening and ready to get to work, all the details are inside the envelopes for when you get there and who to contact. The Italians on the other side will be ready for your arrival. Just ask for Julianna at the Iberia information desk when you get to El Dorada and she will arrange your flights.' Before Eddy had even finished, German interrupted his brother. 'Business class I must add, we like to look after our top sicarios, eh?' he laughed.

"Business class" Meant absolutely nothing to me and judging by the look on Jorge's face, him neither.

'So what have the two of them done?' my future holiday maker of a partner sat there beside me asked. Dressed, curiously in a full blue

Adidas tracksuit and sneakers. For Jorge this was unusual as I couldn't remember the last time I hadn't seen him decked out in his trademark white t-shirt underneath some opened up wild shirt that generally required sunglasses to even look in his direction.

'They stole, well technically he is the thief but you know the rules, Jorge. A message will now need sent out accordingly so, his wife needs to go too and believe me. The further this drags on the more his family and friends will become targets.' German said as he poured out another glass which saw him pour the whiskey out then stop for a second to assess the situation with how much was still left in the bottle. This produced a shrug of his shoulders before going on to pour out what little there was left into the glass.

'He has a computer disc and it is muy important that you recover it before you kill them, you understand?' Eddy enforced on us, pointing at the contents of the envelope on the table. I picked it up to flick through the paperwork once more and found a picture of if not the actual disc, a similar small computer floppy disc with plastic casing protecting it.

'Freddy will pick you both up tomorrow morning to take you to the airport' Eddy said with his back to us as he looked inside a cabinet drawer, closing it once again and turning round with two stacks of sealed American Dollars. Throwing one to each of us onto the table. 'You can exchange that for pesetas when you get to Spain.'

'Thank you, Don Eddy' We both replied at the sight of which, on a guess, must've been around ten thousands dollars each. This being what was our "expenses" and would allow us to not exactly have to dine at McDonalds when away from home. That was what was cool about working for Eddy and German. Jorge and I did not carry out assassinations for them through fear of upsetting the cartel. We carried the work out because they were good guys and paid us handsomely for it.

'Unless you have any other questions then that will be all for now, enjoy your night' Eddy added in a tone that suggested that whether we did have any further questions or not. We in fact "wouldn't" have any further questions.

Jorge and I stood up, German along with us and we all exchanged warm hand shakes before departing the room. The two brothers wishing us the best of luck on our trip and for us to check in with any information as and when we obtained it. As we reached the door, with Eddy showing us out. German shouted out for me.

'Gilberto, come back here for a second' Jorge and Eddy continued on as I doubled back towards the boss. 'Sit, sit' he asked which showed me that his "second" was looking like being just a figure of speech. 'Whisky?' he offered. With him appearing in a charitable mood I asked for a cerveza which was duly served up to me by Mariana who had been stood there in the corner the whole time we'd sat talking. Just waiting for an order to have been given in her direction to perform.

'I wanted to speak to you in private,' German said. By this point Eddy had now rejoined us. Jorge now on his way. 'It's about Jorge, you know what he can be like? He likes to party, he gambles and then there is the women. We're concerned that being sent to Europe he may not be able to resist some of the "attractions" that Barcelona will tempt you with.'

I paused for a second as I pictured all of the trouble that a colourful character like Jorge had brought over the years before answering him back. 'When you put it like that, maybe Jorge might not have been the best choice to send on an assignment to Europe, si?' I offered, feeling conflicted by it as I couldn't help but feel that I was knifing him in the back by potentially seeing to it that he would have his plans to travel with me snatched away from him. For what it was worth though, whether it was a case of knifing him in the back or not it was without any doubt, the truth. PLUS it was going to be me, after all, who was going to have to somehow oversee things when he was faced with all the ways that Barcelona could steer him in the wrong direction.

'Oh no no no, Gilberto. I wouldn't employ anyone other than you two to carry out this job. You're my best men, the very best. I just need you to make sure that Jorge doesn't forget *why* he is there in Europe. Keep him away from casinos, brothels and the nightclubs. I'm sure that having the nickname of "player" it is a most appropriate one for him. Sure, once you've taken care of the targets and secured the disc. You can stay up all night long fucking señoritas if you desire but until you get the job finished. Professionalism is what we demand and it is what we expect. We're making you responsible for Jorge during this assignment. There will be no discussions.'

I thought about asking them why Jorge couldn't be responsible for Jorge but sensibly decided better of it.

'Yes, Don German,' I surrendered despite the fact that inside I wasn't happy at all about the fact that I had effectively been made responsible for the loosest of cannons in Jorge "El Jugador" Lozano.

'It will be very, very bad for us *all* if you do not recover the disc. It contains sensitive information about the cartel and how it operates within Europe.' Eddy said with a stern face back at me before he fell even more serious. 'Now Gilberto, failure is not an option with this. If you and Jorge do not return having assassinated the targets and be in possession of the computer disc then you may as well not come back to Colombia at all.'

It was an ominous way to end this brief chat but it was all the time that they were prepared to give me. Straight after I was then on my way out of the room for the second time with thoughts of intercontinental flights and where the hell my suitcase might have been, now replacing any designs I may have had on beers at Adolpho's.

Chapter 11

Zico

I don't think anything could have prepared me for the madness that was waiting to greet me on arrival back from the Netherlands. I'd caught a wee nap on the flight back but nothing too substantial, likes. The plan was to get myself back to the vila and sleep the rest of the night and be fresh for getting back on the horse again the next day in time for my set at Space.

On the surface, things appeared pretty normal when I walked back through the door to the villa. I hadn't even been spooked over the sound of the TV being on as it really would not have been out of the ordinary for myself to have left the fucking thing on the whole time that I was away. You know? Even when I saw the attractive girl sat there like she'd made herself at home with her feet up on my sofa. I didn't immediately have it down as *that* strange. She looked around about the same age as me. With the frazzled and sleep depraved head that I had on me. I hadn't exactly ruled out this girl being someone that I had completely blanked out on having ever met before but one in actual fact that I had.

This I realised not to be the case the moment she saw me enter and hesitantly asked 'Stevie?' - 'Aye, and obviously since I've walked in to my house to find a strange woman sat on my sofa I'm going to have to ask who you are. Why are you here and how did you get in?' I was taken aback over how confident and assured she was in the way she just laughed at me. 'I'm Eva, I'm here with your dad. He's told me all about you' She sat smiling while patting the sofa to the side of her to get me to come and sit down beside her.

'My dad? He's here in Ibiza?' I asked, this news taking me by surprise and in a way where I didn't know whether I should've been happy over him being here or absolutely bricking it due to the "whys" of him appearing out of the blue.

'Where is he?' I asked taking a seat beside her and reaching immediately for the Rizlas. I fucking needed a seat and a joint after receiving this news. Hadn't seen him for years, not since that whole unpleasantness with Nora back at the start of the decade. We'd kept in touch by phone though and had spoken off and on. That in itself had been a much bigger improvement on how things had been like previously between the two of us.

He'd went off the grid in recent times though and that, combined with me being in Ibiza, had led to us having not had any contact in months. Even the fact that they were here in Ibiza to see me was confusing the fuck out of me because the last time I'd spoken to my pops I hadn't been given the Space residency. I guessed that I'd find out all of the details as and when Pedro Duncan wanted to share them. Actually knowing where he was would've been a good start.

'Him and your friend, Simon have went out for a few drinks. He had no idea what time you were getting back from Amsterdam so he told me that if you got back before them then you were to, keep me company.'

Obviously my head was wrecked, at least I recognised this because I don't know? The way she said "keep me company," I felt there was something else in it. Almost like she was coming on to me but obviously, she couldn't have been?

'Which pub did they go to?' I asked impatiently. With the news that my dad was in town it felt practically impossible to suggest that I would just sit and chill with his girlfriend (?) while my dad and best mate are out there getting up to all kinds of capers. 'I really don't know, Stevie they just left with Peter saying that they wouldn't be gone long.' All that she had been able to offer me.

Sensing that perhaps I'd not exactly provided the warmest of welcomes to this girl. I decided to just relax a little. Sit down, have a puff and get to know Eva while finding out that she was actually my fucking stepmother. Quintessential Peter Duncan. Bags a wife decades younger than him and doesn't even bother to tell any cunt. She was from Manchester and had a proper mad ferrr it accent to go with. Once I'd gotten over the shock of everything I found that she was admittedly quite likeable.

Manchester being a city that I had a bucketful of points of references. We were still going through them when Si and my father walked through the door of the villa. I instinctively stood up to greet him, Si not so much. It had been the first time I'd seen him since the Ketamine episode and, admittedly, I still wasn't exactly his biggest fan. Everything just seemed all off though. At odds with how friendly and relaxed Eva was. He, despite seeing his son for the first time in six years, could not even muster a fake smile. Even just to keep up appearances, likes. He looked lean and mean and like the last time I'd seen him. The South American sun gave him a nice healthy glow, despite the mass quantities of Ching that he was more than likely knocking back.

Aye, his face looked like he had the task of solving peace in the Middle East *and* finding a cure for cancer within twenty four hours or else the bad guys were going to kill his family but Si's coupon was even worse as he trailed in behind him. He was looking at me from behind my dad shaking his head with eyes bulging. Actually reminded me of Gary Lineker the way he was caught looking over to the bench when Gazza was a man on the edge in the World Cup semi final against Germany. I took these visuals from Si to indicate that I should just drop whatever was going on with my dad and that I'd appreciate the nod that he was trying to send my way.

What could I do otherwise though than to react in the way that someone would when seeing a parent for the first time in over half a decade?

'Pops? And what brings you here to sunny Spain? Colombia not sunny enough, aye?' I smiled, opening myself up for a man hug while catching a look from Si which seemed to say something along the lines of "I tried to fucking tell you." I clocked the uneasiness between the woman who I'd only just learned was his wife and him before he even began to answer me. *Now* I was picking up what Simon had so very much tried to put down for me.

'What? Can't a father not pay his son a visit these days?' He replied, having regained his poker face but coming nowhere close to pulling it off with me. 'Well that normally applies when father and son live within the same postcode as each other, not when they live in different continents' I joked back at him while trying my best to mask any concern over what was going on with him. 'And anyway, how did you know where to find me? We've not spoken in months.'

He looked over towards Eva and Si, who had plonked himself down on the sofa beside her, and answered my question by ignoring me and telling (as opposed to asking) Si that he'd be cool keeping his wife company while him and I went out for a few drinks and a catch up. Si, who since that time many moons ago in Blackburn when he first met Peter Duncan thought the sun shined out of his ring, had no issues with complying. 'No problems, Senor Duncan, we'll be fine here until you get back' he replied as he started the makings of a joint with the contents that I'd had left lying around on the coffee table.

'Come on then, Son. Let's take a walk' He said having, in his mind, made the decision of what happened next and turned and started walking towards the front door. After Amsterdam I could barely stay standing, fuck, was I tired. I just needed my bed, badly. What a contrast to that taxi ride back from the airport. Shattered, drained, spent. Ended. However you would like to describe it. I just needed to know that I was soon going to be home. Just like The Warriors trying to get back to Coney Island from Manhattan. That moment where they were on the very last train and knew that, after the most punishing of nights, they had almost made it home.

They weren't safe though. Still had that radge creepy cunt with the bottles to worry about. Actually *did* make me out like one of those gang members when you think about it? Aye, I didn't have the boy with the bottles waiting on me when my taxi got me home but I did have a cartel connected old man and a wife that I didn't even know about waiting on me.

Given the choice I'd have taken my chances with the "Stevie come out to play" option with the creepy, manky looking cunt in the film.

I followed him outside. Whatever was coming was never going to be good, that much was assumed every bit as it was expected. You couldn't exactly not notice that something was up with him. Weirdly, Eva seemed to be quite happy sat there talking to me before dad and Si had came back. It was only when I was walking behind him down the stairs that it dawned on me that whatever he was about to tell me was now going to impact on me in some way. My perfect plan for a summer in Ibiza playing and partying all shot to pieces because of that unpredictable dick of a dad.

'So how you doing anyway, Stevie? He asked once I was side by side with him while keeping his face fixed on the street in front of us. 'Bit of a better state of affairs to when we last saw each other anyway, dad' I answered while my memories propelled me back to that night down in Blackburn inside that old factory where, in the most unlikely of circumstances, we had "bumped" into each other. These words, I could tell, had sent him off down a rabbit hole of reflection as he went a little distant on me.

'Seems such a long time ago now Stevie, doesn't it?' He replied appearing back in the room again. 'Well, technically it was considering it was over five years ago' was all I had back for him. I worried that it had come out as some kind of a dig in his direction which it hadn't been. The years that had followed father and son reuniting on what was the most improbable of chance meetings hadn't exactly been textbook on my side and that was just me, the one out of the two of us who wasn't working partners with the fucking Bogotá Cartel. It was probably for the best that I didn't know what he'd been up to all those years since we were last in each other's company. Way too incriminating.

'Yeah time flies does it not' he said rhetorically before adding 'come on, let's head in here for a sit down' as he unexpectedly chose a bar for us to find some shade to sit in and catch up over a beer.

He'd picked a pub, Trigger's. Somewhere I'd passed almost every day since I'd arrived for the summer. It was one level down from a full blown official Only fools and Horses theme pub. I'd have put on my whole three months wages from Space though that I'd earn over the summer on the fact that not one single cunt involved in the making of the TV show would've been even aware of the establishment and the money that they were more than likely due from the business venture, mind.

Tacky with a fifty foot flashing neon light letter T. Drinks and meals named after about every character in the show. Don't get me wrong though. I could watch episodes of the show one after the other until the fucking cows came home but sitting down to a bowl of Micky Pearce's Mac and Cheese washed down by shots of Trigger's Tequila seemed a little excessive if you ask me.

Still, for the purposes that we required at the time. It had cold beer, a dimly lit area and was air conditioned. It was everything that we needed. Six strategically placed televisions all running the same episode of Only Fools for its patrons was something that wasn't needed but came with the territory all the same.

I'd felt that there wasn't so much of an elephant in the room with us and more a herd. Through that I felt like I was sitting in the middle of Kruger National Park in South Africa than a piece of Peckham in the Balearics. 'So what brings you to Ibiza then, Dad and don't give me the can't a dad visit his son nonsense?' I asked in an attempt to find out just what was going on as it was clear to me that this wasn't anything close to the scenario of a husband and wife taking a much needed holiday to somewhere nice and warm like every other British holiday maker out in Ibiza trying to leave behind their otherwise dull and uneventful day to day life.

I'm not sure if I'd asked the question in some kind of prying way or not but was met by a father who had immediately went right on the defensive. In any case. I wasn't prying I was literally asking him outright and in a way that was asking him to remember that you can't kid a kidder and that all I wanted was the truth the whole truth and nothing but the truth so help me God.

He fell quiet for a second as if to make sure that what he was about to say came out right because he was only going to have the one chance. I sat there not taking my eyes off him waiting on him to answer me.

'Ah, just some politics back in Bogotá, son. It's nothing really. We just wanted to get away from things for a while' came the weak as piss reply. Now while this approach would have most likely worked on seventeen year old me out of his nut on Class A drugs. That was the thing though, I wasn't. I'd done a whole lot of growing up since then and he wasn't talking to his kid anymore whether he'd pegged onto this or not. Even so, I was socially skilled enough to know when and where not to press something. Deciding to drop it I searched for something that was safe and middle ground enough for to move on to.

'How's Mikael getting on? Is he back in Colombia while you're over here? Tell me he's not over here with some page three stunner trailing along' I laughed, genuinely hoping that actually he was along on this trip. Really good lad, likes and if it hadn't been for him I wouldn't have even met my dad that night inside the disused factory down in England. I definitely had a lot of time for the man and it would've been really good to have caught up with him again. A right dead sound cunt, Mik. That's when it all came out though and I found that actually Mikael really was a *dead* sound cunt. As in he had fucking expired.

I wasn't prepared for my own reaction but felt it weird in itself how impacted I'd felt when learning the news over who, in the facts of it all, was someone I'd only met just the once and had spent three hours tops in his company. Even so, I felt like I'd taken a couple of slugs to the chest when the words came out of my dads mouth.

It was as much the implications of him being dead as it was him actually being dead in itself. When you find out that someone with cartel connections has unexpectedly croaked. The tendency is not to look at it like "old Elsie passed away peacefully in her sleep, she'd had a good innings" and so on.

Aye, as far as my dad had planned to keep me in the dark over matters. All it took was one mention of Mikael from me for his plan to fall apart. As soon as I spoke his name, Peter's face dropped. It was a weird feeling but I just knew he was going to tell me that Mik was dead. It was like his face told me everything apart from the details which, to be fair. I'd rather not have known and once I did I was seeing why my father was trying to keep it from me.

'Mikael's dead, Stevie. They killed him' he said after what felt like an hour long silence. The words came out no problems but he appeared miles away. So much so that he hadn't bothered to check his volume levels. Padre speaking about someone being killed, unsurprisingly turning some heads at nearby tables. 'Fuck' I replied. Not really sure how to respond to this news from him. Before continuing, and with more self awareness than he was clearly showing, I had a wee look around to see who was trying to listen in. I locked eyes with this guy in his forties in a Leeds United top sat there with a full English and a pint. I got the impression that he'd been trying to listen in on the conversation but by making eye contact it appeared to be enough to get him back concentrating on his food and drink again.

'Who killed him?' I asked almost in a whisper, completely overcompensating for the fact that discretion needed applying where we were sat. Whatever it had been that was holding my pops had loosened its grip and he had pulled himself out of the trance that he'd been momentarily in. 'Some business associates of ours' he said, looking around the room himself.

'Why? What had he done?' I asked, by then conscious that whatever I went on to enquire would quite possibly provide me with answers that in hindsight I possibly wouldn't want to know. 'They slit his throat and then pulled his tongue through it.' He agonised to me with a helplessly defeated look on his face. Aye, that was definitely one to be filed under "didn't want to know." 'Fucking hell, dad. That sounds brutal' I said, left in the unavoidable position of picturing what it must've looked like. Having only met him the once I had no choice but to picture him in that fucking radge "pirate meets Michael Hutchence" rock star get up he had on in Blackburn, there with his throat slit. Disturbing stuff to have inside one's head and no mistake.

'So what did Mik do to deserve that then?' I asked again. The way I saw it. No cunt slits your throat like that just because their PlayStation is broken and they're at a loose end for things to do. Plus, I'd had a feeling that the way he had been killed indicated something. I wanted to know, had almost assumed to be the case by then anyway, if Mikael's murder was why my dad had suddenly appeared in Ibiza while I was there.

'I don't know, son. We weren't up to anything illegal' he said convincingly. 'Well, apart from facilitating the import of narcotics into Europe on behalf of a powerful and ruthless South American cartel' I said sarcastically, trying to inject some gallows humour in amongst the conversation but it really wasn't the time for it.

I was feeling dangerously tired and the irritable part to me was in the post and, insensitive as it sounds, I bluntly told my dad that I wasn't a kid and or was neither a fucking mug so he should just stop glossing over things with his deliberate vagueness and tell me just exactly what the fuck was going on. Adding that he just didn't pop up from nowhere after six years on the same Spanish island while I was there for the summer just out of pure chance.

I (correctly) assumed that this would take some time once he got started so ordered another two San Miguel's from the bar for us and got myself settled Jackanory stylee.

He spilled on a lot more detail of the intricacies of the work that Mik (RIP) and him did alongside the Bogotá Cartel. They were responsible for the flow of shipments to three European ports. Barcelona, Naples and Rotterdam. With the cartel having business links with the Italian mafia this saw Barcelona and Naples as friendly ports. Through my dads connection with the Turkish mafia this saw Rotterdam also used. According to Peter, this was an arrangement that had went on for years and had made everyone concerned a shit load of money. Walking in on Mikael and finding him like that had been a major red flag with regards to Peter's future job / life security.

'Mikael and I were partners. The Ramirez brothers had only ever dealt with the pair of us. As far as they were concerned. The two of us were one and the same thing. Seeing him sliced and diced like that. I wasn't going to stick around to find out what my own fate was. When you think your life is suddenly at risk. The fact that you're thousands of miles away from home becomes all too apparent to you. My instinct was to grab some essentials, get Eva's arse into gear and we were off out of the country. Let me tell you, son. I hope you are never in the position of having to break it to your wife that she has ten minutes to grab what she needs before leaving her house, most likely for the very last time. You have no idea what earache that brings you.'

'Understandably' I laughed. Looking like he was taking a second to assess it all and how fucking mad it must've been for his wife to be on the other end of it, he laughed back.

'But, with you skipping the country, does that not make you look guilty considering you haven't actually done anything?' I asked trying to make some sense of it all. 'Sounds simple when you put it like that but when your closest friend and business partner is slain in that way and you know that you're then going to have to speak to the people responsible for it. Meeting them while knowing that the chances of you not leaving again is sitting at the eighty percent mark. Would you go or would you grab your essentials and get the fuck out?'

'Touché,' I thought to myself. William Hill would probably be offering odds of a million to one on me sticking around to find out what the Hampden was, the bookies are never wrong either as they say.

He explained to me that they'd had to fly to Barcelona to fix out some financials and that he'd be staying in Ibiza until his lawyer had sorted everything out on his end. That all of this seemed to be the pre cursor to the whole escape plan being activated. He'd been under the impression that he would be able to just drop in on his lawyer unexpectedly and have everything arranged that same day but with the depth of how far his money had been hidden it was going to take days, plural.

'Why did you come to Ibiza though? How did you even know that I was out here just now?' I was hitting him with questions thick and fast. When you find yourself in the position of your father informing you that he is on the run from a notorious and dangerous criminal organisation you really do find yourself wanting to know as much as you can about the subject. How bad things are and if in turn they're going to affect you directly.

'Well it was more convenience than anything else' he replied. Well thank fuck for that, I laughed to myself. For a moment I had started to believe that he had actually wanted to spend time with his son!

'There's too much mafia in Barcelona, too risky to stay there while Sal arranges all my money. I honestly had no plan on where Eva and I were going to go. We left Bogotá in such a hurry I didn't have the luxury of planning our next step after Barcelona. That was when by pure chance I saw a vendor n Barcelona selling boat trips down by the beach. It was for a two day trip that involved going to a couple of nightclubs in Ibiza and that's where I saw your ugly mug on a poster. Looks like those record players I bought you are paying off eh?' He explained away his sudden choice of destination to me.

Putting aside the whole cartel killings, Italian Mafia and "criminal" lawyers moving illegally gotten cash for a moment. My response, out of everything, was an almost star struck response of - 'My face was on a poster in Barcelona?' - 'Yes, Stevie, for that club you play at, Spaced. I felt no need to correct him. Considering all that he had spilled since we'd sat down I was hardly going to be making an issue out of an extra letter D added incorrectly to a fucking word.

'So we hopped on a boat here to hide out while the finances are put in order and chances are I might need to go under the radar for a while. You might not hear from me for a while. Don't call me I'll call you, you know what I'm saying?' He continued. Maybe it was the sleep depravity on my part but I found the apparent sincerity that he said it to me hilarious.

'Fuck, that's a bit of a blow likes dad because if anything you were known for your easy access and constant availability. You know? Your door is effectively always open twenty four seven. It's going to be weird not being able to reach out to you for a while.' The look on his face was a unique display of hurt mixed with resignation. It then hit me again that this was the first time the two of us had spoken in person in so long and the last time we had I was seventeen, already a couple of Eckies into my night and coming up on an ill advised amount of MDMA crystals when we'd sat and had that chat. It had not been a fair fight in terms of a supposed conversation between two adults. This time though he wasn't speaking to someone with the memory levels of a goldfish. He was also not speaking to his seventeen year old son. Instead he had a twenty two year old who had had more drugs than he'd had sleep over recent days and an entirely different prospect.

'How did you find out where I lived though? You and your wife, thanks for telling me you got married as well by the way, thought I might've got a personal invite to that, likes' I trailed off not knowing if I wanted to ask questions to him or simply make points of no real insignificance in the grand scheme of things. When you have a cartel after you everything else kind of gets relegated to the realms of insignificance.

'Stevie, son? How do you think I've managed to operate in my line of work over the years without being resourceful? Finding you wasn't exactly a challenge. Two phone calls was all it took and I had your address. Eva and I were there within the hour. The door wasn't locked so I assumed that you were in your bed so we just let ourselves in. It was only when Simon came round that we found out that you were on your way back from Amsterdam. I called the club that you work for and they put me in touch with your agent, Lee. Bit of a mouth on him has he not? Thinks he's the consummate cockney gift of the gab. Anyway, after him asking me about the story of how I got you your first set of decks and where my funds had come from and me reminding him that only a fucking moron would talk about stuff like that over a telephone, we were straight. After that he happily pointed me in the direction of the pad that he had fixed you up with.' As always with Peter Duncan, he had an answer to everything.

'And Eva? What's the score there? I mean, congratulations and all that' I said trying to make sure that he kept his focus. Not only is it everyday your pops appears hiding out from drug cartels but also does he not generally appear with a wife who is closer to your age than she is to his. 'Eva? She's brilliant isn't she?' A huge smile washed over his face. 'Aye, she's really sound' I replied. I could've also added that she was actually really fucking tidy but that, I felt, would've bordered on the weird in terms of what a father and son would sit and talk about.

'She's made a lot of sacrifices for us, Eva. It was her that decided to take the chance and leave England to move out and be with me in Colombia. Getting married was a spur of the moment thing. Some men go out and buy a Porsche 911 when they hit their mid forties. I went out and got myself a wife half my age' he laughed even though I had already taken him as speaking the truth while masking it as a joke.

'Talking of Eva, obviously you can see that she's ages with you. While I'm here I'm going to try and undo this mess that I'm in and I was hoping that you could help keep her company for me. Take her out, show her a bit of Ibiza.' I tried to explain to him that I was there for work purposes and that I was mainly getting by on an existence of sleeping and playing at Space but he (correctly) responded by saying that I'd still have plenty time between all of that.

'Just show her a good time, Stevie. You'd have a better clue on how to do that than me. I've almost forgotten *how* to have a good time. She's been shacked up in that hacienda for weeks at a time with no one to speak to other than me and even then it's not like I've always been around. She doesn't know the extent of how bad things are, she only knows enough to keep her on her toes. If I was to tell her everything she'd walk for sure.'

I didn't bother to reply any further. Already knowing that I would indeed, in some way or other, end up roped up in looking after my dads weirdly younger (and wrong of me to think or admit but hot) wife.

'So look, cards on the table time' I had already moved my thoughts from the vagueness of Eva and how this twenty something girl from Manchester had ended up married to my dad and living in Colombia. 'How far will these radge cunts go to find you? Are you safe right now? Am I safe?' I felt a little stupid at even asking the question but it's where my head was at. I'd watched too many drug films with Mexicans and Colombians not to give myself a clear point of reference.

'Of course you'll be fine' he laughed back which I found in no way convincing and was actually the last thing I needed to be seeing as far as calming my nerves. 'I was careful leaving Bogotá, alternative passports to cover tracks' it was the first time in my life that I'd seen someone use the word "alternative" instead of fake and I'm not even sure why but I found it impressive. 'The only person that knows we're here is Sal my lawyer and my whereabouts is safe with him. We're only going to be here a few days, three tops and we'll be on our way again. We're checked into the San Antonio Garden just down the road from you.'

I was relieved to hear the last part as had feared that he was going to be asking me if I could put the two of them up. With his money he'd have been getting told to get to Falkirk as well, likes.

'Well you know what, dad? That's quite a story you've told me. I assume that by the look on Si's face it's also one you shared with him?' My dad nodded, allowing me to continue. 'Well that would normally be enough to completely spook someone hearing something like that but even without you I've got Si with some scary English gangsters on his case out here. I've got him giving me the wrong drugs before performances, too many hours partying and not enough sleeping. This additional interruption into what I thought was going to be a summer paradise is just one extra thing for me to think about and unless some Colombian hitman is going to kill me in my sleep anytime in the next ten hours I'm going to my bed and will leave you, Eva, Si as well, that cunt. I'll leave you all to go about your day and we can have a cool off period and catch up tomorrow.'

It felt strange to be the one who was more assertive in the father and son conversation but it was nothing personal. I'd have spoken that same way to Mother Teresa if I'd felt that she was the one standing between me and my bed that day. 'What are you and Eva going to do for the rest of the day?' I asked while settling the bill for the drinks. 'Fucked if I know, son' he replied in a way that showed that he wasn't exactly looking forward to a day and evening of "holiday making."

For someone who had told me that his other half was "brilliant" he didn't exactly look like someone who took much enjoyment out of being with her. Upon getting to mines he'd fucked off with Si and left her there alone and then on returning to find me there he, without even speaking to her, fucked off again instantaneously. Now though he was left with the prospect of some quality time with her and, by the looks, not exactly relishing the prospect of it.

For a brief second I pondered what it must be like for a forty five year old man to consistently try to sit and speak to someone half his age, like him and Eva. Trying to work it out just how two people with such an age gap could get on day in day out began to blow my mind so I sacked it. That alone suggested that it might well have been a bit of a head hurter though. 'Anyway, that's my papa's problem and not mine, 'I thought, passing the buck, mentally.

'Come on, I'll walk you back to get Eva' I said standing up. Regardless of the fact that we'd only seen each other twice in the space of ten years or something. The countless phone calls we'd had, what he'd done for me back at the start of the decade which undeniably turned my life around. With the amount of shifty characters I'd come across in my time. I "knew" my dad because I knew people "like" my dad.

I could tell that he thought that he could just appear unannounced and whatever I was doing I would drop in order to babysit his wife. This enabling him to spend his afternoon frantically on the phone to South American drug lords trying to plead for his life or tracking down some mental Bosnian paramilitary security team to protect him and Eva from the aforementioned South American drug cartel.

Not a fucking chance I was playing ball though. The reality being that his pre planned mark of a son had been burning the candle at both ends. Earning a crust and spending it as soon as he'd gotten it. Coming back from The Dam it was a case of no sleep til Brooklyn for moi and like I said to him. Short of the threat of being killed in my sleep then no cunt was going to stop me from going to bed. Even then I'd have likely checked into some random hotel under some "alternative" name and got my head down.

'Sorry dad, I know you needed me to take care of things today but there's other factors at play than just what's happening your side. Trust me, if I'd known that I was coming back to this I'd have just went to bed in my hotel in Amsterdam last night instead of staying up all night.' - 'Fuck, had I known what had been waiting for me in Ibiza I'd have just not bothered going back there at all,' was the inner thoughts on it all. 'Anyway, I didn't and now I need to go to sleep. I'm not exactly going to be much company for Eva when I start drooling, forgetting whatever the fuck that we're taking about and eventually passing out on her. Trust me dad, the hiring of a stupid fucking Fiat Panda from the rental place across from my villa and a drive along the coast with Eva while you work on your shit isn't going to happen.'

The fact that he didn't even bother to protest showed that he knew I had his number.

'See what Si is up to, you know what he's like. He'll help if he can, current embroilment in on going drug war, excepted' I offered him as some kind of olive leaf which was based on nothing more concrete than the fact that Si was currently already sat there back at mines getting to know his wife.

It wasn't any concern of mines. In the next ten minutes, and despite the baking heat that was sucking the oxygen from me. I'd be back at the villa and in bed and the three of them could do whatever the fuck they wanted for all I cared. With the greatest of respect, of course.

Chapter 12

Zico

Do you believe in love at first sight? It's a question I'd seen asked on the telly and in books but hadn't really thought about it personally until what happened that night at Space. It wasn't like I'd thought about it that way at all until the next day when I was lying in bed thinking about her. What *had* popped into my head while there inside the club was Michael fucking Corleone in The Godfather when he got hit with "the thunderbolt." One minute the lad is just minding his own business while keeping his head down over in Sicily hiding out and the next minute he's absolutely smitten with a girl he knows the square route of fuck all about. Michael Corleone > Me.

It had been a full day leading up to my set on the terrace. Predictably I'd been landed with the position of chaperone for Eva. Well, I did once I eventually surfaced for the day. While I'd told my dad, Si and Eva the day before that I was heading right to my bed after they'd left mines. I ended up having a change of mind by collapsing on the sofa and watching two James Bond films in a row. Live and let Die followed by The spy who loved Me. I know that it can get you a kicking in some parts of Scotland if you don't agree that Connery was the best Bond but I'm not giving a fuck. Roger Moore was better. There I said it. Even now with me being a bit more clued up in life and being able to look back. I'm still willing to give him a pass over those fucking campy pastel coloured safari suits with the big belts.

It actually highlighted how good he was with the women that he could cut about looking like that and *still* have them falling into bed with him by close of business. Proper legend. Once I'd watched the first film I'd actually felt more awake than I'd been for days so ended up sticking the other one on at the back of it. I'm not sure who the fuck had stayed in the villa before I'd moved in for the summer but they'd left a shit load of video tapes lying around in a cupboard when they'd moved out. Half of them were in their original boxes so you knew where you stood with them but the other half had been recorded onto blank tapes you get from shops like Woolworths.

I'd been a wee bit nervous about sticking them into the video recorder though. Bit of a mystery box, likes. The first one that I'd shoved in to try had left me a mixture of intrigue, fear and excitement. I didn't know if I was going to press play and find someone riding their wife or on the other end of the spectrum some sick snuff material. Actually was a bit of a let down when I'd found that it was only French Connection Part Two taped off the BBC. I think part of me was left disappointed that it wasn't a home made porno or a snuff movie, actually.

When I'd eventually woke the next day the first thing that struck me was the noise through in the living room. Having a think to myself. I wasn't able to remember physically taking myself through to bed or what I'd done at the moment but hearing the TV on I took it that I must've left it that way when I'd went to bed after the second film had ended.

Instead, taking myself slowly through to get the TV off before it received an empty bottle of Corona going through it's screen. I found Eva sat there in an almost instant replay of how I'd initially encountered her when arriving back from the airport the day before. Before I even spoke to her I found myself trying to work out just what the fuck was happening with my door to the villa and more pertinently, how the fuck were people seemingly getting in without my knowledge or consent?

My dad had mentioned to me how they'd let themselves in and twenty four hours later they'd apparently done the very same thing while I lay sleeping and blissfully unaware. I fucking swear I'd locked the door both times and yet they've still managed to get themselves in regardless. Not that it was important at the time but just before I'd wished Eva a good morning (only to be corrected and informed that it was no longer morning) I made a pact to myself that the next time I locked the fucking thing I would be triple checking just so I'd remember that I'd locked it to ensure that I wasn't actually losing my mind. Well, not through the subject of the unlockable front door, at least.

The look on her face as she told me that we were now into the afternoon left me with the impression that she wasn't exactly happy with me. Now no one wants to wake up and within seconds be getting the death glare from anyone never mind a woman that you just met the day before, stepmum or not.

It felt plain weird though to have the feeling of being in someone's bad books in the same way that say, a husband finds himself with his other half when he didn't know when to say when the night before and has woken up the whole house on getting back. Only then to compound things further by being discovered as having taken a piss in the kitchen pantry while mistaking it for the bathroom.

The clear and hostile atmosphere that I'd woken up and found myself thrown into was not exactly welcomed by moi but admirably I was able to keep a lid on it. Instead of going with my gut instinct of asking 'what's wrong with your coupon?' I decided to try and go the adult route and instead, actually talk to her to find out. Admittedly had I known her and of her existence for more than twenty four hours I would have most definitely just went with my gut response.

Once I'd sat down beside her while I gradually came to. I started to get to the bottom of why she was heavy on the attitude with me. It was fair to say that I wasn't exactly knocked down through sheer amazement upon finding that my dad appeared to be the reason for it. It just so happened that it was his son that was receiving the sharp end of things rather than the culprit himself.

As we began chatting I found out that she'd actually been hanging around the villa for the best part of four hours while I slept through in the bedroom like a bambino. She explained that the previous day, after I'd gotten rid of them all from the villa. Peter had "offloaded" her onto Si for the day and part of the night. Actually spoke volumes about Simon and how he had been more than happy to help and look after her for the day. This in itself sounded more interplanetary than it did foreign because as good a guy as Si was, it didn't really sound like him.

I still hadn't had the luxury of talking directly with the lad since arriving back from The Netherlands so was not in on whatever him and my dad had been talking about before I had arrived home but there was possibly some kind of side deal between the two of them that I wasn't aware of. Si, she said had been the perfect gentlemen over the day. Treating her to lunch at a restaurant down near the beach called Leonard's which was followed by a small tour around San Antonio. While it was a restaurant that I knew of it hadn't been one that I'd ever visited myself.

This was more down to the fact that it was some five star establishment that normally attracted the rich and powerful who were on the island. Not unknown deejays who had a habit of spending more money than they earned while in the Balearics. This, by extension, automatically ruled out unemployed part time drug dealers who were only on the island through being friends with unknown deejays who had a habit of spending more than they earned.

She actually wouldn't shut her pus when it came to my former associate football hooligan of a mate. It gave me a weird feeling after around the thirty minute mark when it felt almost like a bit of jealousy on my part over the fact that this was someone that was married to my father and Si already seemed to know her better than I did. For some reason, I felt that it should've been the other way around. 'So what's Si up to today then?' I asked her in a defensive way that I didn't like. Trying to make the point of, well if Si's so fucking wonderful and such a great guy why aren't you with him now instead of sat here with boring stinking me.

'Oh, he's running an errand for a friend over to the other side of the island. I asked if I could tag along with him so I could see a bit of Ibiza but unfortunately he was going to be riding there on his motorbike and said his license didn't extend to having anyone ride pillion.' Now "this" sounded more like the Si that I knew and loved. No shelling out on fancy five star meals but plenty of complete fabrications when talking to a woman. For one, he had an insane fear of motorbikes due to his cousin knocking him down with one when he was four years old. Just a random story that he'd told me over the years when we'd been sitting around wrecked at an after party but he had left me without any doubt that they gave him the fear big time, understandably.

This had only came about when a few of us were talking about the Mods and Rockers and how my theory had been that all of the ravers in the UK would've been Mods and your typical Glastonbury cunts would've been the Rockers. That was when Si admitted that he couldn't have been either as he was scared of anything related to motorcycles. Lie number two to her was the whole "running an errand for a friend" as I was his only friend in Ibiza and that this was just a lazy euphemism for going on a drug run.

His hat trick was this pish about his license not allowing for another passenger on his motorbike. It would've helped if he'd actually had a license in the first place but that was taken from him just before he flew out to Ibiza after getting caught doing sixty in a twenty outside the high school that afternoon. He'd already been sitting on six points as it was so it was a case of goodnight Vienna to driving for a while which all added up to none of what he'd told her being remotely true.

Trying to get into his mind I can only guess that he hadn't wanted to tell her about the drug run while safe guarding things incase she'd asked to come along for a ride. Before he knew it he was inventing laws on motorbike licenses. I can't but help love the guy despite all of the nonsense that comes along with him. What even made him think that he had to cover up the fact that he was driving a few bags of Ching over to someone when he was sat talking to the wife of a man who (quite possibly) played a direct part in it even fucking GETTING to Ibiza in the first place?! I honestly felt he'd have been quite safe if you ask me.

We sat speaking for around half an hour until I, sensing that it was now getting close to two, agreed to go and take a quick shower and get ready to take her out for a while. Even as I stood there in the bathroom with the water crashing down on me I had not the first idea of where to actually take Eva.

All of this making the most of the day and the good weather outside stuff while in Ibiza was a concept that was foreign to me. Most of my days had either been spent sleeping or delving into the pile of videos in the villa to watch something on TV. I'd fast adapted a Dracula like approach to how I spent my days. In the chicken and egg type scenario I'd arrived - partied really hard that same night - had the worst of comedowns the next day while playing for the first time at Space later that night - and so began the cycle of late nights and the following recovery periods. Once in it was a cycle that I'd found difficult to get myself back out of.

Thanks to my padre, wherever the fuck he was and whatever he was doing, I would be pulled right out of that comfy hermit like bubble that I had easily become accustomed to. It took me until the point of putting my clothes on for me to pluck the idea out of thin air of taking her for a walk on the beach and then a boat ride so that she could see the coast. With me performing later on I had to watch my time anyway so as unexciting as a boat ride might sound to you or I. It was still something that I'd felt would be ideal for killing a couple of valuable hours.

By the time we'd got ourselves down to the beach my mood had lifted. I'm not denying it, I was pissed off at my dad for just landing her on me for the day without any kind of a warning and I hadn't been able to suppress myself from showing it. How did he know that I hadn't already made plans? Maybe had a girl round spending the night with me? The point was that he didn't but by just going ahead and doing so he was executing a plan of action exactly in the way I'd thought he would when we'd sat speaking the day before in the pub.

The thing is I'm total shit at hiding my feelings. Aye, I might not speak the words at the time occasionally but I can't do fuck all about the look on my face so with her being pissed off at me for sleeping into the afternoon. On my side moi not taking too kindly to the news that I apparently had had my day mapped out for me before I even got a chance to wake for the day. It wasn't the best of starts.

Once I'd spoken a bit more to her and got some extra intel about my dad. Things that he wouldn't have thought to (or wanted) to share with me. I managed to get my head around the fact that she wasn't actually "choosing" to be getting dropped off at my current abode in San Antonio. She wasn't choosing to even be *in* Ibiza.

Fucking hell, days ago she was lying reading a book outside her mansion by the pool without a care in the world only for that radge cunt of a father of mines to rock up and give her what was effectively the ten minute warning. Must've blown her mind, that. Imagine just doing your thing in your settled life and someone coming along and saying that it's all over and you need to grab what you most treasure and then get yourself to fuck? No cancelling the phone line or electricity, fuck all. Too mad to even try to comprehend it.

She was pretty much nothing other than someone caught in the crossfire of being closely linked to Peter Duncan. He'll do that though.

'So where is he today that he's not with you?' I asked her as we walked along S'Arenal de San. Along the way, side stepping this young kid with a cool-box strapped round his neck that was almost the size of him. 'MELONI MELONI MELONI PIIIIIINAPPPPLLLLLEESSSSS' he shouted to the hundreds that were lazing around on sun loungers and the council version counterparts, towels. I wasn't quite past him when he'd begun shouting out his repertoire once more with the first "MELONI" going right into my left ear.

'Aye, ok then, pal' I said angrily looking back at him while Eva was trying to reply to what I'd just asked.

'Fuck yer Meloni, mate,' I heard a nasally Glaswegian accent shout back at him as we continued, moving ourselves away and out of earshot over what may have followed. 'I honestly don't know, Stevie. He said that he had some business to take care of and that it wasn't fair on me to not enjoy Ibiza for however many days that we're going to be here for, that it wouldn't be much fun sitting around alone in the hotel while he was working and that with you being on the island we could take advantage of this and get to know one another. I don't think he even knew where we were going and then once he found that you were in Spain too, that's what brought us here.'

I'd suspected that if my dad had reverted to type then Eva would, without question, have been fed a doctored version of what was actually really playing out in her life and how it could affect her, never mind her husband. I was certain that what he'd shared with me over those beers would have been a diluted version to what she'd have been given. Even myself having sat down with the man. I had come away unsure of what still remained that he hadn't told me.

With me having that little extra clarity than her. I played my cards close to my chest while gently probing her to obtain extra information. She, being the chatty type, was happy to tell me not just about the previous three days and why she was walking along this Spanish beach with me but her life in Manchester and the alternative lifestyle of Bogota married to a Cartel associate. That part came across as a lot more boring than I'd have ever imagined it to be although that was probably, in part, down to my dad telling her absolutely SFA about what he was up to.

Aye, she was good looking, Eva. But she wasn't the stereotypical bimbo along with it. You could tell by the way that she spoke that she was intelligent as much as she was confident. She left me with the impression that she knew exactly what she had been doing when she decided to hook up with my papa. That makes it sound like I'm calling her a gold digger but that's not what I'm saying at all. Just saying that she looked like she was smart enough to know the risks of marrying someone who, whilst clearly earning a lot of money, was receiving it from the underworld. No income tax no vee ay tee.

'If you don't mind me saying so, Stevie. It doesn't exactly look like you're too pleased to see Peter. When we were on our way to Ibiza he was saying that it had been around four years since you'd last seen each other' She asked me as I slowed down to take a look at some of the boats that were docked and waiting to leave. 'Typical of him' I laughed back, telling her that it had been six but apart from me who was counting eh!

'It isn't really the case that I'm not happy to see him, Eva. It's the fact that I don't hear from him for months at a time and then when I least, would or could ever expect it. He appears with a wife I don't know about and on the run from Colombia while I'm already trying to keep my head above water with regards to the lifestyle shift that temporarily moving to a place like Ibiza you can find yourself dealing with' I said, trying to give her complete transparency with regards to my feelings towards my dad.

She laughed at this before admitting to me that she was from the Acid House generation herself so she "got it," winking at me for emphasis. 'And anyway' Eva's face briefly lit up. 'I can't actually believe that I'm just having a casual day out in the presence of an actual Space DJ. Only a few years ago I'd have died at the prospect of that and then look at now. I am and he's my.' She hesitated for a second. 'Step son.'

It really was the stuff of farce that we could only just laugh at the facts in the way that she'd come out with them. 'Ach, it's only a spot on the terrace, just to warm up the crowd.' I said playing things down a little more than I really needed to. 'Peter's really proud of you' She added. I couldn't tell if she was saying it just for effect in the way that"mums" do or not but I accepted the sentiment all the same.

As for the glass bottom boat? The one that we'd been reliably assured by Paul, the tanned and bleach haired Yorkshire lad who was doing a half decent job of sweet talking potential passengers onto the boat, that it was the best boat in the bay? Well that was clearly a lot of bollocks on all counts. Absolutely robbed of the best part of four thousand pesetas so I was. Of course, it might've helped matters if the cunts who owned the fucking thing could've been arsed maybe giving the glass a wee clean now and again, mind. Could barely see fuck all through it. While I have never worked in the glass bottom boat game I would've still thought that cleaning the one area of the boat that pulled the public in might have been key?

The organisers of the trip seemed to think that us managing to barely make out a sunken ship down below us was the piece de resistance. I said to Eva that if they didn't get us back to the shore within the hour there was going to be another fucking sunken ship for holiday makers to vaguely squint at.

A criminal like waste of time and money. Two out of ten from me as far as a tourist attraction goes and they only got the two because I got a free swig of Sangria out of this traditional communal Spanish leather pouch. Swerve it as an activity though. You'll thank me later. Absolute shit.

Once we got ourselves back on dry land again it was time to address what was to happen with regards to Eva. As far as I could see I'd done my portion for the day. That in itself almost comes across like I'd seen it as a chore but she was actually a cool girl and spending the day with her had worked out a lot better than the signs had pointed to when my day had only just started. Still, wherever he was I was of the opinion that it was now time for my father to step up. If any cunt could find him that was, of course. I'd suggested a quick bite to eat before we wrapped up and it was while sat there in Delgados, a small tapas bar situated down near the West End, that we launched a joint effort to try and track him down.

It was futile really though because if he didn't answer the phone to his bread knife then he obviously wasn't going to pick up for his fair weathered son. By the time I'd finished off my Patatas Bravas which had been the last dish of many left on the table with food still on it. We still hadn't heard back from him so, explaining to Eva that I needed to prepare for my set. I agreed to take her back to her hotel.

In my own mind I'd envisaged some kind of a romantic evening out for Eva with my dad, once she'd finally been reunited with the slippery cunt. I'd figured that with him leaving her to spend the day with me he'd have been on a make up mission for the latter part of the day. Whether that was his intentions or not, Eva had other ideas. As we stood outside the hotel saying our goodbyes. While telling her that it was going to be a big night especially with Paul Oakenfold playing she just laughed back at me.

'Of course it's going to be a mad one, why do you think I'm going as well?!'

'Now hold on a fucking minute,' I thought to myself. Fair enough, do your bit for the familia like I'd done over the day. Do your piece, muck in and all that. It's only to be expected. To be asked to extend that to taking them to your fucking work with you? Nah that's not going to happen and it was only right as I was going to go on a major strop about it when she told me that Si had already said to her that he was going and had asked her if she wanted to go.

Classic Si, why think of the fact that this woman is there on holiday with her husband and that maybe just maybe. She might want to spend it with him. Instead, he invites her out for a night of Class A's in one of Ibiza's most legendary nightclubs.

'He said that you get a taxi through most nights and that him and I would go with you and come back again when you're ready for returning to San Antonio,' she continued. Fair play to Si, he had it all worked out, apparently.

'Well I'll see you later on again then,' I said, shutting the conversation down. It was too humid to stand chatting there any longer, stood at the bottom of the steps that led up to their majestic palace of a hotel.

'Good luck with your set, Selecao' she giggled.

It was the same giggle that I'd heard hours later as we all sat around Space following my set. From the moment that the taxi had pulled up outside the club I'd went my separate ways from Si and Eva. Fast forward then to a few hours later when I'd caught up with them again and was left in no doubt that the pair of them hadn't wasted much time in letting their hair down. It didn't take a drug counsellor to work out that Eva had necked one or two pingers while Si had evidently been dipping into his own wares as was carrying about that whole air of superiority that screamed Cocaine.

Eva, instead, was the furthest thing away from arrogance. She looked happy, incredibly so. One would not have been able to tell that she hadn't known Si or I for more than the couple of days that she had by just looking at her the way she was interacting with the two of us. She'd definitely begun to grow on me and sitting there following my set it really felt like I was sat there with a mate on a night out. Not sitting with my fucking stepmum.

With my performance out of the way, I'd decided to get myself into the party spirit along with Eva and Si by necking a wee Eckie myself to try and catch up. Si had seemed a bit miffed by this decision of mines although that was probably more to do with the fact that he was missing out on the lucrative sale of some Ching with me electing to purchase something that was the monetary equivalent of a fillet steak dinner in a basic San Antonio restaurant. Eva simply looked like she was having the better time out of the two of them and I wanted in.

The set had gone brilliantly and I was in a barry mood so fuck it, eh? I'd actually played back to back with an Italian DJ called Marco B. That scenario had been sprung on me when I'd arrived for the night. To tell you the truth, the only reason I wasn't happy about it (initially) was that I thought the cunts were going to pay me less for the night because I'd only covered one of the decks. Obviously that was nonsense and I would still get paid the same wedge regardless of only doing half a shift, so to speak. Plus, the Italian was quite a sound lad.

His English was better than mines which was a good help because I'm not sure that firing him names of Italian fitba teams and players names would've been conducive to an ideal partnership behind the decks for a couple of hours.

Between the pair of us, the crowd were absolutely doing their dish by the time I'd spun the last record. Fucking blew everyone's minds with my "Ibiza" last track of the set. Ally's Army! Too mad. I'd pinched the seven inch record from my cousin's record collection along with a select few other tracks that he had while I'd been planning all of these radge songs to end my sets with. Almost chose the eighty two World Cup song "We have a Dream" but I didn't think it was anywhere fast enough to drop on an unsuspecting crowd.

Ally's Army though? Fuck me, it went OFF out there. Did the majority of the crowd going crazy out on the terrace in front of me know the origins of the song and how a nation had been hypnotised into believing that Scotland were going to the World Cup and were actually going to win the fucking thing? It was merely a formality and that song was the anthem for everyone in the country to merrily sing while waiting on Ally Macleod and the boys to bring the trophy back home? I imagine that no, most, if not all, Si excepted, would not have heard that song before in their entire puff. Did it matter in that moment when they heard that accordion start up and then the beat kick in? Of course it didn't. It was Ibiza.

I invited Marco over to join me with Eva and Si but he was heading across the island to another set he had booked at The Ku. We'd gelled so well over the few hours we'd spent though that we parted ways with phone numbers exchanged and an offer from him for me guest at the club in Rimini that he was resident of. I know that it would take a lot of sacrifices from me to have to go to the trouble of going to a beautiful part of Italy on someone else's Lira and then get paid to play records in some club but for my art I guess it would be a sacrifice I'd have been willing to take.

Choking on my traditional post set smoke. I walked him out as he made his way towards the waiting car. Noticing that I'd just pulled a joint from out of my T-shirt top pocket. He popped his head into the car to indicate to the driver that he'd be a few minutes. We walked back away from the taxi and the crowds waiting to get inside the club and shared a few words as we smoked.

He was a really interesting boy, actually. Turned out that he had two younger brothers who were both signed with Fiorentina. The older one out the two had just been called up to the first team for the new Serie A campaign by the coach Claudio Ranieri. I was as impressed by this as Marco was nonplussed. This, I bet, was likely down to how often he'd get that reaction from people upon learning about his two footballing brothers.

He told me that he was a decent player also and had been the Italian equivalent of a schoolboy signing with Bologna but had been bitten by the house music bug and wanted to be a DJ instead of a professional fitba player. Fair play to the boy. I like to think that I'd rather be a fitba player in Serie A than a DJ. *Then* I think about all that I've been up to over the past six years and how it hasn't exactly been the life of an athlete and just how much a contradiction to how a fitba player is generally allowed to live. That's when my feelings on the matter become a bit more confused.

'Now don't take this as the drugs talking here, boys but I just want to say a massive thank you to the two of you for the past couple of days.' Eva said in that accent that made me think of Coronation Street any time she opened her mouth. Even though the Mitsubishi that I'd necked had completely taken a grip of me and was about to make me its bitch for the next couple of hours. I still thought I had a bit about myself to see that actually she was, in fact, just pouring out some Ecstasy induced shit, just because. As she continued however. I soon saw that I was wrong about that. A little later I'd see that I was also wrong about me thinking that I had a bit about myself as well!

'The past two days with you two has made me feel like an actual real living person again. Having conversations, laughing, feeling stimulated, meeting new and interesting people, meeting human beings of any description full stop. Tonight? I can't even remember the last time I went out and had fun and I'm not talking going to Space and getting out me tits either. I almost felt like a prisoner in that house.'

It was like when you see one of those Formula One drivers when they're up on the podium and they're shaking that bottle of champagne and eventually pop the bottle and it goes off all over the place and can't be stopped once it starts. Aye, that was Eva once she'd started speaking. Si and myself exchanged a quick worried glance at each other. Almost trying to work out a plan telepathically between us that would avert this impending car crash of a conversation topic.

The thing was, this wasn't just being around someone who was pouring out their feelings while leaving you not close enough to them to fully deal with their predicament. This was a lot more closer to home considering it was in relation to my own dad.

'I'm not saying that Peter is a bad person or husband, I know he loves me and I have wanted for absolutely nothing since leaving Manchester to be with him but it's just such an empty life, you know?' She continued. Looking like she was going on to add some other thoughts only to stop which, knowing how many hours she was into her pills. I put down to her forgetting what she was about to say rather than thinking better of it and remaining silent.

'Well, looks like you'll not be going back to any emptiness in Colombia anytime soon, Eva.' Si said, subtle as a fucking brick by going with the novel approach of trying to make someone feel better about something by reminding them of the worst part of what's going on in their life.

I went with the tried and tested tactic of moving over and giving her a big hug, kiss on the head and telling her that all of this stuff happens for a reason and that it always works itself out to how it's all meant to end up. I'm not even sure I believe all of that shite myself but it sounded good at the time and with how the Eckie was working on me, it really was as good as it was going to get and it wouldn't get that good again for a number of hours.

She hugged me back even tighter. Of course she fucking did. Who doesn't love a big cuddle and some nice words in their ear on a pinger?! 'Awwwww I love you Stevie, you too Si' she said reinvigorated. Once she'd let go of me she lurched over towards Si to give him one. 'Right, drinks?' I said to the two of them as I stood up, after a bit of effort due to how light headed I was from the pill. 'Just a bottle of water please' Eva answered while snuggling into Si from the side. 'Another beer por favor, Senor' Si confirmed, shaking his empty bottle for emphasis.

My head had been starting to take off during the latter part of the conversation and at least for a few minutes. I wanted to deal with what was going on inside there away from any Trisha style sofa confessions that was going on with Eva. Due to circumstance more than anything else I hadn't had a pill in months and either my tolerance had been temporarily lowered or those Mitsubishis had been designed by some Dutch madman. It could easily have been a bit of both.

Saying that I'd be back soon. I left them to it as I gratefully took off for the drinks. This, a vow that I would end up not entirely sticking to.

Without any intention of doing so I ended up almost involuntary circling the room for a while. Speaking to someone I didn't know for five minutes here. Someone that I already knew for twenty minutes there. I completely lost track of time and that I was meant to be buying drinks for friends. I ended up with a beer for myself from somewhere although had barely touched it.

I'd never been a fan of mixing alcohol with Eckies. I always thought that it defeated the purpose of it all. If you want to have a swally then fucking well have a swally and if you want some Class A's then knock yourself out but mixing the two doesn't do either substance any favours. Almost the equivalent of having the world's fastest racehorse ready for running in the national but having Bill Werberniuk pencilled in as the jockey.

This bottle of San Miguel was fuck all other than a prop and I needed to get rid of it as soon as I could. Clocking a colourful round Mexican mosaic style table. I happily stuck my bottle down on top of it. Glad that I was finally free of carrying the thing around with me which, because of the pill, felt like it weighed a tonne.

'FAHKING ELLLL, WHAT THE' The table screamed in a cockney accent as the bottle fell off the side of it and smashed onto the floor. That's when I realised that it actually wasn't a table at all. Alarmingly so I had been initially more confused by the fact that despite placing the beer slap bang in the centre of the table and it had STILL fallen off the side rather than the actual table itself talking to me.

Borrowing a line from my favourite Prince song. That's when I saw her ooh then I saw her. Drenched in the cerveza that I'd inadvertently tipped over her, glass shattered all around her sandalled feet. She should've been raging at me, she wasn't though. Maybe it was my pitifully pickled state that was staring back at her which had saved me. Stood there apologising to her as I in no way helped matters by patting down the soaked parts of her dress while I tried to work out how I had managed to mistake a girl from London for a drinks table.

She was beautiful, I mean absolutely stunning. Prettiest girl in the room, whatever wherever the room, material and despite the fact that I'd dispensed with a bottle of beer while using her body to do so. She was actually there smiling back at me.

I felt this forceful instant feeling of being grabbed by something, completely smitten. The only time I'd experienced an equal had been that night in Nineteen Ninety when I discovered the absolute witchcraft that was the combination of House music and Ecstasy. Aye, that's how powerful it all felt as I stood there looking back at her.

Obviously there was the Ecky at play but this was by no means the first time I'd spoken to a member of the opposite sex while having partaken in MDMA, obviously.

'I thought you were a table' I said in what could only have come across as a mixture of sincerity, embarrassment and bemusement. Of course, I was forgetting the fact that this would all be crossed with a stupid spaced out grin on my face that didn't exactly suit my embarrassed state of mind, safe in the knowledge that I had made an massive cunt out of myself. Having been provided with a moment of reflection I was able to clock that what I'd thought as a table was in actual fact a big fuck off Mexican sombrero that was on top of her head while she sat. This had given off the impression that it hadn't been a person and instead was a table. Well, that was my story and I was fucking sticking to it.

'You thought I was a table?' She replied back to me once she'd stopped laughing in my direction. Practically repeating my words for confirmation. I liked her instantly. There she was wearing a bottle of San Miguel courtesy of moi but her tone of voice and the look on her face was showing me that it hadn't done anything to dampen her night, despite dampening other parts of her.

'Well, aye, obviously. You mean you've never been mistaken for a piece of furniture before?' I laughed back in a cheeky way that I'd had the feeling that I'd able to with her. 'Apart from my primary five performance in the school nativity play, no, not really' she answered smiling back at me which I took to be in reference to her potential wooden acting skills. It couldn't have been literally in connection with her having the role of table in the play, I thought. I suppose technically it could've been but that wouldn't have said much for her or any kids acting skills for that matter if they'd been handed that as a role. Put it this way, if I have any kids and they end up getting that as a gig for a play I won't even be leaving the fucking house for that particular performance. Waste of time, that.

'Can I buy you a drink?' I asked. - 'Well if you think that you could manage to get yourself to the bar and back again without sitting down on top of someone because you think they're a chair or something like that and *then* can manage to pass me my drink without it going all over me then yes, I'd love one. Spiced rum and coke please. I'm Flo, by the way and while we're at the introductions stage you're going to have to tell me your real name because I can only pronounce your DJ one when I'm straight. Add one pill and then you can forget it.' She laughed, indicating her willingness to carry on with the chance meeting.

'I'm not making any promises on that,' I laughed with her. Safe in the knowledge that there was probably an even higher percentage of a chance of me sitting down on some poor cunt than there was of me thinking someone was a fucking table. 'I'm Zico, pronounced zeeee-co' I added with the same sarcasm that she had treated me to. Screwing her face back at me in the same way I left to go to the bar telling her I'd be back in a few minutes. Unlike the previous "few minutes" that I'd promised Si and Eva. This really was going to be stuck to.

'Nice hat by the way' she said as I left her for the bar. I wasn't even sure if she had been taking the piss with that or not purely down to the fact that I'd already had Si and Eva ribbing me over it. During my set earlier on. A girl had come over to the booth and handed me what looked like one of those Zorro style traditional black Spanish hats with the red ribbon that you'd often see cunts wearing while cutting about dance floors with castanets in their hands. Dressed all in black. Those type of cats. I'd stuck it on my head the moment that I'd been handed it and by the time my set was over. Myself and the hat had become inseparable. The more Si and Eva slagged me over it the more I wanted to keep it on my head. Just to annoy them. Pushing back against them, I'd said that I was going to wear it for the whole of my set the next time I was playing at Space.

'I should lay off the Eckies more often if this is going to be the results,' I thought to myself while standing at the bar waiting on being served as I clocked how strongly the Mitsubishi was impacting on me. Was I only taken with her *because* of the pill and the wonders it was working or was she really that special in the way that this Michael Corleone style thunderbolt was electrocuting me with?

That was the one major question I was trying to get my head around. I also found myself considering that she knew who I was. That fact alone still freaked me out a little. In that people knew of me because of the DJ thing. I suppose the bigger deejays are all used to it but it was still something that took me by surprise at times. In my frazzled state having the thought of her knowing me. I had somehow connected that to the psycho Spanish lass.

I batted that thought away easily enough though considering this had not been a case of her flirting her way into talking to me. Instead she had literally been minding her own business when I'd gatecrashed her evening. She was only in the position of talking to me because of my own actions. That fact alone told me that I didn't need to have any worries on that score. End of the day, I didn't know what the fuck was going on, pill or no fucking pill. All I knew was that it had been me who had made an absolute twat of myself in front of an extremely attractive girl. She'd then made eye contact with me in a way that almost left me on my arse and yet despite all of that. There I was carrying drinks back for us.

We sat chatting and getting to know each other a little more. The one thing that had stuck out that I'd liked was that rather than the predictable conversation that I'd normally have found when speaking to a stranger inside Space. Mainly centred around the fact that one of the two people taking part in the conversation was a DJ at the club. We never.

It was like we didn't need to go there such was the rapid connection that appeared to exist between us. No need to frantically reach for a mutual topic that two strangers can grasp on to speak about while searching for a happy medium to ensure that there would be no awkwardness. Difficult conversation was the least of our worries. It was more like one of those rare occasions where you speak to someone for the first time but it feels like you've already spoken to them countless times. Like you already know them.

I'd found out that she was there with her friend Elle who at the time was outside looking after some spaced out eighteen year old kid she'd found who had taken his very first pill and hadn't been handling things too well. With how precious seats and tables were inside the club Flo had agreed to stay put so that they didn't lose their spot. They were over from England for their annual summer three week blow out on the island. This being only their second night of the holiday. Her star sign was a Scorpio, she had an insane fear of birds and her favourite DJ was Erick Morillo.

I resisted the natural urge to tell her that I'd actually filled in for her favourite DJ just before she was flying out. She was from Kingston which was just outside London, apparently. Her age was just a couple of years younger than me at twenty. It was their second summer in a row out on the island. The previous year being so good that they had booked up for the next summer before their sore heads from the previous trip had even cleared.

I just let her go on and on and when she stopped I would ask even more questions. It felt so refreshing to have a normal conversation with someone in that environment. One that wasn't anything to do with me or Space. It was something that I one hundred percent endorsed as much as I embraced. I literally couldn't take my eyes off her as she sat there talking to me. That smile, the glow. Her colourful dyed Tizer red hair that she had up in a bun of sorts. Beautiful brown skin and the body of a swimmer or a runner, definitely an athlete anyway.

I know a lot of things can become more attractive when under the influence of MDMA but she really was taking the piss. She had a sense of style that was right up my street. I'd complimented her on the short flowery dress that she had on to which she'd taken enjoyment out of in addition to the pride she displayed when she told me that it was one of "Stella's graduation collection." This, I admit, would've had a lot more impact had I known who the fuck Stella was. Spilling that I didn't know what she was talking about. She explained to me that it was a dress designed by Paul McCartney's daughter and was the only one in the world that existed.

I'd heard of Stella's dad at least and while, having my mind body and soul ruined by the Mitsubishi. Trust me, it was an achievement of sorts to even remember the names of the four members of The Beatles.

We were still there talking when her friend Elle came back to join her. I could tell from the introduction that Elle didn't know who I was. For all she knew I was simply just some guy who had been trying to get off with her friend, having noticed her sitting there on her own. Soon after that, the three of us moved over to join Si and Eva to officially kick off a night of epically messy yet monumental proportions.

The mix of the five of us spending the night and morning together was like the perfect fucking storm. The two cockneys were a riot which then pitted them against the Scottish patter from Si and moi. Eva? Get a couple of pills inside that lass and she's the life and fucking soul. The Mitsubishis were returned to over periods of the morning until just around midday when we crawled out the place to the waiting black and white taxi. It had been easily the latest I'd left there since starting the residency. A night of talking the biggest amount of bollocks, laughing until a little bit of piss was in danger of escaping, smiling until my cheeks hurt and dancing (with Flo) the most I'd had in all the years of me getting behind the decks.

Despite how scarily well her and I had clicked. This was not your predictable thing where the two of us would end up back at mines to finish things off. First up it was fucking lunch time when we left. That fact alone pretty much done away with the whole 'want to come back to mines' way of doing.

Secondly, the pair of us were completely wired. There wasn't going to be much "action" back at mines other than me getting home, necking a couple of blues and getting my sorry arse to sleep for the next twelve hours. Disregarding any of that though. I can't explain it because I'd never really had that feeling before but from the minute I met her. I had the feeling that she was different. That she was better than taking home at the end of the night with the sole intention of having sex with.

The five of us all travelled back to San Antonio although only after a small to medium sized bribe from Si had been given to the driver after he had clocked five of us getting into his four seater Peugeot and had lost the head with us over it. The journey was filled with full on lunacy. I felt a little bit sorry for the guy behind the wheel, actually. He had the three girls all singing along to the pop tunes that were playing on his radio, Si telling him to slow down a bit as he was trying to have a bump in the back of the car on some clipboard he'd found.

Meanwhile, I'm trying to be the sound cunt and talk to him about fitba as always. Asking him who he supports, the usual routine you do with strangers, like. He was more worried about the singing though by the looks. 'Callate el infierno,' he shouted looking round at them. Only turning back around in time to steer the taxi away from going right into the back of some fruit lorry that we had been heading towards at speed.

Whilst my fingerprints were embedded into the dashboard of the car. The use of my voice had apparently been taken from me. I had tried to shout and warn him about the oncoming crash but without success. Quickly glancing at me he casually shrugged his shoulders as he overtook the lorry, speeding past it before pulling back into the other lane again.

Eva, Flo and Elle got the message after that. They behaved. I know that normally the man is going to then have to step up and get the taxi driver told but in all fairness to him. They *were* extremely nippy, especially at that time of the day. In that heat after being up all night on the chems with their high pitched off key singing that no doubt was not the version that they were actually hearing in their own heads.

When we got back to town I was first out the car although I wasn't for getting out until the driver had given me a couple of pieces of paper from the pad that was stuck to his window so that Flo and I could take care of the formalities in exchanging each other's details. Tentatively agreeing that maybe, but only maybe we'd catch each other later on at night once we'd both grabbed some R & R.

With the worst double vision and head that was starting to split, spin and overheat through the combination of the pills and the temperature of the afternoon sun. I popped my head into the window of the side that Flo was sitting at and gave her a gentlemanly peck on the cheek while saying a quick adios to everyone else in the car. I was still stood there in the sweltering heat as the car disappeared out of view while I tried to figure out just how I was going to pull off those forty or so steps from the kerbside to my front door and back inside the villa.

Chapter 13

Zico

Seeing her later that night was always on the high end of hopeful. Being able to actually get myself to sleep would've been a good start when it came to any post sleep plans. It didn't come easy my way. The amount of MDMA that was still running through me coupled with thoughts of this Flo lass had been enough to leave me a very twisted bright eyed and bushy tailed individual. I'd lay tossing and turning through in the bedroom. The couple of Diazapam I'd taken before slipping into bed appeared not to have even touched the sides. Apart from leaving me feeling a little groggy and slowed down. They had done absolutely fuck all in the way of putting me to sleep.

Eventually, frustrated with the tossing and turning in addition to the absolute nonsense that was inside my head as the chemicals tried to work their way out of my system. I got back up again. In my logic, the pills hadn't been enough to meet the MDMA head on and knock me out so I felt a plan b needed enforced. Deploy the alcohol. Figuring that even just a couple of beers would've been enough to push me over the edge. You know all that pills and alcohol stuff. Do not drive do not work any heavy machinery and all of that guff?

Despite the genuine trepidation over the torturous heat that was going to be waiting on me outside. I put on some shorts and a DJAX Upbeats t shirt and ventured out with the sole intention of getting a couple of nectars down my yak and back to bed as quick as I possibly could. I was not built for "outside." Not then, not that day.

It was only when I walked into the nearest bar, Fat Tony's, that it dawned on me that it was officially the first day of the European Championships. I thought something had to have been up because you generally wouldn't have found as many people inside a bar, any bar, at that time of the day. Once inside I found a large group all huddled in the corner staring up at the large TV that was fixed to the wall.

My head was that fried from Space I couldn't remember which game was scheduled to kick the tournament off. Instead of any fitba at that point on the screen it more resembled the last night of the fucking proms than it did pre match inside Wemberley. Fucking 100 piece bands, trumpets, clarinets, bassoons the lot while cunts in the crowd were all waving their union jacks with great gusto.

I don't have any time for those opening ceremonies for major sporting tournaments. They always seem to come across as nothing more than pretentious as fuck. It looked like Euro Ninety Six was reverting to type. What the fuck had Les Miserables to do with fitba anyway? I asked the barman who England were playing. I'd already assumed that with it being the opening game they at least would have been one of the teams to open the tournament.

Even though the TV was already switched onto the coverage from London and the fact that pretty much all of the customers were inside there specifically for the game, the bartender didn't know. Overhearing this between us. Another guy, some middle aged chap who had that lobster red look about him which suggested that he'd made an arse of the whole suntan thing on day one of his holiday and was now going to have to hide out in shaded areas for the next two or three days until things calmed down, shouted down the bar to me that it was England - Switzerland. The second he did I knew that it was something that technically I'd already been aware of since they were two of the teams in our group. Through that calculation, Scotland versus Netherlands was going to be the other match to complete the two opening games in the group.

Tucking into the ice cold bottle complete with lime shoved into the neck. I noticed that they were now starting to clear the instruments from the pitch ahead of the game starting. Through the heat in the poorly air conditioned bar, I downed the beer inside two long swigs before asking for another. With the game almost ready for kick off I decided to stay for the ninety minutes before then heading back to the villa for some kip.

Assessing the room, it was clear that the crowd inside were pretty much exclusively English. All packed inside there to watch their boys. In an environment such as that, while throwing in the tribalistic nature that fitba can bring out in people. I wisely decided to keep my mouth firmly shut while sitting there. Pragmatically I knew that my accent could well have presented a problem at some point over the game to some of the crowd that had assembled inside there.

I'd had way too much experience when it came to that side of things abroad when finding Brits from all corners of the island mixing in the one place. What, out of everything that had placed me on my guard from the very off had been the vibe that the group in the corner had been giving off. Proper Rule Britannia two world wars and won World Cup we've one, sorts. A couple of them in Union Jack shorts on which in itself was always the most red of flags. From personal experience I'd always found that if you ended up engaging in any kind of handbags with English guys wearing Union Jack shorts then it would either end in violence or at the very least some pieces of furniture being thrown indiscriminately in your direction.

"INGERLLLUND INGERLLLUND INGERLLLUND" the lads in the corner started up as the teams emerged from the Wembley tunnel to a noisy capacity crowd. As far as my own interests went. I thought a draw between the two teams would've been perfect for Scotland in their attempt to get out of the group stages. I couldn't see it though and on home soil and in such a big match with the whole of the world looking on. There really was only going to be the one outcome which, in my mind, would've seen Terry Venables' men take all three points. No disrespect to the Swiss either but I'd always seen their strength's lie in other areas like watch making and boasting the best dodgy banks for even dodgier people to use.

It looked that way even more when Alan Shearer put England ahead with an absolute thunderbastard of a shot in the first half. I had to laugh at everyone in the room following the goal. All singing his name like some favourite son when, as far as we'd been made aware in Scotland. Shearer had been taking a heavy amount of grief from the press and fans because he'd not scored for England for a while. The minute he scores though he's suddenly a Ballon d'Or winner in their eyes. If the bastards don't want him I'm sure the SFA could magic up some kind of fugazi Scottish grandparent for the boy.

That's one thing though that I'd never understood, the English press. Looks like they're never fucking happy unless England are shite which, fortunately for Scots, the players and management over recent years had been happy to accommodate. That Graham Taylor experiment a few years ago? Fucking hell! Still though, a few weeks before the tournament began they were getting fired right into Gazza because he'd had a swally with the rest of the team when they were abroad. Probably their best player and the press are trying to nail the poor cunt right before the tournament had even began?

It was midway through the second half and I'd sank four beers by then and wasn't exactly feeling too clever. Any kind of effect from the Mitsubishis was long gone and had been replaced by the general lazy sloppiness result of the Diazapam mixed with the beers in addition to the all too obvious fact that I hadn't left Space until lunch time. I told myself that I'd have one more for the road and there was not one iota of a chance that by then I wouldn't be sleeping within minutes of getting back into bed again. I wish I'd fucking stopped at the four now though.

I was taking care of the toe nails stage of the bottle of Corona and with just under ten minutes to go and the match still one nil to England. I decided that once I'd finished my beer I'd just head as by then I wasn't exactly trusting when it came to where I was going to be from one minute to the next, mentally and physically speaking. Through the spacey head that I had on me I wasn't clocking as much inside the bar as I'd been earlier on. I hadn't even been watching the game anymore while I finished off my beer.

That's when I heard a series of loud expletives and groans behind me. Hopes instantly soaring, I wheeled round fully expecting to see the Swiss players all piling on top of each other by a corner flag celebrating. Instead, I was looking at Stuart Pearce (I think) with his head in his hands having, in all probability, surgically removed one of the other players limbs. Penalty to Switzerland. Fucking hell, didn't see that coming. Then again, it would've been a challenge to see anything when you have your back to the TV screen. This though presented me with a whole new different problem, other than the already pre existing one of just exactly how I was going to make it back to the villa from the pub. Motor skills were at an all time low by that point, the fear was starting to creep in and I should've been well removed from all other forms of human contact by that point. Now there was a new issue to be concerned with.

Don't fucking celebrate if Switzerland score, DO NOT make a sound, nicks nada, Scottish Fitba Association. I told myself this as I sat there along with the rest of the bar in complete silence waiting on the Swiss player to take the kick. It felt like time had stood still as he waited to take his run up.

DO NOT CELEBRATE I offered myself one last gentle reminder as he ran up to take the kick.

'YESSSSSSS YA FUCKING BEAUTY GET IT RIGHT FUCKING UP YOUS' I bawled, leaping out of my chair. What looked like all of the bar turning round to see who was making the noise in this sombre of moments that had descended upon the room. 'Oh do one you fucking Jock prick' one guy who'd went all in for the day and, despite the fact he was in thirty degree plus weather was dressed in some fucking fancy dress King George chainmail. 'Yeah fuck off you fucking sweaty sock' this fat blonde woman shouted at me. Wearing a t shirt way too small for her. England badge and 'it's coming home' written on the front. Whatever that was meant to have meant.

My protests that I wasn't the stereotypical "Jock" who would support the IRA if they had eleven decent players and were up against England at fitba and that I was merely celebrating in a tactical sense over hoping to get out of the same group as them. A draw was, after all, the optimum result that Scotland would've chosen to benefit themselves before kick off. Those protests didn't prove as successful as I'd hoped. Through the combination of the threats of violence towards me and the very real fact that I would not have been able to punch my way out of a wet paper bag by that point of the day. I decided to leave before I ended up with a chair over my head or something. My head was sore enough as it was.

I didn't even make bed in the end. I couldn't remember what happened other than, well, nothing. No recollections of getting back from the pub to Casa de Selecao but I must've done just enough to get myself in the door and no more. I came to on the sofa still in my flip flops and shorts and t shirt.

Fuck knows how but I'd managed to drop half a smoked joint that had been lit onto the front of my t shirt where it had then burned a hole in the material. Then, managing to melt itself to the shirt. I didn't even realise it was there until I got up for a pee and noticed half a fucking joint stuck dangling to the front of me. I worked out that I'd been sleeping for almost 15 hours which was a decent amount of kip in anyones book apart from a sloth I suppose. Those cunts know how to kip and no mistake.

I was walking back from the bathroom when I noticed the slip of paper that was lying on the floor on the inside of my front door. Like it had been pushed under it from the outside. I walked over to pick it up, almost cringing at what might be on it. Obviously I hoped that it had been from Flo but I was realistic enough to know that it could have easily been something on the opposite end of the scale like a message from my dad telling me that I had to leave Ibiza within the next hour because there was a Colombian death squad on its way to kill me. It was from Flo.

'Stevie, I'm free today if you fancy doing something together? Call me, Flo xx'

I'd only seconds before finished reading her note and was running through to the bedroom to find what I'd had on at Space with no real recollection of where I'd put the piece of paper I had with her phone number and hotel name written on it. It was in the very first pocket I tried which saw the very next action being for me to look for the phone to give her a call. When she answered she was sat at a restaurant about to have something to eat and said that she'd call me back.

'How close are you to mines?' I asked before hanging up. - 'Not too far' - 'Well I'm going to jump in the shower and get changed, have your lunch and then come over here and we'll go out for the day' I said getting ready to hang up. 'Oooh sounds good' Flo replied while also saying something to a waiter on her side of the phone. 'Do you have anywhere in mind?' - 'Not a glass bottom boat anyway.' I laughed. Unable to recall if I had told her about my recent trip on the waves.

By the time she'd arrived I'd already decided on the destination of Ibiza Town. It was a place I'd only ever visited at night to go to Pacha but it had looked a nice historic and chilled place and one perfect for her and I to get away from tourist infested San Antonio. When she arrived at my door any niggles I'd had over the night in Space being MDMA assisted were pushed aside. Those mad fucking butterflies revisiting me all over again at the sight of her when opening the front door.

She was wearing a pair of cork wedged shoes along with a mini dress and had these big gold hooped earrings that you couldn't not notice. You could've almost volleyed an Adidas Tango right through the fucking things. Exactly like the first time we'd met though it was her massive smile that grabbed all the headlines. 'Sooooo where you taking me then?' She asked excitedly while I sat there tying the laces on my ZX 600's. 'Well how would you like a day out over in Ibiza Town? A wee stroll, couple of drinks, something to eat and who knows what other blanks we can fill in and capers we can get up to along the way?' I said looking up and meeting her smile with one of my own.

Flo admitted that she'd only ever seen it at night and even then that had been largely restricted to the taxi ride to Pacha which had me laughing over the fact that her experience was pretty much a carbon copy of mines in the sense that we could've almost went there in the same car for all we'd both seen separately.

Borrowing Si's car, well, I'm not really sure what it's called when your friend leaves their car outside your house along with the keys with no intention on anyone driving it. We got on the road across to the other side of the island and the old town. I took the opportunity on the drive for her to find out a little about me. I'd found out so much the night we'd met that had it not been for the vague level that the memory operates at after Ecstasy I'd have probably been able to provide you with her first pets name, bra size and mother's maiden name. I on the other hand was more the mystery man by comparison.

Completely imbalanced, apart from my name and that I spun records at Space every other night she barely knew nicks about me. I took the chance to address that over the journey that took us from the West Coast of Ibiza to the East.

'Jesus H, babe! Well that was entertaining. THAT was better than Enid bloody Blyton' Flo said in a semi amazed kind of way as I pulled into a space down by the marina as we arrived in Ibiza Town.

'The worst part is that at least Blyton's stuff was made up' I laughed back at her while contemplating some of what I'd told her. She'd been hit with the epitome of randomness when it came to finding out more about me. She'd effectively started it by asking what had led me to be playing to the rich and famous as well as the skint and infamous on the terrace over in Playa den Bossa. To answer that question in the way that it deserved I took her all the way back to Shroom. The first all-nighter six year before that I'd went to in that farmers field. I told her how that one single night on my first Dove had led to a whole chain of events that almost sent me right over the edge before I was even legal age to buy a fucking drink.

How, with the discovery of Acid House and all the delights that it had in store for me, it had been the most exciting time of my short life yet in "perfect" harmony alongside it. At all times had been the crippling worry over how the story with Nora was going to end. Her reaction when I got to the part of who it was that came to my rescue in that respect and how they managed it was priceless. Almost spat out her fucking lemon Fanta when she heard the part about Si and moi completely spangled inside a disused factory in Blackburn stumbling across my fucking absent cartel dad who went on to not only provide us with an obscene amount of narcotics for a doggy bag but who would go on and readjust my whole equilibrium of life.

Si had tried calling me about halfway into the car journey but when I'd noticed that it was him as the caller I decided to let it ring out. The chances were medium high to high that he'd come to get his car and found it gone and considering that this aged Volkswagen Golf (soft top though, likes) was key to the day away from it all that I had planned for the two of us. I felt it foolish to answer the call and in doing so have no choice but to admit to him that I was in possession of it.

Since, apparently, any cunt on the island could get themselves into the pad that Lee had rented out for me, I'd assumed that Si had got himself in, went to where he'd left the keys. Found them gone and got out his my first calculator and managed to add a couple of twos together and place me firmly at the scene of the crime. I put it to the back of my mind and got back on with the drive and the severe tongue lashing that I was giving Flo as we tucked into the block of Hash that Si had ever so conveniently left lying around in the car's centre console.

I don't know? Most girls I wouldn't have even told half of the story to. Let's face it, *most* girls would've ran a mile from a fella once he started breaking out stories involving soccer casuals and narco fathers but Flo hadn't ever given me that impression. That she was one of "them" and such was proved with the excited way she would bounce up and down in the passengers seat laughing out loud and asking further questions to get more background.

It was a task in itself keeping my eyes off her while driving. The combination of me having never driven to Ibiza Town and myself not exactly proficient in driving on the right hand side of the road. I wisely kept my eyes off her for the most part.

The old town of Ibiza was beautiful. It actually freaked me out just how different it was despite only being half an hour away from San Antonio. The area that I'd driven us to was a world away from the rows of pubs that offered full English breakfasts all day long and a happy hour that lasted all night. Restaurants that you'd be risking spending the rest of your holiday inside your hotel toilet if you'd ate from and tourist shops that would sell you a Spanish donkey and a pack of German hardcore pornography playing cards in the blink of an eye.

Nah, this place was, different. An absolute masterpiece of an idea. We got out to take a walk around as I lapped up the beauty of the surroundings. The stark contradiction of the old buildings within touching distance of all the modern super yachts that were docked at the marina. The whole vibe was so much more quieter. No PR reps no eighteen to thirty cunts and no stupid fucking lassies who've ended up getting drunk in the afternoon and have no idea just how nippy they're coming across to the general public. Fuck, there wasn't even any looky looky men which was, weird. There was the added bonus that Spain were playing Bulgaria in the Euros so there was a decent buzz about the place. Lots of natives kicking around with their faces painted and flags around them.

Completely cheesy as fuck I know but I bought the two of us an ice cream for walking along down by the water. We spoke about what her plans were for the rest of her and Elle's holiday while left not in any way surprised by her answer.

'Space, Amnesia, Ku copious amounts of Ecstasy and sleeping it all off on the beach. That and spending some time with my new DJ friend' she replied with a cheeky smile while putting her arms around me and giving me a big kiss on the side of my face. Leaving the remnants of her latest lick at her Naranja sorbet resting on my cheek which she then proceeded to swipe off with a finger and in the most suggestive and ridiculously sexy of ways. Shoved it into her mouth and licked it clean. Which for someone like myself who was wearing a tight pair of Jimmy Connor's Tachini retro tennis shorts, wasn't exactly cool there and then, ken?

'Well, if you start to enjoy yourself too much and don't want to go back home to Ingerlund at the end of your three weeks then you can sleep on my sofa' I joked with her, well technically that wasn't exactly true. I was more serious than I was joking but well, that was mental. Barely knew the girl didn't I but that fact was for some reason being overlooked by moi.

She well knew what she was doing with that whole looking at me seductively while talking to me with her eyes and licking and sucking on her finger. I'd have had to have been a level one novice to have not picked up on it. I was just about to enter into the absolute worst of patter sex analogy involving her finger and ice cream being a much more appetising prospect than a Ninety Nine (Which didn't even fucking make sense by the way) when my phone went off. Si again, around an hour after his last call. Like before, when I clocked the name on the phone I put it back in my pocket. I dodged an analogical bullet thanks to that beautiful bastard. Not that I was ever going to pick up his call though, mind.

She'd noticed the call when we were in the car and how I'd not answered it and now the same thing had happened. That's when

I had the epiphany that it might've come across as, to her, that I wasn't picking up the calls because they were from another girl or it had been something that I was trying to hide from her. 'I can't promise that he's not going to call again, that's twice now' I said shrugging my shoulders to her. Words I simply would not have spoken had it not been for the epiphany seconds before. 'Who's that, babe?' - 'Si' I answered in the kind of way that you do when you're talking about someone that you can't live with but can't live without in equal measures.

'Give him a call, Stevie, it's fine' She said, coming across like she'd thought that there was a chance I wasn't answering him because I was with her. 'Nah it's cool, Flo. I'll speak to him later on, I really can't be arsed with all the "where's my car" stuff right now. Too busy enjoying my day out, eh' I said trying to show her that everything was fine on that front. As we walked and chatted about everything and anything I took us into this quaint wee bar to cool down over a drink.

We managed to get the last table in the place which was jam packed with locals all staring up at the wee telly with the game now into the second half. The mood inside the bar wasn't exactly carnaval'esque and was quite a shift from what the Spanish fans had been like pre match around the town. One look up at the corner of the screen that was showing Espana 0 - Bulgaria 1 offered up an explanation for the apparent mood.

'Hristo Stoichkov just scored with a pen a few minutes ago, both teams down to ten men too' I heard the Birmingham accent come from behind me. I turned around to find this old guy. Mitchell Brothers folically challenged head and wearing a Birmingham City away top. Sat there at the next table with his wife who looked bored out of her tits but you could tell that with this being an old school relationship he'd pulled rank so he could have a couple of refreshments and watch the match.

'Just wait until she finds out that there's another two fucking matches to come today,' I laughed away to myself. I looked back around me to make sure that he wasn't speaking to someone else because of course it would've been completely mental to just offer such information to a complete stranger when they've innocently walked into a bar with a girl but aye, he actually had been speaking to me.

I didn't want to be rude to the gadgey or nothing so just offered him a 'that right mate, aye? Nice one' before turning back around to Flo. 'Bulgaria's flooded the midfield you see, the Spaniards aren't getting a second on the ball' he continued. 'If this cunt thinks that he's now got himself a fellow British fitba fan to sit and chat with during the game then he can get to fuck,' the opinion I sat there with.

I was sitting there in the process of working out what kind of a response I was going to give him when the Spanish equaliser went in. The waitress was just in the process of bringing Flo and I our drinks when some big lad wearing a Matadors beret in the colours of the Spanish flag celebrating Alfonso's goal barged into her. Sending the drinks flying. In amongst all of the celebrations it had barely registered with the locals who were a mass of limbs all over the place.

Birmingham man's wife definitely registering. Most of Flo's red wine going over her face and hair. My fresh orange over her striped vest which, in my opinion, had been a poor wardrobe choice in terms of matching her reddish sun tan but I digress. She was fucking livid, wasn't the girls fault though. To be fair to the matador hat lad. Once he'd clocked what he'd done he was over apologising to anyone that would listen. 'Makes a change from it going over you anyway eh?' I nudged Flo which had her giggling.

We stayed there for a couple of more drinks as the bar emptied at the final whistle. Leaving the place to ourselves. I felt bad for all the Spaniards trooping out at the end with their faces tripping them. I wanted them to win as it would've been party time outside and would definitely have been a bit of a spectacle. Obviously the Spaniards would've expected to beat a team like Bulgaria too and that would've heightened their whole sense of anti climax after only drawing the game. Not that the Bulgarians are mugs either though. Made a few people view them differently a couple of years before in America. Ze fucking Germans know all about them, anyway. That boy with the baldy napper sorted them out big time, likes.

The two of us were in the middle of looking through the tapas menu, and apparently ordering every second item that we came across. That was when Si called again. When it comes to your mates. Sometimes you know them more than you know yourself. A simple thing in others eyes but Si calling me for a third time in such a relative short space of time. I felt that I should've answered it on his latest attempt.

'I'm just going to take it this time because it looks like he's just going to keep trying me' I said holding up the phone to show her whose name was showing as the caller. 'Fine, babe. I'm just going to continue ordering pretty much all of the food that this place has inside its kitchen, ok' she smiled back as I pressed the green button to answer him.

'Audi, Si, happening mate?' I casually answered giving off no vibe whatsoever of someone who had just stolen their mates car and was now about to have the conversation that was inevitably going to follow such an action. Effect follows cause, always.

'Forgive me if I am short with you here but time is very much of the essence, Zeec. Where's my fucking car, mate?' In all the years I'd known Si I'd never heard him like that, he sounded rattled but then again I suppose you should be when you've been given a loan of a car for the summer from some Spanish drug syndicate and you find it has went missing.

'Aye it's cool, Si. I just borrowed it for a couple of hours to go out with Flo for a wee while.' I replied, trying to put him at ease. It instead, only heightened his state of mind further.

'Zeec, you should've fucking asked, I need the car, like four fucking hours ago need the car. You're my best mate, I love you and would go into battle for you, and have done many a time but whatever you're doing right now even if you're hanging out the back of that London girl. You need to drop it and get back here to yours. You've left me right in the fucking shit here, lad and the sooner I get the car the sooner I can start digging myself back out of it, where are you anyway?' He asked, expectedly.

I braced myself for what was now about to come.

'Emmmmm we're over in Ibiza Town, Si' I said, wincing and looking to the side at Flo who sat with a concerned look on her face over the obviousness that my phone call wasn't going too well.

'Fuck's sake, Zico that's fucking miles away. Fuck fuCK FUCKKKK' He screamed. Not exactly at me but I guess more over the circumstances he was faced with. - 'What's up, everything ok, likes?' I asked, a wee bit worried over what the fuck he'd potentially gotten himself into this time. 'It's too much to explain, just get yourself back here post fucking haste' - 'On my way, I'll still be around an hour though mind. Place is fucking hoachin because of the Spain game' I assured him while also kicking him in the balls with the news that I wasn't going to be there anytime soon regardless of whatever he was needing the car for.

'Oh aye, what was the score? Forgot it was on, likes' He asked. He's some boy is Simon. Comes on the phone sounding very much like his whole existence is at stake, for whatever reason, yet amongst it all he can still take the time out to enquire as to how a game of fitba turned out.

Listening in on what was going on, Flo was already onto the fact that it appeared like we might well be on our way unexpectedly. A clear sign of this being that she'd put down the tapas menu for one thing. 'K k we're leaving now, mate. Be with you when I'm with you. Help yourself to my Hash when you're waiting on me. I haven't exactly been shy with yours that was left in the car so fairs fair, eh' I laughed before hanging up.

Flo, as chilled a girl as you could come across was already standing up with her bag in her hand as the call ended. No drama, no pouting because their day out had been brought to an abrupt end.

'Thanks, Flo' I said, appreciative. 'I'll explain on the way.'

Chapter 14

Si

You know those times where you could quite literally kill someone that is close and dear to you? You always manage stop yourself at that invisible line though, don't you? I'm not entirely sure that Zico appreciated just how fucking lucky he was over the existence of that same line. I'd been unexpectedly summoned by Ivan. When he called, he had told me that he was just about to go out on the golf course for a round but needed me up there to meet him at the clubhouse by the time it was over. He seemed irked. Couple of hours he'd said which was at least a bit of notice compared to some of the other times I'd had those out of the blue business calls from him.

I'd taken the small walk from mines to Zico's to get the Golf. Figured I'd grab the car and then head to Cabballero's for a Jamon Bocadillo and one of those rocket fuel triple lattes that had already saved my skin on more than one occasion when finding myself one step away from death after the excesses of the night before.

Only, once I got onto the main strip. Outside of Zico's pad I could already see that the car wasn't in the spot that I'd left it in the night that Eva and Zico and I had travelled over to Playa den Bossa. On seeing this a wave of fear and panic swept over me in such a full on way that it turned my legs to jelly. The world started to spin around me.

The fact that the car didn't even belong to me was left in the shade next to who it was who actually *did* own it. I hadn't even got to Stevie's door and I was already trying to work out how the fuck I was going to break the news to the boss of a Spanish crime family that the car he had so generously loaned me had been stolen. As far as my mind was concerned *that* in itself was a justifiable reason for me going missing along with the fucking Volkswagen.

Once I got closer to the house I was able to see that parked in the space was now some battered Seat that looked like it hadn't been washed in years. The Golf really was gone.

I tore right up to Zico's front door. Didn't even bother with the formalities of knocking and waiting for a reply. Desperate times, desperate measures my friend. Stevie could've been shagging Julio fucking Iglesias live for state television for all I cared there and then. I shouted out for him as I entered but the place seemed dead. I went through to his bedroom just in case he was still kipping but he was nowhere to be seen. Still no idea why the cunt doesn't lock his door likes. Way too many times I've let myself into that place when he's not been around. Lee sorted him out with those Technics for his stay here. Them alone would fetch a few pesetas if someone was to "break in" and have a sniff around the place. Knowing Zico though he probably wouldn't give a fuck about the decks but if any cunt took any of his clothes he'd go so radge it would likely result in extradition back to Scotland.

The reality that the car was missing had now very much been taken on board. The more pressing issue now was who had taken it. Police? Tow company? Zico? Some, at that moment in time, unidentified thief. I made right from Zico's bedroom back through to the kitchen to where I'd last seen the keys. Miraculously despite all that we got up to that night and all the way through to the next afternoon at Space. I was still somehow able to clearly remember that just before the taxi had come to pick us up I'd had a line on the kitchen bunker. Following that I had fixed out my money and drugs for the night and stood there with the car keys in my hand. I'd felt that there was no point taking them as I'd not be needing them anyway so figured they'd be safer there in Zico's kitchen.

YES, I cried out when I got through there and found the keys were missing. My assumption being that by adding two plus two it would lead me to the answer of Zico having taken a loan of the car. It hadn't been like him as he would've generally done anything to avoid driving abroad, he hated it. Said that driving on the wrong side of the road was too confusing. Straight away I tried calling the cunt but couldn't get an answer.

The fact that the keys were no longer there in the kitchen at least lowered my stress levels. It was the only real logical explanation but until I physically heard Zico tell me that he had the car then of course, I wouldn't be fully in the best of places. As long as he wasn't too far and he called me back soon enough then things would still be cool for me getting out to the golf course to meet Ivan.

I sat down for a while on his sofa. The initial thought once I'd plumped myself down was to make myself a joint while I waited on the call back. That very same thought deconstructed in seconds once I remembered that the Hash I had (and as far as I was concerned was going to be reunited with once I got the car back) was inside the missing automobile. Luckily for me though Zico, when making a spliff, at times resembled a hippopotamus wearing boxing gloves and through that there was around the equivalent of an eighth lying scattered around his coffee table mixed in with what looked like the sum parts of ten Regal King Size cigarettes.

I'd stubbed the fucking thing out on the other end without Zico still having not called back. I tried calling again with the same end result as the first time attempt. Where was the cunt anyway? He very rarely ventured out during the day time. He'd been almost hermit like since we'd got there and the most we'd seen of each other had been in the evenings. The boy thought he'd hit the jackpot when he moved in and found that big pile of English speaking video tapes. I've seen him watch a whole eight part series in one afternoon and evening following his shift at Space. Who does that? Like, watch a whole fucking series, one episode after the other?

I wouldn't have the attention span for that nonsense. Takes me to fucking watch a film all the way through. He fucking makes me laugh though with all of this "I was working the night before so need to chill all day long" stuff. He wasn't exactly doing anything much different from me on a night out apart from playing a few records. We're matching each other for drugs every fucking step. He cracks me up, makes himself out as the professional and how he has to stay straight for when he's playing. Aye, he makes sure he shouts that loud and clear for any cunt that's interested in listening. Doesn't shout too much about what he gets up to after he's finished playing his records though.

Still, it was strange that he wasn't either in bed still sleeping or lazing around on his couch watching The Darling buds of May or whatever the fuck it was he had on the last time I saw him. It wouldn't have surprised me if he was off doing something with that cockney girl from Space a couple of days before. The two of them seemed to be getting on pretty good over the course of the night. Hushed conversations between the two of them while the group all sat there, that kind of thing. We were all a bit well on with the Mitsubishis by that point but he'd told me that the two of them had started speaking because he'd tipped his beer over her but I took it that he was having a laugh with me.

Regardless of if he intended to answer or continue to blank me. Zico was literally my only fucking hope Wan Kenobi so I would keep calling until he was either worn down by it all or switching his phone off all together. I could've done without Camacho's call. It came out of the blue as I'd had no contact with him since getting back from my unplanned meeting with the O'Hallorans that night. I'd been absolutely bricking it walking into the restaurant. Let's face it, informing the boss of a crime family that his kids lives were being threatened was something that was never going to be a piece of piss soaked cake whoever the deliveryman was. In reality, It wasn't that bad.

I suppose in times like that, you can't fuck about. You just need to be straight and to the point with people like that. Don't fanny around. My face gave the game away before I'd even been able to open my mouth. 'Problem, Simon?' he said as he clocked me walking towards his table having first exchanged a few words with Sergio and Guillermo who were blocking the way into Ivan's special dining area of El Tonto Cangura. 'The address I was given for the drop off? It was an O'Halloran property. They had guns, but didn't take the gear, that's still in the car. They only let me go so that I could bring this to you.'

I handed him the flyer for the kindergarten. I expected some animation from him but instead he cooly sat there looking at one side of the flyer before turning it over and staring at the message that had been scribbled in felt pen. 'Thank you, Simon. I imagine that it must've been concerning in there with those English pigs, especially with what they have already done to some of our men so far. I apologise that you had to be subjected to whatever you were, I assume they did not just hand you the note at the door and then send you on your way?' He said sitting there without any break in his composure. He reached into his wallet and started to count out a stack of pesetas for me.

'A little extra for you for tonight, I appreciate that you came straight to find me. I need to make some calls and put some plans into place so if you will excuse me. I will be in touch.' It was his composure that stuck out for me. I expected fireworks and hysterics. Instead he was the epitome of cool.

With that I was sent on my way again. It all though, left me in a bit of a hole. After what had happened with the Scousers, that was me. In my own mind, done and dusted with that particular game. I'd only agreed to the work because it was easy money but having fucking shotguns shoved in your face? That wasn't something that had been explained to me during my induction period. Telling Ivan there and then though was never going to be an option.

It still left me in a bit of limbo though all the same. I suppose it wasn't a job with an employee number, paid holiday and company provided healthcare and benefits so therefore I wouldn't have imagined that there was any kind of notice to work before leaving.

It wasn't my first game of Space Invaders though. Regardless of the fact whether I'd worked in the drug game before or not. You only needed to watch a couple of films to see how charismatic, likeable but ultimately just how unpredictable cartel gaffers could be. Smile at you one minute and give the order for your murder the next. Camacho and I had sparked from minute one and I'd only ever felt nothing less than comfortable around him despite the clear and obviously different worlds that we were from but how much did I really know the guy? How would he take what might've been viewed as rejection from me? Fuck, I'd once watched a documentary on some Colombian boss who threw people to his alligators to warn against disloyalty to him and his organisation. I'm not sure if Ivan even had any alligators but I wasn't really in too much of a hurry to find out either.

On top of it all I'd had a well decent day planned my side. Three Euro Ninety Six matches in a row and I'd already arranged to meet up with a mate, Shaky, who was over for a couple of weeks holiday and had reached out to me a few days before he'd been due to fly out to arrange to meet up. Looked a right barry day on the sniff and sauce though. Spain against Bulgaria to start the day followed by the Germans and the Czechs and the evening match, Denmark v Portugal. That one phone call from Ivan threw a massive spanner into the works though.

I'd definitely miss the Spain game but depending on what he needed me for. There was still a chance that I'd make it back to join Shaky and the rest of his mates for the remaining matches. Some boy, Shaky, like. We were good mates when we were younger but once I'd chosen to run with the Utility at the weekends we didn't see as much of each other as that whole casuals thing wasn't his cup of Earl Grey. We'd always kept in touch though. We nicknamed him Shaky back in primary school due to one day when him, myself and Pete Sturrock were in his bedroom after fitba practice. He'd went downstairs to get his tea and left the two of us up in his room. Of course, as kids do (fuck, adults as well I suppose) we'd had a wee nose around his bedroom. Pete found this wee black book with the word "Autographs" embedded in silver writing into the front cover in one of his drawers.

Our excitement over what we found inside the book was anti climatic to say the least when all we found was one solitary autograph on the front inside page belonging to Shakin fucking Stevens! It's scenarios like that where nicknames are handed down to people for life. Whether they like it or not. Give it another twenty years or so and he's going to have a hard time explaining his nickname to people (especially the younger generation) when no cunt can even remember who the fuck the Welsh singer even is anymore.

Talk of what matches I'd manage to see or not over the day was what could only be described as moot until I was given the clarification of just exactly where the car currently was. I tried Zico again but once more, no answer on his end. It was starting to do my fucking head in. If there had been one time in my life that I truly needed my reprobate of a mate answer my call it was right there and then. It was Stevie who was pretty much standing in between me having to tell Ivan Camacho that his car had been stolen. I didn't even want to entertain the possibility that it *wasn't* in his possession and as far as any hopes that I had, they were completely (and without question, unfortunately) placed as all in with Zico. What a man to have responsible for you and your hopes when they're hanging by the slimmest of threads.

I started to get another joint together with all of Zico's surplus that he had lying around but time was now starting to work against me. Ivan would've been well onto the back nine of his round by then while I was nowhere further forward than I was when I'd taken his call at the start of the afternoon. I started to think of alternatives for me getting myself to the course but given the circumstances the only moves open to me would have been to either go with the car or just not go at all.

Impatience getting the better of me I tried again soon after and stone the fucking seagulls he actually answered. How royally pissed off I was with him upon learning that he actually had commandeered the Golf was, momentarily at least, replaced with a wave of relief that I wasn't going to have to report a stolen car to the Camacho family.

The relief dipped levels below though when he informed me that while he had the car he was fucking miles away on the other side of the island in Ibiza Town with the girl from London. The struggle not to go completely radio rental at him over the phone was real but what good would it have really done there and then? Bollocking my best mate while possibly making me feel a lot better wasn't going to ensure that the car was back in San Antonio any quicker.

I settled on leaving him without any shadow of a doubt, informing the boy that regardless of what he was in the middle of it had to be dropped and that he had to be back to the West Coast faster than the speed of fucking light and sound put together. Without going into any of the "whys" over the phone he appeared to pick up on the urgency that I couldn't help but reek of and within seconds was telling me that the two of them were already on their way back.

With no choice other than to sit tight I got comfy and took my chances with the mystery video that was already sitting in the player. An old episode of The Bill. I was going to be late for my meet with my drug lord boss but yet even so. I still felt that I was winning.

Chapter 15

Peter

Life's just a series of bridges that you have to cross isn't it? In between them you're just doing your thing, living the dream if you can. That next bridge is always looming though. You're always a better man for crossing it and in some cases a different person with vital lessons learned along the way. Putting in that eventual call to Bogota though? That was a bridge I was desperate to do anything to avoid going anywhere fucking near.

I could only imagine how I was being looked upon by Eddy and German Ramirez all those miles away back in Colombia. All those years of working together, the money that we all made out of it. Obscene amounts of capital. All the trust, and I mean that both ways, that we'd built up. Gone in a relative sixty seconds.

When Eva and I had fled South America I hadn't ever envisaged that I'd be wanting to put a phone call into Bogota to the cartel. That's about the size of it though. I didn't want to call the brothers, my hand had been forced.

From the "safety" of Europe I'd got to work in trying to fix whatever mess I was in. Of which, the full extent of things I'd still yet to find out. All the while trying to keep Eva at bay and off the scent of the danger she was potentially in. I was on the phone half of the time trying to track down the type of people who didn't want to be found. Luckily the boy and his mate Simon were good enough to look after the wife while I was making those type of phone calls that you really didn't want your wife to be around to hear.

I was grateful for their help in that respect as I was in a bit of an awkward position. Pragmatically I knew that there was a chance, how high I didn't know but a real chance all the same of our actual existence being on a shaky peg. That, I'd had no alternative other than to accept but this was also a topic that I didn't want my better half to know too extensively about. She's not stupid though.

Yes, of course she's the epitome of a trophy wife, on the surface. She's intelligent though and as always, you can never discount the power of intuition in a woman. That side to them is quite scary when you think about it and Eva's was gold standard. I knew that sooner or later she was going to want to talk about it. Women always do. My plan was to have everything rectified before we got round to that particular chinwag.

I wasn't exactly too happy with the boys though when it came to taking Eva out to Playa den Bossa that night. I'd been away on business so to speak and (without Eva's knowledge) wasn't even on the island the day that they all went out. I'd left around four in the morning that day with Eva fast asleep and by lunch time I was in Cadiz. By the time I arrived back to San Antonio Bay it was approaching six the next morning. With me having been posted missing for over twenty four hours it was fair to say that I'd accepted that my wife was going to have a few choice words to say on the matter. After the long trip and the sickening news that I'd been given while there in Cadiz, the last thing, the very last, I needed was grief from Eva.

It was with a completely random mix of emotions when I got back to the hotel room. Hoping that I would be able to slip into bed without waking her. Only to get inside and find that she wasn't actually there herself. I had the relief that I might just have gotten away with my long term absence but at the same time the question of why she wasn't in bed was obviously needing addressed. Where would my wife be at that time of the morning? A more pressing question I'd had though was more in connection of *who* she was with at that time of day. I tried calling her only to then hear the ringing of her phone from through in the bathroom. Daft cow hadn't even taken it out with her. She's always like that with that phone. Probably lost a dozen of the things and then when she does have one she would never have it charged.

I was still lying sleeping in the room when she eventually walked back in around one o clock in the afternoon. Insanely out of her plastic surgery enhanced tits she was. Dancing to a song that wasn't playing. Jaw swinging like Tarzan through the jungle. Really happy to see me in that way that can only ever be achieved through the properties of Ecstasy. Excitedly telling me what an amazing day and night that she'd had in amongst repeatedly telling me that she loved me. Also, as far as Stevie and Si went in her opinion? Salt of the earth the pair of them.

My own opinion on them was an alternative one to Eva's. If I'd been around Stevie or Si right about then there wouldn't have been any telling what I'd have said or done to them. I couldn't have it all my own way though. I recognised this as I watched her doing a kind of half dance and half undress move as she got herself down to just her thong before slipping under the sheets with me. I was happy enough to dump my wife on Stevie and his friend and was doing so under no illusions what they were getting up to while in Ibiza. It was pretty much the focal point of why they were even on the island after all. Even though my anger was real I couldn't really have been too hard on the pair of them. You don't leave a loved one alone with monkeys for the day and then expect them not to throw shit at you the next time you see them, I conceded to myself.

You couldn't make it up though could you? I'd had Eva living in the land of Cocaine with a husband who had access to limitless supplies of the stuff in addition to him being partial to a dabble every other day. Despite all of this I'd managed to keep her from getting into the stuff herself. Fuck, it could've been an easy habit for her to slip into being shacked up in that hacienda all day and night. I purposely kept her away from the type of parties where the stuff would be available on tap. I never used it when I was around her at the house. Two minutes in the company of my son though and she turns into Keith Richards.

My friends in Bogota? I'd had some alarming news on my trip to Cadiz. I'd been left with no choice but to to endure the less than welcome traveling there because the absolute one person that I'd needed to speak to (after Sanchis in Barcelona) had been Miguel Gallego.

Gallego, who I had struggled to track down, was one of my longest running connections in the business. I'd been sent down a whole series of rabbit holes through the series of calls I'd put in to Madrid to try and locate him after it had become clear that he wasn't for taking my calls. The attempts to ring him weren't even reaching the ringing stage. Only the sole option to leave a message, which I did only to be told (once I'd recorded it) that the mailbox was full and my message could not be saved. Eventually I had a touch of luck when someone I hadn't even thought of to call on account of him not being local, called me.

'Hi, Peter! How are things my friend? Said the unmistakable Dutch Accent. - 'Nicky van Bosman! How's tricks yourself? I'm good, good,' I lied. - 'Oh life is just beautiful, Peter. I am in Bora Bora at present, just a small holiday. We need to reward ourselves treats from time to time don't you think?' - 'Oh of course, Nicky. What really would be the point of it all otherwise if we cannot treat ourselves every now and again? So what do I have the pleasure of a call from my man in Amsterdam may I enquire?' I said trying to cut to the chase. I had a lot more serious issues to be addressing other than a small talk filled catch up with someone that there had been absolutely no requirement towards catching up with in the first place.

'So I was hearing that you were looking for Gallego, Peter' The Dutchman asked. Yes, that got my attention. 'Yes, friend. I've been desperate to get in touch with him. Can't reach him by phone, don't know where he is and you know Miguel? He could literally be in Madrid and not just wanting to answer his phone, in Colombia taking care of some business or at Disneyland in Florida with his wife and kid.' I could feel the hope building inside of me as I spoke to him.

'Well don't worry about things, he's in Cadiz. I don't know where about but that was what I heard. I am not sure if that's any help Peter as it's still all a little vague but I thought I'd give you a call to see if it could point you in the right direction. Look, I know that it's still no way close to being evens for how you saved my skin from the brothers over that missing suitcase and I *will* fully pay that debt to you but just treat this as a friendly gesture all the same.

Well yes, Cadiz was a major step in the right direction. Actually by simply hearing that name it all clicked into place in my mind. I knew EXACTLY where Miguel was going to be. I just needed to get myself there.

After hours of traveling by boat and car I arrived at what Miguel regarded as his sanctuary from the craziness of running one of the largest narcotics rings in Europe. Gallego's syndicate overseeing the delivery of the shipments and then the redistribution back out of

Spain. The thing is, as a head honcho of a crime organisation like that. This secluded mansion of his had been, understandably, kept to a minimum in terms of who actually knew about it. It really is the only way when it comes to that side of the business. Because of the long running friendship we'd had over many years I was one of the privileged few who not only knew about it but had actually been there on occasion for parties. Then again, when you're the godfather to Miguels kid. That kind of already shows that you have already achieved the status of being placed inside the inner circle of Miguel Gallego.

I got to the front gate at the bottom of the long drive and pressed the buzzer. Already having decided that whether it was answered or not I was still getting in and I didn't care one way or another if that meant casually walking through the large iron gates or desperately climbing right over them.

If there was one man in Europe who knew what was going on back in Bogota, it was Miguel Juan Gallego. Knowing him as long as I did and also the Ramirez brothers for just as long. I had to unfortunately combine the two. Knowing that the Ramirez brothers knew how good terms I was on with Gallego I'd have stuck all of the millions that Sal was currently in the process of moving for me on the fact that Eddy, German or both would've already been in touch with Miguel to ask if he had seen or heard from me.

They're smart guys. You don't build a billion dollar company and not have some kind of smarts, especially of the street variety. The intel that Miguel potentially had was something that I needed to hear. So much so I'd been prepared to board a boat to go see him. Now that I was there outside his house I wasn't going anywhere.

Eventually after a wait. Once it had been answered it wasn't by Miguel, or either Catarina his wife who, as far as standard of trophy wife goes, made my Eva look like third rate. No disrespect to my wife either when I say that, even if it is a touch insensitive. Instead, it was a security guard who answered. At first he wasn't for entertaining visitors. Telling me that the owners of the property were not home, that I was on private property and for me to leave the property.

I'd had enough years experience in dealing with hired goons with automatic rifles. From the jungles of Colombia to the streets of Juarez. Behind the rifles and the jobsworth attitudes though is generally one brainless drone of an "employee." We are not talking cancer curers here you understand.

'Look, señor, when Don Miguel finds out that the godfather of his son, Luque was outside asking to speak to him and that you couldn't have even been bothered to let your boss know about it never mind let him in? Well, I'm not sure just how Don Miguel is going to react to it. Especially when it wasn't just some friendly visit and that it was on urgent business. If you've got any kind of sense inside you, you'd go and tell Don Miguel.' I said confidently.

There was a brief pause while the cogs inside his head slowly began to turn. You could almost hear them.

'Wait one moment' he said, breaking the silence.

A minute or two later the scaling iron mechanical gates sprang into life. Parting and allowing me to make my way in. For his age, lifestyle and infatuation type addiction to Wimpey burgers, Miguel looked really well. He had hair slicked back and a goatee that weirdly didn't leave him looking like a complete arsehole. When he set eyes on me I was instantly given this sudden feeling that the way he was looking at me was what it was like when people found themselves face to face with a ghost.

He had felt no need to even enter into any shape or form in terms of pleasantries when we came face to face.

'You shouldn't be here, Peter. I mean this with no disrespect, you know how close we are to each other, but you should not be anywhere near me or my familia.' He spouted before we'd even reached the handshake stage. 'They're coming for you and I'm sure you can understand when I say that I do not want the trail that you are leaving behind you leading to me.'

Despite the many years that the two of us had been friends for I had never seen him so spooked over something and when it came to the

Cadiz operation. Miguel generally always had something or other to be spooked over. Not that he ever let himself be affected by it all.

"They? Who are they, specifically. Obviously you are referring to some Colombian associates?' I asked, looking for clarity. By this time we were inside Miguel's kitchen. 'You best take a seat, Peter' he said gravely as he reached into the fridge for a couple of bottles of beer.

'I had German on the phone two days ago before I left Madrid to come here. He was fishing to see if you'd been in touch. Knowing our history I was an obvious choice of person to call, I guess.' He said as he sat down on one of the other spare high chairs at the breakfast table I was already sitting at. 'Yes, and that is exactly why you, Miguel are the one person that I've been searching for. I'm not in a good spot right now' - he pulled a no shit Sherlock face at that admission from me - 'and I'm trying to see if there's any way out of it.'

'Can I be blunt, Peter?' He replied in what sounded to me the blueprint for the term "ominous." I nodded my head, words not exactly required. 'Gilberto Martinez and Jorge Lozano are already in Europe, they arrived in Barcelona days ago.'

He fell silent, leaving what he'd said hanging in the air like the most foul of smells. The news he'd broken left me without words. I had no response. La Cobra and El Jugador being sent from Bogotá to look for me was quite literally the worst news imaginable and in itself displayed just how far things had escalated since Eva and I had left Colombia. This was a complete game changer.

In Gilberto and Jorge you had two sicarios who would, without question, chase me to the ends of the earth if the job was required. My head was sent into a tailspin over it all. How did the Ramirez brothers even know that I'd flown to Barcelona? What had the two hitmen found out since? *Who* had they spoken to? Did they even live to tell the tale after having been paid a visit by the two South Americans? Thoughts inevitably turned to Sal.

There wasn't a doubt that if Gilberto and Jorge had visited one person and one person only in Catalunya then it would have been my attorney. I was concerned. While I'd had no qualms about Sal when it came to doing the dirty on me in relation to law enforcement. I had never envisaged that he would have ever been put in a position where La Cobra and El Jugador would have been at his door in connection with me. THAT changed the whole landscape of things. I'm almost sure that I would grass MYSELF up if put in the same room as the two of those nasty bastards and had them on my case.

While I'd been calm over Sanchis when it came to knowing his place with regards to giving out intel in relation to me. I wasn't so sure if that could have ever been extended to when face to face with two of the scariest, psychotic and cold blooded killers to come out of Colombia.

I feared the worst.

'Fuck, amigo. That changes things.' I eventually managed to find some words. If I'd not already been sitting I'd have needed a seat. I felt lightheaded and nauseous. It's hard to explain but for someone who wasn't even remotely close to claustrophobic. When Miguel had given me the news it felt like the walls inside the kitchen had began closing in on me. Gilberto and Jorge were, what I could only have described as, rockstar hitmen. Their names (and reputations) went before them and were known throughout the whole of Colombia. Almost boogie men mythology. I'd imagined mothers and fathers telling their kids that if they didn't behave La Cobra and El Jugador would get them.

In all of my years working with the cartel I had never seen them leave Colombia for a job, save for the occasional trip to Mexico on loan from the Brothers to the Sinaloa Cartel for select, specialist jobs. Never, ever thousands of miles from Bogotá. As far as the Ramirez Brothers sending out a message. I'd received it loud and clear.

'I have never heard German so angry and agitated in all the years I've known him, Peter. What the fuck did you do? He told me that it was a matter of great importance that you be found and that there was the potential for someone to make themselves a very rich man while buying some goodwill with the Ramirez family if they were to provide your location.' Miguel continued to fill me in on some of the blanks although I fully admit that there was an element of white noise due to the dark thoughts that I was having my head filled with. Yeah he was talking but at times I couldn't hear any words as my mind was miles away.

'What the fuck did I do? Well that's the best part, Miguel. I genuinely don't know.' I replied.

I went on to fill him in on everything that had taken place since the moment I had walked into Mik's pad and found him there mutilated. How I had panicked and was on a flight out of Bogota within hours, my position with the cartel brought to an abrupt end.

'No way could I stick around to see if they had the same tactics in store for me like they had with Mikael' I almost pleaded to Miguel as if he was tasked with putting the bullets into my head personally. 'Quite understandable, my friend only now you look guilty *because* you ran.' My Madrista friend was not in any mood for dressing things up but that was exactly what I needed. Realism. Not to be told what I wanted to know in that everything was going to be alright. That would've been clearly a pile of shit. Things were a far fucking way from "alright."

As you'd expect from a good friend, Miguel told me that the very first thing he'd tried to do after speaking to Bogota was call immediately to issue the warning but had been unable to reach me. Having now moved onto a burner phone I was operating on the basis of that if I wanted to be in touch with someone then it was going to be done on my terms only.

Once I'd gotten all of the information out of Miguel that I needed I was on my way again. I apologised for how short a visit it had been but obviously there was stuff going on to which he told me that for a man in my position I really had no apologies to be making to him.

As I left, Gallego walking me down the drive, the two of us had what could only have been described as "a moment." No words were spoken on the subject but it was all in the eyes. It was a goodbye where both people knew that it might be the last time they would ever be in each others company. I left Cadiz for Ibiza broken and trying to come to terms with the fact that YES this was happening and YES it wasn't going to go away just because I'd flown thousands of miles from Colombia.

In some cases the world simply isn't big enough to hide. Despite having a few cards up my sleeve, the thought of the Ramirez brothers' finest hitmen on my trail had put the fear of god into me. These two men were not the type of people that would come pay you a visit and sit and talk things over with cups of tea and plates of Custard Creams.

On the boat back I found myself thinking about just what a stupid move it had been to come to Ibiza. Potentially I was now putting my own son at risk by being in the same vicinity as him. One thing the cartel absolutely fucking loved was when there were kids on the scene that they could then exploit to help manipulate business associates. I'd not exactly been the model father when it had come to Stevie. I hadn't even spoken to him in years never mind seen him until that night we were reunited in Blackburn but even then, admittedly, I was only there through business. Meeting my son there had been nothing other than coincidental. My long lost Steven was the very last person that I'd ever have expected to bump into. I'd tried to make things up to him since that night, keep in more regular contact, take an interest in what was going on in his world, that kind of thing.

As much as I tried, wanted to try. Life in Bogota didn't exactly lend itself well to keeping up relationships, of any kind. Since the last time I'd spoken with him I'd gotten married, hadn't even told the kid about it never mind invite him over to Colombia for the wedding. Yet I thought nothing of just gatecrashing his life when he least expected it along with a wife pretty much his own age that he didn't know existed and two demented killers following closely behind.

It was much like when someone is given x amount of months or days to live and they go through all the stages of grief. Bargaining being one of them. That was me, I was sat there on the boat back vowing to myself that if I could get myself out of this I was going to be a better dad, a better husband to Eva. Ah that old chestnut when someone already knows the horse has already bolted. Pathetic, really.

With everything that was at stake. I'd been given no choice other than to call German and Eddy. The were a pair of wily bastards. You don't stay on top in the Cocaine business in Colombia without being so. For all I'd known, German had engineered things by calling Miguel. Already knowing that out of loyalty to me I'd have been told about the phone call. Fuck, with that line of thinking maybe the two sicarios weren't even *in* Europe and their names had been merely dropped into the conversation in the knowledge that it would have been enough to bring me out of hiding.

Well it worked, didn't it? Even so, I was a bag of nerves when I picked up the phone to make the call.

'Well if it isn't the little cockaroach himself' Eddy said down the phone to me after hearing my voice. As far as starts went, it wasn't the best. The choice of insult he'd used was measured and meant specifically to let me know where I stood in his eyes. A dirty disease ridden bug that needed stepped on.

'Where are you, Peter, oh where oh where can that soon to be dead Scot be? Where in the world, huh? Iceland? South Africa perhaps? Maybe even back in Britain with your shit weather and tasteless food' He had entered into drama mode and keen to stamp his authority all over the call.

'Awwww come on now, Eddy, I think you know a bit more about where I am than you're letting on. Someone with your resources, you could find a man if he was hiding on Mars.' I responded. I don't know where I found the balls from but I found them all the same. 'Ohhhhhhhkkkkkkkkkk you got me' he laughed before continuing. 'Now what say you tell me *exactly* where you are and I have some friends come and meet up with you. Give back the computer disc and then we can all put this behind us, si?'

'Well when you describe it as amicable as that how could I possibly resist such an offer' I laughed back at him. 'There's just the small detail about that if I come face to face with your friends they'll be the last thing that I'll ever see which is stopping me from fully getting on board with this proposal.' I said with mock scepticism.

'Oh, Pedrito. After all we've been through. Would you really think that I would have you killed? And I thought that we were friends' He replied arrogantly. His sarcasm now beginning to grate on me.

'Well, I thought you and Mikael were friends as well if we're on that same subject' I replied bringing a bit of realism back to the conversation. - 'Yes, that was, unfortunate.' He said, sounding almost like Mik's murder had happened so long ago that I'd just asked Eddy to recall it even happening.

'Yet, you sound surprised, Peter? Surely you realise that when I found out what the two of you had been up to there was going to be some kind of a response from German and I, no?'

'Up to?' I replied with nothing other than bewilderment and surprise for him. 'I don't follow you, Eddy.'

'Oh come now, Pedrito, the time for lying is now over. We are not interested in fabrications from ratas. All I want now is vengeance and, of course, the disc back.' He spat, having apparently already decided for himself that I knew what he was referring to and that here he had a case of just another sorry fool in the business trying desperately to save their skin.

'Eddy, you're talking in riddles, brother. Rats? Discs? Help me out here' I pleaded, surmising that if he was to give me some additional information I might well have been able to contribute to what was being passed off as a conversation.

'Must we play this game?' He sighed back at me. 'Are we really going to pretend that you have no idea that your partner, the man that has stood side by side with you in all the years we have known each other had been talking business with Don Munoz.' You could sense the anger percolating inside of the man now that he found himself on the subject.

For the very first time since I'd discovered Mikael sat there carved up in his living room. Something made sense and when I say that. It was confusingly a case of something making sense while completely *not* making anything close to sense. I'd replayed it over and over in my mind just why they could have done something like that to Mik. That was the one thing that was causing me such a headache. There was no reason for it to have happened. Well, that's what I'd thought anyway. Things were perfect. We were making more money than most professional footballers. In Bogotá we were treated like film stars and politicians. The many perks aside. To upset business partners such as the Ramirez brothers would have been nothing other than professional, as well as personal, suicide.

The phone call between the two of us required the fastest of thinking on ones feet but from what Eddy had just accused Mikael (and myself) of, there was simply too much for me to digest.

'Eddy, I, I .....' I couldn't even finish what I'd tried to say. That was mainly down to me not even knowing what I was even trying *to* say. I had to say something though, anything. Remaining silent would have only added weight to the belief that Eddy apparently held that whatever Mik had been engaging in prior to his killing. It was a joint effort along with his business partner.

I didn't know what to think or feel. I wanted to show anger towards Eddy for having my friend killed. Wanted to disagree with him over the fact that Mikael wouldn't have ever done what I was now being told of. In those initial thoughts I felt disgust at a supposed close friend like Mikael for leaving me in such a position. I didn't know what to believe. Despite being behind the order of thousands of murders over the years as cartel boss, Eddy, in my opinion, was a gentleman. He respected the case of right and wrong. When a button needed pushed however he never shirked from pressing it. If an example required set or a lesson dished out he acted imperviously. His reputation demanded it but also his reputation was one of fairness.

He had always said that if you wanted to know how to dine from the top table when it came to running a narcotics empire then you should always look at what Pablo Escobar did and do the exact opposite. Yes he made a lot of money but running his cartel in such an unpredictably violent and carefree way was what was ultimately his undoing. You cannot rule entirely through fear and terror and Eddy (and German) recognised that. What is it they say about how you catch flies?

I felt a little dirty as well as disloyal to find myself cursing Mikael for what he had done (and on appearance, having now left me to mop up) while he was no longer alive to offer any form of defence to counter things. My heart told me that Eddy was mistaken but deep down my head as well as my gut was telling me that it was the truth.

'Surely you're not suggesting that I had anything' I continued but Eddy, who I guess had held numerous conversations like this in his life had already guessed what I was going to say cut me off.

'You know, Peter? Less than a week ago I would have laughed had someone told me that you were plotting behind my back with a business rival.' - 'EXACTLY' I interjected with relief over the tone he'd began with. This, however, seemed only to provoke some anger from him for the first time.

'QUIET' He asserted himself. Letting me know who exactly was in control of the conversation. 'Then again, I'd have laughed if someone had suggested that Mikael would be a rat and go against German and myself. Only, he was. I received a call last week from a source in Medellin that Don Munoz's La Comuna were going to make a move on our Sinaloa arrangement and, specifically, from there the European routes. Some of the information that Don Munoz came by? Well, that is what led German and I to, ohhhhhh who is it that are the ones that make the European shipments run smoothly for us? Care to remind me, Pedrito.'

I remained silent, I wasn't sure if he was finished or not. Regardless, anything that was about to come out of my mouth was sure to only fit his vision of someone trying to talk their way out of a precarious position. I was realistic over the fact that me genuinely pleading my innocence to him was not going to come anywhere even close to being able to cut any ice with him.

'I know how this works, Eddy. My partner has left me in all kinds of shit that is now on me but I just want you to know that if you look hard enough you're going to find that I have had nothing to do with any of this. I don't know if you have contacts within La Comuna that will confirm it. I'm just asking you to please explore all options before you do something that there's no coming back from. I know you,

Eddy. I know that if in say, a years time you find out that I wasn't part of it but only after you've already had me killed. I know that you won't just shrug it off.' I'd hoped that with me delivering this whilst staying as far the fuck away possible to begging or pleading that it would carry a bit of credence. That I'd been able to confidently offer solutions to him while displaying, what I'd felt, authenticity and sincerity.

'Well here is where we all find ourselves. When I received word about the mole who had been loose with their tongue over our Europe routes the finger was pointed firmly at you and Mikael, so I had Kiki tap yours and Mikael's phones.'

This would've explained that Wednesday, the week before leaving Colombia, when I'd arrived home in the evening and Eva had told me about Kiki, the head of security for the brothers and how he had stopped by. He'd told her that he was there to make a security upgrade to our phone line which would provide it with some form of extra encryption.

'After a few days of listening in. Kiki intercepted two phone calls from a Medellin network code to Mikael's number. That, was the confirmation that we were looking for.' Eddy continued. 'And as you will know, no phone calls to or from Medellin on my phone line' I couldn't help interject. I tried for subtlety but got nowhere near.

'I'll get to you in a minute. Don't think you are out of the woods, Pedrito' he barked the darkest of warnings at me. For a brief moment I'd almost lulled myself into a false sense of security that with him mentioning our calls being monitored I was hoping that I'd be completely exonerated on that front. I was wrong by the looks.

'Kiki traced the number back and it was located right in the heart of La Comuna tengo trece. Gilberto and Jorge visited Mikael the next morning. You know the rest.'

I didn't want to ask but was dying to scream out over where all of this involved me. Despite already having had the misfortune to be the first person to walk in on Mikael and subsequently have that image etched into my memory for, in all probability, the rest of my life. Despite how horrific it all looked, I now had the image of La Cobra and El Jugador carrying out the attack and it seemed to add new levels to the terror I'd already felt almost anytime I'd closed my eyes since the day Eva and I had fled.

'And that now brings us to you, Pedrito' he said. About ready to put me out my misery while no doubt sending me into a whole new fresh kind of pain and suffering. 'I was undecided with you, so was German. Kiki had not picked up any suspicious activity through your phones, incidentally that wife of yours and those calls back to England must be bleeding you dry, but I digress. Peter, you know you are part of this. Maybe you thought you were more clever than Mikael by keeping a distance from Medellin through telephone contact but we both know that you were in this with him. We know you have the computer disc.' Eddy was finally getting to the point with things, even if I didn't strictly follow what he was getting at.

'Computer disc?' I asked. - 'Don't test my patience' he spat back at me. I hadn't exactly been fooled by Eddy's passive aggressive start to the phone call and now it appeared that he'd decided to completely do away with his whole act.

'Mikael was in possession of a disc that, we discovered days later, had been stolen from Ariel Maturama's office. And who had held a meeting in Sandro's office around about that very same time,' Eddy said rhetorically.

Ariel Maturama was the cartel's chief accountant and it wasn't uncommon for Mikael to visit him in connection with the flow of money from Europe to South America that Mik and I were helping generate. That was more Mikael's expertise and generally I let him crack on with it.

'Now at the time, we hadn't discovered the disc missing so there was nothing unusual but the same day that we finally made the Medellin connection to Mikael, Kiki listened in on a call between you and Mikael where he told you that he had accidentally dropped a disc in your car and how it was urgent he got it back and could you make sure that you gave him it back the next day when you were meeting up.'

Now that I *did* remember. The disc was down the side of the passengers seat beside the door just as Mik had said it would be. I never got the chance to give it to him though. I'd popped it in my briefcase ahead of driving to meet him but by the time I'd got there, as I'd then since learned. Jorge and Gilberto had beaten me to it.

'Before he was killed and was, naturally, pleading for his life, he told Jorge and Gilberto that you had the disc, Peter. Kiki's recording only confirmed that once we'd pieced things together. Can you see how this does not look too good for you, Pedrito? You running from us? You see how guilty that makes you look? Innocent people do not run, amigo. That is not the biggest concern right now to me though. The disc is.'

Knowing what I did about the inner workings of the Bogotá Cartel and the brothers who ran the operation. I'd already arrived at the conclusion that things had went too far and that it was a situation that I wasn't going to be pulling myself back from. Well, specifically, I wasn't going to be recovering from if I simply rolled over and played dead. The trust that we had built up with each other over the years had been shattered into millions of tiny pieces the moment Mik did what he did and was caught out over it. Eddy, understandably, did not have any trust for the man who had suspiciously left Colombia still in the same clothes that he was wearing when he'd abruptly decided to run while in possession of something that was vital to the future of the cartel. Obviously, it didn't look good.

Trust is something that goes both ways however and through that, over the space of that one phone call. I was facing the facts that neither could I have trust in anything that Eddy or German now said.

'You, DO, have the disc, Pedrito' Eddy enforced. I took a moment to decide what exactly would next come out of my mouth. That's when the lightbulb moment came to me. Eddy, out of character, had naively played too much importance on this computer disc that Mikael had stolen. Through this mistake of his I saw the potential for opportunity.

Potentially the disc could be the one thing that would keep me alive. If anything it would be a slim chance but a chance all of the same which was better than a kick in the cojones. Matters truly had been reduced to beggars and choosers.

'Yes, I have it' I offered without any further forms of commitment on the subject. I felt the less I said, the more vague that I was. The less cooperative I acted the more it would be beneficial to me. Choose the correct bluff and it could literally be what would keep me above ground.

'Ok then, that's good. Pedrito. Best news I've had all day. I've already had to deal with the word from Miami of a DEA bust that took out a shipment that was meant to keep half of North America supplied for the next six months. Knowing that you've got the disc is a turn for the better.' Eddy's spirits were suddenly lifted. I couldn't help but notice that he had now flipped back to a more non aggressive tone.

It sounded more than that though. It almost felt like the Eddy that I had spoken to thousands of times before in my life. That's the thing though. I knew him. It was patently obvious that I shouldn't have just suddenly trusted in the fact that a magic wand had been waved and that everything had been reset and was all ok once again. I already knew that when it came to the Bogotá Cartel and myself, things would never be ok again.

They had mutilated my best friend in the world, in part over this floppy disc. Whatever was on it must've been incredibly important to the cartel. The fact that a, normally, supercool customer like Eddy had lost his usual cool and calmness over the subject of the disc told me that there must've been a serious amount of bodies buried on the files contained inside it, figuratively and literally. That was nothing more than guesswork on my part. Whatever it was it had to have been something incriminating and strictly on a need to know basis. I hadn't looked at the disc. I didn't have a computer for one thing but even if I had been the owner of a PC I still wouldn't have been able to do anything with the fucking thing. That was something I left up to Mikael. Computers and all things technological like that.

Mik was right into his internet. He'd been the first person to even show me what the whole song and dance was. Showing me different websites that ranged from funny videos of swearing parrots to hardcore porn. He also showed me him sitting chatting with his daughter who lived in Helsinki. I could barely believe my eyes. I didn't know this whole world existed. I have to admit though the most enjoyable part of the internet when he was showing me around was always when he'd pull up our business bank accounts. He'd sometimes make a few payments or check if we'd received any that were due in from Europe. It was like we were in the future. He's sending a quarter of a million dollars to someone thousands of miles away at the touch of a few keys. Absolute witchcraft!

I wasn't so much for that though and to my own disadvantage I was in possession of this piece of software, didn't know what the fuck was *on* the disc but for the purposes of trying to stay alive I was going to have to at least pretend that I *did* know.

I wasn't sure if I would be dropping Gallego in it with the cartel if I'd let on that I already knew that La Cobra and El Jugador were in relative close proximity to me by this point. As a result I decided to keep that one to myself as I attempted to see just what Eddy was now going to do with the information that I'd given him over the disc.

'So, what's your thoughts then, Eddy?' I asked. I'd already assumed that he was now going to be the consummate nice guy again but call it extreme paranoia or a passionate will to stay alive. Whichever, I knew that I couldn't go along with it, whatever he was going to suggest. This was cartel business. We were too far past the point of just going back to business like nothing had ever happened. You know what? If Mikael really did all the things that Eddy said that he did then as sick as it may sound. He deserved what he got. He should've known better and that was the thing, he fucking well did. Even so, do you really think that I would want to go back and work for the people who had killed my friend?

That really all was pointless anyway because there was more chance of Gary Lineker getting a fucking yellow card than there was of me going back to Bogota and picking up where I left off with the cartel without finding myself sprayed by bullets on the street from two sicarios on a motorbike within five minutes of me being back there.

'Well, Pedrito, it is very simple, si? Just tell me where you are and I'll send some men to meet up with you and collect the disc' he replied. It was the casualness to how he came out with it that struck me.

Like he already didn't have two killers fuck knows where but not exactly thousands of miles away on standby. I'm not sure if he realised it or not or, once again, my paranoia levels at a dangerous high but he had not mentioned anything regarding me just bringing the disc back to Bogota. His option being that wherever I was he was going to send some "people" to recover the disc spoke volumes to me. It was a classic example of him killing two birds with the one stone. Retrieve the disc and make sure I don't live to tell the tale of what was on the thing.

'And what about me?' I asked? I'm still the man who went into hiding from you while holding this disc. How do you know that I've not made more copies of it, even if you do get this one back?'

I didn't wait for his response. I knew that he was going to come out with some bollocks about bygones being bygones. Anything that would be enough for him to get what he needed. I thought I'd poke the bear with a stick figuring I was already in the shit with the bear anyway.

'Pffft I know that you haven't made any copies, I do not need to worry about that' He laughed in dismissal before telling me that Kiki had protected the content on the disc which enabled it as read only and that it was impossible for copies to be made. All high tech James Bond kind of stuff that I didn't understand. With that being a subject that I was less than comfortable in debating I had no option but to discard with the angle involving making copies. Whether it was wise to remind a cartel boss of the reasons that they may want to murder you over or not I felt that they were elephants in the room that I wasn't down for "talking" about in Bogota and instead were best left for discussing at a safe distance of over five thousand miles.

'You will be fine, come back to Colombia, Pedro. You choose your new partner and we draw a line over the whole sorry Mikael episode.' He almost got me, such was the reassuring manner to his tone. Those with less experience may well have been taken in by him. 'Well, Eddy, considering this is a situation that was not of my own choosing, nothing would please me more than be able to come back to Colombia with Eva and get back to normal life again. We should be back in Bogota in the next couple of days, I'll bring the disc to you, amigo.' It felt strange to be speaking to him the exact way that I would've normally yet right there it was nothing more than an act just to see what his reaction would be. It was telling.

'No, no, no that is not suitable. I will have my people come and get it from you.' Eddy was not interested in any debate over it. To his extreme disgust he got one.

'See, Eddy, that doesn't really work for me.' - 'Funny, it sounded like you were disagreeing with me there' He arrogantly talked down to me. 'I know this might sound a bit crazy but I am where I currently am because I thought my life was in danger from you and German. It would almost defeat the purpose of the exercise if I was to then tell you where I am so you can then track me down. As mad as this may seem I have some major suspicions that when you do catch up with me then, well, you know.' I guess by that point of the conversation he'd either just got tired pretending or I'd provoked him further but his next response was to let me know where I really stood with him and the Bogota Cartel.

'You don't have a fucking choice, pendejo. I'm coming to get the disc and whether you tell me where you are or not I'll find you and your whore wife soon enough' he said menacingly. 'And what makes you think that I actually *have* the disc on me. When you're in possession of something with information like what is on that disc, the tendency is for to try and put as much distance between it and you as possible.' I answered, trying to bluff him.

'Meh, I'll leave that to La Cobra and El Jugador to work out. That's why we pay them the money that we do.' Eddy paused before adding, 'oh, didn't I say who the two associates were earlier? Excuse me, brother.'

'No you didn't say but Gallego fucking did so that whole striking fear into me thing that you were going for has well and truly been usurped,' I thought to myself. 'Well next time Jorge and Gilberto are in touch, oh and by the way tell them I said hi, you can let them know that I am not holding the disc but it *is* in a safe place with instructions for it to be turned over to Julio Gaviria at El Tiempo should anything happen to me or say, I was to simply disappear off the face of the earth one day. '

'The smart play here Eddy is for you to recognise that I am a man of my word. I have been so from day one in our friendship, business and personal. I will personally guarantee to you that if you call off your men that disc will never see the light of day. You won't ever get it back but neither will anyone else. Call it an insurance policy. You have my word that no one will see it. Surely you can see from my point of view, Eddy. Once I give you the disc, I have nothing. You're a smart man, you know that what is on that disc and you do not want the media getting hold of it, or worse. Colombian newspaper stands for El Tiempo shouting about your business for all the country to see.' I was chancing my luck the direction that I was steering the conversation in.

'FUCK YOU, AND FUCK EL TIEMPO' he raged down the phone at me. It wouldn't have exactly been a stretch of the imagination to suggest that Eddy Ramirez generally was not used to being threatened or blackmailed. That was his area of expertise after all. 'Once Martinez and Lozano catch up with the two of you, whether you have the disc on you or not. When they find you, they've found the disc, you know this.' Eddy said with assured arrogance. Like the prospect of his two sicarios finding Eva and I as a mere formality. I wasn't sure if my bluff had worked or not. I'd have been surprised if he'd reacted to it in front of me even if the prospect of me releasing the disc to a newspaper was one that had knocked him off guard.

'Oh well then Señor Ramirez, uno to tres you don't find me and quatro to siete you do. Roll the dice, my friend' I laughed as I hung up on him without affording him the chance of a response. I had business to attend to.

Chapter 16

Gilberto

'So how many games did Maradona actually play for la Blaugrana?' Jorge, stood there asking the tour guide inside the Nou Camp stadium. To any onlooker he was just another giddy day tripper to one of the most famous football cathedrals in the world. The home of the mighty F.C Barcelona. The ironic thing that technically he *was* an excited tourist there in the stadium. I'm going to go on and take an educated guess however that a very high percentage of visitors on their Nou Camp visit have not carried out mass murder only an hour before their guided tour.

He'd been like a fucking nino over going to the stadium. Can we go to the Nou Camp? Can we go to the Nou Camp? Can we go to the Nou Camp? He wasn't any better than Emiliano my son on days out with his "are we there yet papa are we there yet papa.' He'd taken out at least a couple of hours of the flight from Bogotá to list all the reasons for why he wanted to go on the stadium tour. He'd wanted to sit in the same dressing room as all of his heroes like Johan Cryuff and Diego Maradona. How it had been a dream as a boy to stand on the Nou Camp turf and look up to the stands as if he was one of the players. Like the archetypal football tourist. He was at almost wetting himself stage over the prospect of being able to visit the club shop and get himself and all the family kitted out in the latest Barca shirt. Over the conversation I was beginning to think that he'd actually forgotten why were really were sat on a flight to Spain.

The brothers back in Colombia would've went loco for sure if they were to have learned of guided tours around football stadiums while officially on the clock working on the much more important business of tracking down Peter Duncan and his wife. Even so, I'd have liked to have thought that Jorge and I also had some kind of artistic license when working away from home. If the pair of us were to get the work done then who really should have a care when it came to our extra curricular activities?

The main worry on that front really was over the type of scenario that would involve us not finding and terminating our targets and it then somehow getting back to German and Eddy that when we were both in Barcelona (while absolutely not finding the Duncans) we'd still managed to find time to pop into the Nou Camp for a photo opportunity with the European Cup. Knowing the pair of them from back in the days of when they used to sell cartons of cigarettes outside the various factories in the city and surrounding areas. It wouldn't have taken much guesswork to know that they would have had something to say about that little tourist attraction that we had indeed been attracted to. Then again if we're talking how understanding the Ramirez brothers may or may not have been over the football trip they'd have been a whole lot less appreciative about what we'd been up to while in Barcelona if they'd had any kind of insight into the goings on the night before we paid Salomon Sanchis and then the Nou Camp a visit.

Red light districts, clubs, brothels, casinos and (for one of us) no sleep whatsoever before going on and taking care of the task in hand with the visit to Duncan's attorney. In defence, this was all enjoyed in the evening part, after our extensive search for the couple had been wrapped up for the day. With a dead end until getting hold of Sanchis, we awarded ourselves some us free time.

There was this football tournament going on in England which, after having it explained to me, was similar to our Copa America that we have in South America. I figured a good meal somewhere on German and Eddy's peseta and then some drinks watching whatever match was playing would be the ideal way to unwind while making sure that we'd be prepared for the next morning and hitting the attorneys office.

Driven by Jorge though I knew that there was no real chance of that being reality. A night could not ever be so simple as that with him. Yes, I'd been asked, well told really, back in Bogota that I was personally responsible for Jorge, keep him away from, everything basically. It wasn't like I was ever going to be able to respond to that request from them with a no. I just nodded my head and agreed with them that I would personally see to it that I would look after the operation while we were in Europe. This including keeping Jorge in check.

That's what you say to a pair of drug lords when they tell you to do something. You say yes you will. The reality of the situation was not (and wasn't ever going to be) so simple. Asking me to stop Jorge Lozano from fleeing to the nightclubs, casinos and brothels that the city centre of Barcelona could throw at him was nothing more than the equivalent of asking me to take a hyena for a walk down Las Ramblas without a lead or muzzle and asking me to ensure that it not bite anyone.

'Diego Maradona played just under forty matches for the team' The girl in her official Barca branded bottoms and polo shirt, who had been leading the tour, replied to an attentive Jorge who had been hanging on her every word as we moved from area to area of the stadium. It had been nothing short of a medical miracle for the therapeutic properties that the Nou Camp had apparently held for Jorge. He hadn't slept all night, couldn't see or walk straight and had what appeared to be the worst hangover known to man. This all contributing to the mess he went onto make inside the attorneys offices. Yet inside the stadium, there he was more alive than anyone else in the room. Just walking through the front door of the stadium had seemingly invigorated the man.

'She knows her stuff, Gilberto. That's over ten years now since he played here and yet she can still give out that kind of information' Jorge said, purposely loud enough for the girl to hear even though he was talking exclusively to me. 'Well, it is Maradona, not exactly an unknown who played a couple of Copa del Rey matches and was never seen again' I responded. I didn't want to piss on the girl or Jorge's tortillas but I felt that possibly anyone who were a Barca fan would have known the basics of when the greatest football player the world has ever witnessed was at their club. Having seen a hungover Jorge shoot three people inside the space of a minute I decided to stop short at ribbing him over the fact that he didn't know the answer himself given he was such a passionate fan of the team.

Jorge seemed a little put out over me offering anything other than agreement that yes, this girl in the Barcelona polo shirt with the pony tail that was so tightly pulled back across her head that her eyes looked like they were being forcibly pulled up was indeed the greatest female in the whole wide fucking world. All because she knew a simple stat about Diego Maradona.

'Hold on a minute, you're neglecting to mention that while yes Diego Maradona is hardly a mysterious figure on the world stage, his time at the Nou Camp was not what you would describe as glossy. It's crazy I know but, and I may be wrong, but I think he scored almost a goal every second game' The girl in the polo nodded. 'Gracias, Bonita' Jorge acknowledged in her direction before carrying on.

With the girl being partially inside this conversation between Jorge and I she hadn't moved on from her standing point inside the dressing room which had most of the visitors inside there milling around her listening in on things. From the accents I'd heard that had consisted of English, German and a few Scandinavians from those on the tour along with us. I got the impression that they wouldn't have been able to pick up on what we were talking about in any case.

'Yet despite a goal every game his time here was viewed as a major let down. Here on their hands they had the brightest talent in the world and a player who was years away from becoming the best and yet they didn't know how to manage him. He had the bad injury and then came the Cocaine' he continued while I started to question if the road he was starting to go down was going to be appropriate for a family friendly tourist attraction. The guide finally started making for the door with the tourists all following behind like sheep. As we walked behind, Jorge pulled himself closer to me and whispered 'Of course, Diego dabbling in our country's finest export might've been bad for Barcelona but their loss was Colombia's gain, eh' We both laughed away at the private joke as we left the dressing room and out into the narrow corridor that led us back into the maze that was the inside of the Nou Camp.

As she took us all from the dressing room towards the steps leading down towards the tunnel. We passed framed pictures of legendary players from throughout Barca's history which were hanging up on either sides of the walls of the tight corridor. I could see them as we walked on down behind all the other tourists. Johan Cruyff, Michael Laudrup, Bernd Shuster, Zubizarreta, Neeskins. It was quite literally wall to wall of some of the best players the world, not only the Nou Camp, had ever seen. I couldn't concentrate though. I was, in my mind, seeing the trail of destruction that we, ok Jorge, had left behind in the offices of Sanchis.

The image of all the blood that had been left splattered all over the walls of Sanchis' office walls. Covering all of his framed law degrees on one wall in addition to some of his wife and kids on the other. The terrifying shriek like noise of that poor girl who looked like she was still only in her teens when it dawned on her that Jorge was going to kill her. Taking a bullet in her head for no other reason than her screams were giving a dangerously and delicately hungover El Jugador a sore head.

I've killed a hundred people with Jorge. It is not a pretty job to do but Jorge and I have made our peace with this as the life that we chose. Even so, regardless of the fact that him or I have killed more people than you have had hot dinners this year. Sometimes there is still a little wriggle room for ethics to be employed. Seeing the nonchalant regard that Jorge had displayed for that young Spanish girl's life was over the line.

The way that he had warned her to stop screaming by waving his gun in her face was a tactic that I couldn't see having any success. She was too far gone. The fact that he did not even have the patience to wait and see if it would or not was something else completely. Promptly putting a bullet in her head and looking at me with justification that "she had been annoying" was something that had unsettled me.

So had the smell that Sanchis had made in his trousers when shitting in his pants. This coming directly after telling us where our targets had gone to and moments before Jorge had unloaded into him.

The attorney had to go. He knew too much but his two staff that were in there at his quiet offices which, incidentally, were conveniently only walking distance from the football stadium of a tourist attraction that had also been on the things to do list of the two sicarios. The girls didn't need to go. Jorge had different ideas. He'd said that through some calls he'd made he'd found that Sanchis' reputation was one of a tough customer and that menacing characters like the two of us would not necessarily have been a guarantee of putting him in a position of compromise. Instead, Jorge felt that the way to go was one of, upon entering, grabbing the first staff member he could find. This turning out to be a very pretty and stylish looking woman who looked to be in her mid forties.

Dragging her into Sanchis' office before announcing that him and I were there to obtain some information from him and that if he wasn't prepared to give it to us then he would be dealt with exactly like his employee. The words barely out of Jorge's mouth he then put the Ruger to the woman's head and blew her brains out and over the wall. Murdered for no reason other than Jorge using her as a shortcut to getting what he was there for. I couldn't help but feel that had he enjoyed the luxury of an early night, good sleep and a piece of breakfast to start the day he'd have been more willing to entertain the prospect of some clear and measured thinking.

I was angry with him there for the approach he had taken. The man was good at his job, I would never deny despite all of his faults away from his work but this was just sloppy, unnecessary and simply, work that I did not want my name associated with. I had to bottle up the feelings I had as it all took place. He had taken an innocents life with such a flimsy attitude for no reason other than to give someone else a message. That before the young girl was then killed for, once again, a cut price reason for a life being taken. Falling out with Jorge thousands of miles away with the job still not completed would however bring nothing good our way. The prospect of me having to return to Bogota without the heads of the Duncans was not one either that I was willing to contemplate.

No one could say that any of this hadn't been telegraphed. The fact that German and Eddy actually asked me to look after Jorge. Surely that should've been the sign to say that maybe just maybe someone else should go with Gilberto to Europe? Nobody really knew Jorge like I did though and I guess it was only myself that was fitted with the foresight of what putting Jorge into an exciting and world famous city like Barcelona would result in. It was always going to be a place with too many distractions and that was proven not even twenty four hours of us having arrived in Catalunya.

Yes, no partying would've equalled no gangland massacre in some quiet legal office, I was in no doubt of that. Had we visited Sanchis' offices in less of the fragile state that Jorge had been in. The job would've been carried out with the expected professionalism that the Ramirez brothers had hand picked us for. Instead of "professionalism" the offices were left resembling as if Eddy and

German had blindly drawn out two teenage street thugs like bingo balls to carry out the assignment. Sure, a murder inside an attorney's office in a modern and advanced city like Barcelona would always be something considered newsworthy but the triple killing and specifically the age of the young girl. It would inevitably be something that would draw extra scrutiny. In our line of business scrutiny was neither welcomed or invited.

The night before, the two of us had been separated from each other around two or three in the morning. He'd been sat there at the blackjack table of this casino called, Suerte. He seemed settled so I decided to go get something to eat. I could've had something brought to me there at the table by a waitress but sitting watching Jorge play blackjack wasn't as exciting as you may believe. I decided to go for a walk on La Ramblas and get myself a McDonalds instead. I'd also not had a smoke since leaving Colombia but had been reliably informed that the Africans down the southern area of the long stretch of city centre boulevard were the men to speak to so decided to take a look for a dealer after getting some food into my belly.

I never saw Jorge again after that until around ten the next morning when he staggered back into the hotel room. I was already out on the balcony trying to shake off the effects of the night before. Having my first cup of coffee of the day as I finished the joint that had been sat leftover in the ashtray from the night before.

Watching him through the glass sliding doors from outside. I had the luxury of observing while he, disorientated as he was, had no clue at all that he wasn't the only one in the hotel room. Once he noticed me, tipping my coffee cup towards him from through the glass, a huge smile came over his face as he staggered towards the balcony doors to come and join me.

As I sat there battling with the polarities of the strong effects of the joint, kicking in and assaulting my brain once again while dealing with a clearly worse for wear Jorge shattering the peace I had been enjoying, he weaved me a tale. Some of it highly incriminating if we weren't planning on getting out of Barcelona and in all likeliness never to return again.

After him and I had parted he lost his way, somewhat. He'd left the table looking for me after he'd noticed I'd been gone a while. Myself, most probably sitting down on the beach near to where I'd bought some skunk from a young Moroccan boy. The teenager who I'd noticed making a sale as I was coincidentally walking in his direction, happy to provide for me.

After he couldn't find me it appeared that he had then went completely nuts. Tequila, which any true friend of Jorge's will always stop him from getting to, for his own good, Cocaine and brothels. As he was standing there telling me all of this he then started to pull out an obscene amount of pesetas from his suit pockets. Even he had a look of bemusement on his face as he came to terms with how much money he had. Way too much for a wallet. Shit, I didn't think that even ten wallets would have held it all. He'd literally had it crammed into all of his pockets, some rolled up into balls, others just indiscriminately pushed in.

'God looked down on you at the table, brother?' I asked him but his response was not one of someone who remembered the exact part of the night where he'd had the equivalent of a small bank vault shoved into every part of him that could hold something. Then came the twist of his tale that went beyond the whole boys will be boys and what happens in Europe stays in Europe point of view.

From his vague recollection of what had gone on during the night. He had gotten into an argument at a brothel with the owner. According to Jorge he had been with the same prostitute for over an hour and before he was finished some guy had came into the room and told him to wrap it up as the girl was needed elsewhere. Well Jorge had taken exception to this which resulted in a brief exchange of views which were only brought to an end through Jorge shooting him.

Now while Jorge, who quite matter of fact like had told me about this, did not fully appreciate the full implications of what he'd done, I did. Yes, Barcelona was not a city that neither Jorge or myself were that familiar with but it really did not take much to assume that, like anywhere else in the world. The brothels of Barcelona would have been connected to organised crime in some way or other. Money laundering, illegal trafficking of girls or even just plain old protection of a business owner who couldn't go to the police for such matters.

Regardless of what connection there may have been to the local mafia. Jorge had shot (he was not clear over the state of the patient) the owner of a brothel. Behaviour like that is always a sure fire fast tracked way to having all kinds of unsavoury characters suddenly asking questions about you and looking in your direction. As a rule it's not something that someone tends to get away with without there being some form of reckoning. Considering it was the Barcelona mafia who had been assisting us since we'd arrived from Bogota, ironically them who had armed us with the Rugers and enough ammunition to last the whole of the summer. It would have been embarrassing at best had they found out that it had been one of the Colombian sicarios who had carried out the shooting.

Whilst ordinarily troubling his news was when it came to potential ramifications at some point down the line after someone had begun to start joining the dots. I knew that we couldn't let that hinder us when it came to taking care of Sanchis that same morning. If everything was to go to plan we would've been off on the scent of Duncan before any of the fingers started being pointed in the direction of the Colombians over what Jorge had done.

Ill prepared we were for the visit and Lord oh Lord how it showed but I guess in the line of business as ours, the ends justified the means. Before he checked out. Sal Sanchis, as he sat there in his leather chair behind his desk said one word. Ibiza. Jorge got the result he, we had been looking for. Just not the way I had personally wanted.

Ibiza though? Despite the clear pitfalls of being in tow with Jorge in what, I was led to understand from some articles in magazines, was the party capital of the world. That aside, I was beginning to like Peter Duncan's choice in destinations.

Chapter 17

Zico

'OH FLOOOOOR O SCOTLAND WHEN WILL WE SEE YER LIKE AGAIN. THAT FOUGHT AND DIED FOR YER WEE BIT HILL AN GLEN. AND STOOD AGAINST HIM, GUESS WHO! PROUD EDWARDS ARMY AND SENNNNNT HIM HOMEWARD TAE THINK AGAIN.

THE HILLS ARE BARE NOW AND AUTUMN LEAVES LIE THICK AND STILL. O'ER LAND THAT IS LOST NOW WHICH THOSE SO DEARLY HELD. AND STOOD AGAINST HIM, GUESS WHO! PROUD EDWARDS ARMY. AND SENT HIM HOMEWARD TAE THINK AGAIN.'

The audio levels of my living room was resembling the Wembley Stadium that we were all staring at on the TV as we stood there singing the national anthem as the camera panned its way along the Scottish starting eleven for the game to end all games. Scotland versus England. Andy Goram between the sticks, the flying pig and a goalkeeper who through his height and less than athletic frame managed to defy logic season upon season. Colin Hendry, the most Scottish person in the world and as the camera got to him was showing a face of someone who was ready to fuck shit up if any cunt came near him.

If UEFA rules permitted such behaviour then there was absolutely no doubt in my mind that he'd have come out with the fucking Braveheart face paint on. Shearer and Sheringham would've fucking shat it. Then to the eye-catching ginger hair of Stuart McCall. Someone as Scottish as a fucking Russ Abbot Jimmy Hat but a decent player to have in the starting line up to give him his dues. Then the captain Gary McCallister. The man that on the day was hopefully going to be a key figure and keep a lid on the rest of the team. It was surely going to be a day where tensions would run high and cunts would need to keep the head. Not do anything daft. Especially when you've got a

European ref in charge. You never know what those unpredictable mad bastards are going to do from one minute to the next as far as giving a decision.

Seeing the Scotland line up and then England's. There was no denying that on paper they had a far superior team. Then again so they fucking should when they've got fifty million more of a population to cherry pick from. Pure common sense would dictate that Scotland were the underdogs in this match up. That fact however had most definitely escaped myself, Si and the rest of the crowd that had been assembled over the hours leading up to the match. Forget the fact that England were, obviously, going to be swept aside. Si, actually went as far as to describe Terry Venables' side as nothing more than an inconvenience on our march to the final back at the same stadium. Copious amounts of Cocaine and alcohol can do strange things and offer up alternative perspectives to some. I say in defence of not just Si but myself every bit as much. Since the dawn of time Scotland and England had always had their yearly get together for what was, while technically meaningless, a friendly match that never dipped below the levels of the exact fucking opposite of "meaningless."

It was nothing more than about bragging rights but was a fixture that, any Scot who had an interest in the beautiful game, was never not in their calendar. The thing is, and considering part of my youth I can't be too judgmental here, cunts can't behave themselves can they and as far as away from Hampden Park or Wembley it was never a case of both sets of fans all sitting round in a circle stopping traffic as they collectively sang Kumbaya My Lord.

Eighty Nine was the moment though where things got too radge. A decent sized mob of English hoolies came up to Scotland. Kicked some cunts in, got some of their own kicked in. Fairly standard stuff in the ballpark to what I saw when running with The Utility. Maybe it was because it was a much higher profile match than Motherwell versus Dundee United on a midweek but anyway. They stopped the matches after all of the capers that had been going on that day. Before during and after the match until the English mob had been sent back home again.

The country was devastated. The match between the "Auld Enemy" was, much like a place at the World Cup, almost looked upon as our birthright. Through time, everyone became used to not playing them and the games against England was just like anything else that used to exist but didn't anymore. No different to the Dodo or a Marathon.

Only, after seven years of not playing them and the two teams being drawn in the same group to play each other at the European Championships in England. The country of Scotland went into complete meltdown. Then came the waiting. Where you knew the game was going to arrive and when it did it was going to be fucking massive. Until then however it had been looked upon as something that you just had to put to the back of your mind. Safe in the knowledge that it would come around when it was time to do so.

Sat there on the sofa surrounded by everyone. Most, due to the combination of the drugs and drink and then having the molotov cocktail of an England Scotland match thrown into the mix, already by then a rabid mess who had been worked up into a frenzy before a ball had even been kicked. I couldn't help but imagine the same states that people were working themselves into back home in the thousands of pubs across the country.

Apart from Si and moi there was also my dad and Eva. Flo and Elle had come too. Joining ranks with Eva for Team England. Then there were the four others who I had never seen before in my life until Si showed up with them in tow at my door. Him vouching for them which, as always, was good enough for me. Well, unless he's already been wiring into his supplies. Which he had.

The boy who seemed to be the one most friendly with Si was called Shaky. Apparently the two of them had been pals from as far back as primary school. I'd never met him before despite how close they were due to the fact that Shaky hadn't had any interest in the casuals back when Si was running with the Utility. Had he been up for it then he'd have been a character that I'd have surely met years before Along with him were another three of his mates. Wisey, Biscuits and Locks. Just regular lads the four of them with a shared common goal with myself and Si which was to get in as much of a state as quickly as we could leading up to the match and then beyond.

It was Biscuits though out the four of them who had caught my eye. He looked scarily like the boy behind the bar in The Simpsons, Moe. Same curly hair and everything. It wasn't even the fact that he looked like a cartoon character that had grabbed my attention about him though. It was more to do with the fact that when he walked into mines I could actually hear him jangling with change from his pockets with every step he took. Think someone with new shoes with the squeak that they have with every step and replace it with the sound of copious amounts of coins clashing together. Mental it definitely was. Both of his pockets were fucking bulging.

'Been giving the bandits a battering mate, aye?' I asked him as he was introduced to me. Looking like he'd started on the swally hours ago he just laughed back with a glazed look on his face. Not that he had that distant look on his coupon for long once Si started dishing out the goods.

It was a decent party vibe inside the villa. Thanks to the girls getting a wee bit of notice they'd turned up with with face paint in the colours of the two teams. Si had "borrowed" a flag that had been flying outside a Scottish pub when he had been walking home the night before and had it hanging from my window looking out onto the street, slightly waving around in the gentle breeze outside.

Si, daft bastard that he is (even if his heart is always in the right place) had actually went to the trouble for our "Scottish Day" of getting some haggis from a guy that he'd gotten to know who worked in Jock's, this San Antonio Bay Scottish pub. Si doing this so that we could make haggis sandwiches for half time. His face was a picture when, once everyone was in place at mines for the game, I'd asked him just how many of the revellers (Coked out of their nuts) would be taking him up on the offer of a haggis sandwich.

Fucking hell, haggis being as an acquired taste that it is would never guarantee a high uptake in takers even without the fucking Ching being taken into account. I appreciated the sentiment though even if it was never really going to get itself off the ground. You'd think a dealer would've sussed that out for themselves though?

It would've been an understatement of the highest order to state that I had been buzzing for the day coming around. With all of my own stuff I had going on with Ibiza and Space. I'd admittedly slept on a lot of the Euros build up as it had approached. There was a time where I could've rattled off to you what teams were playing on which dates, against who and in which stadium but that was a different time. A less complicated time, a less complicated me. You get a wee bit older though and other things begin to take importance than fitba. That aside, the date of the fifteenth of June had been etched in the memory from the moment the two teams had been drawn together in Group A.

That highlighted by the fact that I had not only for the first time since being in Ibiza set an alarm for the next day before I'd went to bed but had also woken up before the fucking thing had even got round to going off such was my Christmas day style excitement. Before I'd even got out of bed I gave Si a bell. It was still early doors likes but that cunt had woken me up enough times in my life so I called him without neither fear nor favour.

'What time is it? he gruffly answered after what was getting close to the point that it was going to go to voicemail which I wouldn't bothered to even have left considering the soft lad doesn't know how to listen to them. It wasn't exactly like he was some nugget who didn't know how to work a phone though. He literally *couldn't* get his voicemails because he'd locked himself out of them. One night when he had a bit too much of too much he'd been fucking around with the phone. In a moment of paranoia he had set a pin number function to his messages like you would a bank card. Only, by the next day he'd forgotten what the fucking pin number was that he'd chosen so from then on. Leaving him messages was a waste of time.

'Time you were up Sonny Jim' I merrily replied. Way too bright for someone who had only woken up seconds before. 'Today's the day that the English get their tatties, Simon,' I laughed, while believing that fact a lot more than I should've done. 'What's the plan, when you coming round?' I asked.

'Well I need to quickly get ready and drive out to Can Bellotera (I had absolutely no point of reference to where that even was) to collect something so I'm thinking that I'll be back and over to yours by around twelve.'

Fucking hell, around four hours until kick off. There would most likely be untold damage done before the teams had even walked onto the pitch.

'Aye, no worries mate. Bring lots of supplies, it's going to be a marathon not a sprint.' I in no way intended for the words that came out to be as ominous as they sounded but knowing what I did about the pair of us when together with hours to kill and alcohol and hard (as well as) soft drugs at our disposal. It fucking well IS ominous!

'Oh, by the way Zeec, is it cool for me to bring a few mates along with me today for the match? I said it would be cool but obviously making sure with you before, likes' he asked. Doing so just as I was about to hang up on him. 'What mates?' I replied, not that I was going to say no to him anyway but just wanted to know out of interest and in advance of them coming. Any mates of Si are mates of mine. Corny as fuck but true as fuck also.

'Eh, an old pal, Shaky. Him along with the lads that he's over on holiday with. Good boy, Shaky, you'll like him' - 'Aye, of course, Si. the more the merrier, absolutely fucking buzzing for today, mate' I said, giving the go ahead while letting my own emotions get the better of me. 'Right back at you, man. It's been way too fucking long since we played these bastards. You were just that wee bit too young and weren't running with the casuals the last time we played England. I was through in Glasgow that day along with quite a few of the Utility boys to see if we could play some part in the madness, which we did. Such fun, mate. Good times'

I'd heard that same fucking Scotland England story from Si a hundred times over the years but at least he was telling it on a day where it was actually relevant compared to all of the times when it wasn't.

'Right, I better get moving if I've to get over there and back in time,' Si continued. 'Same here.' I agreed, I'm heading out for breakfast and then going to the supermarche to stock up on provisions. I'll see you when I see you.'

With my own plans in place for meeting Flo for breakfast I hung up and headed straight for the shower to get my own arse into gear.

We'd agreed to meet at Los Pepes, a restaurant near enough equidistant between my villa and Flo's hotel. When I'd arrived there, although not disappointed in any way. I could see Elle sat there at the table along with Flo. I wasn't naive in any way that would've saw me expecting Flo to spend all her time with me while there in Ibiza. It wouldn't have really said much about her actually as a person had she been so willing to ditch her mate on a holiday that they had probably saved up for all year together and looked so much forward to.

'Audi, Girls. Como esta and all of that shite' I laughed as I sat down beside Flo at the table. They looked a tad rough. 'Fucking hell, you two are still wrecked' I laughed having had the benefit of further inspection.

'Yeah we've not been to bed yet' Elle said behind a pair of shades that by then I could see were not only wrapped around her to guard her eyes from the sunlight. 'Amnesia' Flo added while lifting her own pair of sunglasses up from over her eyes to show me that hers were like fifty fucking pence pieces. 'So I'll just start pretending that I hadn't received both your RSVPs for todays Euros party then because no way are you both lasting until the afternoon.' I made light of the fact that I was being realistic of the facts that there would be neither of them in attendance at mines for the match.

The two of them just laughed back at me but more in a dismissive sense as if they were taking it that I thought I was talking to two Ibiza novices. 'We'll be just fine, Meesta Selecao' Flo said with a cheeky wink. 'Yeah we were planning on staying up until evening but then having the earlier night that our bodies are crying out for so that we can be recharged enough for getting back on things tomorrow night. You need to pace yourself out here' Elle said as she picked up her glass of fresh orange and had a sip which brought an almost orgasmic look to her face.

'Actually, don't be so sure about the early night, babe' Flo said looking across the table at her friend. 'This boy here is on at Space tonight, I wouldn't go ruling out a naughty trip over to Playa den Bossa, we could leave early though and still get *some* kind of sleep' She continued. The tone that came across was not one of "we'll see" and much more one of having already been decided whether they'd agreed on it yet or not.

'SELINA WALLINGTON!! Can't you go one day of your life without being a bad influence on me' Elle giggled in some faux act of trying to make out that she was the innocent one out of their friendship. They'd have to fucking go some to still be in the land of the living by the time I took the decks on the terrace later on. Shit? 'I'd have to go some to be in a fit enough position to fucking be standing behind the decks by then never mind "on" them,' I thought to myself as I gave the waiter standing over me my order of a cheese and onion toastie and instructions to bring me the biggest glass possible of the same orange juice that Elle had been drinking. Flo instead was sat with a cup of tea which I thought was a bit mad considering how hot it was, even for that part of the day. The girl must've really liked her tea, I guess.

Of more importance to me wasn't whether they were going to have the lasting distance to get themselves to Space for my set. I'd have been fucking astonished if they did in all honesty but what was more pressing was the name that I had just heard Elle call Flo. Assuming that even was her name. She'd called her Selina so with my powers of deduction it appeared that quite possibly her name actually hadn't been Flo. I had to be sure.

'So, eh, what's with the Selina stuff then?' I asked, laying out my ignorance for all to see. 'What do you mean, Stevie?' Elle replied, looking genuinely puzzled by my question.

'Well, you called this girl here, Selina,' I said playfully nudging Flo. 'You're possibly not aware of this being Scottish but down in England we have this thing where if someone has a name, and that pretty much means everyone, pets included. From time to time we might actually call them by it. Weird, I know right?' Elle replied sarcastically but with a smile that had me smiling at her impudence.

'So your name's not Flo then, Flo?' I said, looking at her while thinking inside of all the things her and I had done in the short time we'd known each other and I hadn't even known her real name!

'Well, no,b b but I'm pretty sure I told you my name the night we met in Space' Flo said with a look on her face that suggested she was only a certain percentage of how sure she was saying this as fact. 'To be fair you probably did, that was a night for the scrapbook and no mistake' I laughed back at the memory of it.

'So why do you get called Flo then?' I asked while we were on the subject. Whatever her real name was it wasn't going to matter a fuck in any case as I was just going to keep calling her Flo, regardless.

She lifted up both hands so that they were on show for her and Elle although both of them were looking at me for my response. Which was blank. Aye, nice nails she had, I noticed them the first night I'd met her. Really colourful with not every nail the same colour. Something which stuck out about her. The way she would talk, expressive with her hands and you having had several Mitsubishis ended up with mix of her at times leaving a rainbow like trail behind with her hand. I still didn't get the point that was being made though and by then Flo had realised this.

'Oh for fuck's sake, Stevie' Flo said in mock exasperation to me, nodding down at her nails. 'Florence Griffith-Joyner, Flo-Jo' She said leaving it at that for my lightbulb to be belatedly switched on. 'AHHHHHHH I GET IT!' I replied happy as fuck that I was now in on it all. It was obvious really but sometimes you just can't see those woods for the fucking trees.

'WELL DUHHHH' They both said at the same time giggling. We sat eating and drinking, me mainly doing most of the eating which was anything but coincidentally as they filled me in on their antics from the night and morning they'd spent at Amnesia. After my recent trip there. Even just the name of the place brought a shiver down my spine. Once we'd finished our breakfast and the gallant side of me had paid for everyone's meals. We went off on our separate ways again with the two of them confirming that they'd be around to mines a few hours before kick off. Leaving me thinking to myself just how cute it was that they actually believed it.

I'd stopped to pick up a case of San Miguel and (in all probability, stupidly) a bottle of Jose Cuervo before heading back to the villa. It wasn't long after that when the bodies started to appear at the door. First Si along with the other lads he'd mentioned earlier, then pops and Eva. I'd been surprised when they'd both agreed to come for the fitba related party at all. Due to the unconventional relationship my father and I had I didn't even know if he even liked fitba or not. Considering all the shit that he was in, as well as the other stuff that I no doubt didn't even know about. I'd have thought that the very last thing that he needed to do be doing was to surround himself with a mob of boys half his age who were going to be indulging in chemicals and alcohol and, without question as the day went on, increasingly becoming more and more hard work to be around.

I was pleased to hear him say that they'd both be there. I hadn't seen the happy couple together much since they'd arrived in Ibiza and gatecrashed proceedings. I couldn't believe it but Peter had made such an effort for the day that he'd actually went to the trouble of securing a Scotland top to wear. It was one of those fake ones that you see being sold in tourist shops where the badge is actually the same fabric as the shirt.

It even had a name and number on the back of Nine - McCoist. I was impressed and it left him escaping the ripping that he (or anyone for that matter) would've and should've had for wearing a snide shirt. The two of them had obviously planned all of this because Eva was wearing the same fake style fitba shirt only hers was the famous white of England with the three lions. For the record, while her husband was the cheeky chappie of the Scottish game, Ally McCoist. His wife was going by the name of Shearer.

It was a nice touch from the two of them and it showed me, if anything, that just because a dangerous Colombian drug cartel are on your case. Life as you know it doesn't have to just suddenly grind to an abrupt halt while you wait on meeting your end. Soon after they'd arrived. So did Flo and Elle, remarkably.

'How the fuck did you two make it?' I asked in genuine amazement as I stood staring back at them as they waited on me letting them in. 'Oh, nothing a little disco nap couldn't have fixed out' Flo laughed as they both walked past me and into the living room to receive some good natured booing from every single Scot that was already in place. 'Fahk off you Jocks' Flo said back to them while motioning her hand in the international sign of "wanker" which left everyone pissing themselves at.

As for the English contingent in the room. It was going to be a day where thick skin would be required, even if the vibe was one of nothing other than friendly. Scots simply cannot be trusted to behave during a Scotland versus England match. This is fact. Comments will be made, patter that, if not taken in the correct context, might well prove to be offensive to those born south of the wall. With Flo, Eva and Elle representing for England and, I assumed, never having watched an Auld Enemy match in the company of such a crowd. They would be in for an education.

With everyone in place we then set about getting as supremely fucked up as much as we possibly could before kick off. No, it wasn't big and neither was it clever but as Scots safe in the knowledge that we might never play England again in our lifetime. It was our national duty to make the most out of the chance we'd been given.

As we sat enjoying the afternoon with the clock fast approaching kick off, Flo had heard enough of the anti English invective and decided to ask the question.

'So why do you hate the English so much?' She pretty much asked the whole room minus of course Eva and Elle. 'It's your fucking media, Flo, your commentators, all this fucking nineteen sixty six pish. Thirty fucking years ago by the way, thirty years and yet every single fucking time England play a game of fitba they mention it like it was yesterday.' Si, who had been talking at a rate of a hundred words per minute as it was, happily jumped in and obliged her.

'He's right, babe. The fucking BBC and ITV when it comes to World Cups or Euros are insufferable. You'd think that England were the only British team that is ever playing in them. I mean, look at most Scots, they've got a favourite English side that they follow during the fitba season. If they hated the English you really think they'd have an English team they support? Nah, it's your commentators and their arrogance that winds cunts up.

England have absolutely no right to think that they're going to win a tournament as they're nowhere near good enough yet every tournament they're in we've got to sit and watch the telly and be told that they're one of the favourites. It's a fucking nonsense' I backed Si up. 'Don't forget Jimmy Hill either, fucking poof' Si added, name checking the BBC man who, back in eighty two, had managed to alienate an entire nation just through how he had downplayed a Scotland goal against Brazil.

One of Shaky's mates, Locks, this wiry looking boy had sat shaking his head as Si and I offered up our reasons for why Scots didn't like the English.

'Nah, you're wrong lads. We've hated the English for hundreds of years. It didn't just start because of Brian Moore and Jimmy Hill.' He said, finally speaking up. He'd pretty much kept quiet in amongst everyone else as we'd been sat there drinking and sniffing but he looked like he was on one with this particular subject. 'The bastards have raped and pillaged Scotland for years, stolen our land, taken our oil. The fucking Tory Party look at Scotland like a piece of shite on its shoes but are quite happy to take our fucking dosh. Look at what they did to us with the poll tax. Cunt's, absolute cunts'

'Keep it fucking light mate,' I joked as I literally watched the spit spraying out of his mouth as he spoke. He was right about the Tory party though, mind.

'I fucking hate the English' He continued with so much venom I knew that this was now a situation that was going to have to be dealt with. All stemming from what was nothing more than an innocently curious question from Flo.

Si locked eyes with me and I could see that he was thinking the same and it was really now just a question of who dealt with it the quickest. With it being my pad though I felt it was my call.

'Well if you hate the English so much then you won't be wanting to watch the match in the presence of my dads wife and my girl then.' I said, already getting to my feet to make my intentions felt. 'Same goes for the other three of you. I know we all have a wee bit of banter about the English when it comes to the fitba but he's went too far.' I continued, pointing directly at Locks. The other three just sat shaking their heads to confirm that they were staying put. Whether that was down to the fact that they agreed with me or that they knew it was now too late to get a good spot in a pub by then in time for kick off was anyones guess.

'N n n nnno I wasn't saying anything against the girls, Zico, no disrespect mate, totally' he tried to backtrack. Almost sobered up in that moment, faced with the implications of his words. It was too little too late, he was going. The one thing that was for certain was that if that was the state he was in ten minutes before kick off he was only going to get progressively worse over the rest of the afternoon. When he realised that he wasn't getting to stay, his mood turned back again and it all got a bit silly. Resulting in Si giving him a couple of digs outside the house and away from the eyes of his three mates so as not to escalate things any more than they needed to be.

We never seen or heard anymore from him after that. Funnily enough.

Once we got settled again that was the teams finally ready for going out onto the pitch. Flo, who I'd been sat beside the whole afternoon leaned into me and whispered into my ear 'That's the most gallant thing anyone has ever done for me' - 'Stop it' I giggled back at her while not in anyway sure if she'd been sincere when she'd said it or was simply having a laugh. 'And did you just call me your girl?' She teased.

I was saved from having to answer her by the teams coming out onto the pitch and the room suddenly erupting with an outpouring of emotion over seeing the players walking out from the tunnel. The massive release after all those years of us having gone without it.

The ninety minutes of the match felt like they'd put five years onto my life. The Ching and the booze obviously wasn't helping but the match had it's dizzy highs and the most sick and twisted of devastating lows.

As is often the case. Something like Scotland and England that is highly anticipated, it can tend to be an anti climax and the first half of the match had lived up to that. Still, nil nil and all to play for. I'm not sure if it had been the same for the players but the first half had flown in. Then again, they weren't taking some of Bolivia's finest. I would've hoped not anyway.

I had an interesting conversation with Biscuits during the half time break. My curiosity had gotten the better of me and had asked him about all the change that his pockets were bulging with. His reason blew my fucking head clean off! He fished his hand into one of his pockets to collect some of the coinage before putting his hand up to my face for a closer inspection. He was holding a pile of standard British 2p pieces.

'Why the fuck are you carrying coppers around in your pocket, mate?' Was the inevitable follow up question because I fully admit, he had me scratching my head. He then went on to tell me that the previous year in Ibiza he'd been paying for a packet of fags from a vending machine and mistakingly had put a 2p piece into the slot and in doing so. The machine, instead of spitting the coin back out again, credited the copper as an actual 25 peseta coin! Fast forward to the next summer and the boy's brought his fucking piggy bank over with him! Brilliant.

After the regulation fifteen minutes break. The teams emerged back from out of the tunnel to take that long walk across the track and onto the pitch. We'd taken advantage of the break ourselves to refuel courtesy of Si and my dad's contributions. There was no way that the second half was going to be as low key as the first had been. With the Ching hitting in all the right places we were ready. The question of would Scotland be ready was really more of importance to matters.

'KEMONNNN SCOTLAND' Si was seriously losing his shit, veins sticking out in his neck and everything as he shouted his piece before picking up his beer and trying to settle himself again in preparation for the assault on the senses that was heading our way. Whatever bubble that we had been living in that we would beat England had a sharp pin taken to it not even ten minutes in when Shearer scored.

It didn't even make sense but the thing that seriously annoyed me over the goal wasn't the conceding of it. Or the sight of Shearer running away with that trademark boring as fuck celebration of his. No, it was the close up shot of Gary Neville celebrating the goal. I couldn't even explain it but he had me in two minds about putting a bottle through the TV as the camera zoomed in on him celebrating towards the England fans. I just needed a target in the heat of the moment I guess and it just happened to be the Manchester United full back. The room felt the blow of the goal every bit as much as the Scotland side themselves. Spirits definitely dipped. The girls, sensing this, didn't go overboard with their celebrations. Which was sensible as far as they were concerned.

England almost made it two which would've finished us off had Goram not pulled off a wonder save. As Scotland always do though, they kept themselves in the game despite being up against it. Then came our own wee spell. "Juke Box" Gordon Durie nearly scored with a header that Seaman almost panelled himself against the post in keeping out. The boys kept plugging away though while keeping the English out at the other end.

Then it happened. If you're talking moments of destiny then aye, this was it. A couple of minutes that no Scot will ever be able to wipe from their memory for the rest of their lives. Attacking down England's left, Stuart McCall's managed to put in a decent pass into the box for Durie, who was in a race with Tony Adams for the ball. Juke Box got there first, Adams last and down went Durie.

'PENALTY' screamed around the room. It felt like an eternity before the referee eventually pointed to the spot. Cue bedlam inside the living room. People ending up on top of each other, beer knocked over and lines of Coke sent flying into the air. The fact that Tony Adams hadn't even complained about it told its own story as that lad protests more than Amnesty fucking international.

I'm not really sure where I went for that following minute after the award had been given. I, momentarily, left the room with elation. I imagine most of the room did also. This was textbook Scotland. Up against a superior team but stay in the match and then score from a set piece and pull off a shock. It was a film I'd seen many times before that it was almost as if it was in our footballing DNA.

Once I came back to earth it was to see Gary McCallister putting the ball down onto the spot. My first reaction was that Ally McCoist should've been taking it. So fucking what if McCallister was the captain and the assigned penalty kick taker. Ally McCoist was like Roy fucking Race. The type of player who suffers horror leg breaks and in his return match from injury scores winners in cup finals with overhead kicks. Scotland against England and the opportunity to be the hero was simply written for the man. I even said so before the kick had been taken. My father, much too old (and full of Ching) for that jumping on top of each other caper, told me that McCoist and McCallister had had a little difference of opinion over who should take it only for the captain to pull rank.

We were a bag of nerves as the Scotland captain stood there waiting on the whistle. We weren't going to get too many chances in the match. This was THE chance. Shaky couldn't even bring himself to look and instead had stood up and walked over to the kitchen to get a beer from the fridge while it all took place.

With the whistle blown, McCallister began his run up. Just when he was about to go on and strike towards the goal I could've sworn that the ball moved slightly. Maybe it had been blown by the wind although it had looked a baked in sunshine London where the match was taking place. Possibly the ball had been balanced on a little piece of raised turf and had fallen off? Whatever the fuck the reason. I was positive the ball had moved. McCallister? Well he couldn't have been too concerned about it all because he just cracked on and melted it anyway right at David Seaman who somehow got the ball over the bar for a corner.

The pain of that moment. The knowledge that with nothing more than a better placed kick we would all have been experiencing unadulterated delirium instead of pain. Pain? Watching him miss the penalty, hard as it was to believe, we didn't even know true pain, yet. We hadn't even been awarded the opportunity of processing and coming to terms with the penalty miss when Paul Gascoigne was suddenly racing up the other end of the park looking to be played in.

Understanding the torture of being a Scottish fitba fan. You just knew what was coming next.

Gazza has made an absolute fanny out of Colin Hendry. Sent the poor cunt for a hotdog with one flick of his boot before then hitting it first time past Goram on the drop. Without a doubt one of the most, if not *the* biggest kick in the balls I'd ever felt in my life that came at the end of those crazy couple of minutes. I wanted to be sick. Looking around, everyone knew that it was fucked. It was the nature of it that was what stuck in the throat and that was evident once we'd all managed to get our head around over what had just happened and start to process things. That's when the anger started to filter out. All in the direction of McCallister.

'Selfish bastard should've left it to McCoist, wanted to be the fucking hero though eh?' Si shouted to no one in particular.

'Fucking wanker' Shaky chipped in 'His fucking da should've pulled out and done everyone a favour. Better still, he should've have went anywhere near his slut of a mum' he kept on. That was probably a bit much though but passions were running high. I got it.

'The cunt should never fucking play for Scotland again in his life' Biscuits said jumping up pointing at him on the TV whilst about two pounds worth of coppers spilled out of his pockets.

'SCRAMBLE' I shouted at the sight of the coins hitting the floor to try and take the sting out of things but everyone was too far gone with their own gripes by that point. Everyone apart from the girls and my dad. It was only while everyone was losing their heads that it had dawned on me that he'd barely said two words all day despite doing a healthy amount of Charlie. Obviously the man had plenty on his mind but the one thing I knew about him was that he'd talk about it if he wanted to and not a minute before so I shrugged it off.

To our devastation the match ended two nil to England. Compared to the bedlam that had greeted the two teams coming out for the start of the match inside the living room it now resembled a morgue. You had Flo and Elle who were by this point leaning against each other and one step away from crashing out. Si still moaning about Gary McCallister.

The three lads looking like they were shaping up to be leaving and my dad and Eva sitting there in silence. Fucking hell, what a let down.

Within the space of half an hour everyone had gone. Flo and Elle assuring me that they would be back in time for a lift to Space while Si mentioned he would possibly be in line for going through. For some reason Eva stayed silent on the matter but it was written all over her face how much she wanted to be going along with everyone else. Shaky and his mates, before they left, apologised one last time for their mate's behaviour. I told them not to trip about it while jokingly asking Biscuits for enough spare change for a couple of packets of cigarettes which he duly obliged by handing me twenty pence worth of coppers as he was walking out the room.

Left there alone with my own thoughts I was heartbroken over the result. Utterly depressed by the way that it had panned out. It would've almost been easier to take had England given us a doing rather than that fucked up few minutes that would've ended someone with a weaker heart disposition that we'd all had to go through. The last thing I wanted to do was to go and stand in front of hundreds of happy party people and make them dance with me and my coupon tripping me over the result but it wasn't exactly a valid excuse for not going into work was it? Sorry gaffer, team lost, can't come in today. No cunt would have a job.

I did exert a tiny bit of pleasure from my set later on the terrace when I'd ended it with the Sex Pistols track "God save the Queen." Apart from Si, Flo and Elle there couldn't have been anyone else in that crowd who could've known why I'd ended with such a diverse tune on the decks. I didn't care. I wasn't playing it for them.

Chapter 18

Gilberto

After touching down at Ibiza airport. Our very first destination was a restaurant called El Bandido Borracho. Before we'd checked into the hotel or went looking for the Duncans I was intent on visiting "The Drunken Bandit." It was an indulgence that after all of what I had had to put up with back in Barcelona, I felt I was due. Jorge, I think, sensed this and offered up no resistance when we were forty five thousand feet up in the air when I was telling him about the famous Ibizan restaurant that it was said served up the finest paella in the world and how it was going to be the very first thing on our list of things to do.

A guilty pleasure of mines years back had been watching El Viajero Hambriento which followed presenter, "Chucho" on his travels around the globe trying out the local cuisines. One of the episodes saw him in Spain focusing on the coastal seafood restaurants. As part of the show it had him in Ibiza at one of the island's most famous restaurants. It was so small it only had ten tables inside. All the film stars holidaying on the island apparently take time out to visit when there, so popular it is.

Once we'd cleared baggage collection and found ourselves stood outside the terminal. We got into the next available taxi to pull up in front of us with the basic instruction of 'El Bandido Borracho por favor' given to the driver. A gruff 'si" from the front confirmed he knew where we were headed as the car pulled away from international arrivals.

I'd assumed that with the flight from Barcelona arriving at around ten in the evening we'd have one, possibly two hours left before the restaurant was ready to close. With the promise of extra pesetas thrown in his direction if he stepped on it. The driver turned an estimated thirty minute journey into a seventeen one. Jorge and I were impressed enough with this to make sure he could've taken the night off if he'd so wished through the tip handed his way.

I'd taken it for granted that such a small, intimate and by all accounts, very exclusive restaurant would have been booked up months in advance and due to this there would not have been any tables available upon our arrival. Yes, I appreciate that I could have easily obtained the phone number to the restaurant and called from the airport to ask the question. This however would have been a complete waste of everyones time. They would have told me that there were no tables available and asked me if I'd like to book for another time. To them, all I would be, just another voice on the end of the telephone. Someone they could wave away with a hand. I was Gilberto Martinez though, La Cobra. Not the type that you easily dismiss.

I'd always found that in our line of work, especially with who our employers were. Doors tended to open for you. While it would have been all too easy to turn me down over the phone, dealing with myself and Jorge face to face? Yes, not so much. Given the haste to get to the restaurant, we had not even picked up our weapons from the contact that the Italians had given us but securing a table in a restaurant was hardly going to be the stuff that would require firearms. Considering what I'd had to put up with in Barcelona when Jorge last had a weapon it was possibly even a good thing that neither of us were carrying.

We entered through the small front door, both of us having to duck for to get through and inside. A well dressed man who looked to be around early thirties greeted us with an initial smile which the shine could've blinded you with if it was to hit you at the wrong angle. Then the smile, instantly dropped. I assumed once he'd had an extra couple of seconds to appreciate the two customers who had just walked in. I swear that I was able to detect the exact second in his mind when, faced with Jorge and I and the vibe that we apparently give off, he realised that he was now the one with the job of giving us the news that there were no tables available.

'Buenos noche, senor. We would like a table, por favor' I asked, already knowing what would follow.

'Oh I am afraid that a table for tonight is quite of the question. As you can see, we are full' He said but without actually looking Jorge or myself in the eye as he did so. Happily diverting attention from being on him to surveying the small dining area. All tables occupied by couples sat surrounded in dim lighting aided with large candles. With us being invited to take a look, which we did, it led to some of the diners looking back at us before looking away again immediately the second they locked eyes with us.

'I think you've made some kind of a mistake, check again' I responded. Calmly and charitably giving him the chance to catch up with the situation that he was now involved in. His next response. To ensure that the restaurant was fully booked for the rest of the night and that they could not possibly accommodate the two of us showed, unfortunately, that he wasn't understanding things too clearly.

'Wait, did you check under Paco Herrera and Juan Pablo Munoz, the Colombian cartel party of two?' Jorge asked.

'Ummmmm no, those names are not there in the reservations book sir,' unbelievably he checked the list after he'd given him the names. That's when Jorge's patience ran out, I guess. Maybe that could've been put down to tiredness through flying. That can bring out the worst of us at the best of times can't it? Then again, it was more likely a result of Jorge being a dangerously horrible bastard.

He grabbed the host by the collar and dragged him away and to the side of the eating area so that the diners now couldn't see what was about to take place. That purpose was pretty much defeated anyway with them all having seen the host being dragged away from his podium in the first place.

The look on the hosts face was one of someone who was not expecting this reaction. I guess in restaurants customers generally act with a lot more decorum when they are given bad news such as no available tables or that the sticky toffee pudding is sold out. Most restaurants do not have a Jorge Lozano wishing to dine in them however.

'Look, pendejo. My friend has come all the way from Bogota, Colombia. The first thing and I mean the very first thing that he's done after getting off the plane is to get in a taxi and come straight here. You see how important this is to him? Even far away in Colombia he has heard about your paella and this is why we are here right now. And you are saying no? THIS is how you treat him?' Jorge scowled, his face inches away from the host who was now a quivering wreck. I do believe we'd have been given exclusive access to the whole of the restaurant for the rest of the night if we'd asked for it after that. No doubt the diners would have already been a bit spooked over the turn of events that had come along and shattered their peaceful cosy candlelit meal and that in itself would free up the table situation.

'If you'd only phoned ahead before leaving Colombia I would have been happy to have reserved a table just for you.' He replied in amongst his struggle to breathe. Unbelievably I couldn't help but feel that there was still the tone of him maintaining that there was no tables for us. He had balls, big fucking balls. I will give him that. Either he was ignorant to the ways of the cartels or he was officially the world's biggest idiot. Either way he wasn't reading the situation the way that he was meant to be. How *everyone* did when plunged into a scenario as this.

Jorge and I were used to the clarity that people would have with us. That we came from the plato o plomo way of living and quite literally. If you weren't happy to play along and accept the silver then you'd then be seeing the lead accordingly. It was this knowledge that fast tracked so many situations. Unlike there inside the Drunken Bandit.

'Are you fucking loco?' Jorge spat at the guy while taking an even tighter grip on him. 'Now my friend is starting to get hungry so lets stop fucking around, ok? You're going to fix us up a table. How you do it that is up to you but you're going to arrange one for us. If you don't, do you know what I'm going to do?'

The host, looking confused wasn't sure if he was meant to answer Jorge or not remained silent while still finding himself grabbed by the collar and thrown from side to side.

'I'm going to slice you up into tiny pieces and then my friend and I are going to have your chef put you into the food. Let's see how fucking famous that paella is of yours once that extra ingredient goes into it. You may think I am not serious si? I am serious, I assure you, amigo.'

Jorge is good value to watch at times. A true master of his craft. Even the words chosen. Spoken by a different person they would undoubtedly have much less of an impact but coming from El Jugador. They arrive with the threat that he appears like he will actually carry out what he says he will. Which in reality he absolutely positively would see through to the bitter end if the requirement was there.

'Oh and would you need me to advise you that if you were to think about calling the police while we dine, that is when we start to talk about your familia, si?'

I think Jorge managed to get his message across. I myself was moments away from offering the host a large payment to facilitate us a table, one that he would not, could not have refused. Jorge, saved me paying out a single peseta through his eagerness to secure us one. My way, I felt, would have been a lot more sensible but Jorge is going to be Jorge.

We were sitting down at a table within minutes. It turned out that one of the couples, despite their dessert having just been served up, had decided to leave early. This freeing up a table for Jorge and I. Naturally word had spread amongst the staff over the latest customers to join them for the night and it was with extreme wariness that the waitress approached us. 'Don't be shy, señorita, come, come' Jorge assured the young girl. It was impossible not to draw the parallels of her age and the teenage girl in Barcelona.

'Can I get you a drink?' She hesitantly asked, eventually stood beside our table.

'Si, a bottle of your best Rioja' I replied. 'And we won't be needing the menu tonight, Paella de Marisco.' - Looking from me to Jorge and back again she seemed surprised at this. 'But señor, Paella de Marisco is a special meal for six diners' She said, evidently doing her sums in her head based on the imbalance of people sat in front of her to what the meal was actually intended for.

'That will not be a problem. Paella de Marisco' I smiled back offering her some closure on the order I was placing. 'Ok, Paella de Marisco, I will bring your wine in a moment, please excuse me' she smiled back, appearing to be a lot more at ease with us than she'd been when first approaching.

Jorge and I sat talking about how we'd now, unexpectedly, found ourselves in Ibiza. If anyone had suggested that to us last week it would have been so far removed from reality it would've been deemed laughable. It wasn't exactly a destination that had ever been on Jorge or mines lists of places to go before you die but even as far away in South America. Ibiza had a reputation as a wild and vibrant island.

Not that we would be experiencing it. I'm sure Jorge would have loved nothing other than a night out to see what the island was all about but as far as I was concerned. After a nights rest at the hotel, we'd get to work the next day and if things were to fall into place we could well be on our way back out of Ibiza within twenty four hours and on our way back to Bogota. We were in the middle of planning the next day and remarking on how the very first thing that needed done was to collect the guns when the waitress started making the preparations for our meal being served up.

It was brought out soon after. While in reality it was being served up with background music of a guitar soloist stood in the corner of the room to provide the restaurant's ambience. This grand meal surely deserved something much more fitting. A hundred trumpet fanfare, at least. It was a sight to behold as the girl, with great difficulty, placed it down onto the table. I'd never understood the expression "eat with your eyes' before until seeing the paella sat there in front of us.

Squid, eel, three different versions of shrimp, mussels. It even boasted SHARK and OCTOPUS. We could see more marine life in front of us on the big bowl than Jacques Cousteau in his little submarine. This was a paella for the ages and was worth the thousands of miles travelling and the unfortunate menacing tone we'd had to adopt to be offered a table. It was worth it all. You always question if TV presenters are simply acting for effect such as in a food show but on this occasion Chucho hadn't been lying when he had dropped by for some paella. He'd actually downplayed it if anything.

While we *had* been discussing the plans for the next day in relation to tracking down Duncan and his wife. The Paella, and Rioja, which by then we were onto our second bottle, had taken over. By the end of the meal I'd ended up demanding that the chef be brought out to the table. After Jorge's show with the host. I fully appreciated that it would've been an apprehensive walk out from the kitchen to us that the chef must've had.

He had no fears on this. I simply, after having what was without any question the best meal of my life, wanted to meet the person responsible for such a creation. To meet and be in the presence of greatness. The look of relief on his face when he realised he was out in front of us to receive praise instead of some crude spontaneous indiscriminate violence was something that Jorge and I found quite amusing.

I passed him twenty thousand pesetas while whispering into his ear that this tip was just for him. The rest of the staff would also be taken care of. He was visibly grateful for the money but equally was just as happy to disappear back to the kitchen from where he'd came from.

'So as we were saying, the plan for tomorrow?' Jorge asked as he scooped up some rice along with a piece of shrimp and crammed it all into his mouth.

'A couple of phone calls to make in the morning and then we see. Duncan has some close contacts in Spain so we start there. Who knows? If things move quickly for us maybe we have time to see for ourselves what this Ibiza nightlife is all about.' I settled with him while dangling a big fat juicy carrot in front of his face. He lit up in the exact way that I knew he would had I suggested going out to a nightclub would've done. That was why I hadn't shared with him the knowledge of someone who may have been key to us locating Peter and Eva Duncan. The exact reason for that because of the fact that the specific individual was going to be found in the very last place I would've wanted to take Jorge to.

'Si, Jorge, maybe we see this famous Space.' I said, safe in the knowledge that once Jorge got inside a place like that I would not be able to control him. Pragmatically though I knew, and after doing my homework had long established, that with a slick customer like Peter

Duncan he personally wasn't going to make it easy for us. The easier option for us was always going to be through the boy.

Chapter 19

Zico

'Oh my god it's DJ Selecao' I heard the girl shout loudly behind me in the line inside Kentucky Fried Chicken. It was the kind of scenario that while in no way a daily occurrence *was* something that I was becoming no stranger to either. Generally what followed would be an exchange where the "fan" would simply just want to have a quick word, usually to do with a set I'd played that they were at or someone wanting to know the name of a particular tune.

That in itself never failed to leave me laughing due to the combination of them trying to imitate an electronic dance track while at the same time doing so from a memory that would not have served them too well from the actual moment that they'd actually heard the tune. It was never, ever replicated in the way that they'd thought it would be.

I was still a couple of customers away from being served so turned around to see just who exactly had shouted my name so publicly and fan girly in a way that, by the looks, had grabbed the attention of not just me stood in the restaurant.

'NO FUCKING WAY!' I shouted back at her which was as much if not more louder than the way she had screamed my working title at me initially. Staring back was the unmistakable smile of Shan, Si's ex from years back. An absolute diamond of a girl and admittedly I'd been a little gutted when the two of them split up as she was so much fun on nights out and also (and never let it be forgotten) was always a good shout for getting the best quality in narcotics, primo like. As is always the case though. When your mate splits up with their other half, no matter how well you got on with them, that pretty much means that you've split up with them as well.

'Shit?! How are you, babe? I haven't seen you in a fucking minute' I said taking her in while my mind was being assaulted with tens and twenties of memories from mad nights and even more deranged mornings in her company. Those excited bouncing all over the car road trips on our way to, at times, mystery destinations to dance for twelve to twenty four hours. The nights in each other company where you simply thought that life could not possibly get any better than that. Those return road trips where, still out of our minds on the cocktail of Class A's we'd taken, at times it had seemed like that it had been the collective will of everyone in the car that had gotten us home safe and sound with Si behind the wheel.

She'd put on a little more weight since I'd last seen her but for Shan that was most definitely a good thing as she'd have had to run around in the shower just to get wet, so thin that she was. Thing is if she was in Ibiza for the reasons that I thought she was then that weight would be right back off her by the time she got on the plane to go home again. Back in the day you would literally have found more meat on the proverbial butchers pencil than you would've done on her. Somehow she'd managed to get her whole wires crossed over the whole "eat sleep rave repeat" mantra. What she lacked in the eating though she more than made up in the area of the raving.

'I'm good, Zico' She said grinning from ear to ear. 'You're looking good too' She said / possibly outright lied. 'The Ibiza sun and lifestyle must be good for you' - 'Are you fucking joking' I laughed out loud at her. 'I've been here for weeks now and I've only had about nineteen hours of sleep and Dracula saw more sun than I've done since getting here.'

It really felt good to see her again. I'm not sure if it was even one hundred percent to do with her and more of what a period of life that she represented to me. The fact that the only time I would ever see her would just happen to be during some of the best nights of my life. It meant that I associated Shan with nothing other than in the best of nights and times.

We were interrupted by the guy behind the counter trying to get my attention so that I could place my order. Once I'd taken care of that I asked her if she wanted to sit with me and have a catch up. I'd planned to just take the food back to the villa but meeting her in there altered that. She said that she was on the food run for "her and the girls" so wouldn't be able to sit and eat but was happy to hang with me for a few minutes before heading back to her hotel.

Reaching this compromise we were sitting in a booth having a catch up within minutes. As, had easily been already assumed, she was over for a couple of weeks of sun and partying. She had her list of which deejays and the nights they were appearing already set in stone like it had all been planned with military precision. I joked with her about if a trip to see DJ Selecao had been pencilled in. Shan with her cutting and dry but very funny sense of humour replied that if I was going to be appearing on one of the nights that they were already scheduled for then yeah, she'd be prepared to go into Space a little earlier to hear me.

'It's been dead weird, but in a really good way, to see you making a name for yourself over recent years. I've even been to a few nights that you were appearing at' She sat there unable to resist dipping into the bag that was sat in front of her. Randomly pulling out a chip from inside every now and again and nibbling on it. 'Aye, it's been a bit of a ride the past few years,' I agreed. 'Still pretty low level though as far as this industry, babe but really? You think I'd swap what I have here for three months back in Scotland?'

'AND you're getting paid to be here' She said which was delivered like it was meant to be some kind of cherry on top. 'To be honest Shan by the time I leave this fucking island I'm probably going to be in more debt than I was before I came out, most of it to Si.' I said, regretting almost every single fucking word of it. Aye, if she'd asked about Si then I could've told her but not only had I straight up mentioned her ex boyfriend's name but had insinuated that he was also out there with me and dealing.

'Si's out here with you?' She asked, a little surprised. I knew the minute that I mentioned his name there would be no throwing of squirrels in her direction. 'Aye, the daft bastard jacked his job to come out here with me, not that we've seen each other twenty four hours a day. I think he was just looking for an excuse to do something like this and found one through me.'

She sat there giggling but you could tell that her mind was elsewhere, even if it was just for a few seconds or so. 'I haven't seen or spoken to him for a couple of years and even then it was because I'd randomly bumped into him at the Blur gig through in Glasgow.'

'Aye Si's just, well, Si. No different to the boy that you went out with,' I said, conveniently leaving out the part about the dealing for a Spanish crime family and the run ins that he'd been having with the Liverpudlian underworld. 'Can't live with him and can't live without him, eh?' I added which in the scheme of things when talking to someone who had actually managed to live comfortably without him for years, possibly wasn't the most sensible of ways to form some speech.

'Well, I'd like to think that after all these years since we split up that is a complete pile of pish, Zico' She laughed back at me with complete validation. 'Tell me about it' I laughed before proceeding to go on and tell her the (edited) story of the night at Amnesia. Truly the real impact of that night could only have been appreciated by someone who knew both the properties of Cocaine as they did with Ketamine and with Shan I was safe with that. She'd sat there with a horrified look on her face, open mouthed before bringing a hand up to cover it while displaying eyes that were about to pop out of her skull.

'He did fucking WHAT?' She screamed. 'Aye, things were frosty for a few days between us after that episode although he done his best to avoid me to escape all the shit he was in' - 'Typical Si, that' Shan agreed rolling her eyes back at me.

'Look, Zico, I'm going to have to get back with the food, it's not like we've got a microwave or cooker in our room,' Shan said almost apologetically over the fact that she was going to have to go. 'Nah, cool, cool' I assured her. 'Listen, what's your plans for tonight with your pals? How's that schedule looking?' I enquired, hoping that since we were both in Ibiza at the same time this chance meeting wouldn't be the last that we'd see of each other again.

'Just a quiet one, we have Masters at Work tomorrow night at Pacha so are just staying here in San Antonio for a few quiet drinks tonight' she replied with a look that hinted that she'd rather have been doing something a little more energetic. Then again this was Shan. Of course she'd have wanted that.

'Any chance you could persuade them to go on a trip to Playa den Bossa tonight instead? Entry and the first six drinks on me' I threw the cat amongst the pigeons. 'And there's also the small matter of Moby if you're not already grabbed by the prospect of DJ Selecao.'

The look on her face at this offer told me way before she even opened her mouth in response that she was open to it. 'Well you know me so well, Zico. All of that is all you needed to say. The girls might take some persuading as they're all on their arse's after KU last night, hence the comfort food which incidentally the colder it gets the less "comfortable" it's going to be. There is one thing though that I better tell you before I go though. Lisa is one of the friends that I'm out with, I thought It would be sensible to say before you go putting names on guest lists.'

I didn't expect that. Aye, Shan and Lisa had connected like a house on fire when it was the regular couples night out to the raves that the four of us had travelled to across Britain for the best part of a couple of years before things had all started to go tits up. I'd never considered that Shan and Lisa would have kept in contact after both their boyfriends had fallen by the wayside. It made sense that they had, considering all that they'd had in common. Still, it was not something that I'd even thought of entertaining when the "fantastic four" had been broken up years before.

I didn't have the luxury of seeing what my reaction had been to this but it had been enough for Shan to make her own assumptions. 'Ok, so I'll take it that it *is* a problem that she's here with me' She said with a completely neutral tone to her. 'No no it's fine, I'm just a bit freaked out that the two of you are out here in Ibiza together. I've not spoken to Lisa for a while now. How is she? She good?' I tried to show that things indeed were cool as far as I was concerned.

'She's great, she's a bit fragile after last night but you know her as good as I do. She'll be raring to go by tonight' Once I'd taken it all on board that they had continued being friends I took on a feeling of one that was of being supremely happy that the pair of them had carried on the friendship long after Si and I had departed from the scene.

It could've been said that two guys like Si and I deserved each other, and the trouble that we brought each other. That applied every bit as much for Shan and Lisa. They definitely deserved each other for friends with whatever benefits it brought them such as summer holidays to Ibiza together.

'Have you met anyone on your side since you and Lisa split by the way?' Shan asked as she stood up and grabbed the brown paper bag from the table. Instantly I thought of Flo. The fact that it was her that had been my first thought was an inescapable fact even though I knew that there had to be elements of "summer love" that had to be taken into account when it came to this girl from London.

Lots of people meet and connect on holiday but taking it further than that isn't always that easy I would imagine. Take yourself away from the hedonistic chemically modified romance filled anything is possible vibe of Ibiza and really? What would be the chances of me being able to regularly see a girl from London? Yet still, when the question was asked, it had still been Flo that entered my mind.

'Nothing too serious Shan but aye, there might be someone' I said non committal which I knew would've done her head right in with me deliberately leaving out the details of it all. 'Seriously, babe. As long as Lisa is cool about it and your other mate I'd love to have you as guests tonight. A lot of nights I've just been going home after my set but I'll be sticking around once I'm finished to see Moby so it would be quality to have a bit of a night with you and Lisa for old times sake. There's no guarantees that he'd be there anyway but you're asking me about Lisa, how would you feel about seeing Si again?' I turned it on its head.

She wasn't fazed by this in any way.

'Just stick my name and plus two on the list, we'll be there.' She assured me as she made to get herself moving. 'Emmmm I'm not even sure if this is embarrassing or not but it needs to be asked, what's your second name?' I said taking my chance while it was there in front of me. She looked at me for a second in thought before, I assumed, realising that actually yes I might not have known her second name. Surnames weren't important in those days.

'Jacobs, Zico. Ok, really need to go, we'll see you tonight' she said quickly. Giving me a quick peck on the cheek as I sat there with part of a chicken burger still being chewed inside my mouth and then was on her heels. Making her way out of the place leaving me there to finish my meal.

The front door could have barely closed behind her before Si was answering the call from me to give him the news of the chance meeting I'd just had. If planned in advance and executed in a sensible fashion. The night itself had the makings of being a good one, epic even. Almost a class reunion of sorts with us all having moved on and (hopefully) capable of being civil to each other.

Placed in a situation that was well removed from the likes of randomly bumping into each other at the supermarket and being forced into some painful smalltalk. Of course though, there was equally the chance of it all going completely tits up with arguments following the past being brought up and Si at the very least needed some advance warning of things. Like I'd said to Shan, it wouldn't have even been certain that Si would've even been planning to be at Space that night but knowing him privately like I did. What *was* certain was that when he learned that Shan was going, listed by me. The fucking A-Team wouldn't have been able to keep him away from the place.

Chapter 20

Si

I really didn't need Zico putting stuff like Shan being there in Ibiza into my head that day. Things had reached boiling point between the Camachos and the O'Hallorans and I really did not need to be thinking about ex girlfriends. The day that I'd met up with everyone else at the golf club I'd learned that, completely going against the message that I had delivered to Ivan. He had, and despite his kids having been threatened, decided against calling the Scousers. What road did he choose instead?

Instead of getting around the table and talking things through he went the other way. He kept supplying on the island and discreetly installed four of his finest men as security at the kindergarten that his kids went to. This was discovered by the O'Hallorans when, after days of inactivity when it came to contact from anyone representing the Camacho family, decided to make good on their thinly veiled threat and sent some of their men to pay a visit to Bambino's.

I'm not sure if anyone really knew what their intentions had been. Could've been just a bit of a reconnaissance. It also however could well have been with more sinister of intentions. They never got a chance to carry out whatever instructions that they'd been given by the Scouse brothers. Chased from the premises by a couple of Camacho soldiers with extremely itchy trigger fingers who had been watching the front entrance, strapped with newly issued Uzis that had been delivered as part of a larger shipment only the night before that they were just waiting on the chance to try out.

No doubt that would not have went down well with the Scousers and judging by the two brothers I'd sat and had a chinwag with. They didn't look like the type that would've been the ones to take something like that lying down. I'd have expected retaliation. So did Ivan.

That day at the golf club he rolled out his plan of action. Until the thing with the Scousers had been brought under control. He was going to be scaling down operations on the island. Choosing to make wholesale supply trades which would be heading back out of the Balearics and towards mainland Spain. That news suited me. It ruled out having to make any more deliveries. Something, after my experience with the Liverpudlians, I was trying to avoid doing as much as possible.

Opposite to that, however. I wasn't exactly chuffed when, as part of him telling everyone the new strategy, he informed us all that he was issuing us all with our own weapon. The O'Hallorans had crossed a line by bringing the kids into things and Camacho intended to react to this in a way that it was certain would not have gone down well with the Scousers.

I wasn't entirely sure what he expected me to do with the handgun that I'd been given to me inside the function suite of the golf course that day. Scratch my back with it? Hit a Liverpudlian goon over the head with it as a cosh? I took the weapon anyway with the advice along with the rest of Ivan's street team that it would be better to have one and not need it than need it and not have it. I stored it in the boot of the car underneath the spare wheel. Figuring that I would be safer with it in there than in my pocket. Chances were I'd have blown my fucking leg off before the day had finished otherwise.

Zico's call to tell me about Shan had come ten minutes after my first call of the day which had come from Ivan to give me the heavy news that Zubi, one of the kids that dealt down the West End had been abducted right as he was in the middle of selling to some tourist. Thrown right into a BMW and sped off into the night never to be seen again until found dragging himself into a local hospital through nothing other than sheer upper body strength the next morning having been shot in both knees. This in addition to other medieval type shit that he'd been subjected to.

Ivan admitted that he did not have any intel with regards to making any kind of retaliatory strike but was most insistent in me being on guard for anything that might come my way. With me not, and never having done so, doing any street dealing I felt that I would have been safe but was still respecting enough with senor Camacho that I would keep my eyes out.

Lying there thinking about poor Zubi and the pain the cunt must've been in. That was when Zico called. Apparently full of the joys of summer telling me tales of how he had just bumped into Shan. It was probably the last fucking thing that I thought he'd be banging on about when I answered his call. I hadn't seen Shan in a good while with the exception of that awkward as fuck time that I bumped into her when I was through in the Weeg to see Blur.

I hadn't even wanted to go to the fucking thing in the first place. That was the ironic part. There was a girl that I'd been trying to get fired into who I'd been talking to at work and she'd mentioned that she fancied going to see Blur. Suddenly I was the biggest fucking fan of the group after that. Rattling off name of songs and albums (after some intelligence work around HMV on Princess Street) and full of talk of "maybe the two of us could go through to the SECC and see them on their tour."

Of course, on this date away to see a group that I couldn't have cared less about all in the name of having sex with someone at a (hopefully) yet to be arranged time. I end up bumping into my ex who I had broken up with under less than cordial terms and in fact, the last time I'd seen her had been one of the worst moments of my fucking life.

I'd be the first to admit that I blew it big fucking time when it came to Shan. With her, I had a princess and threw it all away. She was loving and loyal. She was supportive. She also got the best drugs that I'd ever taken in my life. Put up with me as a soccer casual with The Utility. Nothing that she wouldn't have done for me, Shan.

I fucked it though. Just one night I cheated on her, if you could even call it that. One fucking night. It wasn't like I'd been having an affair behind her back like you see in Eastenders and TV shows like that. Just one night where I made a stupid mistake but fuck me, how I paid for it. I was in Fat Sam's one night, having stayed down in the city centre after a United match with Zico and I keeping ourselves out after the game for a few drinks.

We reached a point where we should've went our separate ways and got ourselves home in time for Match of the Day. Instead, Zico ended up buying ten pills when we were in a boozer which, due to its proximity to the train station, I'd initially thought was the last pub we'd be in before he got himself on a train back home to Fife. Him buying those pills changed things, entirely.

Fast forward to a few hours later and the pair of us were inside Fattie's, two Eckies deep into our night. Any hope of Zico getting on a train having now left the station so to speak. We were talking to these girls, like you do when you're on a pill or two. Just having a wee dance and exchanging a few words. Everybody's in the same boat when it comes to the pills and the music eh? Well the next part I wasn't to find out the full extent of until months down the line but one of the girls in the group that we'd been talking to?

The best way I can explain. It was that the pingers got the better of the two of us at the exact same moment. Which I'm in no doubt had been brought on by the piano break from that FPI Project track. Fucking gets me every single time. Anyway, the two of us, knocked out by whatever shit had been collectively going on inside of us, coupled with that irresistible piece of piano. Ended up kissing each other there on the dance floor. Proper big fucking licks as well too Was no peck underneath the mistletoe type stuff. It was nothing more than a spontaneously unplanned moment.

It didn't go any further than that. It was almost like the pair of us had known that all it had been was a case of the chemicals taking over. We'd barely even said two words to each other but standing there with our hands in the air face to face. It just happened. A smile exchanged, a piece of eye contact that could not have been taken back.

It must've been around six months or so when it all came back to haunt me when one weekend when I was playing Sunday league for Frews Bar. Shan appeared midway through the second half and ran right on the pitch screaming at me while the game was still going on.

When she invaded play she left me in the most surreal of positions. One where I had an opposing midfielder running towards me with the ball and just as I was preparing myself to tackle him I then saw her over his shoulder. Further up the pitch with a face like a Pit Bull chewing a jaggy nettle. Didn't know what the fuck to do, whether to challenge the other boy or not. Taking one for the team, knowing that I had a few seconds before she'd made her way up the pitch. I took the boy out with a challenge that, admittedly, had been more industrious than I'd planned. I'd only wanted to break up the play likes but had ended up catching him a nasty one on the side of his ankle.

This in itself provoked a bit of a response from some of his team mates with me getting shoved around with the referee in amongst us all trying to make sure things didn't escalate further. I stood there trying to deal with these cunts while all the time knowing that, for a reason that I was about to find out, there was far worse to come than a bit of handbags from low level fitba players who were still half pished from the night before.

'WHO IS SHE, SIMON? WHO THE FUCK HAVE YOU BEEN SHAGGING?' She screamed while punching hard on my chest. Both sets of teams and officials not to forget the watching crowd all stopping what they were doing to watch the show unfold. Of course, I didn't have a fucking clue who she was talking about. I hadn't been riding anyone behind her back after all so it wasn't like I had an immediate point of reference to call upon.

A cold hard fact of life however is that if your other half is there accusing you of being up to no good, they've obviously got this from somewhere and in their mind then aye, what they are saying is gospel. When you deny it, like I had done stood there on the pitch. Then as far as they're concerned, of course you're going to fucking deny it. Mad frustrating though when you know that you're innocent, like.

'Babe, I've not been shagging anyone, where you getting this from?' I said trying to calm her down, running my hand up and down her arm. 'DON'T YOU FUCKING DARE TOUCH ME,' she shouted back with some right manic eyes on her. Clearly not in anywhere near to a rational stage of talking. 'And don't fucking lie to me either. I've SEEN you and her together in a picture, oh I've seen the pair of you, Simon.' This didn't make any fucking sense to me but when your girlfriend goes full scale tonto and invades the pitch during a game of fitba then you have to assume that they've got some highly credible shit on you.

'Look son, you can't be doing this on the pitch. We've got a game to be finishing here' The referee, who to fair had been put in a spot that there was no fucking way he'd have been advised on when taking his SFA badges to become a match official, voiced his concerns. I remember that section in Shoot Magazine, "You are the ref" but I definitely don't remember it ever taking on the whole players girlfriends invading the pitch with accusations of infidelity narrative.

'YOU CAN GET TO FUCK AS WELL' Shan turned her attentions towards the ref over his attempts at butting in. He didn't quite know what to do next judging by the look on his coupon. Couldn't exactly give her a red card could he? 'He's right though, babe. This isn't exactly the place for to be doing this.' Risking further mouthfuls from her. I decided to back the ref up. I could hear all the laughs and snide comments from both the crowd and some of the players there on the pitch. I could've done with the ground swallowing me up and just claiming me there and then. Actually, I don't think that there has ever been a more appropriate moment in my life for that to have happened than that morning.

'Look, there must be a mistake here, Shan. Don't worry babe, we'll fix it. You want to hang around until after the game and we'll talk afterwards' I said, wrongly as it was to turn out, thinking that she was now a little more calmer and ready to see reason.

'There isn't going to be any "afterwards," Simon. It's fucking OVER. You know what I told you when we started going out. The ONLY thing that I told you not to do was cheat on me. I put up with your casuals stuff, you looking like a human punchbag half of the fucking time. I never said a word. All I asked was that you didn't cheat You couldn't fucking stop yourself though.' She said, more measured than the ranting she'd been doing initially but you could now see that she had started to cry.

'Right, come on now, enough's enough' The ref said tapping me on the shoulder. - 'FUCK. OFF' I shouted in frustration at him. The penny starting to drop for me that Shan actually was, in fact, in the middle of ending things with me. Through my choice of words I think I managed to gift wrap the decision that the ref was looking for to try and end this situation.

'Right then, son. You know I'll not have that on the field of play, you're off' he replied as he raised the red card triumphantly in the air. It was almost a relief when I saw him pull the card out of his back pocket as I couldn't have stood another second more of shame out there on the pitch. Getting dumped in the most public of ways. Shan and I both left the pitch, me trying to ask her what picture she was talking about while maintaining my innocence to her that I hadn't been cheating on her. She wasn't interested in debating, her mind was already made up by the looks.

Once off the pitch she started walking off in the direction of her car that was parked up beside the pavilion. 'Talk to me, babe. I'll swear on anything you want that I haven't been shagging anyone.' I pleaded with her but was just getting stonewalled. 'The time for talking passed the moment you went behind my back with someone else.' She finally broke her silence as she fiddled with getting her key into her drivers door. 'LOOK, FOR FUCKS SAKE, I HAVEN'T DONE FUCK ALL' I shouted back at her, frustration and the fact that none of it made any sense, by then getting the better of me.

Finally unlocking her door and opening it. Before she got in she paused and looked back at me. 'Oh really? Tell me that after your next visit to Fattie's.' She got in the car and sped off leaving me stood there still in my muddy kit trying to figure out just what the fuck she had even meant by that.

One trip to the club the next weekend and all was revealed to me. Talk about the worst of luck. Inside Fattie's appeared to be some kind of a new promotional campaign going on. As part of this there were posters up in the reception area and also inside the bathrooms. Fairly standard stuff. The posters showing the Fat Sam's clientele all having a good time. Lots of people dancing, big smiles on their faces, that type of deal.

It was one of the posters though where, despite showing a good fifteen people in it dancing, upon further scrutiny you found that there was more than just people dancing in it. Captured also was myself and the girl I'd had that kiss with when Zico and I had went through those ten pills that night. In what had been the personification of bad timing. In the seconds that her and I actually had kissed for, some hired club photographer had taken a picture that none of us were even aware of. In doing so losing me my fucking girlfriend.

I'd had a few drinks after the United match that Saturday. Was already pissed off because Aberdeen had beaten us two nil and to make matters worse the police had managed to keep us and the ASC away from each other outside the stadium after the match. THEN getting inside Fattie's and seeing the poster. It tipped me over the edge. I went looking for management to tell them that I wanted the posters with me on them taken down. Eventually I got this girl who looked like she hadn't even seen her twenty first birthday but anyway she was telling me that she was the manager. I told her that the poster had been used without my permission and I wanted them removed from their promotional campaign.

She asked which poster it was that I was referring to. After pointing it out to her and specifically where I was in the photo. As cocky as you like, she told me that they didn't need my permission to use me because it wasn't a full face photo, only the side. 'Well you and your fucking campaign have just lost me my girlfriend over it,' I answered her back. I don't know why I even bothered. To absolutely anyone it would only have appeared that I *had* been cheating on my girl and was trying to clean things up. Nothing more.

I tried to call Shan so many times following that night to explain to her the whole circumstances of that night but all attempts to call her were knocked back. It was the worst feeling in the world, the feeling of splitting up with the love of your life. That one single person that you wouldn't ever want to live without. Even all of that was heavily eclipsed by the feeling that none of it needed to have happened.

Eventually I got the message though and stopped trying to call her and hadn't seen her for a good while from that morning down at Fox Park.

Of course, the easiest option would have been to just keep the head down and concentrate on not getting shot and killed from some Scousers and not get side tracked over ex girlfriends. I've never been known for taking the easiest of options however. When Zico called me with the news about Shan and Lisa. I didn't even think twice about saying that I'd be there at Space that night.

Chapter 21

Zico

I had been uncharacteristically nervous before my set at Space. It couldn't have been because of the fact that Lisa was going to be there, could it? Well, I tried to convince myself that was the case, at least. At the same time though I could neither deny that the only thing different about the night ahead *was* that Lisa and Shan were coming to see me play. It had been so many years since we had all been under the same roof or, in some cases, in the middle of an agricultural field.

Obviously I couldn't speak for any of the two girls but in the time since we'd last partied. I personally had done a lot of growing up while, impressively, still managing to frequently find many more lessons that still needed learned. Not that I'd be sharing that side with Lisa or Shan if I could. If the pair of them were looking at me, out in Ibiza playing at Space for the summer in the image of someone who was doing well then who was I to stop them.

I honestly could not have seen any upside in telling them that while yes I was playing at Space. I also had a best mate out with me who didn't know the difference between Ketamine and Cocaine. A reprobate who was running around with a firearm while in the real world couldn't even make it past the first level on Virtua Cop. And also, there was, of course, no need for them to know about the whole messy business of whether my dad had some dangerous Colombians chasing after him. Doing good for oneself? Aye, I'll crack the jokes.

It's funny though how someone can be so far out of your mind and then a situation, like bumping into Shan, places that person firmly right there in the front of your mind. That's what it was like with Lisa. At least for the first few years I thought about her quite often. Just those random thoughts that you have no control over that takes you to all types of places. Eventually though those thoughts were popping up every other day, then every other week. That's just how things go, isn't it? Seeing Shan and knowing that I would be seeing Lisa again, however?

It naturally left me raking back up all of those old memories from when the two of us were together.

Me trying to hide from her that when I was going to the fitba I was running with the Utility. Coming home some nights having been booted around some Scottish city, other Saturdays returning back without a hair out of place on my middle parting. The first time the pair of us had sex and how I'd lied to her that it wasn't my first time. Me not thinking that she would want to go to that very first all night Acid House party. Instead, her going with me and life not being anything remotely close to the same again for the both us. That night, quite literally the Big Bang. Year zero of a journey which had taken me to playing records in Ibiza.

Aye, Lisa and I had history and there was no denying that. A time of life where you truly start to find out who you are and the type of person that you want to be. Where you want to go and what you would like to do with yourself. Years later you can often see that the two people have progressed and deviated in their own ways on their individual paths. New priorities, needs and outlooks compared to when, still just effectively kids.

I found myself wondering if she'd met anyone. I second guessed that had she been with another guy then she'd surely be on holiday with him instead of Shan. It wasn't through any sense of jealousy or possessiveness, fuck, of course it wasn't. That ship sailed so long ago it could've navigated the circumference of the globe times over and I'm sure that she felt the exact same on her side. On that subject I knew that there wouldn't have been any issues when it came to Flo who, along with Elle, I expected would more than likely be putting in an appearance for my set as they had been doing since we'd met that first night.

There hadn't been any acrimony when Lisa and I had split. No one had stabbed the other in the back and disrespected the other. There wasn't any reason for ill will or wishes of the other running into any difficulties in life. Just a case of something not working out for two people. Happens every day across the world doesn't it and just because you're not with the person any more doesn't mean to say that you want a world of shit for them with you not being part of it. Well, unless you're a massive cunt, like.

Aye, I was looking forward to seeing them again but it was mixed with a little piece of apprehension which I couldn't work out exactly why on that score.

I guessed that it was nothing other than my own pride but for that specific night I wanted everything to be perfect. I wanted the set to be on point, the records complete bangers and crowd pleasers. I even made more of an effort for what gear I was wearing for the night when generally a pair of ZX on my feet and shorts and t shirt was enough. I couldn't stand the heat there inside the booth to wear anything further than that.

For that particular night though? I found myself planning on what to put on and before I knew it I had the white Stone Island long sleeved shirt on, the one that I'd been too fucking scared to even wear after purchasing it. This based on the fact that it was so crisp and white I had the fear that I would destroy it after one wear. Dirt from the less than clean DJ booth. A burned hole from a hot rock. Some pisshead being sick over the back of it. I was no better than one of those cunts who buys a classic car and then doesn't want to take it out the garage in case a bird breathes on it never mind dropping its guts.

And yet without barely any consideration I'd found myself shoving it on my back. Once that was chosen there was no stopping me. Next was my special pair of Valentino chino shorts that (in my own fantasy world) I'd had over with me in case of a very special occasion. In my own delusions. That special occasion was going come near the end of my stay on the island.

I'd have made my bones behind the decks at Space on the terrace and eventually received the invite to play in the main room. I'd figured that being there for the best part of three months. I'd have been in with the bricks by that point. A pair of Adidas Stockholms on my feet and I was ready for the off. I'd had to leave earlier for Playa den Bossa as Lee had arranged for me to meet up with him for something to eat before my set. Ever the sound cunt, he had let me choose where we ate so I had opted for La Boca. A place that I swear you would rob your own own gran with a hypodermic needle for the money to have one of their Argentinian steaks with Chimichurri sauce.

I travelled through alone to meet him with everyone else following later on in the night in their own groups. Setting aside the fact that I was being offered the chance to have a big bastard of a steak on the house so to speak. I had held some resentment towards Lee's timing of his plans as it was clashing with the evening match from the European Championships. With his gift of the gab though he could literally talk you out of going to your mum or dads funeral if he had the motivation to do so. He was banging on about how he'd not had a proper face to face with me for weeks and since he was in town for the night he wanted to meet for dinner.

Yes, technically we hadn't seen each other since that night of Amnesia that I'd spent as much of my free time as possible trying to forget but it wasn't like he'd exactly been a stranger either. Barely a day would go by without Lee calling for some reason or other. Reasons for him calling me would range from motivational speeches telling me which big gun European nightclub and event owners would be in attendance to see me play to checking that I was taking care of the basics like eating and sleeping.

When I arrived, Lee was already sat there at the table sipping on a glass of wine. With the waiter showing me to my seat and asking what I would like to have to drink. Lee had no hesitation in butting in and telling the waiter something 'non alcoholic.' 'Just a Coke por favor' I said as I sat down. 'Professionalism is all that I offer and it is all that I ask, muckah' he winked at me. 'Of course, of course. You know me, Lee. I just say no, almost as if I went to Grange Hill' I laughed back. - 'If only that were true you little lying bastard' he said, both jokingly and seriously. He took his eyes off me and picked up the menu.

Already knowing before I'd even left San Antonio what I was having. I took a moment to look around the place. It had charmed me from the very first time I'd visited with its stone walls that looked like if you breathed on them chunks of stone would fall out. The walls themselves painted in the blue and yellow of the Argentinian institution, Boca Juniors. I'd never been to Argentina in my life but just by being inside there it gave you the distinct feeling that, at least for the duration of your meal, you could as well have been sitting in down town Buenos Aires.

'Not hungry?' Lee asked peering at me from over the menu still in his hands. - 'Very much so, Amigo' I assured him as I clocked the waiter approaching with my my bottle of Coke. 'Your drink, señor' he said with a nod, setting it down on the table for me. 'Are you ready to order now?' He asked. With me sat nodding my head at this before telling him that he just needed to bring me the biggest size of steak they had in the kitchen.

'Jesus fahking aitch, Stevie. You should've given me advance notice that I needed to remortgage the house before taking you out for dinner, mate,' Lee joked. - 'Oh aye, which house would that be then? The one in London, Manhattan or Madrid?' I joked back reminding him that if any one out of the pair of us could afford to spring for a steak dinner it was him. 'Touché, smart bastard' he laughed back before looking up at the waiter and confirming that he also had nailed down his order. 'Carbonada for me and another glass of Cabernet Sauvignon, Senor'- 'Excellent, hombres' the waiter smiled as he collected both menus from back off the table and disappeared again in the direction of the kitchens.

'So what's been happening, my son' Lee said just before polishing off what was left in his wine glass in anticipation of his second glass being poured. 'How's the villa? How have you been getting on with everyone at Space? Been doing any networking so far? Is your father still here on the island? You recovered from the devastation of our boys beating you Jocks at Wembley yet?' He continued while leaving me without the first fucking clue what he wanted me to answer first.

That was classic Lee though. The man moved and spoke at a hundred miles an hour, always. The ironic part being that he contained all the hallmarks of an amphetamine or Cocaine abuser but in actual fact was more anti drugs than Nancy fucking Reagan. To be fair, considering he did business in the sector that he did. Where drugs were a staple ingredient to how it all worked. He could've chosen a better vocation.

'Ehh, aye, all good, Lee.' I replied not even sure myself which question I had answered. 'The villa's tree men dos, as they say around these parts,' I continued. Now I wasn't looking for him to physically piss himself right there in front of me but I thought my well planned out way of working a Spanish pun into my answer would've at least raised a smile from him. Too intelligent for him, my own guess.

That or he probably wasn't listening and was already thinking about something else that he needed to do for one of his other roster of Deejays who were anywhere from Ibiza to India and Moscow to Melbourne. The only man I know that needs to carry a spare battery for his phone as it always runs out on him each day. I don't know how he manages it considering my phone would normally go two to three fucking weeks before needing to charge it up?

'The only thing about the villa is that I can't seem to fucking lock the place up. I mean, I'm sure the place is locked when I leave but there's been times I've got back and it's been unlocked and people have been in. Not robbers and shit like that though, don't worry about that. Just Si and my dad.' I said which was more to cover my arse if some cunts *did* rob the place and take the decks that Lee had acquired for me than anything else. 'Yeah no worries, Stevie. I'll get a plumber round to look at it in the morning, don't worry we'll get it fixed' he answered me back. By doing so, completely validating my suspicions that he hadn't been paying attention.

Before I could correct him he started up a new line of conversation by asking how things had been going with my dad. 'Barely seen him, Lee,' I said which was a convenient truth as I sat there with him. I couldn't be doing with talking about Pedro Duncan. The bastard had been making me tired all over and there was just this nagging feeling that there was more to what he'd sat and told me that day. It hadn't been a lie though to say that I had barely seen him. Technically I'd seen his wife more than I'd seen him since they arrived.

'I wonder if someone like your dad when it comes to employment. Needs to plan their holidays in advance, you know? Submit a request in writing so they can then go on and book their trip?' Lee said, trying to by funny but, being honest. His whole fascination towards my dad's line of business had started to wear a little thin with me. I totally got it at first as there's undeniably a novelty factor at play but he'd had enough time for that to wear off by then. It wasn't like I had told him much in the way of details anyway. Just that my dad worked in South

America and was involved with a cartel. That was where it ended. I'm not exactly wise in the ways of narcotics syndicates and how they operate but I'd have thought that one of the golden rules was discreetness. I was hardly going to be running around stopping traffic to tell the drivers that my dad Peter Duncan worked for the Bogota Cartel in Colombia, was I?

'I'm not sure, mate. Maybe send a fax to the cartel's human resources department and I'm sure they'll be able to tell you.' I said, intending on coming across as sarcastic but by doing so still had Lee laughing back at me. 'I'm not even sure that he's doing it anymore going by what Eva his wife was saying.' I tried to throw a wee bit of piss onto Lee's bonfire.

'Eva, your mum?' he said, attempting to rib me. 'How's it working out having a mum that would've went to high school with you then by the way?' He asked which I guess was one of the more obvious questions that are just waiting there to be asked when the topic of Peter and Eva was on the menu.

'Confusing, mate. So very confusing.' Pretty much all I could reply back on the subject.

Over the course of the meal we got talking about how things had been going professionally. The feedback he'd been getting from both the owners of Space and from other deejays about me had been one of a positive nature in terms of the impression I'd been making with my sets. 'You know the way this game works by now, you're a fucking snowball Stevie and you're only going one way my friend. This time next year you'll be back here on this island but wait and see the crowds you'll be playing to.' Whether he was talking some Arthur Daley bullshit or not I couldn't help but smile at his sheer energy and enthusiasm he had towards me.

'What about Amnesia though?' I asked, with good cause. 'Let's not kid ourselves here, Lee. Amnesia was a fucking disaster. Worst set I've ever played in my career. How many fucking times did I leave the room without any music playing? I launched a cup at the crowd. As far as when I was in Carl Cox's dressing room? I've done all I possibly could to erase that particular memory and it is still there haunting me.

I've heard that some Romanian gypsies can do things to you which chases bad memories and nightmares away and I'm one step away from going down that road to tell you the truth. Who the fuck knows what Carl Cox has went on to tell people about it. Si and I almost came to blows over it mate and him and I have *never* been close to that stage in our life. Surely Amnesia must've sent me sliding back down that fucking snake, no?'

In reality, my performance had probably been forgotten by the next day for the majority of people who had been inside Amnesia that night. Through their rose tinted spectacles. All they would remember was that they had an Eckie and went out and had the best night ever and they would then be looking forward to going out later that night and doing it all over again and having another best night ever. It was more the people that weren't out their tits partying that mattered more on a night like that where a best first impression was the numero uno priority.

Deliver on a stage like that when you're opening for a House Music legend inside one of the scene's clubbing cathedrals and there's no telling what that does to your career. Instead, I quite literally lost my mind while in the presence of said House Music legend and threw a missile at a paying customer inside said cathedral. 'Well that's the thing, mate. You'd have thought that eh? I'll be honest, I was shitting bricks that night. I'd talked you up so much. I had you filling in for Morillo for fahks sake'

'When I walked into Carl's dressing room. The first thing I noticed was the look on his face, not the fact that you were clearly away with the fairies' - I cringed at the thought of it all over again, well, the fuzzy flashes that I could recall. K holes are not the best places to be receiving too good a reception from the outside world and I feel that I may be grossly understating that fact when I say it.

'BUT the Amnesia forum on the internet the next day was going crazy about you. I don't know how you managed it but that abomination of a set actually has had everyone talking about you. As you know, that wasn't the average set that you'd normally see.' Lee said, almost in disbelief. 'What the fuck is wrong with people?' I laughed while still very much asking the question.

'I'll be expecting a call from Amnesia soon to book you, mate. They're so predictable. Don't worry about Coxy either. We've known each other since way back before Acid House. I called him the next day to apologise for anything you'd done.' He assured me. 'Yeah I was going to call him but was too embarrassed so left things,' I interrupted while on that subject.

'He actually pissed himself laughing, like proper belly laughs down the phone when I told him the full story. He said that you'd tried to tell him about that as well as a lot of subjects but that you weren't really capable of gathering thoughts and then putting them into a way of delivering them from your mouth. Carl said that it was a minor miracle that you managed to go through with your set.' Lee continued in such a chilled way that it instantly had the same effect on myself.

'So him and I are good then?' I asked, digging for that last bit of confirmation which Lee would possibly have already assumed I'd pegged onto by then already. 'You're sweet as a fahking nut, Zico. He's talking about getting a slot for you at this big top event in Finsbury Park in London next month if we can work it out between your duties over here.'

What a boost he'd given me. Probably just the exact thing I was looking for and whether it was only just mind games from Lee to up my morale and nothing more. I wanted to believe him, so did. You never know with him. There's times where he can be like the fitba manager who tells his rank rotten striker that he's as good as Maradona.

Noticing that time was beginning to get on. I asked him if he was taking a taxi up to the club with me. Instead, he said that he was actually heading to Ibiza Town as he had some important business to take care of at Pacha. He was flying back to England the next morning but said that he was over again in a weeks time so would catch a set from me then. I was still waiting for the taxi arriving when the waiter brought the bill out. It had been worth traveling through earlier in the night just so I could have one of those steaks but the cherry on the cake was seeing his face when he clocked the fucking price of one.

It brought up a memory of a family tea for my birthday once that I found myself looking back a lot more fondly then than I had at the time. 'It was worth every single peseta.' I laughed, already sensing that his reaction to the bill had been related to my choice of meal. 'What? all those thousands?' he asked, seriously.

'Well, you get what you pay for. my friend,' I said in justification. 'Yeah and that's why you get paid peanuts you cheeky little cahnt now get your skinny arse up to Space and do the Ragamuffin Agency proud. I'll see you next week but will bell you in between then.' He replied, completely burning me in the process. We exchanged a brief man hug before I left. Lee almost starting to call someone on his phone before we'd fully let go of one another.

With time having run away with itself back at the restaurant. I only walked through the front doors of Space around five minutes before I was due on. A wee meal with Lee and then up to Space for a catch up with everyone before me heading into the booth had been the original plan. Lee talks some amount of pish at times, though. If it's something that you could sum up in a couple of sentences he'll take ten fucking minutes to tell you. Also has about half a dozen topics going on at one time and like Billy Connolly he would always get himself back to the original thread, eventually. Add in the fact that the size of steak I ordered should've technically taken six hours for a human being to eat but I'd rushed it! This all meant that I was only arriving right at the end of Jalisco's (the local DJ that was on before me) set.

Due to the unusually large crowd that was out there that night. It was around four songs in before I made them out in the crowd. I can't even describe how surreal a feeling it was to look out there from the booth and see Si beside Shan and Lisa. Big smiles on their faces and all going for it on the dance floor just like those early years of Acid House. The only thing that was missing down there was moi.

Obviously I had other duties to attend to. Seeing them all like that though was enough to give me the type of rushes that it would've generally taken a Class A to provide. Despite always having my set planned before I went out and played. Seeing my friends like that out there soon had me digging out some older tunes from back in the day. Our day. Doing so just out of the buzz I'd get at their response when they heard whatever random tune being mixed in. Outlander - Vamp, Moby - Go, Human Resource -

Dominator. The fact that the rest of the crowd were responding in the most passionate of ways was merely an added bonus. I was playing for my three mates whether anyone else liked it or not.

Around forty five minutes into the set. I noticed Flo and Elle on the other side of the room dancing away with each other. Flo had this fluorescent necklace around her but from what I could see, it had leaked because she was glowing in the dark in certain areas of her hair, parts of her top along with the more consistent glowing ring that was around her neck. For a second the two of us caught each others gaze. I tried to point towards her top but I was out of international sign language. How the fuck are you meant to say silently that someone has what looks like radioactive material on their top? She just smiled back at me with one of those chemically assisted grins that for a moment looked even brighter than her necklace.

By the time it was approaching half an hour to go of the set I was, by then, just itching to join everyone else and get on with the night's capers. Seeing Lisa with Si and how friendly they all looked, not to mention the fact that they looked like they'd all had a pill or two. I already knew things were going to be cool in terms of speaking to her. The first thing I was going to be doing was to get hold of Flo and Elle and take them over with me so everyone would be all in the one place before things started to get messy. That again was another thing that I knew would be fine. The me and Flo thing and Lisa being part of the group. It was hardly like Lisa and I had just broken up the week before.

I was only half a dozen songs away from the end of the set though when I found Si in the booth beside me. Not even fucking sure how he'd got in there but I'd turned my back to pick a record out of my box and the next thing he was stood there. Weirdly for someone who'd been getting fired into the pingers, stood there with a straight face to him.

'What's happened?' I automatically asked. Whatever it was, I already knew I wasn't going to be much a fan of. 'Look, I think something's about to go down, Zeec and you need to get out of here, pronto' he said urgently. 'Eh? What you talking about man?' I said laughing while hoping that whatever he was on about was just him fucking about with me.

'I'm fucking serious, man,' He replied. His face appearing to back up the words. 'Listen to this. I was having a pish in the mens and there was these two older guys in there. You know when you just see someone and you just know there's something not right? Well there was *nothing* fucking right at all with these two cunts. Absolute beasts, the pair of them. The clothes they were wearing was absolutely fuck all like you'd ever expect to see anyone wearing at a place like this, not even like some of those radge Germans in their vests and stuff like that. They didn't exactly look like they were here for a night out their tits listening to their favourite deejays, put it that way.'

Still not sure where he was going with all of this. I told him to hang on a moment so that I could take care of bringing the next tune in. As part of my unintended trip down memory lane. I'd went with Liquid - Sweet Harmony. The spontaneous reaction of the crowd to the piano break that I brought in, more frenzied than if it had been dropped at The Eclipse or Shelley's at the beginning of the decade. All those smiling happy faces in the crowd. No doubt the combination of the piano break and the MDMA attacking their senses taking them to a place that was so at odds with me in the booth. Stood there knowing that Simon had something for me that I probably wasn't going to want in any shape or form.

'So I'm washing my hands and next thing. One of them joined me at the sink to my left and then the other on my right. Two big bastards, like. Anyway, one of them turns to me and starts asking me about you. Didn't talk about you by your DJ name though and that was what set the alarm bells ringing. The man actually asked if "DJ Duncan" was playing and at what time.' - If it hadn't been for the fact that it was a couple of big looking cunts that were looking for me that DJ Duncan part would've probably been mildly amusing but Si wasn't getting any laughs from my direction. 'Annnnnd' I pressed him.

'Well I'm not fucking daft am I, mate? Two scary looking cunts talking with Spanish accents in broken English looking for you? I'm hardly going to say that you're up on the decks but to hang about as you'd be finished in a few songs, eh?' He said, erratically considering I'd never accused him of doing anything of the opposite in the first place. 'I told them that you were due on the decks in about half an hour but that traditionally you normally arrive just as you're due on so to avoid being hassled by fans and that if they wanted to catch you for a word they'd need to hang around. As far as they're concerned the DJ after you *is* you but you need to get yourself to fuck before they find out otherwise. Look Zeec, Peter's told me a wee bit about some of the shit that's going on and why he's in Ibiza. You don't think that.' He didn't bother to finish, unable to find the words but they weren't required in any case.

'I'm not sure I should hang around to find out. You going to stay here with the girls? Find Flo and Elle and tell them why I've disappeared as well, and for fucks sake be creative please, mate. If you can at all avoid telling them the fucking truth then it would be very much appreciated. Oh and mucho important here. Maybe give it half an hour after I'm gone but go to the front door and ask for Nando and describe the two that were in the toilets. He'll take care of it.'

I'm not sure where I was able to even find such clarity but it had dawned on me that if these men knew to come to Space looking for me then what would be to stop them from coming the next time I was playing, or any other time. I figured that Nando and some of the other security would find the two of them and then from that point on they'd have been wasting their time trying to get into Space at any point from then on. He even had the nickname "Elephante" due to his talent for never forgetting a face.

It could all have been just a whole lot of fuck all but with the way things had been with my dad. Personally I had been waiting on something happening in whatever varied ways that could have meant. Being told that two strangers with Spanish, and by that loose definition, South American accents were looking for me was just the exact type of thing that fitted into that category of "something."

'Cheers mate, lucky it was you that bumped into them than some loved up and helpful clubber who would've been only happy to assist.'

I said, thanking him as I got my records together having already signalled to Alberto, who was on after me and already standing patiently in the booth waiting, to get himself ready for taking over from me.

With there being no such thing as too much paranoia. I got hold of the first security that I could find and asked him if he could let me out by a different exit other than the front one. Once outside, I jumped into the first taxi that I saw with the orders of 'just drive' handed to the driver.

I wasn't exactly chuffed over the fact that I'd been robbed of the chance to have a night with the old crew mixed with the new one. The expression bigger fish to fry was inescapable though. This, I felt was what looked like the beginning of whatever the fuck my father had set in motion back in Colombia. That whatever shit he had landed himself in was so big that it had been enough to follow him from continent to continent. Over that taxi journey back to San Antonio I'd tried to convince myself that I was overreacting and that this was all just a combination of all the Ching I'd been doing since getting to Spain. A case of what details my dad had given me and my mind taking that and running with it. Possibly these two men were owners of another club and had come to watch me play, I surmised? My gut, as well as my head, knew better though.

Chapter 22

Zico

'Buenos dias Stevie my lad, what's going on?' came the cheery voice down the other end of the phone. Unnaturally chipper for my dad all things considered. By the time him and I were done with the call however. I was quite sure that he was going to be left in a whole lot less sunny of a mood than when he'd answered. 'Oh you know the score, pops. Living the dream eh. Sun, sea, sand, getting paid to do what I love. Being hunted by dangerous looking South Americans, you know? All standard stuff really'

That got his attention.

'What happened, son? You ok?' he asked. Suddenly sounding nervous. The wind well and truly removed from whatever sails he'd had. 'Well for now I am but the question is what the fuck are you going to do about this?' I'd never spoken to my dad in such an authoritative way in my life but then again. Him nor I had never encountered such a unique situation like this as a father and son. I wasn't in the mood for letting him speak. This was a call where he was going to be doing the listening and I the talking.

'I knew the moment that you appeared out of the blue with tales of things going wrong in Colombia that everything was going to turn to shit here and well, here we are.' - 'Who' was all that he managed to get out before I continued. 'Two guys came looking for me in Playa den Bossa last night and if it wasn't for Si then fuck knows how it would've all turned out. I managed to sneak out before having to face them but I'm assuming that this won't be the end of it. The main question I have is that why the fuck are they coming looking for me when it's obviously YOU that they're after, actually don't even fucking answer that because I'm not sure that my head would be able to handle what the reason is.' Once the words started they weren't for stopping.

'How do you know that this is connected to me?' Was all he could say back. His response was disappointing, really poor stuff. Can you believe the nerve of him? Oh aye, every single day of my life I have menacing looking gangsters looking for me. Normally before I've even had a chance to have my breakfast. 'Are you fucking serious, dad?' I shouted back at him in a mixture of disbelief that he'd try that shit and disgust that rather than take ownership of the situation. Instead, he was appearing to try to excuse himself from any blame.

'You seriously trying to suggest to me that you appear on the run from Colombia and the next thing strangers are snooping around looking for me through what my surname is and that the two things aren't connected?' I rammed my point home to him. It felt so strange to be talking to him in such a way but this was where he'd brought us both to.

'I think you should stay away from the club for a while, Stevie' he eventually spoke up. Conveniently skipping past the part about me being correct and that yes he had indeed caused all of this. Choosing to neglect all of that. Fast tracking himself right into concerned parent mode. 'Dad? That is the *exact* fucking reason why I'm here. If I'm not at Space then I'm not getting paid and well, there's not much point me even being here if that's the case.'

'Yeah I know, I know but if these two are who I think they are then they're going to be like a dog with a bone, son.' I wasn't liking what I was hearing. The tone of his voice had such a threatening side to it. 'So fucking sort it out then?' I shouted in exasperation, letting the fear and frustration inside me boil over.

'I'm afraid it might be too far gone to fix, Stevie.' He said, sounding utterly defeated by the situation. 'If they've come as far as Ibiza then I'm imagining that they haven't come all this way for a couple of beers with me before heading back home again.' I couldn't believe how relaxed he sounded despite his obvious concerns.

'It's fucking despicable what you've done by coming here. All the places in the world that you could've bolted to and instead you head towards the one part of the world that I was in. KNOWING that there was a chance that cartel would be following you. I knew you were selfish but didn't realise what an elite level you were operating on.' I went off on one at him. 'What kind of a fucking parent does something like that? Should be ashamed with yourself but of course, you won't be.'

'Now you hold on' he tried to interrupt. 'No you fucking hold on, dad. I'm over here trying to make a go at something career wise and you appear with secret wives my age and Colombian hitmen chasing after you. I'm trying but failing to see any part of that which you may have thought was a good idea to come here.' It wasn't like my father was a stupid man, quite the opposite actually. With that in mind he would've full well known the risks of what he was involved in and what repercussions would follow. So to then head right in my direction was a pretty poor move on his part.

'Look, Stevie, I know emotions are running a little high right now and you're saying stuff that you don't really mean but you need to listen to me here. These people are dangerous. This isn't football hooligans here, you understand? At least for the next two to three days you need to keep your head down, lay the fuck low.' I was listening to every word he was saying but despite the fear that he was doing a pretty fucking job of striking into me. I had no intentions of going hermit.

It would take some ten commandments plague of locusts type scenario to stop me from making the most of the potential for the debauchery of Ibiza, and anyway. Don't go anywhere near the club. Keep my head down? If the Colombians knew where the rented vila that I was staying at was. They could've quite literally let themselves in like every other Tom Dick and fucking Harry if they'd wanted to.

It was hardly a fortress that I was living in with a fucking moat around it and drawbridge. If these two Colombians were determined and skilled enough. They would eventually work out where I stayed if they couldn't find Peter. It didn't really matter if I stayed away from the club or not. There was nothing about any of it that was reassuring.

As far as the call to my father had went. I'd called him with the sole intention of seeking reassurance and by the time it was over he'd only left me even less assured than when I'd picked up the phone.

Chapter 23

Eva

'Oh come on Peter, not again' I cried out to him in disbelief. Well, possibly not quite "disbelief" because that hubby of mines really was capable of anything. It was all I could say in response to his sudden news that, once again, he was giving me a warning to get my things together because we were leaving, and fast.

He'd taken a call from Stevie which, without knowing all of the content, I had been still able to hear and see enough from Peter to know that it had heavily impacted on him. He'd went to make a call immediately after the one with Stevie had ended but then hesitated for a second before walking out onto the balcony. He slid the door behind him before he continued with making it.

It was when the glass doors slid open once again that he came back in announcing that it was time for us to be checking out. 'Look, Eva. This hotel was only meant to be a stop gap until Sal had sorted things on his end. Until then though I don't think it's too good an idea if we stay in the same place for long. I've sorted out a villa for us just outside San Antonio Bay, now get yourself packed.' He said in that same commanding tone that I'd heard back in Bogota. This time around it was a lot more easy for me to read between the lines of his erratic behaviour. It was also a damn sight easier to pack. It's quite simple when you barely have anything to pack.

I knew more of the background so was fully aware that whatever it was that he wasn't telling me. It was likely a case of being something that, for the purposes of getting some sleep at night, would have been best I didn't know. I complied and quickly started throwing the sparse belongings that I had into the suitcase. It wasn't even just the fact that this was an almost identical scenario to the one that had seen us flee Colombia that had made all of this feel, normal.

I'd watched the failing of the man over the previous days, weeks even until it had got to the point that there wasn't much that he was going to say or do that would've registered with me as *out* of the ordinary. What even was the ordinary any more though? Stuck here in Ibiza with no idea how long for and even less idea where the next destination was going to be. All the while with a husband who would come and go more than Karma Chameleon.

The paranoia, the sheer unpredictable and randomness to him and then there was the amount of Coke that he had been doing. It was rare enough to see him do it around me but from arriving in Ibiza he had taken off and went in the completely opposite direction on that front. It would've been foolish of me to not see that the paranoia and the erratic behaviour were not exactly mutually exclusive when in the same post code as the Cocaine.

You try telling a man who is on the run from a Colombian cartel and is carrying god only knows what thoughts around in his head that he is doing too much of the white stuff. I tried it once, didn't work and I won't be trying again thank you very much. I saw a side to Peter that I'd never seen before or would wish to ever witness again the afternoon that I had broached the subject on his excessive use of the powder.

Just that one "suggestion" that I felt he had been hitting the powder a bit much turned him into a raving and snarling nasty piece of work who completely unloaded verbally on me. There was nothing there at all stood in front of me that came even close to resembling the man that I fell for, changed my life over and married. I literally didn't recognise him as he unleashed hell on me. Shouting that I didn't get to decide when he'd had or hadn't had enough. In an attempt to prove his point, racking up an extra large line on the bedside table in the hotel room and destroying it there and then in front of me before continuing with his tirade.

I, apparently, did not understand the pressures that he had been under since we had fled Colombia. All of what he was facing and dealing with to try and keep him and my owns heads above water and to keep us in the black. We'd had some major fights over the years and no mistake and when we entered that arena. I certainly was never what you could describe as a wallflower.

That day though? What he had in his eyes and the razor sharp venom that he delivered his monologue with. I felt that only bad things was ever going to come out of me fighting his fire by grabbing the jerry can and pouring petrol on top of it. Truth be told, he scared me that day for the very first time in our marriage.

'ALL THE FUCKING RISKS. ALL THE DANGER I'VE WENT THROUGH FOR US. FUCKING POLICE, D.E.A, INTERPOL, FUCKING SNAKES THAT YOU NEVER KNOW IF THEY'RE GOING TO KILL YOU FROM ONE MINUTE TO THE NEXT. EVERY SLIMY MENDACIOUS FUCKER THAT WORKS IN THE BUSINESS THAT YOU HAVE TO CO-EXIST BESIDE. YOU WALK AROUND IN YOUR FUCKING LOUBOUTINS WITH NO CONCEPT OF WHAT IT TAKES FOR THEM TO BE ON YOUR FUCKING FEET YOU CLUELESS CUNT. NOW UNLESS IT'S ESCAPED YOUR ATTENTION. YOU AND I ARE IN A PILE OF SHIT HERE AND I'M TRYING TO GRAB HOLD OF THAT SLIPPERY SHIT COVERED ROPE TO TRY AND PULL OURSELVES BACK OUT OF IT SO SPARE ME THE FUCKING LECTURES OVER HOW MUCH COCAINE I'M PUTTING UP MY FUCKING NOSE.'

He shouted at me, so close that saliva would occasionally spray my face due to the ferociousness he was yelling at me with. I actually thought that he was going to hit me at one point such was the rage that he'd flown into. The speed of zero to sixty that he exploded. All from one concerned comment from me was staggering. Had he actually hit me then that would've been something that he would not have been able to talk his way out of. I know some wives and girlfriends can live with that kind of shit but I aint the one.

Instead, I think very much aided by the fact that I was not retaliating and most probably stood there with a frightened look on my face. Once his temper had began to simmer he appeared to realise just how much he had lost it with me and was instantly regretting the extremities of his actions. Not that this incident changed things in any shape or form. He carried on with the excessive amount of Cocaine in terms of daily intake and like I said. I just chose not to mention it again at any further point.

In the early days of us arriving on the island I'd been spending more time with Si and Stevie than I had been with Peter so I had never really had the chance to see whatever it was that he'd been getting up to. With things ever changing though. Stevie meeting Flo and understandably wanting to spend time with her before she would go back to England, Si had his work that he did during the day. I was more forced to be around Peter or at least see him at intervals over the day before he dashed out to do something or other.

I actually followed him one day without him realising it. Threw on the biggest pair of Elizabeth Taylor style shades that I had and popped my big straw sun hat on my head and carefully tailed him. I followed stealthily behind at distance as he walked along the vibrant San Antonio street full of restaurants, bars and tourist shops until he stopped to take a call. After putting the phone back into his pocket, instead of carrying on along the street he stayed put. Standing there by the side of the kerb.

It was a few minutes later that the car came whizzing down the road and screeched to a stop right beside him before the driver reached over and opened the passengers door for him to get in. I instantly recognised both the car and driver. It was Si.

I'd felt it slightly strange. If he was meeting up with Stevie for a chat or something like that then that would've been all perfectly normal but Si? Why would Peter be arranging to meet up with Stevie's mate? Why the secrecy also? I'd found it suspicious that he had been picked up somewhere other than right outside the hotel. Why hide something like that? So many why's. It was only days after that when Peter was in the shower when his phone had went and I answered it for him. A Scottish accent asking for him. I, assuming that it was Stevie said that his dad was in the shower and I'd get him to call back once he was out.

'No, Eva, it's not Stevie, it's Simon' he corrected me. We spoke for a few minutes of small talk before I, attempting to get to the bottom of this thing with him and Peter, asked him if I could pass on a message.

Not, I'll have him call you back but a very definite what is the reason for this call.

'Ehmmm, nah Eva just get him to give me a bell back when he has time, like' He replied in the most cagey of ways. He obviously wasn't much up for spilling any beans but I could tell that he was hiding something so I went in on him while he was still semi rattled. 'So you two are getting pretty pally aren't you? How did all that come about then?' I asked, knowing that if he didn't give me an answer to that inside an acceptable amount of time then it would once more provide further evidence that the pair of them were up to something.

'Ehmmmmm, well, like, ummmmm' - I felt was not exactly the best of starts from Si if his intention was to leave me believing whatever was next about to come out of his mouth. 'I think that like, you know, all the stresses he's had recently. He could really do with someone to talk to, a friend like, you know? He finally managed to pluck some words out of fresh air. It actually did make sense what Si was saying though.

We all need someone to talk to about something at times and on some of those occasions that person that you can let it all out to might not always be the most obvious one that you think of. If he couldn't speak to me then fair enough. I'd almost have been willing to give Peter the benefit of the doubt over the fact that he probably didn't feel like he could talk to Stevie about it. Any self respecting father would've kept things away from Stevie as much as they could so it made sense for him to get things off his chest via Simon.

I'm not buttoned up the back though. I could tell that he was lying to me, making it all up on the spot. Peter at no point had mentioned this "friendship" between the two of them. I decided to humour him though and said that I'd let Peter know he'd called and that hopefully I'd see him and Stevie soon for another night out at Space which he was in full agreement over.

The clincher was when Peter eventually came back out of the shower to get himself dressed for the day and me telling him about missing the call from Si. His reaction, to me, a disappointing act of scratching his head while rhetorically wondering why Si would be calling him. Like all the other things that were undoubtedly going on behind the scenes and under my radar, I just looked the other way while praying that somehow it was all going to start working itself out. What is it Dolly Parton said about if you want the rainbow you have to put up with the rain?

The darkness though, clearly still ruling the skies while I found Peter, with the fear of god on his face, clearly agitated over whatever that earlier call had entailed. Telling me to get my stuff together as we were leaving for the villa he'd rented. None of this had the feel that things were entering the crock and of gold stage.

Chapter 24

Si

One goal, one miserly fucking goal. That's all we needed. One.Fucking.Goal! It was the very first thing that popped into my head when I came to in that, for those initial moments of waking at least, strange hotel room. She wasn't lying beside me and I could hear no signs of noise coming from anywhere else in the room. This in itself was not a bad thing. Actually on the contrary, it was most helpful. Waking up the next day in a strange bed with a marginally lesser strange woman was never a winning situation so to find yourself waking without her in attendance? It was definitely a sign that the gods were looking down on me that morning.

Unsure of how long she had been and would be gone for. I decided that I shouldn't look the gift horse in the mouth I'd been presented with. Throwing my clothes from the night before back on, and even quicker than they'd been removed. I exited stage left before there was any requests of an encore. I walked down the corridor almost certain that I was going to bump into her on her way back to her room. Apart from this fat guy carrying an already inflated lilo who was taking up the whole width of the corridor there was no one else between myself and the lift. At the very last second I decided against getting in just in case she was going to be standing looking back out at me when the doors opened on that tenth floor.

In these times where cunts only seem to be getting lazier and lazier. I thought the stairs would be the safest option. No one takes the stairs. Within minutes I was out of the hotel and back onto the street in textbook fashion. I'm sure she'd have coped with the loss of me not being there when she'd returned. Fuck, for all I'd known she had purposely removed herself from the environment just praying for me to be gone by the time she got back? I couldn't really remember that much about her as I walked along the street with the sole intention of simply getting myself as far away from the hotel as I could. There was barely a recollection of what she looked like. That was something that I would need a quick refresher over the morning once things started to come back to me. I remembered that she was from Nottingham although that was only because I had started to call her Maid Marion. That, I could remember.

She'd been nothing more than a consolation shag on what had been the most heartbreaking and bitterly disappointing of nights that had led to me getting myself into a bit of a state to compensate over. One fucking goal though. Just that one vital goal and the whole night would've been completely different.

It had been Scotland's final group match of the Euros. As is, was and will forever be the fucking case, things were complicated as far as us making our way out of a tournament group stage for the first time in our history, but it was possible. Left in front of you like a mirage in a desert. Zico, had already committed to something with his manager so missed out on the game. I headed to Loon's, a Scottish pub that I'd been in a few times since arriving. It was owned by this sound as fuck sheep shagger that I'd already had a bit of United - Aberdeen banter with and had seemed the perfect venue for a night like a Scotland match.

The place was already half full an hour before kick off when I'd arrived. I'd hoovered up a couple of gargantuan sized lines before leaving my pad and practically flew down the road to the Scottish theme pub. Despite all of the uncertainties. I had been absolutely one hundred fucking percent sure that this was going to be the time. After all of those failures. We were going to make it through to the next round of a major tournament for the very first time in history. The wonders of Cocaine, eh? Fuck, if they'd been handing that stuff out to all of the Scottish internationalists from yesteryear we'd have brought the fucking trophy back with us decades ago never mind trying to make it past three matches.

The pub was absolutely bouncing. Loon, the owner had stuck on a tape with all the Scotland fans favourite tunes to sing along to. Well, technically, what someone, somewhere had decided was what (in their head) a compilation of songs that Scotland fans would like to sing to. I say this without any shadow of a doubt knowing that I have never heard Scotland fans singing Rod Stewart's

"Maggie May" at Hampden Park. Didn't stop the whole of the fucking bar from belting it out (me included) when it started coming out of the speakers though, mind.

With five minutes until kick off I fucked off to the toilets to sneak in a couple of lines to see me through to half time. This was Scotland, I'd be needing hard drugs to get me through it, at the very least. Aye, who me kidding eh? It could've been Portugal versus the Czech Republic for all I'd have cared. I'd have still had the lines. I heard the whole of the pub singing its hearts out to the national anthem while I was holed up inside the cubicle chopping out onto the porcelain of the toilet. It gave me a wee bit of a rush hearing them like that, throwing in the fact that I'm inside there listening to them and how it would have been easy to forget that I wasn't inside the bathrooms of a boozer back in the motherland right there. Made me feel all patriotic, like.

I came back out a new and improved man. The couple of pints that I'd had since arriving had given me a bit of a dunt to the head. Have never been the worlds best with alcohol. Class A drugs? Aye, different fucking proposition all together. Proper mad though that I could neck a couple of Eckies or tan a whole gram of Ching to myself and be able to work heavy machinery or drive like a pro yet fire a couple of pints of beer into me and I'm slurring my words and left with jelly legs when trying to walk. The couple of lines restored parity and sent me back into the pub ready for whatever fresh new torture the national side was about to inflict on me and the rest of the country.

Even before the sniff and the beer. My head had been fried by the permutations of what could or would need to happen for Scotland to qualify. Well first of all we needed to win but even then that wasn't a guarantee that we would go through. England and The Netherlands were both on four points and were playing each other in the final game. A cynic might've said that the two of them just needed to play to a convenient draw and they'd both go through. Leaving whatever we did on the night as irrelevant. Seen it happen tones of times where teams play for a draw. Fuck, the last ten minutes both sides completely stop playing all together. Shouldn't be allowed likes but what can you do eh?

If one of those two teams *did* win the match though and, as hoped, Scotland beat the clock makers then it would have come down to goal difference which once again wasn't even really much fucking help considering after two games Scotland hadn't fucking scored any. As long as man has a little bit of hope in his heart though as they say.

That was only placed into a heightened state when within the space of around fifteen first half minutes both England and Scotland had scored. When Ally McCoist opened the scoring with an uncharacteristic screamer of a goal. The bar was a sea of bodies and drinks flying all over the place while I, the man who had been sniffing up some primo half an hour before. Stood motionless while celebrating in my own special way via the most intense rush up the back of my head. Standing there motionless with my hands in the air like I was savouring a piano break inside a big top in a field back in Britain.

Still, it was just one goal but it was a start. It was pleasing to see that in the England match they weren't sitting back. Through me not being able to handle all of the possible permutations of how to qualify. I had completely overlooked the minor detail that there was a massive goal difference between us and The Netherlands and England. Which even the most optimistic of Scots supporters would admit to you. It was kind of hopeful to suggest that it was a scenario that you would see Scotland turning the deficit around.

We reached half time. Aided by the Ching I'd sunk another couple of pints without barely even noticing. Never touched the fucking sides although the impact was felt on my bladder big time. The second the ref's whistle went for half time I was back in the cubicle taking advantage of the situation that saw me entering into what had felt like the worlds longest pee by sorting out a couple of, smaller, bumps. It was only half time for fucks sake but I could see how the night was going to turn out if I didn't rein it in a little. Fuck knows what I must've looked like. Guiding the end of my cock towards the toilet with one hand while, in a semi kind of crouching position. Leaning over towards the porcelain while I chopped out the two lines.

The second half? Fucking hell! I'd never seen the likes as a fitba fan in terms of nail biting drama. Whilst we'd had our chances to increase the lead at Villa Park in Birmingham the scoreline remained one nil which wasn't much of use when you had four goals to claw back. Then it all turned surreal.

The news came through that Teddy Sheringham had made it two nil to England. Then around five minutes after that Shearer had made it three. Suddenly with more than half an hour to go. Scotland were in the position of only being one goal behind the Dutch. Score another against the Swiss and we'd done it. The dream was most definitely on. The pub was in danger of having its roof removed, such was the racket inside there. I almost feared for the establishment, full stop, if Scotland actually was to go on and get that goalden goal.

Then the moment, which would rival any feeling I'd ever had before. The buzz of chasing the ASC around their own city. The rush of your first white dove. Any of that endorphin filled beautiful stuff met stiff competition the moment that, now for the forth time of the evening, the bottom right hand corner of the screen flashed up with footage from Wembley. Straight away you could see that it began with England in possession, confirming that this looked pretty fucking much like the impossible was about to happen and that England were about to score the goal that would send Scotland through.

Teddy Sheringham you beautiful bastard you! After a fumble from the Dutch keeper, Sheringham was on hand to scoop the ball into the net to put England an outlandish four nil up. If all scorelines were to remain the same in Birmingham and London then we were through, officially.

'WEMBLEY WEMBLEY WE'RE THE FAMOUS TARTAN ARMY AND WE'RE OFF TO WEMBLEY' the pub danced and sang in what was just the best of carnival atmospheres you could find without the infiltration of illegal substances. Fitba as a sport never, ever fails to surprise. Take how happy that everyone was inside Loon's at how the night was surprisingly progressing yet it was all down to the one international team that they hated with a passion and would eternally wish for whoever was playing England to beat them. "Anyone but England" as some say.

Aye, anyone but England ...... unless they happen to be in a position to do Scotland a favour, to be exact.

Anyway, our southern neighbours were doing the business for us in the most unexpected of ways. Another goal from Scotland would've saved some finger nails though. I sat calculating with the knowledge that with around half an hour left and on a night that anything could happen (and technically, had) there was still plenty time for further drama to come. It would have been absolute peak Scotland for England to freakishly beat a world superpower like The Netherlands four scud and then Scotland to lose an injury time equaliser to send us out just when it looked like we were in.

The remaining minutes of the match began to fly in with still no additions to either scorelines. As time ticked down, the party spirit and confidence that had swept the bar began to make way for a tense nervousness. Looking at the screen through the cracks in the fingers when the Swiss would attack, almost finding yourself right up in front of it when it was Scotland. As if you were able to put the ball in the net for them remotely from an Ibiza boozer. All done so while praying that the right hand corner of the screen would not be flashing up with any further goal alerts from Wembley.

With around ten minutes left though a fifth goal alert flashed up in its (by then) usual space on the screen. The sight of the Dutch in possession made me almost want to spew there and then all over the bar, projectile levels. The sinking realisation that whatever I was about to see it was going to leave Scotland one goal out of reach from qualification again. Big Paddy Kluivert slotting one away from an angle to put the Dutch back in the driving seat to jeers and howls from most of the pub. The rest stood with their heads in their hands.

A few minutes later, with Scotland still coming up blank on their side in the pursuit of that one goal that would change everything again. That was when the shouts of conspiracy then started up. Somehow, despite the fact that England had taken four fucking goals off the Dutch, when we most needed it. It was England's fault that we were now looking like being eliminated because "they'd lost that goal on purpose so that we wouldn't qualify." There was still five minutes left to save things so I decided to concentrate on that rather than remind these fucking cranks in the bar that our country was now approaching two hundred and seventy minutes worth of fitba with one single fucking goal scored. If, as was looking, we went out after our obligatory three group matches then the last place to point fingers at would have been at Terry Venables and the English players.

The goal never came. Scotland won one nil but still went out on the night in what was apparently a completely new way they'd found of twisting the knife. When that final whistle went at Villa Park it didn't so much feel like a boot in the balls and more a case of some cunt tying them with a rope then tying the other end to the clapped out Fiat van that was parked outside the bar and it driving away with me still sat inside drinking my beer.

As fucking always. Scotland were out the tournament. Our casuals had done themselves proud though so at least there was that. I'd spoken with Carson, one of the younger Utility boys that were coming through just as I was getting out of it all. He'd filled me in on what had gone down the day of the England match with him and a lot of the Utility lads down there to join in the fun. Battle of Trafalgar Square, he'd called it. Sounded like our boys done their country more proud than the actual fucking players.

The night spiralled after that. I left Loon's straight after. I felt quite depressed with how it had all ended but in my warped sense of logic. I decided that the night could still be salvaged. That was when I ran into those girls from Nottingham. I'd had way too much Ching and alcohol and absolutely no doubt about it, was being annoying as fuck. I was probably pestering them, the more I thought back about it but well, the pestering must've worked because I ended up going back with one of them. Perseverance is underrated.

With my head in complete pieces as I walked away from the hotel. I headed off in the direction of the beach to sit and soak up some of the early morning sunshine before continuing on back to my pad for some real rest and recovery. The beach was around an hour or so from being packed with the hordes of holiday makers and locals who would descend on it each day.

Apart from the occasional person walking their dog along it or the various traders getting themselves set up for the day that were in the vicinity, I had the beach to myself. I discreetly got a joint together for myself and sat there on the warm sand enjoying the feeling of the sun's rays washing over me. Having sparked it up and taken a few tokes. I sat there with my eyes closed, oblivious to everyone and everything around me.

'Don't you know that Hashish is illegal in Espanya, friend' my peace was broken by an unfamiliar voice next to me. I squinted my eyes to see this Spaniard standing over me. Dressed in a pair of shorts and an opened up Lacoste short sleeved shirt.

'Who the fuck are you, like? The Hash police?' I replied, mildly pissed off at him for breaking the peaceful state that I'd descended into as I'd sat there on the sand. - 'Well, no, just the regular police.' He said with a smirk as he produced his badge from out of a pocket in his shorts. Looking past and over my shoulder, with his other arm, he motioned for someone else to come over towards him. I looked round and there was a Guardia Civil van parked up beside the public toilets with two policemen stood outside it having a smoke.

I knew I'd fucked up. My only relief, that I'd ran out of Coke the night before. Ivan had taught me from day one that if huckled by the local constabulary to always offer them a bribe. Having played the big man by buying all those drinks for the girls from Nottingham all night though. I was rooked with barely a peseta to my name. I thought to run but considering it takes me to adequately walk on sand. Running was always going to be a bad idea. In any case, without even a pause for thought. The two officers were over and with a hold of each of my arms. Frogmarched me back over towards the van beside the toilets leaving the guy with the shorts on still standing there on the beach.

Once in the van I found myself getting the mother of lectures from an English speaking officer telling me how much trouble I was in and how the locals detested the fact that tourists had turned their home into a drug playground. He left things with a warning that I was soon going to find out how they dealt with tourists like me. I sat in silence mulling over all the of possibilities that were about to come my way. A possession charge? Deported and an abrupt end to my yearly trip to the Balearics with a huge question mark then left hanging over any future returns? Stuck in prison on remand

and not getting to go back home until a trial? Nothing seemed to be out of the question as far as my own mind estimated.

Sat there in the back of the blacked out police van. I assumed that I was on my way to the local station so was initially confused when the van eventually stopped and the back doors opened. I could see nothing but another police car parked right behind the van and what seemed like hundreds of trees in the background.

There was a policeman sitting on the bonnet of the car behind my van looking straight at me as I got out of the back. He had a big bushy moustache. The type you'd see in an old Panini World Cup sticker album from years back and was puffing away on a cigar that would've choked a horse. Standing up from the bonnet and taking a long puff of the cigar. He moved forward towards me and blew the smoke into my face before starting to speak to me in Spanish.

By now, I'd become desensitised towards foreign people speaking to me in tongues that I couldn't understand. If he thought that he was going to intimidate me then he had the wrong man. As he ranted away I looked around, trying to see exactly where I was. Not a sign of a police station so it left me thinking that the officers had decided to go down a different road of serving justice. Barely out of the van the three of them started pushing me around the area we were stood. Me inside the triangle that they'd formed. They seemed in quite a jovial mood the three of them as they all took out their batons. You've got to love what you do, I suppose.

The first blow I took, straight into my stomach, had me doubled up and falling forwards into the officer stood in front of me. He, stopping me from falling further, very kindly adjusted my balance by dishing out a hard whack on one of my knees. Knocking me backwards and onto my arse. Once I was down, they took a more carte blanch approach with regards to laying into my body and legs. It seemed like a good 10 minutes but was more than likely only a minute or two.

Once they finally stopped and, with me lying there in the foetal position, they shouted a little more at me in Spanish before all bursting out laughing and casually turning around and making their way back to the vehicles they'd arrived in. Starting the engines they slowly began to move off. The "keepers of the peace" taking one last look at me before driving off laughing. Leaving me there still on the ground, lying there in shock trying to take in all that had happened over the previous hour.

The ten miles or so that I limped my way back to San Antonio in that blistering heat, the irony that I'd spent the previous days, alert and on the look out for receiving a paggering exactly like I'd just taken. Just not from the fucking bizzies though, eh? It *did* go to show though that whatever country you find yourself in. The same rules always apply.

All coppers really are bastards.

Chapter 25

Zico

As far as Flo and I were concerned, that last night was always going to come around and, in an Ibiza sense at least, the two of us had been living on borrowed time before reality finally bit. All of the adventures, laughs and fun. The instant chemistry that only deepened by the day. Then there was the sex. Fuh-kin-ell, the sex with Flo and her flexible stretchy and bendy sexy ways. Should work in the circus as an escapologist or something like that, her. All good things come to an end though. No matter how much resistance you may have towards them.

Of course, we'd made a pact with each other that we would continue what we'd started with each other once both back in the UK but then again so did "Stacey from Ripon" and I back when I was ten years old in Mallorca at the Magaluf Park kids club and we never heard from each other again.

Then again, that was back in the days where if you had wanted to get a message to your "sweetheart" you would've needed to bring in the the Royal Mail for assistance. Despite my knowledge about all of this internet stuff being so small you could have probably written it down on the back of a packet of Benson & Hedges. I'd remembered an episode of Tomorrow's World in which the presenter had said that one of the features of the internet was that it would be perfect for people to keep in touch with each other, almost instantly.

It was mind blowing, the way the guy had explained it all. He was also predicting things like being able to buy your shopping straight from your computer. Imagine getting a computer to sort out some new clothes and save you the train journey through to Cruise in Edinburgh?! Them and their stupid fucking bell to get in. With that piece of intel there was some real hope that Flo from Kingston was not going to turn out to be another Stacey from Ripon. Then again, it took me to load up a game on my Commodore VIC-20 when I'd last owned a computer. With that in mind it probably would've been a good policy to not get my hopes up too much.

Flo leaving the island was definitely going to equal her presence heavily missed by my good self though and no mistake. Of course, it was maybe just all some fortunate coincidence but from the moment that I'd met her. It had appeared that a lot of the craziness that had been following me around in Ibiza started to disappear.

Sometimes that's all it takes for a man though isn't it? You just need a good reason to toe the line and it all falls into place from there. What after she was gone though? Back to the night in night out madness that had been considered as standard or would I resort to becoming a hermit who would periodically only appear for two hours of a set on the Space terrace before mysteriously going missing for the next few days until his next again performance? Ladies and gentlemen place your bets.

Obviously it had been mainly Flo related but not entirely exclusive. Elle was a good lass herself as well and the two of us had been brand new with each other. Realistically I could not (and would not) have expected that two pals would save up all year for their annual Balearic blow out and then get out there and one would ditch the other for a man she'd only met two minutes before.

As a result I saw Elle a good chunk of the time over the two and a bit weeks they'd been in Ibiza after Flo and I had met. It was the repetition of it all that I enjoyed. The feeling of, I don't know? Normality I guess. It's good meeting new and exciting people but that is somewhat devalued when safe in the knowledge that, while you're meeting and exchanging words with a new face one day. The chances are you'll probably never see them again after that. If you don't get the chance to build relationships and friendships with those certain people that come into your life then what really is the point?

In an ideal world I'd have managed to get Elle paired off with Si which would have provided the best of happy mediums but with Si's activities since arriving with me in Ibiza. I could not have consciously, and in good faith, brought another person into the car crash of the world that he had slipped into. He seemed to have latched on to some kind of delusions that saw him take the attitude that whatever he had been getting up to while in Ibiza could simply be reset back to zero, simply by catching a taxi to Ibiza Airport and taking the flight back to

Edinburgh. Like I'd said to him that night we had a heart to heart over him, the Camachos and this fucking mad family of Scousers. What would he do if his time ran out and he was still kicking around the White Isle when the moment eventually arrived for the excrement to hit the air cooler?

There had been a major adjustment to life for the both of us since the days of us running with the Utility boys. I'd like to say that since the football hooliganism days I'd straightened up and flown right but that wouldn't have exactly been the truth. The occasional violence and danger had been cut out of my diet however and that was a very good start. So had Si to be fair, once he'd got himself out of the firm. He took his time right enough but I got it. Being a casual was effectively a lifestyle choice but once chosen. That was when you found out the sheer addiction to it. The buzz of a Saturday afternoon with the rest of the boys was something that wasn't easily taken out of your system. Years later I still found myself missing it but this was always tempered by the knowledge that had I continued I could just as easily have been sat in a jail cell (or worse) instead of playing records out in Ibiza.

Years on from those Dundee Utility days though. The only danger to me was from myself and not the members of the Capital City Firm or the Motherwell Saturday Service. While there was now around ninety nine percent less likelihood of me lying in a pool of my own blood on a Scottish train station platform or adjacent street of a football stadium. There were other pitfalls to be found. Getting into a pickle through copious narcotics consumption, waking up with psycho girls and dealing with an unpredictable loose cannon of a papa were now my kink.

The moment Si mentioned the O'Hallorans I fucking warned him straight away about them. The ironic thing was that I was hardly considered as informed when it came to the whole gangland stuff. Instead, when I heard the name O'Halloran mentioned it plucked a random memory out of me from the year before when watching The Cook Report on STV. Fucking right radge cunt is old Roger, like. Putting on those mad disguises and infiltrating all kinds of dangerous crime gangs. It's a wonder that no one has done him in by this point but fair play to the boy, I hope that he's getting a decent wedge out of the gig.

Anyway, who did he happen to infiltrate in this episode I'd watched but this Liverpool crime family who were running a major drugs ring and protection racket in Merseyside. They were anyway until Roger turned up and threw a spanner into the works. Apparently they'd had to flee Liverpool after the expose and, according to Cook, had been driven to the Costa del Crime of Espana. Obviously I never thought further of it and being honest, I only found myself watching it because I was high as Yuri Gagarin and the remote control was just that tiny bit out of reach from me. You know how it can be? Some brave soul could climb Ben Nevis in a wheelchair but someone stoned can't find it within themselves to get off a sofa to pick up a TV remote control.

I just didn't want to see Si in trouble. If it's your best mate you do what you can to steer them in a different direction to the impending nastiness that was surely going to rear its head at some point. A turf war he'd ended up getting himself involved in while he had been looking to make just a few easy pesetas a day to subsidise his stay on the island. Once you get sucked into something though there's always the risk that you can get stuck in a moment that you can't get back out of. That was what it was looking like from my direction when it came to the Si and, after all. No one knew him better than me.

Aye, when we were out partying at Space at night or the rare occasions that we would just sit and hang out in the villa and set the world to rights aided by San Miguel and the finest Moroccan Hashish. That was the real Si. There were too many examples though of a pseudo version. The times that he would go missing for a couple of days at a time. The excessive use of the powder. When he would be around you but not really around you at the same time. Miles away despite being right there. I dunno, I just think that it was not the Si that I thought would be flying out to join me for the summer.

I just wanted my wing man to be returning on that flight once the summer season had been wrapped up for another year. With still several weeks to go I, in my own honesty, could not confidently rate his chances at a hundred percent. The again with all of my nocturnal activities mixed with the undertones of potential menaces from Colombian hitmen. What were my own particular odds of making that flight back in one piece?

With it being Flo's final chance to go to Space before heading home the next day. I'd put together an extra special set in honour of the girl who had completed taken me by storm since that fateful night where I'd mistaken her for a table. Through all the many music related discussions we'd held while hanging out. I'd learned that two of her favourite labels were quite inconsistent in terms of the opposites of them. Strictly Rhythm from America and R&S Records from Belgium.

Through knowing this. I put together a collection of tracks for the night just for her that was going give her the proper send off back to England. Dominator, Energy Flash, Stella and for my last record I was going to make an exception and not play something completely non house related. Choosing instead to hit her with what she had confessed as her favourite track of all CLS - Can you feel It which, in the way I had formed the set in my head, was surely going to blow her head off after a few final Mitsubishis.

I'd last spoken with her earlier on in the afternoon when I had been sat there in my pad digging my way through stacks of vinyl. Looking for those specific tracks that I had decided on but equally, the majority not exactly registering on the "seen recently" list.

Fortunately I had a lot of older records out to Ibiza. With me figuring that, being out there for such a long time. I could hardly just travel out there with the thirty or "forty flavour of the month" tracks that I'd been rotating with back home. If I was going to be in it for the long haul then I thought that the best policy would be to plan for any eventuality. One of the beautiful things about Ibiza was indeed its capacity for surprise and if for some obscure reason the requirement was for a one off Belgian techno night then I'd be ready.

Flo had seemed quite merry on the phone despite it being her last day and one that she had already told me way in advance that she had already been dreading. She said that her and Elle were doing a bit of last minute shopping to get the obligatory presents for the folks back home that predictably had been left until the very last minute to procure. I didn't want to intrude on their last day plus I was busy seeing just how exactly I was going to pull off a set of Belgian techno and American house music on short notice so had left her to it and got my head stuck into my preparation.

After shopping, they were then on their way for a meal at the tapas bar that they'd eaten at pretty much every single night on their holidays. It made sense I suppose, when one of your main consumptions during your holidays just happened to be chemically processed narcotics then on the rare occasion that you're going to actually find yourself wanting to eat something then, what better than tapas. The absolute perfect food to make it look like you're actually eating something, even just for appearances, while in reality a couple of spicy prawns in a dish isn't exactly the stuff of three square meals a day.

She said that after their meal they were going to go back and get ready for the night. I offered the two of them a lift through to Space in my cab but with them deciding to go out for one last set of drinks in the West End before going home. Flo said that they'd be happy enough to make their own way to Bossa and catch up with me there.

The same went for Si. Him telling me, euphemistically, that he had a couple of things to take care of and wouldn't be in a position to leave San Antonio as early as I needed to. The mind boggled when it came to what things were being attended to by him. He would've told me had he wanted me to know and I simply couldn't be bothered by asking.

With me having gotten everything done on my list. I awarded myself a couple of lines and a heavily packed spliffter as I sat chilling watching some of the Euro Ninety Six recaps. Scotland, of course, were already back home as-per-fucking usual but it was still a bit sore over the whole what might've been. With the tournament now getting near the end of things where the, and absolutely LOTS of disrespect to the SFA, wheat had been separated from the chaff. Things would now start to get a bit more interesting. The whole England side of things had been starting to get a bit more conflicting.

Whilst it was all too easy, while marooned in Scotland, to take on the attitude of "anyone but England." This whole DJ thing was taking me into a world where I was actually beginning to meet a lot more English and that's the thing. They weren't a bad bunch. Exactly like us I suppose, only with a stupid accent. When you become friends with some of them though. It does make it slightly more difficult to adopt that whole William Wallace attitude towards the English. That said though, if I was to have said that my preferred team to go on and win the tournament, since the might of Scotland (sic) had been eliminated, would've been England then I, my friend, would've been fucking lying.

Eventually I'd managed to get myself into a position where I could get myself dressed and ready for leaving. Lee's zero tolerance winners don't do drugs just say no policy now respectfully in effect. I jumped into the taxi and was soon on my way to Playa den Bossa ahead of Flo and Elle and their tapas and drinks and Si and his fuck knows whats. I briefly thought about Eva. It was a night that she'd have been right up for and would've been a welcome addition but considering how things had been left with my dad during that last call. I wouldn't have thought it exactly appropriate to have then went and tried to invite Eva while her husband was evidently left in a spin over some news that his son had just delivered by telephone.

Eva was a really nice girl and I and everyone else had warmed to her. She was completely a fish out of water though in terms of being in tow with my father and all of his capers. She was just a normal Mancunian girl who liked to have a bit of fun. Normal and in reality, just needed another normal man as her other half. Someone Peter Duncan wasn't even close to being. In a weirdly conflicting scenario of morality. I'd found myself hoping that whatever was about to come her and my dads way, and it was practically certain that "something" was coming. That out of the two of them Eva would be the one that ended up safe. She didn't deserve ending up with a Colombian fucking necktie. As for my dad? Well that was something that the jury might well have been out on due to my suspicions that since he had arrived he had not exactly been free with the full facts over what was all going on.

I set off on the journey to Space sat there in the back of the cab with a strange mix of excitement over how special an occasion it was going to be while tinged with the sadness that it would be the last time I would see Flo out there dancing. I'd always looked out for every single set I'd played and once spotted I would barely take my eyes off her while I stood and let a track play. That smile of hers would always give me an almost Ecstasy like rush any single time I saw it.

Despite it only really being a relative short space in time in the scheme of things. I had gotten used to her being out there and it was going to be strange, moving forward, not seeing her out here in the crowd.

There was one last time left though and it was one that I planned to make the absolute most of every single second of it.

Sat there in the taxi though I was also dealing with an increasing amount of apprehension over my appearance on the terrace. Those Colombians? What if they'd done their homework by this point? Now knew who I was and what time my set would be scheduled and they'd be ready for me? What if it was a different set of doormen on for the night and no one recognised them on entering the club?

I felt like a fucking president who had been issued with a death threat in advance of a speech he was about to give but, not to show any weakness, would then go ahead and deliver it in defiance and a show of strength to his people. Well aye, I felt a bit like that when the taxi pulled to a stop outside Space. Not that I had around fifteen Secret Service bad bastards in suits talking into their cuffs protecting me or fuck all, like. I didn't even have any cunt that would go and get me a drink from the bar never mind being willing to take a fucking bullet for me.

After exchanging a few words with some familiar faces and some not so on the way in. I was up and ready to to take over from this young DJ who I didn't catch his name but apparently was only sixteen. This Danish boy who had won a mixing competition on local Ibiza radio. On my way to the booth I ended up having a chance meeting with an old mate of mines from back in Fife, Ecksie. Sound boy likes and someone I'd known from way back as far as primary school days. We used to muck about together. Even our mums were pals when they were our age. Hadn't seen him for years likes but one of those pals that time doesn't matter when you bump into them.

Despite my evident rush to get myself up and ready for my set. Ecksie wasn't really clocking this due to the clear signs that he'd already started to hit the narcotics for the night. Through this his self awareness levels were non existent. He brought up the England match which, to be fair, was a topic that pretty much any Scot was going to be bringing up with his fellow man at least until all of the fuss had died down even if, in fitba terms, it had now been ages ago. Apparently, he was telling me, that spoon bending crank Uri Geller had been claiming to the media that had moved the ball off the penalty spot - with his mind - just at the precise moment that Gary Mcallister was about to strike the ball.

I fucking said it at the time, I'd seen the ball move with my own eyes but I'll admit that I'd never considered the reason of some Israeli spoon bender. Whether he actually did it or not. What's his fucking problem anyway? He isn't Scottish or English so why's he even sticking his nose into things? Once that (debatable) fact was in my mind it wasn't coming back out again. Nagged at me throughout the set. I was already still sore over how we'd went out the competition so my head couldn't really handle belatedly learning that potentially some kind of witchcraft had been at play to make sure that we didn't get a result against Ingerlund. When you take as many Class A's as moi at times the very last fucking thing you need is a couple of conspiracy theories thrown into the mixer for you to chew over.

The first track I'd chosen for Flo's special set was an R&S Record's banger in Outlander - Vamp which came along with that irresistible piano break that I knew that from minute one the crowd would've been in the palm of my hand. If you can't get an Ibiza crowd behind you with a good piano sample then that would be the moment that you close up your record box and get yourself as far to fuck as possible from the Technics.

After a couple of songs and a careful scan of the room I still hadn't made out Flo, Elle or Si. Normally I'd have picked at least one of them out of the crowd but had came up with nada. Instead I, for a while, concentrated on providing the crowd with the eclectic mix of American house and garage together with some harder Belgian beats. It was by the halfway point of set and with an hour to go that I'd still managed to come up with nothing in terms of Flo and Elle. I'd eventually picked out Si who had been standing with a bottle of beer in his hand dancing away to himself with a glazed eyed but fixed smile. I was more disappointed in Flo than concerned in anyway.

Knowing that Elle and her were going for drinks earlier. I'd began to assume that they'd gotten so drunk that Space was now beyond them. It had been a bit of a let down though. With it being the last night, I had hoped that she'd have made an extra special attempt at getting herself to Bossa for a last crack at Space.

As it entered the final stages of my set I'd stopped looking into the crowd for them. Sticking to my own stuff. I left "Can you feel it' as the last track of the performance which, while Flo and Elle weren't around for it, fortunately the rest of the terrace were every bit as up for it as I'd hoped that Flo would have done, had she been there.

After I'd finished I headed in the direction of Si to ask if he'd seen any of the two girls. His reply on the negative side. I tried calling her but it went straight to voicemail which I assumed was that she'd maybe had a flat battery. Never rang once. I was a bit pissed off over her non appearance once it dawned on me that was how the night was going to turn out. The complete antithesis of what I had began planning as early as that afternoon.

Like my man, Jim Morrison. I felt that there was no need wallow in the mire and proceeded to endeavour to go up as many levels in fuckedupness as possible with Si until the next afternoon.

Those plans changed however the moment I saw Elle walking towards the two of us. Standing out in a secluded area sneaking a quick smoke. I clocked her first and, despite how completely pickled I was. The first thing that I noticed about her was that she was minus her trademark smile.

'Have you seen Flo, Zico?' she said with a frightened look on her face.

'But I thought that she was with you?' I replied with what I can only imagine a head scratcher of a facial expression.

'Well, she was. We were in O'Hagen's. She went to the bathrooms and never came back out again. After a while I went looking for her and she wasn't there. It doesn't make sense. We were sat quite near the toilets so I couldn't have missed her coming back out yet she wasn't in there.' She said, clearly not doing too well in making any sense out of it all.

'What about her phone? Any answer? I asked. Beginning to pick up on Elle's panic about the situation.

'Nope, straight to voicemail,' she answered as I nodded my head in affirmation that I'd had the same result to my attempts in trying to get hold of her. Something felt off about it all. The Flo that I'd gotten to know over the holiday was not one who would have missed the last opportunity to completely have it one last night at Space.

'I'm really worried Stevie that something's happened to her. It's not like her to just go off without saying. She'd only been sat five minutes before when we were having a drink saying how buzzing she was for Space and how being our last night we'd be making it count and to fuck with the broken state of mind that we'd be in on the flight back home. Next minute she's gone.' Elle had started to cry which had the effect of, in that moment, almost completely sobering me from the Double Doves that I had dropped earlier in the night that I had been rolling my tits off through.

'Look, there's no point us going to the West End to look for her as that will all be well closed by now down there.' I said glancing at my watch, seeing that it was approaching seven in the morning and facing the stark realisation that this had once again, been a night at Space where certain individuals evidently hadn't known when to say when.

'We keep trying her mobile, you phone your hotel and ask to see if she's in the room by now. We'll find her, Elle don't worry.' I consoled her. Rubbing her shoulders trying to reassure her while inside privately holding the fear that after around twelve hours of no one being able to get hold of her. Someone acting completely out of character like was the case with Flo. It was difficult not to worry over what exactly *was* going on her side.

Chapter 26

Zico

The first thought I had wasn't the Flo situation when I woke (my body apparently having given up on me after returning to the villa around eleven in the morning) but that fucking Uri Geller. Who fucking asked him to get involved in things anyway? Was it an Asian betting syndicate thing he was part of? Was it a Scot who had called him out on his spoon bending shit as a con and from that point he had held it against Scotland as a country. Just waiting, biding his time until he could pay us back in the most heartbreaking of fashions? Probably not even that exotic. Nothing more than him being just one of those cunts who feels the need to stick their noses into others business.

After leaving Space and getting ourselves back to San Antonio around half seven in the morning. Elle, Si and myself, the last two completely wired after a night on it, searched far and wide for Flo. Checked the hotel about twenty times on and off. Phoned around the local hospitals and medical centres. Went all over San Antonio and San Antonio Bay but collectively came up with the square route of fuck all. I'd trawled the beaches while secretly shitting myself incase I ended up discovering her body floating in the water onto the shore. Twisted on chemicals and searching for a girl who means the world to you but you've managed to convince yourself that they are in some serious trouble. Well, it's not a winning combination, mentally.

We had all searched until sheer exhaustion got the better of us. Elle was in a right state because the two of them were meant to be flying back to England in a matter of hours. Crying that she had no money left for another flight. I told her that there was nothing more that we could do than wait for Flo to get in touch. Elle said that if she went home she would be back out again within days but that she would report Flo as missing before she flew home.

It was a terrible position for her to be left in. I tried to reassure her that if she went home. I would be taking care of things from the Ibiza side. We all went off our own separate ways. I'd only managed an hour of sleep before stirring again and after getting past those initial half sleepy thoughts of fucking Geller. My thoughts then turned to Flo and if there had been any development during my sleep.

I didn't even get the chance to reach for the mobile to attempt to call her before the phone sprung into life.

'Now listen carefully' the voice on the other end of the line asserted itself from the very beginning. Offering me no chance of interrupting let alone even answer the call with a hello. 'We have something valuable of yours and if you ever want to see it again then you are going to to help us with something that is valuable to us' a man with a Spanish sounding accent "introduced" himself.

'Oh aye, and what might you have that's valuable to me then?' Fronting, I tried to play along with his wee game. There was a brief moment of silence and then that was when I heard her voice. 'Stevie, they took me last night, I don't know where I am but they're holding me here and ...' The unmistakable tearful cockney accent said before having the phone snatched from her mid sentence.

'FLO? HAVE THEY DONE ANYTHING TO YOU? DON'T WORRY BABE I'LL' I was in the middle of deliriously shouting down the line at her when the original voice was back talking to me again.

'So, you see, amigo?' came his first words on regaining control of the phone. - 'Listen, whoever the fuck you are, if you don't let her go right now I'm going to fucking open you up like a tin of fucking tuna' I replied back, trying all I could to show some kind of composure and failing miserably. Ranting and raving at him with ride all in the way of coolness about me would never have had any kind of effect with him though. No one ever takes the ranter serious, more laugh at him making an arse out of himself than anything else in my experience. On the flip side however. I didn't think that showing him any fear, and fear there most definitely was, would have helped the situation either.

'Of course you will, brother' he laughed back at me with an air of confidence that hinted that this was the type of call he makes every other day and was already used to the whole spectrum of reactions from people which, no doubt, would have had a similar range as the five stages of grief.

Deflated by the obvious control that this man had over proceedings and that I was left in the position of asking me to jump and being left with no choice other than to ask how high. The tone of my next question was completely minus of any hostility or antagonism in his direction.

'Who the fuck are you and why do you have my girlfriend?' I asked, already resigned to the fact that an answer, at least to the first question, might not be too forthcoming.

Anyone who has ever watched a crime TV show or film that has involved kidnapping and shit like that would know that one of the key aspects is to never give away any potential leverage to someone planning a move on you. Through this unplanned slip of the tongue. I was kicking myself at only strengthening this cunt's position. With the state my mind had been reduced to inside a matter of minutes. I really was all over the place. It didn't take long for the logic to come forth telling me that if this man was calling me while having abducted Flo then he had already done his homework on things.

'None of that is important to you, Steven but what is of great importance is that if you want to see this pretty little brown girl of yours again then you're going to have to do exactly as I say. You understand, si?' He said while maintaining a firm grip on the way the "conversation" was progressing.

I tried to reply with some kind of coherent words but all I could muster was some kind of weird noise that I swear I'd never heard myself make in my life before. It appeared to have been enough of a confirmation on his end for him to continue talking.

'Here is what you are going to do for me, well assuming that you don't want me to start chopping off parts of your beautiful Selina?' I was overwhelmed by an image of Flo. Sat tied to a chair with some sick bastard removing one digit at a time. It was horrifying to think of but the Spaniard was giving me no time for breath and if there was one phone call in my life that it was of paramount interest that I paid attention to it was surely that one.

'I want the location of your father and the disc that he has that belongs to my employers. Now if I know your father, which I do. I know that he would not be so loco as to carry it on him. You wouldn't happen to know anything about where he has stored it, would you, brother?' he said facetiously to me. The implication blatantly being that I knew *exactly* where this disc was. Disc? Fucking hell. That VIC20 I had didn't even take discs! Quel fucking surprise though this was all down to my dad. I immediately felt bad about it but I had the thought that if they were looking for my dad then why the fuck did they not take Eva instead of Flo?

Then again, would my dad do the right thing in such a position? Loveable rogue and all of that shite but deep down if he'd existed in a world like Colombian cartels then who the fuck really knew what such a character was capable of? My mind was a fucking jungle with all that I was having to take in and at such a rate (especially due to the excesses at Space with Si) but he continued laying down what I was vitally expected to pick up.

'Now listen to me, brother. I am a family man so I understand that what I am asking you is a big decision and because of this I am willing to give you some time to make peace with whatever it is that you choose. If it's any consolation to you, your rat father and bitch wife *will* be found with or without your help although let us not forget about the disc that I am here for, si?'

Despite the menace that he'd maintained over the course of the call. He also had a fair bit of charisma to it which confused me slightly. On one hand he was holding someone who had become really fucking special to me and was making, what seemed, all too believable threats to her life yet at the same time was showing a human side to him. Recognising that the position he was putting me in was the most sadistic example of a catch twenty two and that some time to consider my options would have been welcomed.

Save a girl that I'd only known just over a couple of weeks and, in doing so, ensuring that my dad, who may or may not have had it all coming to him anyway, and "mum" were going to be topped in some way or other. Or the roles reversed which would see that an innocent girl, who was only guilty of knowing me for a short period, killed in what would be nothing more than simple collateral in a bigger game that was being played out.

There was also the matter of this disc that he had been speaking about. I knew fuck all about it but the insinuation that he'd projected was that he thought that I did. It was obviously some pretty vital stuff whatever that was contained on it the way he kept banging on about it. It almost felt like the disc was even more important than Peter Duncan to the caller.

I hadn't yet managed to come up with any kind of a response to him when he then altered the tone with the most grave of warnings.

'And, brother. If you go to the police about this, Selina dies. If you tell anyone else about this, Selina dies. If I do not recover both where your father is hiding AND the location of the computer disc. You know the rest, amigo.'

Trying to buy myself a little time. I entered into what what was nothing more than negotiations that I wasn't even sure I'd have been able to agree to / carry out regardless of where it got me with him. Considering I knew nothing about any disc but *did* know the whereabouts of my dad and Eva. I asked him, while once more reminding him of my innocence towards the disc, what if I was to find where my father was but not the disc. His answer was that either or would be looked upon favourably and that he would be willing to offer me an extension to provide the other but was also reminded that with time running out I better give him, something.

'You have twenty four hours, for Selina's sake I hope that you will have made the correct choice by then, brother. When I call tomorrow you make sure you answer. There will be consequences if you do not'

The last words I heard from him before the line went dead. I sat there for what felt like a few minutes. Still holding the phone up to my ear as if the conversation was still in full flow. The shock of the content of the phone call had practically sent me into a zen like state. Lying there in bed frozen in the same spot. Phone resting against my right ear as I stared into space. Trying to fully get my head around what had just happened and the all too real situation that not just myself but Flo (and my father whether he liked it or not) had been placed in.

The collage of thoughts that were alternating through my mind were were enough to make one's head explode. I was lurching from some relating to Flo sat there crying her eyes out having had fuck knows what done to her already by that point, with the potential for far worse. To offset this, on the other hand Pedro fucking Duncan was swanning around in his pink Ralph Lauren polo shirts, chinos and Gucci loafers while putting away more Ching than your average American stadium rock band, without an apparent care in the world. This despite the imminent danger of a Colombian drugs cartel getting ever so closer to finding him.

The thoughts weren't rational though. I'd soon flipped to the complete opposite scenario that saw Flo, finding out that the long distance thing wasn't working for her and ending it with me. Imagine choosing a girl instead of family only for the girl to leave you anyway? There was also the Nora factor. I'm not sure "favours" should exist between family in the way a favour is considered when it comes to the underworld but even so. My dad stepped up and dealt with a period of my life where everything was about to come to a grizzly end and this wasn't something that I'd ever forgotten over the years.

Then again, I also hadn't exactly blanked on that not only did my pops fix my problems when it came to threats from a formidably depraved individual like Nora but he (coincidentally?) happened to engineer that it would happen in a way that would ensure he came out of it all a very rich man.

In those following moments after the phone call I literally did not know what to do. Protect my father and I kill Flo. Protect Flo and kill my dad (and Eva) and considering the matter of this disc, who knew, possibly STILL be killed myself after taking the hardest of decisions set in front of me. Possibly we'd all be killed once we'd served our individual purposes? Maybe that was a case of me having watched too many films with that last theory but I felt that when these thoughts were coming to me it would've been idiotic to have at least not considered them as possibilities.

"Rational" in those minutes following that chilling phone call was a commodity that was rare than your chances of finding some rocking horse shit inside Toys R Us. I couldn't think for myself. Thinking full stop was a challenge over the white noise filling up my head.

I felt a good start would be to call the one person responsible for all of this fucked up situation that I had suddenly been pulled into.

Chapter 27

Peter

I was entangled in one of our all too frequent heated debates of the day when the boy called. The square route of Eva's chagrin being that the swimming pool which had came as part of the villa that I had been forced into renting for us had not been filled with water. As far as I'd been concerned. The prime motivation for us moving out of that hotel and away to the outskirts of San Antonio Bay had been based on our literal survival. Not so that either of us could put in a few lengths of breast stroke each morning. When Stevie had called, I was practically in the middle of reminding her that we had relocated to the secluded villa through the bare necessities of keeping ourselves one step ahead of the cartel and its associates and not because we were busy training for the upcoming Atlanta Olympic Games.

The real irony being that we had a pool fit for Mark Spitz himself back in Bogotá and I never once seen her in it yet. Apparently it would've ruined her hair had she went into it. The chlorine would give her split ends or something to that effect. Give me peace!

The villa itself had been nothing other than a temporary safe house for the two of us. Simply a bolt hole that we could remove ourselves to until finally getting out of Spain entirely. Technically I'd planned for us to have been and gone by that point but things had been held up on Salomon Sanchis' end with regards to my attorney securing the transfer of my stocks and shares. That subject alone had been causing me some major concerns due to him going off the grid. I'd not been able to catch him in days with all attempts at calling diverting straight to his voicemail. Even my attempts at a work around by calling the office reception number had been thwarted.

There was something unsettling about the fact that for three consecutive days I had not been able to get someone to pick up the phone from an attorneys office or to be specific. An attorneys office that was responsible for the safeguarding of a not insignificant amount of capital belonging to me.

My life savings, my money for the obligatory rainy day and ultimately the mechanism for an escape for when finding a couple of psychotic and sadistic killers on your trail. Rainy day fund? By that point it had turned to a fucking monsoon but without Salomon's vital assistance. I was getting near close to having to walk through it without an umbrella. The hard cold facts however were that I may or may not have had to eventually face were that there may not have been any umbrella forthcoming. It had already been assumed by myself that with Gilberto and Jorge ending up in Barcelona looking for me. The natural next step for them would have been to pay Sal Sanchis a visit seeking intel on my location.

Sanchis was loyal, he'd proved this on many occasions over the years and he was the one person that I trusted (after Mikael) within a business where it was difficult to trust anyone. Loyal or not, when you have a couple of unsettling and formidable characters on your case like the finest sicarios available to the Ramirez brothers. Sometimes loyalty can only extend to a certain point and there lay the key question, or questions.

What had he told them? How much? What had they done with him afterwards? Was he even alive? With me not getting hold of him for those three days while not receiving any calls back from the messages that I'd left. The last question of mines was the one that concerned me the most. Most that would've come into contact with La Cobra and El Jugador, within a business capacity, didn't live to tell the tale. I'd even have went as far as to say that if those two psychotic bastards paid you a visit then you were already dead.

I'd be the first to admit that I was devoid of the class to admit any shame over the fact that when pondering the possibilities over Sal being dead that the first thing that I thought of was Sal, his wife and his two kids, his family unit that he proudly displayed via numerous pictures to any visitor to his office. No, it was my money that I was thinking of and my money only. Of course it was.

Yes, the money had been a concern but when you have the finest men at the disposal of the Ramirez brothers on your case. It shows you that money isn't always everything. Staying one step ahead of those cold blooded killers came way before having money in your bank account.

They catch up with you then being wealthy suddenly becomes irrelevant in any case.

Mid argument, when the phone rang and I noticed it was Stevie. I was of a half mind to screen it and call him back but the devil on my shoulder spoke to me. Convincing myself that if I answered the phone call then it would automatically remove me from the argument Eva and I were having. One that wasn't showing any signs of reaching resolution.

Had I known what my son was calling me about in advance I would've screened the call as had previously been thought of as an option.

'DAD, THEY'VE GOT FUCKING FLO, THEY'VE TAKEN HER' he screamed down the phone at me the second it appeared to him that I'd answered. While this wasn't exactly a phone call I had been expecting but with the panic in his voice and the words he screamed out, I knew what had happened. Working as long in Colombia as I had. I'd picked up a few lessons along the way. I wasn't going to be making it easy for the sicarios to find Eva and I to the point that even if we were in the same town or city I would have still been semi confident that they would not be able to find me, as talented as they were. Which they were. The very best you could hire in South America and I assure you. South America is not a continent short of its unhinged killing machines.

No, I was in full on stealth mode in terms of hiding out while waiting on word that the paperwork was all tied up before Eva and I rode off into the sunset. Through Gilles, a contact in Berlin. I'd been given a list of countries that wifie and I could go to and, upon arrival, disappear off the face of the earth as far as anyone wishing to find us would be concerned. "Friendly" government officials would be willing to assist the integration into our new surroundings, euphemistically speaking. All of that was going to take serious outlay however and whilst I still had a more than comfortable nest egg to see Eva and I through however long we were going to be stuck in The Balearics. It wasn't going to stretch to funding a completely new identity and location.

As for Stevie though? While I had used all the tricks in the book to prevent someone who I didn't want finding me to actually find me. Stevie was in the complete opposite of that tactic. Admittedly my lad in no way had ever considered that he would ever be involved in something like that. Laying low and giving out fake names and address' and throwing in red herrings all over the place? He, instead, had his name up on posters advertising which nights he was on plastered all over town. Given the serious nature that Gilberto and Jorge took their work. I could've only imagined that it would've taken them all of half an hour of being in Ibiza to figure out where to find him.

The last time I'd spoken to Stevie had actually been in connection to some heavies coming to the club looking for him. Escaping them that night would've only bought him time. They were always coming back again in some way or other. No question, they'd have concentrated on finding me first but the moment that they started hitting brick walls then that was when they would have decided to make a move towards the next best thing to me, my family.

I'd presumed that they'd maybe taken a day or two to scout things out. Follow him back from the club, see where he lived, who he interacted with regularly. Snatching Flo was a textbook move. Despite not really even knowing the girl. A chill went down my spine at the thought of being held captive by those two sick bastards. On reputation alone I'd have been astonished if Jorge, the looser cannon out of the duo, had not subjected her to some forms of sexual molestation. This was not a good situation for any of us to have been handed though, not just Flo.

'Stevie, look, take a breath son and tell me what the hell is going on here?' I asked while, at that point at least, completely exonerating myself of any reason for this girl going missing. 'What the hell is going on here? Don't you fucking give me that dad, it's BECAUSE of you that this girl's life is in danger' he hit back with emotions running high. Mostly of hostility.

I'd planned to issue yet more futile denials of my involvement but by then my son had managed to form a series of words that were more of a constructive sense. 'This man wants you, Eva and some fucking computer disc and if he doesn't get his hands on all three he's going to kill Flo by tomorrow.'

'WHO is it Stevie? Did they tell you their name?' I asked. - 'Oh aye, dad. The cunt told me his full name including his middle one which was, weirdly Primrose. Told me his interests as well when he's not abducting innocent girls and threatening to chop off parts of their body. Long walks on the beach and reading books, sounds a bit of a boring bastard if you ask me ..... OF FUCKING COURSE he never told me his name' He turned sarcastic which I really hadn't cared for. I'd just taken a big line from the coffee table a few seconds into the conversation starting and didn't really appreciate someone talking to me like that whether they were my son or not.

'That tone's not exactly going to help, son' I said, purposely condescending back to him. - 'Fuck your fucking tones. It was you that came here without warning, hadn't fucking seen you in yonks and you show up, closely followed by fuck knows what kind of dangerous bastards. I'll talk to you in any fucking tone that I want given the circumstances and anyway fuck me or you. This is about Flo, and specifically .. what are *you* going to do about it?'

Stevie had never spoken to me like this in his life. It was throwing up a personality clash against the pleasant and untouchable rushes that I'd been getting from the Coke. Even so, I couldn't help but find an extra piece of respect over seeing the man that my son appeared to be growing up to be. The assertive and dominant response to an absolute disaster of a situation from him was something that I couldn't help but be impressed by.

'So what is it that you expect me to do?' I asked knowing that from experience there wasn't going to be many options that were going to come out of this that would be arriving at a happy medium for everyone. 'Well I don't fucking know, dad. This is your game, not mines?' Stevie said with what appeared to be less than hopeful confidence.

'So what exactly is it that you think I can do to help?' I asked. I wasn't exactly even sure myself which way the words were meant to come out in but I suppose they were never going to go well with my son on the other end. Him, waiting there on me to save the day rather than show myself up as the self centred coward that I was. He really had no clue how dangerous the stakes were. This was every man for themselves time but instead he wanted to play the hero.

'Well you could agree to meet this man who has Flo, give him the computer disc and can all go about your day,' he replied. I knew how street smart Stevie was and frankly, had he actually believed what he'd just said I'd have been most disappointed in him. 'Oh come on now Stevie, I meet this mystery man who is holding your, what is she exactly? Too early to be considered a girlfriend, lets call her a friend, and you really think that it's all going to go cordially? Best case scenario is that he lets her go but if I go to that meeting then I wont be walking away from it again and besides, I don't know what you're talking about with this computer disc.' I tried to give Stevie the facts of the matter, all be it a doctored version, since he was appearing to miss all the points that were staring him in the face.

'So that's your response, is it? Girl with the rest of her life ahead of her is going to be executed by some sick Colombian BECAUSE OF YOU and you give me a reaction of fucking apathy?!?' Stevie was in no mood for letting up the display of his feelings.

'Look son, this is the life that I chose. Innocents have always paid a price along the way through simply being in the wrong place at the wrong time. It's unfortunate but it happens. I mean, you only knew the girl a couple of weeks, son. It's a sad business but you'll get over it' Tact and sensitivity had completely departed me in terms of social skills. The powder more than playing a part in my delivery.

For the first time since I'd answered his call he'd remained silent. I pounced on it with the A material. 'Because it probably doesn't even need to be said but it's not like you would choose a girl that you barely even know over your own father.' I made a purpose of laughing to provide emphasis over how ludicrous the thought even was that my own son would choose a girl over me.

'Well maybe one day we'll sit down and talk man to man about that response you just gave me because I won't ever be fucking forgetting it but, this disc? The way the man spoke to me about it. He said lots while saying very little. It seems like it's worth a lot of money to someone who is in the market to sell it or a disaster to his cartel bosses if placed in the wrong hands like the Federales. If you've not got it do you know who the fuck has? Whatever the fuck is on it quite literally could be the difference between Flo living or dying? Think for fucks sake. Well, since you're not enough of a man to give up your own life for someone else who least deserves it, of course' He pleaded. The last comment stinging but one that I really had nothing close to a comeback over.

'Stevie, for the last time. I don't know anything about a disc and as far as making a trade of me for Flo. I've got a wife to think about here, for fucks sake. I'll try and make some calls to see if I can find out what's going on and get back to you.' I said, trying to come somewhere close to meeting him half way. I knew, however, that there were no calls to make. He needed placating so I obliged. The only way that Flo was getting out of it alive would be if I was the exchange in the deal and that wasn't an option.

'Can't I give this guy your number so that you can talk to him, possibly buy some time for her?' Stevie tried to bargain, evidently racking his brains for any angle that might keep his girl alive. Technically, yes I could've easily told the boy to pass on my number to Gilberto and Jorge. Whichever of the two that had been making the call moments before Stevie had then phoned me. My guess, Gilberto.

To give those maniacs my number however would've have been as good as giving them the address to the new villa that we'd relocated to. With the DEA technology that the Ramirez brothers had procured from some corruptible agent from Miami years before. I would never have ruled out the possibility of my calls being tracked.

'No Stevie, I can't do that. Like I said, I'll make some calls.' I attested. Fully aware that none of this was what Stevie had wanted to hear when he, unaware of the fact that some people in the world have no choice but to adopt the dog eat dog attitude to day to day life, had dialled my number for help.

'So you won't meet with this man in return for Flo's freedom and also wont get involved regarding this disc that this cunt says you have.' He said rhetorically, adding. 'Then there's not much more to say then, pops. I guess I've got some thinking to do.' He ended the call straight after, denying me the chance of a response.

Chapter 28

Zico

Well as far as stepping up and being counted when the McCain oven fries were down. Peter Duncan AKA my father was not someone that could've been considered as pro-active. I didn't know exactly what to expect when I called him with the news that Flo had been abducted and that it was him that held the key to it all but the almost indifference that I was greeted with was a kind of disregardful coldness that made me ashamed to be from the Duncan bloodline.

The right bastard in all of this was that despite my father truly laying his cards right on the table and letting me know just how he operated, what his life involved at times and, the worst part for me. The very lowest of the low, just how cheaply he valued Flo's life. It was as if he had been sucked into the mentality of your Colombian cartel member or associate. Any values that he once might have held before relocating to South America, now gone. Yet through all of that. He was still my dad. The ultimate in flesh and blood, the co giver of life and quite possibly the man responsible for saving mines back at the start of the decade.

All of a sudden however. As I sat trying to figure out some kind of solution over what way out of this could be found. It dawned on me that, despite leaving the hotel that they had been shacked up in since arriving, my dad had not taken the liberty of letting me know where him and Eva had moved on to. He'd not had any problem in completely ram raiding his way into the life I was trying to carve out for myself during my temporary stay in Spain yet at the same time was just as comfortable in disappearing without even a toodle fucking ooh.

If all of this had been intended as some closely guarded secret he'd wanted to keep from me then Eva obviously hadn't received the memo. She'd given me a call to let me know where they had relocated to while stating her intentions that just because they had moved further out of my proximity she would still be up for a night at Space as long as her and Peter were still present on the island. Whether my dad knew of this was anyone's guess.

The initial call from the "Spaniard" who, during the course of the conversation, turned out to be Colombian had left my mind going in all directions. I was seamlessly moving from thoughts of Flo and what she made have been subjected to, as I lay there in bed so early in the morning, to the disgust in terms of how I was viewing my father all the way to the undeniably real facts that I was scheduled for a special extended five hour set at Space later on.

Despite all of the priorities that were right there in front of me I somehow had arrived at the fact that I would need to let Lee know as soon as possible that I would not make my set. I wasn't actually sure what to do about it. Normally you have yourself a job and you phone into the boss if you can't make it in for the day? Being in a foreign country tasked with "working" in a club that does not belong to your own employer. Who the fuck *are* you meant to phone in sick to? My boss was Lee, I guess.

I opted for calling him and in the classic case of calling in sick (regardless of your vocation) to your boss and hoping that they don't actually answer, leaving you the first wish option of just bailing with a voicemail. It went to his answering machine. My wish had been granted.

'You're through to Lee of Ragamuffin Agency. I'm busy right now, most likely attending to my industry envious stable of top deejays but if you would like to leave a message after the beep I will get back to you as soon as I can. Be lucky' came the ever cheeky Cockney message after the call had rang out.

'Emmmm, Lee, It's Stevie here, well, aye, obviously you'll know that but anyway. I really hate to do this mate but I've had a bit of an emergency, family stuff, you know? I don't think I'm going to be able to make my set. Don't worry, Lee it's not drug stuff or anything directly to do with me but I just need to sort some things out. I can't promise that you'll get me on the phone for the next wee while so I'm hoping to fuck that you get this message and it all gets sorted for tonight. I'm sorry but it's a proper emergency and I'll explain later'

I rambled on and on until the recording time expired. In total I'd barely remembered all of what I'd said but it was a mess of a recording, without a doubt.

Weirdly, with me feeling like the insignificant elements of the day had been taken care of. I then felt like I was now able to concentrate on the more important and pressing matters. Like trying to keep as many people alive as I possibly could. Myself included.

I took the next few hours out to try and come up with some sort of a plan but it wasn't as if I'd been handed an array of options to work with. Not even the slightest hint of help from my pops other than the offer to "make some calls" which I can assure, sounded several levels below the sincerity that I think that he had been aiming for. There was nothing that he was going to be doing to help so other than that. What choice really was I left with?

I knew his current address. That was all I had in terms of being presented with some kind of a bargaining chip. The only choice that I had in my locker to use. It was my dad though, to even consider it as an option to use left me feeling like the lowest of the low. I kept seeing visions of Flo though, crying her eyes out in fear, held by who knows what kind of sick bastards. At that early part of the day I could already see that had I been awarded twenty four years rather than twenty four hours I still would not be in any further a position to making a decision.

I eventually got myself out of bed and relocated through to the sofa. Choosing not to switch the TV on. Knowing that all it would do would be to provide an unwanted distraction. I hit the rips with a vengeance seeking some calm. In no uncertain doubt that if ever I needed the strongest of cannabis cigarettes it was right then.

I was midway through smoking it while overplaying the binary thought of "do I or don't I" when Si arrived.

'Any news yet mate?' He asked the moment he walked through my door. Rubbing at his eyes and still yawning as if he'd just risen seconds before. His hair that was sticking up on one corner testifying to that.

What he received back from me was the juxtaposition of him hearing that one specific word (yes) that he had wanted to hear me say while in a visual sense was staring back at someone who had reached the official end of their world. 'Fuck, Zeec. She's not dead, is she?' he said, his face completely dropping as he sat down and joined me on the sofa. 'No, she's not dead, mate. Well, not yet anyway.' I replied cryptically as I handed him the half smoked joint before setting about explaining to him just what had happened to Flo since we'd discovered that she had gone missing.

He sat in silence taking in every word that I said to him. Puffing away on the spliff. Such was the seriousness of the subject of the conversation he, doing away with the general etiquette stuck to by the toking fraternity, smoked it all the way down to the roach without any hint of him passing it back my way.

Any other time he'd have been pulled up about it. This was Flo's life that we were discussing though. The fact that someone had hogged the joint really was neither here nor there.

'We've got to do something about it, Zeec' an animated Si concluded as he jumped back up from the sofa and began pacing around the living room. 'Well, aye, that has already been pretty much confirmed, mate but what the fuck *can* be done without either Flo, dad and Eva dying?' It wasn't a time for sarcasm even if used with a best mate but I couldn't help it from coming out the way that it did.

'Sorry, Si. I'm heavy fucking stressed here,' I followed up with which had him waving the comment away as if I had almost insulted him by feeling the need to apologise to someone who was so close to me as he was.

'What if there's a way that we can get Flo back without any of the three of them being hurt in any kind of way?' he said, still walking around the room to the extent that the cunt was beginning to make me dizzy. 'We could quite literally have Flo back today. Fuck, you could be hanging out of the back of her by tonight mate if all going to plan.' I appreciated the sentiment if not the crudeness that he'd felt the need to attach to his attempt at being a mate in my hour of need.

It was a mark of the hopelessness of the situation that when Si offered up the proposal that he may have had an idea to get Flo back safe and sound, I was all ears. In all seriousness what really could Si ever have been able to do when it came to dealing with cartel kidnappers? We'd fought together on numerous of our own versions of a battlefield back in the day when running with the Utility boys.

We'd never shirked when tough measures needed to be taken. Decisions made within the blink of an eye that potentially could have meant a trip to hospital or a jail cell. This was a different level of trouble altogether though. This was the shit that a Bruce Willis would be handed a couple of hours to figure out. Not some random nobody who doesn't have a weak plot line or lack of attention to detail to help them rescue the girl.

Despite this, I wanted to know what he had to say. Deep down I would have always known that there would not have been a Rangers supporters chance in the old Parkhead Jungles hope in hell that he was going to come up with a workable plan to fix this mess. Yet even through just a hint from him that he had a plan was enough for my hopes to rise as I waited to see what it was. The desperation was so strong that I was more than happy to see beyond all reason. I just wanted it all to go away and if there was a chance that he could make that happen then he deserved the chance of me hearing him out.

After a minute it was already clear to me that with his ideas of guns and double crosses I already knew that he had fuck all in the way of something constructive. In fact, he had dreamed up a "solution" that as far as I could see would have resulted in even *more* deaths than the ones that I was trying to find a way to prevent.

'Well, you know I've got that gun that the boss gave me for protection. It's outside in the car' he said, completely neglecting to mention the fact, which I already knew anyway, that while aye, he did have a gun. He didn't actually know how to use the fucking thing. Had told me that he wasn't sure if the safety was on or not so was keeping as much distance from it as he possibly could for fear of blowing his balls off.

A marksman he most definitely was not. The minute he mentioned a gun he'd lost me as a potential backer of whatever plan it was that he had formed. I decided to humour him though. Fuck, quite possibly by accident there might have been a chance of him coming out with something that actually could be cherry picked from the rest of the nonsense.

'Aye, but do you seriously not think that these Colombian cunts aren't going to be carrying guns either, mate?' I tried to reason with him. We weren't gun types. Umbrella or a pub chair, maybe aye.

'Well all the more reason for us to fucking have one too then, Zeec.' He replied back as if it was all as simple as that. 'In fact, it would probably make sense if you had one as well, mate. I'll give Ivan a call and see if he can sort me out with a loan of another one. He's a sound enough cunt likes. When he hears what's going on I wouldn't put it past him to start throwing fucking Israeli Uzis at us to get the job done.' He carried on with this nonsense.

'Fucking hell the boy's lost his mind,' I thought. Asking me to take up arms with automatic weapons and stuff? I'd always had this image that if I was to fire off a round from an automatic weapon the force would send me all over the place with each bullet fired. Hardly the cold blooded accurate one shot deal that would be required in a dangerous situation such as what we were engulfed in. Fuck, there would have been as much chance of me putting a few bullets into Flo as there would have been her captors. Be as well staying there in the house if that was the case.

'Well taking into account that the only gun I've ever shot has been a fucking air gun at the Links Market in Kirkcaldy when I was a kid. I'd have to pass on the offer Si and anyway. We could call in a tactical strike to hit the cunts with if we had the arms and that's the point, mate. We don't fucking know where they are? I said trying to introduce a piece of realism to what I was already rendering a harebrained scheme.

'And that's where the big bluff comes in my good man.' Si replied with a confident smile. Considering the wreck that I had found myself in since the moment I had taken that phone call. It was his confidence and the fact that he was stood there smiling that I found myself questioning. Was he actually taking all of this as seriously as he should have been? His response of wanting to help was an absolute given. The two of us knew that we would've trusted each other with our lives but I don't know? It was more the smiling, the whole nonchalant way he seemed to be viewing things that left me thinking that he wasn't appreciating the gravity of things. There was fuck all to smile about.

'Bluff? And what could we possibly bluff them with?' I asked, already thinking past and up to the point that these were quite possibly the type to kill you even after you had complied to all their demands, never mind what they'd do if they worked out that you were at it with them.

'From what you say, this computer disc is pretty fucking important to them, aye?' He said confirming what he already knew from the way I had described the phone call I'd started my day with. 'And you said that he'd made a comment insinuating that you knew where it was?'

'Well that was the impression that I'd been given just by the way that he mentioned it, the tone of him, almost condescending in a way. Like he was talking to someone who he knew was lying and just to humour them he was pretending that he didn't. All the while, indirectly fucking with their heads with a gentle nudge of a comment to let them know that they weren't out of the woods just because of them issuing a denial.' I confirmed, replaying the words through my head.

'And that's where we're going to use this to our advantage, Zeec. Aye, you don't have the disc but he doesn't fucking know that does he? In fact it's to the contrary. If he already suspects that you either have it or that you know where it could be found and then you go calling him to say you have it. Is he going to really be that surprised? He's going to look at it like you're someone who has folded like a deck chair at the first threatening phone call from him.'

To give Si his credit. A lot of what he was saying (if you took out the stuff involving guns) was actually making sense.

'So what do you propose?' I asked, figuring that he'd explained most of his plan by this point, not one that I could say that I was fully behind but none the less. The boy was trying at least and I appreciated it.

'You said that unless they get their hands on the disc and your mum and dad then you don't get Flo back, right?' He said while letting out a slight giggle over how he had described my dad and Eva.

'Aye that was about the size of it,' I verified. Cursing at the sheer imbalance of all that they were asking of me.

'The key to negotiating, Stevie my man is never to show all of your cards. While you never bothered with the card schools when we had away days with the Utility. I on the other hand played more poker than fucking Amarillo Slim. When it comes to not showing your hand I'm a fucking master at it and the rules of poker do not always remain exclusively to the game itself. Show your hand too early and your opponent has already won. This is the strategy that we're going to employ in getting your girl back, mate.' He continued with the manner of someone, who in his own mind at least, had this predicament all completely under control.

'When it comes to negotiating a trade. Both parties are looking for something out of it of course but that doesn't have to mean that you give them all that they are asking for straight away. You barter, you get yourself a better deal. You look for some give and take while you intend to take more than you give.' He laid out the rules to business for me as he rejoined myself on the sofa once more and picked up the packet of rips that were lying on the table.

'Aye ok then Donald Trump,' I said, slightly frustrated over the fact that every minute was going to count and he was telling me everything that I already knew and absolutely fuck all in the way of things that I didn't. 'And what bargaining chips do we have to get ourselves a better deal out of this fucked up situation?' I asked, wishing him to get to the point.

'So, what's going to happen Zeec is that you're going to call this guy back again. Tell him that you actually *do* have the disc and that you want to do a trade for Flo and *only* after Flo is safe that you'll then give them the address of your dad and Eva. You give a little you get a little and despite being from another continent. I'm positive that they'll appreciate that whole attitude to trading. That shit is universal, isn't it? Of course, once Flo's safe that's when we take them out. Problem solved'

I couldn't believe what I was hearing. The cunt genuinely thought that this was a film he was in or something. Fucking Charlie Bronson grabbing a couple of guns and going off to "fix shit." Had he not been yawning his head off, rubbing sleepy eyes and with hair sticking up. Evidently someone who had came straight here from waking. I'd have taken all of this confident but crazy talk as a sign that he'd been hitting the lines before he'd driven to mines.

'Mate?' I was in the middle of a response that was going to end with saying thanks but no thanks, I love you and appreciate your help but your idea is fucking suicide so lets not shall we, when his phone went off. Pulling it out his pocket and checking the caller he looked at me and pointed his index finger indicating that he'd just be a minute.

I took over building the joint that Si had started on before being interrupted.

'Ivan the terrible, como esta my brother' Si said, managing to take himself out of the seriousness of what we'd been speaking of. Suddenly taking on the appearance of someone without a care in the world talking to one of their mates. The chipper demeanour didn't last very long.

'Shit, that's not cool, Is he still alive? .... Thank fuck for that.' Naturally this was something that got my attention. 'What? Right now? Emmmmm well I've got a bit of a situation that I'm having to deal with that I was going to ask your assistance with. I need a loan of an extra guitar.'

Fucking guitar? What was he going on about? It was only when he looked at me and mouthed the word guitar while pointing an imaginary gun at me before the penny dropped that it must have been some form of slang term.

'Well that sounds like a plan, amigo. The sooner I get to yours the sooner I hopefully get back and deal with this other stuff. Ok, I'll see you within half an hour, adios' he said, appearing to have worked out some kind of agreement with Camacho.

'Look sorry man but I'm going to have to go. Something has gone down with the Scousers. They've snatched one of Ivan's family and he wants all his soldiers in one place while he decides what retaliation he's going to hit back with.' He was already up and grabbing his car keys off the coffee table and on his way out of the villa while telling me this. 'Shouldn't be gone too long likes so I'll fire right back here. Oh and good news by the way. Camacho said it wouldn't be a problem to sort me out with some extra guns. Don't phone the Colombians until I return but don't worry mate. We're getting Flo back don't you even fucking trip my son.'

I hadn't even been awarded the chance to say one single word back to him before he was out the front door and on his way.

Soldiers, guns, cartel trades and life or death situations. What the fuck was going on?!

With Si departed, I was once again back to square one with me myself and I and the disturbing thoughts that I was awash with. Nothing had changed as far as what had been discussed with Si. If anything, time had been wasted. I was no further forward with things and still firmly deep rooted in the set choice of choosing one person (or persons) over the other and signing the death sentence of whoever didn't make the cut.

It was all too much for me sat there inside those four walls. I completed the joint that had seemed to take a forever to get together and decided to go out for a walk on the beach to see if by clearing my thoughts with all the distractions that the outside world would provide. I could then go back to the Flo situation with a fresh head and maybe, as unlikely as it was, find a way out of it all.

Chapter 29

Lee

The kid had left me worried with the voicemail that I'd found waiting for me after finishing the breakfast that I'd been out having with Rene, one of the management team from The Ku. I'd been trying to get an in at that particular club for "Wilson" one of my other deejays in the stable. I'd always felt that one of my strengths when it came to who I had under my wing was to always be able to pair them with the correct club and the vibe and musical philosophy of The Ku was suited to the boy from Newcastle. Breakfast ended however without any deals struck with Rene which I had been mildly annoyed at having previously been given the impression by him that we were meeting to cross the t's and dot the i's over the deal. This fahking business though, eh?

The disappointment was soon forgotten about the moment I began to listen to Stevie's recorded message. He was calling in sick as far as his set at Space went. While that wasn't exactly ideal. What with how clubs can sometimes view a no show from a DJ. Some, automatically going down the black ball road, it wasn't the end of the world. I had enough connections across the island to secure a stand in. It wasn't the fact that he couldn't make his set that had caused me the concern.

It was the *way* that he said it. That I'd been given the impression that there was a lot more at play for him. His cheeky sarcasm that I'd only ever associated with him was absent. By mentioning that it was family stuff. That, as far as I could surmise, must surely have involved his dad. A man, by all accounts, in terms of being a colourful character. The human equivalent of Joseph's bloody technicolor dreamcoat.

On a personal level. I'd felt that I had almost failed Stevie during the time he'd been in Ibiza. The potential for disaster for a young man let loose in such a kind of island for the best part of three months were there in every direction that you cared to look and it was my job to make sure that he played his sets that I'd booked him while also remaining out of jail and a mortuary. Apart from that horror of a night at Amnesia and the meal that we'd more recently had in Playa den Bossa. I hadn't seen him at any other point of his stay.

I know that it was not much of an excuse, and I would never ever have wished to even attempt to use one as such, but it had been a difficult summer. That would have been putting it mildly. I had one DJ (Patrick Harrison) in what was Ibiza's version of the Betty Ford Clinic due to a drug fuelled meltdown in Ibiza Town where he ate an A4 page sized sheet of Acid blotters and marched into the local police station, announced himself as the son of Peter Shilton and asking if he could have a meeting with Diego Maradona. Patrick, one of my longest standing clients from the early days of Acid House always was a bit of a wild card though but as the years went on I had seen a touch more maturity to him. I'd have been lying if I'd said I saw the whole meltdown with the blotters coming.

We're a family at Ragamuffin though. The moment I was told about his antics I was on the next plane out of Heathrow to Ibiza to take care of him. Make sure that he was alright. No man gets left behind in my agency. Fahking right set of muskahteers we are.

While Patrick was drying out. I also had the fact to contend with that saw Duffy and Vibes, a DJ duo from Bristol that I'd signed the summer before who had been falsely accused of raping a cloakroom girl over in New York. There was never a doubt in my mind that they had done it. Ironically for their line of work you could not have met two more shy and reserved characters. I hadn't signed them for their personality though. Regardless of them being eventually released after being held by the NYPD. It was still a costly inconvenience that I, as much as Duffy and Vibes, could have been doing without. All of this coming right about the same time as the night DJ Selecao almost came close to ending his rising career as a DJ all within the space of two hours at Amnesia when there had been the case of the mistakenly picked up drugs wrap.

On top of that there was just all of the usual other shit that came with the territory with regards to making sure that the clubs and one off events in Europe and beyond were adequately supplied with people to make the crowds dance. Palms to grease, favours to be carried out as well as granted. Lots in the industry with their hands out in your direction.

Sometimes it really isn't easy being me. Then again, each and every one of us could sit there and say that about themselves, I suppose.

I immediately tried to call Stevie back the moment that his recording had ended but after the designated amount rings had elapsed. My call was diverted to Stevie's default voicemail message which resembled a female robot from somewhere like the outskirts of Delaware, America.

'Stevie, call me back mate. It's fine about tonight. There's a local lad that I promised I'd give a chance to the next time an opportunity came up. He'll bite my fahking hand off. Listen, do call me back though, mate. I want to make sure that you're ok. Call me back now, remember, oh oh ohhhh one more thing before I go, CALL. ME. BACK. I know what you're like with returning calls.' I left the message for him before terminating the call. Zico was your classic case of a really good and genuine stand up guy who needs to be around the right type of people for him to be able to flourish on his own personal journey. I could easily have imagined him back in school. Good student and brainy but just stick him next to the class clown and Stevie's focus is suddenly gone. Easily Distracted. B minus.

The boy can achieve anything he wants in life if he holds that focus. He never fucking does though. Of course, having friends like that fahking Simon and a father like Peter Duncan. How the fahk was Stevie ever gunna have a chance to focus? Now I wouldn't be as unfair as to suggest that Simon was actually worse than Stevie when the two of them were together. No, when those two get the wind behind them they are a pair of certified maniacs. You never quite know how far they'll take things with the madness. They are most definitely equal partners in crime and have been for many years now by all accounts but the point that I'm making is that it's only when Simon's around that it all kind of goes the shape of the pear for Zico.

I'd barely even known Simon before the Ibiza summer season but what I did know about him was that on the nights that he would show up when Stevie was playing at, it always resulted in carnage once Stevie's set was over with. The times where Zico was left to his own devices? The lad was always as good as gold. Couple of friendly drinks with some industry insiders after his set and then straight back to the hotel. With that prior knowledge. The consideration of

Stevie and Simon left on that island for fahking months at a time was frightening in the sense of a DJ Agent. A professional who has made a commitment to Pepe Rosello, one of the most important figures in Ibiza clubland at the legendary Space.

All of this way before Stevie's dad and new wife rocking into town without any advance warning. Now I can be pretty fahking persuasive at times, what with it being part of my job description and all innit but no matter what gift of the gab skills that I humbly would admit to possessing. I still could not get anywhere close to having Stevie open up to me about the surprise visit from his dad with a girl who could almost have been in Stevie's year at high school.

The fact that he would go cagey about things whenever I mentioned the subject? That alone, in a behavioural sense, was all the confirmation that was required that something wasn't "quite right" with the kid. Generally he was always happy to give you his news, what he'd been up to, what he was planning so yeah, you'd have thought that he would have been full of all kinds of intelligence in connection with his dad arriving with his surprise youthful wife but nope. Stevie would break with the bare minimums on the subject before moving, uncharacteristically, the topic of conversation straight back in my direction. Deflecting by asking what I was up to and all of that tosh.

I mean, I knew that Stevie and Peter's relationship wasn't what you could ever have classed as conventional. How the bloody hell could it ever be conventional? The son of a father who worked in South America for a drug ring that floods the world with Cocaine? Maybe it's wrong for me to just go on and assume but when your father has an occupation with "employers" such as the Bogota Cartel. It must really put the breaks on a father and son from going football on a Saturday afternoon or sauntering out for a pub lunch on a rainy Sunday before then watching the live game on Sky Sports over a few ales.

Yeah, it seemed like a bit of a love hate relationship Stevie had with his father. I'm no psychologist but on the surface of it with Stevie. He understandably, housed a bit of resentment towards his dad through previously committed sins yet that clashed with the fact that if you were to disregard all facts bar one. Peter was Stevie's dad and that wasn't something the boy was ever going to forget. He was loyal if he was anything.

If only Stevie had simply said in his message that he had some issues and wouldn't make his set or fuck, even just lied to me and said he was sick. I'd have been left blissfully unaware. Settled that he'd maybe just done a bit too much of whatever and would be back to form by the time his next set rolled around but no. He had to mention "family" and given the already pre conceived impressions that he'd already provided me with his father. I felt the combination of Stevie plus family problems divided by his dad being there in Ibiza with him equalled bad fahking news.

Without Zico's honesty and or him fahking calling me back. I was out in the cold. Ironically so while I endured the high twenties temperature as I walked back to my car around the corner from the restaurant. In my head I was trying to work out where he was and what situation he had landed himself in when the silence was shattered by my phone ringing. Lars from Elation in Gothenburg. Normally he'd have called indirectly through his receptionist. This was from his own personal number. It must've been important. Without question a call that I was going to hit the green button on, regardless of my concerns over what was going on in the life of one of my deejays. The beat must go on, always. If the music dies then I'm out of a fahking job. End of.

'Hi Lars ... How the fuck are you, you sexy blonde Swedish bastard. you?'

Chapter 30

Zico

The day had dragged in longer than a week in Saughton and as for the evening part? Longer than a life sentence in a Siberian gulag. I didn't sleep the whole night. Didn't even try. There was too much shit flying around in my head to get anywhere near close to sleep and even if I had managed to? I reckoned the guilt of me getting my head down for a few hours while Flo was in her position would've stopped me from nodding off even if I'd approached that stage. Nah, there was too much riding on things for snoozing.

Really though? How the fuck would it to have even been possible for me to be lying there giving it big zeds while knowing that (barring some kind of miracle) in a handful of hours I was going to be taking a call that was going to result in someone being killed as a result. Not just "someone" either. A girl pretty fucking far on from "just someone."

The whole of the day and then moving into night had been dominated by one thing only. To be fair though, I'd have been well disappointed in my self if I'd been sat there contemplating which team was going to win the European Championships or what I fancied for my dinner. No, my mind literally had barely shifted from that imaginary scene that, once inserted into my mind wouldn't leave again.

That's what I kept getting when I thought of her. Dark thoughts of her tied and gagged to a chair. Threats of having digits removed and or that sexy as fuck body of hers being abused. It drove me up the fucking wall with frustration as it did with jealousy to think of her so vulnerable. Completely at the mercy of any sexual or vindictive urges from whatever sick bastards she'd had for captors.

In truth, through the sheer black and white of it all. Whether I liked it or not. I effectively had the answer for the unnamed Colombian Cartel operative to his ultimatum that he had handed to me at the start of the morning. I guess I had before the first call was even over. I just didn't want to admit to to myself at such an early stage of proceedings. I'd *always* had the answer.

On one hand aye, you had the issue that the Colombians had been threatening the life of a purely innocent girl. A fucking smashing lassie that only ever impacted on others she came into contact with in a positive way and yes, anyone with a conscience who could help in such a predicament, would do so. That would be where I would then step up and be the fine upstanding citizen to use the tools at my disposal to help secure her release.

If only life was as simple. To do so would be to become a Judas in the eyes of my father. Well, for the short time that he would remain alive in between him piecing together who had grassed him up and a bullet going into his head, but really, who the fuck would want that on their head for the rest of their life?

Whether I liked it or not, the playground rules, the type where you would find "no grassing" alongside mates before girlfriends. You would most certainly find one filed away set in stone with regards to family coming before anything or anyone else.

While I wasn't exactly ready to admit it to myself. I could've just given the Colombian his answer straight away during the call. Just went ahead and told him no to the location of my padre and no to this disc that he wouldn't shut up about. Had I done so it would've almost be akin to knocking a dog down with your car and then getting out and finishing it off to put it out of its misery.

That was how I felt with Flo. By allowing the cartel guy to give me twenty four hours to provide an answer and then taking every single one of them and not giving him the response that I was always going to give when it really got down to it. I felt that I was almost being inhumane towards the poor girl.

Over the course of the day I'd found that I had become completely at war with myself. Thinking one thing only to then find myself disgusted for me even entertaining such dark thoughts. Maybe it would be for the best if I were to just call and tell him that he would get no help from me and get it over and done with? Do so and it would allow Flo to be put out of her misery. Allow her to at least spend one less night in such company. It would've been the least that she deserved, I internally bartered before my head almost exploded with the follow up thought.

Deserve? I'm sitting there weighing up whether I send Flo to her grave and I'm fucking justifying it as me doing her a favour? Deserve? What she deserved was to be back home in England safe and sound with the only pain and suffering that she was going through, induced by the fact that she'd partied like Keith Moon for three straight weeks in Ibiza.

Aye, the "merciful" side to me felt that I'd be (somehow) helping her by just getting the whole show on the road in terms of her murder by telling the Colombian cunt to go and do one. The cowardly side to me however was without question wearing the trousers though in amongst the mental indecision and, instead of taking the bull by the horns and forcing the issue. I completely bottled it and let every single minute of those twenty four hour pass by without me coming anywhere remotely close to coming up with a plan.

Si had phoned early evening to say that he was still tied up with Camacho family business and that his plan that we'd agreed on (which we definitely fucking hadn't agreed on) was going to have to be shelved. It was easier for me to just humour him by thanking him for at least trying to help and that I'd just have to work something else out than it was to correct him by telling him that at no point had I ever, or likely to, agreed that him and I were going to tool ourselves up with guns and go and save Flo like we were a couple of Navy fucking Seals.

Say what you like about Colombian cartel operatives, they're punctual fuckers. He called me so close to twenty four hours on the dot from when he'd woken me the day before that his operation could've been sponsored by fucking Casio. It was the paradoxical exchange that I never wanted to have yet couldn't wait until it was over with. To end the phone call with me free to get on with a life of regret, resentment and the perfect soul destroying mix of self pity and self loathing.

'Ahhh, Junior Duncan, I hope I didn't wake you?' came that smug and cocky tone. The exact same as the day before. Even when the phone started to ring. I didn't immediately answer it. I couldn't. I mean, I knew I had to but that didn't mean to say that I could've pressed the answer button on the handset any easier because of that.

I felt strange. It might possibly have been some kind of stage of shock that I had went into but I didn't exactly feel that I was fully under control of things. I had a feeling of detachment from what was going on, not too dissimilar to the effect that the Ketamine had brought about that night in Amnesia. Everything was spinning, leaving me feeling nauseous. I didn't even fully realise that I'd answered the call until his voice brought a bit of realism to proceedings.

He waited for a response while I fell silent, unable to speak. I didn't know what to say or where to start. Deep down I knew that to speak would be to lead towards giving him an answer to his question. The consequences of that, gravely lying in wait. If I didn't speak, Flo would be fine. Obviously this self denial coping mechanism was not one that was going to be transferable into the real world and the man on the other end of the phone call was never going to entertain such nonsense.

'Hola? Hola? Is this piece of shit fucking telefono working?' He said. His patience in waiting on a reply from me having now expired but not appearing to consider that I just hadn't answered him.

'No, no I'm here' I confirmed to him. Saying what was the bare minimum before falling silent again. 'Ah, excellent, I thought we had lost you there for a moment mister DJ and we can't have that, can we' he laughed.

'So, I very graciously gave you twenty four hours to give me a decision and well, time is up, amigo. What will it be?'

I wasn't given the chance to fully digest the question he had asked me before I began to hear screams in the background of where he was calling me from. Amongst the screams I was able to make out the occasional word and short sentence like "stop, no and get away from me." Hearing the terror in her voice, the panic and desperation that she was projecting. It was torture.

'What the fuck are you doing to her?' I shouted, by provoking me, intentionally or not. It enabled me to find my voice. 'Well, that really isn't of any concern to you, brother although as you know. You *can* help her.' As he spoke, I noticed that the sound of Flo's screams were beginning to become less audible. Worryingly though I could still hear them as in they were continuing. It had seemed like all he had done was walk into another room away from where she was being held. Whatever she was being subjected to didn't appear to be at an end and knowing this was tearing me apart.

'Soooo, what is it to be? Tick tock tick tock, amigo' he pressed me for an answer. 'Look, you seem a reasonable man. I can tell that straight away about you. Surely there must be some way that we can work this out, why does the girl need to be harmed. Let her go, and we can talk? Do the right thing.' I said, meeting his question with a collection of questions and appeals.

'Do the right thing? Ha aha haha haa.' He sneered and laughed at my naivety over who I was dealing with. 'I have made it a very long and lucrative career out of not doing the right thing, brother. Factually my job is do to the things that not everyone can or would ever wish to do. I do not mean washing the dishes or going for groceries either, you understand? You asking me to let the girl go and do what is right. I I I Iiiiii don't know? It's like a fucking syntax error on my shit computer at home. Your words do not compute. So let me be clear with you Señor Duncan, There will be no negotiating. No deals to work out. You know exactly what I want from you. Nothing has changed.'

For the first time over the two phone calls. This, I guessed, was me now seeing the other side to this charismatic Colombian. The side that gets the job done just through a series of carefully chosen words.

'LOOK, I can get you money,' I said in a last ditch attempt at shifting gear in the exchange. Coming to the assumption that with my dad being the direct fucking cause of this whole situation. He would help with the money to secure Flo's release. I already knew about the Medellin and Cali Cartel wars and how kidnappings had been rife in Colombia. I felt it was at least worth a shot.

'Oh dear, that sounded very much like a no then. I guess I should not be so surprised. Familia is familia after all.' He sighed, without any real resistance. 'She doesn't have to die, please think about this,' I begged, sensing that the conversation may have been about to reach its conclusion.

'She very much does have to die, brother. You need to excuse my manners but in amongst all of yesterday's excitement I completely neglected to introduce myself. My name is La Cobra and the reputation I have carved for myself is one that is based on trust first, always trust. If I commit to something then I see it through. You must understand? What reputation would a man have if he was not to be taken at his word? You should ask your father when you see him about me and you will know then. After I have killed that pretty girlfriend of yours, well, after having some fun with her of course because it really would be a shame to not take advantage of that fantastic piece of ass you have there, well had.' He spelled it out for me.

As he spoke to me he appeared to be on the move again. The piercing sounds of Flo's screams, once again filling the air. If it was one last attempt from him to play mind games and have me spilling the details of my dad then it almost worked. How frightened she sounded. The knowledge that she was moments away from, well that I didn't even want to consider or comprehend. The whole death side of things was obviously a major fucking downer in itself but to then have to have your head filled with things like Flo being raped by La fucking Cobra. What even was that for a name? Probably because he was some kind of a fucking snake, I'd imagine. As he continued speaking. The sound, the racket that Flo was making had now got to the point where I could barely make out his words. She evidently was right beside him. Such was the volume of her screams and shouts.

He had been banging on about understanding the honour that I had for my family while ominously adding that while I had chosen the honourable route. I had also chosen the wrong option open to me. That I was merely delaying matters and how he would find my dad soon enough with or without my help. He added that I may well also be receiving a visit from him and his partner in due course.

Those chilling words merged with the screams from Flo were the stuff of your worst nightmares. I almost caved and told him where my dad and Eva were in a heartbeat. I came so, so close to doing so in that moment when his threats and the unwanted images in my mind of what was happening to Flo right at that moment started to get on top of me. It was enough to have me singing like fucking Tony Martin. I wanted to but I just couldn't find the words to put it into motion. There was just that unknown element of thought to speech that didn't kick in to enable me to put a stop to it all.

'Speaking of honour, brother. I am also a man who possesses honour. You may have already guessed that by now however, si? Let's be clear, had you been dealing with my partner you would not have received as much understanding as you have from me. I will be honest, if it had not been for me. My partner would have just went ahead and killed your girl yesterday if you had not given him an answer straight away. I know differently, I know that for a decision like that, a man needs time to think, si?'

Just when it began appearing to me that he was sounding suspiciously like he was starting to justify for the fact of what was about to happen he then surprised me by saying that because he was indeed that man of great ethics and understanding. He would allow Flo and I to speak one last time. There wasn't the luxury of time given to prepare for such a phone call before I heard the frantic voice on the other end 'STEVIEEEEEE HE'S BEEN TRYING TO RAPE ME. KEEPS SAYING HE'S GONNA KILL ME. THIS SICK BASTARD KEEPS STROKING MY FACE WITH HIS GUN AND TELLING ME THAT HE HAS SIX BULLETS THAT ARE GOING IN MY HEAD .... I'M FAHKING SCARED, BABE HELP ME PLEASE HELP HEL.. ...'

The line went dead at that point. You could tell that she wasn't done speaking. Fuck, I hadn't even been given the chance to ask her questions, say anything. Not even a goodbye, which I'm not sure I'd have been able to handle had there been the chance for one. Not with me being the one that was signing off on her death so to speak. And on that subject. She was gone. She had provided a connection on a series of levels I hadn't ever thought possible with a girl. It still had only been over two weeks of "connecting" however. In the general every day sense I barely knew her but did know that one way or another. I was going to be left thinking of her for the rest of my life.

The end of the call left me distraught. Utterly destroyed. Gasping for air, the room started to spin again. I felt like I was going to throw up.

Chapter 31

Zico

'FUCKKKKKK FUCKKKK FUKKKKKKKKKK.' I stood there in the kitchen having what was quite possibly the first mental breakdown of my short life. Following the end of the call, which climaxed with the voice of Flo echoing in my ears. I had immediately been sick all over myself and the sofa. It had been quite literally a gut reaction to the serious indication that something tragic was happening right there on the other end of the phone and that it was only the start for her.

Considering I hadn't eaten a single morsel of food for those twenty four hours. I was astonished at just how much mess I had been able to make over the living room. It really is remarkable just how much you can be put off your food when given news that your girlfriend is being held captive by some nasty bastards of kidnappers.

Once the attack on my stomach lining had passed. I then made a poor attempt at mopping up the mess with the three sheets of kitchen roll that had been there in the kitchen the day that I had moved in. Sensing further danger that there might be more vomit in the post. I made an attempt to try and prevent it by going to look for the packet of Polos that I'd bought for the flight over.

It's bizarre, the things that stick with you from as a child. They can often see the more unimportant and innocuous things as unforgettable and the more crucial life lessons relegated to minor. Back in high school when I'd been sick and had ended up in the nurse's office afterwards. She asked me what had happened and if there was any reason I could think of why I'd been sick. I'd told her that I'd been feeling ill since getting out of bed that morning with a dodgy stomach. It doesn't matter what age I live to be, I will always remember her reply.

'Well you should've sucked on a mint then, Steven.' Her response. Imagine my surprise in finding that eating sweets could make you feel, better. I'd spent much of my youth being told that if I ate too many sweets I'd be sick and yet there was a nurse telling me the fucking opposite of that. This was HUGE. A watershed moment for a school kid. I'm not even sure if she really *was* a nurse though to be honest. I think the jury was out on that considering I'd been told that years before I'd started first year. She had been the Modern Studies teacher. Regardless of this I would never forget the advice she gave me that day with regards to what one should do if they ever found themselves with an upset stomach.

Knowing that I was a marginally better flyer than BA Baracus. I'd bought myself a preemptive packet of mints from John Menzies inside the airport before boarding the plane. Only to then get fired into the pints with Si in the departure lounge and forgetting all about buying / needing the mints. Arriving at the villa I had stored a few of the belongings that were in my pockets into one of the kitchen drawers for safekeeping and had allowed myself to gradually forget that they had even been shoved in there.

With the dicky tummy starting a train of thought that led me to the packet of Polos. It had me off into the kitchen searching for them. While standing in that area of the villa that's when the troubling images of Flo (if even still alive by this point) and what she was being put through. The sickening flashes that my own imagination were coming up with, as vivid as they were disturbing, sent me into a downward spiral of self hatred for what I'd done to her. The loyalty that I had showed one person over another and in that particular example of loyalty. I still did not know if I had done the right thing or not. It was too much for my broken state of mind to handle.

When I made to open the drawer to find the mints and discovered that there was something wedged in there that was preventing it from being opened further than a solitary inch. I unreservedly lost my mind. There was nothing reasonable about my reaction. Then again, this was quite clearly more than just a backlash out of the frustration that had been borne out of something so insignificant as a stuck drawer.

In what, I think, is what others would describe as a primal scream. I began shouting as loud as I possibly could. The screams from me intertwined with a level of swearing that would have drawn looks of abhorrence from a sufferer of Tourettes. Anything that wasn't screwed or nailed down in the kitchen was thrown. Dishes, utensils, cutlery, even the fucking microwave was launched with tiny components from it such as the front dials going flying when it hit the kitchen floor.

'FUCKING COLOMBIAN CUNNTTTTSSS AAAAAAAARRRRRRRGGGGGGHHHHHHH.' I cried out, still a long way from getting myself near to a return back to normality. The hysteria had dipped though but only ever so slightly. I recognised this through me eventually running out of inanimate objects to throw around the kitchen and more importantly. Myself then conceding this only to then turn my attention to what I could now go on to damage.

With the red mist still very much providing a screen for my eyes I made for one of the cabinet doors next. Pulling it right off at the hinges and coming close to firing it right through the kitchen window. The small wooden door just missing the edge of the glass and crashing into the wall to the side of it. With no control I focussed on the drawer again that had set me off in the first place.

'FUCKINNNN STUPID BASTARDING FUCKING SHITTY DRAWERRRRRR.' I screamed out. The noise reverberating around the small room as I started to pull at the handle with every ounce of strength that I had left in me. 'FUCKINNNNNN THING' I pulled manically at it, willing it to break free. The actual reason that I'd wanted into the drawer, long since forgotten about. For some reason, that only a psychiatrist could've answered. The only thing important to me was that I got it open. Nothing else.

Whether it was a case of my super strength brought on from the rage that was flowing from inside of me or a simple example of the balance of probability. Without warning, the drawer came free. In doing so, sending me and the drawer flying backwards into the opposite wall. The back of my head cracking itself hard against the concrete. Landing me right onto my arse while still, inexplicably, holding onto the drawer handle.

I sat there on the kitchen floor with my back against the wall. Had it been a cartoon there would have been those fucking whistling birds flying round and round above my head. It took me a few moments before I was able to start coming to again. One thing that couldn't have been denied though was just how much the bump to the head had done to dampen the meltdown that I'd been going through. All that I now could concentrate on was the searing pain that seemed to be starting at the back of my head and spreading its way round both sides. It felt like there was blood flowing from the point of impact but after hesitantly putting my hand up to the back of my head. I found that, fortunately, it was still bone dry.

It was only sitting there that I was able to find the luxury of stepping back and seeing the damage that I'd caused. Fucking looked like the Tasmanian Devil had blitzed its way through the kitchen and then made it a return journey just in case he hadn't made a good job of it the first time around. Plates were shattered into pieces all over the floor. Same with all the glasses. I immediately looked at my feet figuring that it would have taken a Lourdes type miracle for me to have escaped my rampage without having ended up with shards of glass or ceramic sticking into my feet. There was a small pool of blood sitting under my right foot and sure enough, a big shard of what looked like a wine glass sticking into the side of it. I pulled it out, screaming every bit as loud as I'd been doing minutes before in doing so, only this time in pain.

I launched it across the room in frustration. Add the broken microwave which, in all honesty I'd never fucking used and had no intention of doing so. The hole in the wall I'd caused by repeatedly opening the fridge door at speed into, the broken jar of mustard that had been the only food product even sat inside the fridge, now splattered over the white wall.

All the contents of the inside of the drawer were scattered either over me or around me. The ridiculously sized ladle that had been crammed inside. Most likely the reason for why I couldn't get the drawer open. 'Who the fuck puts a ladle in a drawer for fucks sake,' I raged before having no choice but to admit that it may well have been me that had done it.

What a fucking mess. Flo dead, me seemingly a candidate for sectioning and on top of it all. I'd caused enough damage inside the kitchen that it was probably going to take every single fucking peseta earned at Space for me to cover the repairs. Well, if I even played Space again. Who knew what the fuck the Colombians had in store. They'd already been to the club looking for me and since then we'd definitely become a lot more familiar with each other, in the most unwanted of ways.

That's when I realised that I still had the kitchen drawer lying upside down on top of my lap after it had parted ways from the kitchen unit. I grabbed hold of the edge to move it to the side of me. It was only at that point when I clocked it.

On the underside of the drawer was what looked like two pieces of electrical tape, crossing over each other like an X. I pulled the drawer up closer for inspection and couldn't believe my fucking eyes. Very carefully, and discreetly, taped onto the underside alcove system of the drawer was a black plastic computer disc. What followed next was a case of pure instinct assisted by adrenaline.

Through, what I could've put down to concussion. I'd barely even registered getting up from the kitchen and the point of being sat in the living room with the phone in my hand praying to all the fucking gods in the universe that the number I was calling was going to be answered.

The time to completely lose my fucking mind at my excuse of a dad before going on to, without pause, emancipate myself from the bastard post fucking haste would come. So would the trip to the doctors. In my rush to stand up in the kitchen to run and make the call. I'd inevitably ended up with further pieces of glass sticking into my feet. The sheer desire for me to get to that phone would've seen me through or past anything, or anyone. Fire, Mike Tyson, Pennywise the fucking Clown. You name it I was getting past it to that cellphone. Everything else could be looked at after I got to the phone.

'Hola my friend, como esta? I hope that you're keeping well?' came that cool calm and, at that point, fucking arrogant and cocky reaction. -

'AM I TOO LATE?' I shouted down the phone at him. Understandably in no mood for any fannying around. 'Too late for what? There's still so much of the day left, brother. I think the only thing that you could possibly be late for at this point of the day would be breakfast, si.' He chuckled away to himself, clearly enjoying the moment. Initially I was just ecstatic that he'd answered but within seconds he was being an absolute dick. He couldn't have mistaken in my voice, as well as the fact that I was actually calling him, that there must've been some kind of a development on my side.

'LISTEN LA FUCKING COBRA. WE CAN DO YOUR WEE FUCKING DANCE ALL YOU LIKE IN A MINUTE BUT TELL ME, AM I TOO LATE? IS SHE STILL ALIVE?' I repeated the initial demand, diplomacy there and then something I hadn't' the time for.

'Jorge, JORGE …. STOP.' I heard him shout, in a way that almost sounded like he had dropped his usual patter and was actually displaying a little bit of urgency. Seemingly on the move from wherever he had been at the start of our next "catch up" to where his partner apparently was.

I sat there with a stomach like I was permanently on the dip part of a rollercoaster, waiting on some kind of development.

'Oh, brother. You really do not have any idea how close you left your change of heart.' He shared while letting out an actual 'pheeewwww' to go with it. 'Who knows? If this all works out, your girlfriend will tell you herself' he teased.

All this had given me was a little bit of hope. He had picked up my call. Hadn't immediately told me that I was too late and then to reinforce this had then affirmed that I had got there in the nick of time. That was all cool and everything but all of this had still not actually provided any evidence that Flo really was still alive though. This was something I reminded him with my reply which was delivered in a lot less decibels back at him. 'Give me proof she's still alive and then we'll talk about what I have for you. Both the times that we've spoken before I've barely been able to hear you because of Flo screaming and crying and yet right now? Not a sound from her.' Saying the words and the sense that they were making to me suddenly filled me with a sinking feeling that this was exactly the type of stuff that these cunts did for a living. They'd have been mad not to have tried to fool me into a trap of trying to get Flo when in reality, she was long gone.

'Ah yes, of course, there is a reason for it being so tranquilo now. She was giving me a sore head with her screaming.' He said casually as I then heard the sound of the tape ripping right off her face and mouth producing a scream of genuine pain as opposed to the screams that were enabled by fear from before.

'STEVIEEEEEEEEE IS THAT YOU?' She screamed before the phone was taken away from her mouth again. I could still hear her screaming and shouting in the background as La Cobra began speaking once again.

'JORGE, CINTA.' He shouted which I noticed coincided with Flo's screams disappearing altogether from earshot. 'I'm sorry, brother but I am only human, si. The tape had to go back on. I can only take so much of it before I feel like killing her on principle.' He joked (I think) while I sat there elated that Flo was still alive. The feeling was like nothing I'd ever experienced in my life. Now I just needed to on and finish the job and get her back.

'So, Señor Duncan, what do you have for me?'

Chapter 32

Flo

He was, quite verbatim, in the process of murdering me when the other one came running through shouting for him to stop. That dirty greasy, sweaty moustached horrible cahnt who had enjoyed having me cuffed up and subjecting me to all of his fahking mind games. I'd already accepted that I was going to be killed, they'd told me as much and in the most graphic of ways. Well, one of them anyway. The one that had been referred to as Jorge. The other one was ok. Well, if you can class someone who is partly responsible for snatching you from the bathrooms of an Ibiza pub and holding you as prisoner I suppose?

I was grabbed when I'd went for a wee when Elle and I were in this Irish theme pub, Molly O'Hagen's. It must've been a new addition to San Antonio as definitely hadn't been there the summer before. Ironically, especially in Ibiza, Elle and I would always go off to the bathrooms together and shack up in a cubicle and do a little sniff or have a cheeky sweetie. This one occasion though? With the place being especially rammed. We knew we'd lose our seats at the bar if we both were to go missing to the bathroom. Instead, we decided to take turns in visiting the loo.

It was almost a WWF style tag team effort when she had come back from the toilet. Discreetly passing me the small wrap and sending me walking in the same direction that she'd come from. After patiently waiting my turn for a cubicle in amongst the long line of girls all waiting there. House heads, hen parties, timid mice of women who had clearly ended up on the wrong island with their mates but were trying to make the best of it.

I only got as far as knocking out a line onto the toilet top before the door was kicked in, almost coming right off with the the force. I thought I was fahked, the first inclination that the bathrooms had cameras fitted inside them and that I had made the total schoolgirl error of not checking before I got the Charlie out. Bar security now here to take me away and who knew?

Possibly handed over to the police which would've almost certainly thrown a spanner to my plan of flying home the next day. A thought like that, a major supersession to the disappointment that I'd have had at missing out on a last night in Ibiza and a final chance to see Stevie before I flew home. Plus, he had hinted at putting together a special set at Space to mark the end of my holidays. How many girls could say that they had a set at Space compiled with them in mind?

In actual fact. My fears of being busted by the security, potentially thrown in the cells and missing my flight home were completely unfounded. They were far, far worse than that.

With the door kicked in, that was when he poked his head around, followed by the rest of him. Some slick looking man in a white Hugo Boss polo shirt standing there looking back at me. Tanned with some designer stubble and some tended to but greasy hair that could've kept Giuseppe's chip shop running for a couple of nights at least.

'Oh, naughty girl. That stuff is bad for you' He said with a foreign accent and with an almost cheeky kind of charm that unsettled me as I stood there cornered and still clutching the rolled up thousand peseta note in my hand.

'Ok, senora, come.' He demanded, making a grab for my arm. I pushed him off for a second and screamed but what really could I do? He was almost double my size and weight and there inside the cubicle, I had nowhere realistically that I could go. 'Come now, let us not make this happen the hard way,' he expressed a look of impatience veiled with the threat of this situation turning in a direction that I was sure I'd rather have avoided.

'I want to see Elle, my friend's out there.' I pleaded as he took a tight grip of my arm and pulled me kicking and screaming from the cubicle. I was hoping, assuming actually, that there was going to be streams of other girls inside the bathrooms ready to help but the ones in there just stood and watched. I guess, to them all they were seeing was some girl getting busted for taking drugs in the bathrooms of a pub.

'No, Selina Wallington Seventy Five Hayfield Road, Kingston. That's not going to be possible,' he said as he hauled me out of there. It took me a few seconds to fully register what he had just said to me. Something that there was no way that your standard doorman would ever have known. That's when I got that stomach churning realisation that there was a lot more to this than had initially met the eye. No regular "drug bust" here.

Next thing I'm outside O'Hagen's along with him and another man. They marched me right down the hill in front of all the holiday makers and PR staff working the street. Eventually stopping at a car that was parked at the bottom of the busy strip.

It was all over and done with in what seemed like a couple of seconds. Despite my cries for help, shouting to anyone that would listen that these two men were kidnapping me. There was no signs of a Good Samaritan or (what you'd often see tabloids describe) have a go hero. It was difficult for me to notice if anyone's attention had been caught but it wasn't as if I was on the quiet side as it all took place.

Struggling and resisting as hard as I could while making almost as much noise as the speakers inside The fahking Ku. It appeared like I may as well have saved my energy for as good as my unwillingness to go with them was impacting on everyone else who were witness to it. The one who had pulled me from the bathroom opened the back door of the blue Mazda and his partner pushed me into it. Then bundling himself almost on top of me while the other quickly jumped into the drivers seat, started the engine and tore off with the car's engine making an absolute screeching roaring racket.

'Silencio, Senora. We don't want you to end up being hurt here.' The one in the back with me calmly threatened. The smell that came from him was heinous. The foul odour of cheap ciggies and beer merging with one of those unhygienic smells that suggests someone either doesn't really get involved with the whole washing themselves daily rule and or has never heard of the concept that is deodorant.

With him pressing down on top of me to stop my thrashing around. The main concern was more of me suffocating due to the way he was tightly holding me than it was in relation to the smell of the man. No sooner had the car taken off but it went into what felt like an emergency stop. Throwing myself and my captor rolling forwards from the back seat.

'Jorge, get this on her.' I heard the driver say which provoked another struggle there in the back as he made to pull what looked like the kind of tea cosy that my nan used to stick on her teapot over my head.

'Fahk off you fahking cahnt.' I screamed at him as I felt it begin to slip over my head quickly. This sending me into complete darkness as the fabric moved its way down over my eyes. It was quite disconcerting the way he just laughed back at me in a show of total control and of someone who was in no way fazed by any of what was taking place.

'Awwwww don't you want to be friends, sexy? I want to be *your* friend, ohhhhhh si I do mmmmmmm,' he replied, creepiness personified. I almost lost the chicken pasta with pesto that I had enjoyed a couple of hours before we'd hit the West End of town.

'Leave me alone, Nonce' I screamed. My voice muffled from underneath the tea cosy. 'What do you want with me anyway?' I continued. I admit that a lot of what was coming from me was pure front. The real facts of it all was that I was shit scared. 'Oh you will find out when you find out, now be quiet you little crying bitch or you get something to *really* cry over.' Came the response from my road trip partner in the back. It was said with such a sinister tone to it that I subconsciously began to do as I was told. I questioned whether the word "nonce" was actually an internationally recognised insult and that, by calling him one it had changed the dynamics of which direction this was all heading in.

Actually, when it come to where we were heading, in a literal sense. That was one thing that I definitely did not know. Given the fact that they had taken good care to make sure that I wasn't going to be able to see any of the journey. This, I felt, was in some ways was a good sign. By making sure that I could not see where I was going to. It left me under the impression that they were already planning for later events for when I would retell all of the events back to others. I would be left with no real way of describing where exactly I had been taken to.

To counter this, I had obviously seen both of their faces yet, in amongst all of the scattered thoughts during that surreal car ride. I couldn't help but feel that there had been a point to them obscuring my vision and that they wouldn't have went to that trouble had it not been important to the both of them.

There probably was no way of accurately measuring how long we had driven for before the car stopped and I heard the opening of doors. At a guess I'd say it was around the fifteen to twenty minute mark but then again it could've been longer, or shorter. My mind was taking on a lot more pressing issues than one Mississippi, two Mississippi and so on.

'Out' He barked, grabbing the top of my arm and, whether I was ready or not, dragged me out from the backseat. To illustrate this. One of my feet caught the inside of the car which led to me falling onto my knees outside onto some sharp pieces of gravel. Not that there was any sympathy going spare from "Hor Hey."

'Get up, stupid girl, Awwwww you have cut yourself but do not worry I will kiss it better.' He said, smirking. Ramping up the perv and creep factor. Those slight innuendos really scared me. I still had no idea why these two men had taken me. WHY would they have wanted to take me? For whatever unknown reason they had and the sickening realisation that there I was, alone with them. With the alarming comments that the dirty greasy one with the tache had been saying. My mind began taking me to dark places. Pondering the possibilities of what could end up happening before all of this was over.

Whatever *was* about to follow it would probably have been beneficial to me if I was to keep my head, if possible. I was so very scared though. Fahking terrified, actually. The two of them, despite looking completely different to one another, came over as very serious characters. You would sometimes see a couple of "heavies" pop up in the occasional episode of Minder, trying to give Terry McCann a doing. These two fitting that same type of description.

They even seemed to have the good cop bad cop vibe to them with the original one who had grabbed me from the cubicle having a bit of character to him while the other one? I had only been in his company for all of a minute and I could tell that he was a horrible cahnt. He was the one that my gut instincts were telling me was the one that I would have to keep my eyes on. Being able to actually see would have been nice though when it came to things like that.

I meekly surrendered and got to my feet and with vision still blocked, was led a few metres or so before reaching some steps. I heard a door opening in front of me and followed in. It was only after I'd been abruptly pushed down onto a chair. Both my arms grabbed and pulled around the back of it before I then soon heard the ripping of tape. It didn't take a Mastermind contestant to work out where the tape was headed. The pain went shooting up my arms through the position that they had been pulled back in. With it wrapped around my wrists four or five times it was only then that the tea cosy was removed.

It took a few seconds for my eyes to readjust to the new surroundings. Everything seemed so bright, so white. Once I began to focus I saw that it actually *was* white. The whole four walls decked in nothing but white paint with no pictures, mirrors, nothing. It didn't really stop at the walls either. Inside the room there was one chair, which I was sat on and in the corner on top of a small table was one of those silly little TV, video and CD player combos. The TV screen about the size of a small boys head.

It can be really crazy finding yourself in a position like that and the irrational thoughts that you find flowing through your head. Looking at the TV I found myself thinking that if it was there for my benefit then they'd need to move the fahking chair closer because you'd have needed the Hubble Space Telescope to have seen what was actually on the screen from where I was sitting in the room.

'Are you hungry?' The "nice" one asked. Stood in front of me he crouched down so he could look me in the eyes as he spoke. I inexplicably burst out into tears right there in front of him.

'Tranquilo, tranquilo,' he sympathised as he stroked my shoulder which comforted me way more than it should have done considering who had dispensed it. 'This will all be over soon and you will be back partying before you know it, party girl. Now do you need food?' he asked me once again.

'No, I had something earlier,' I eventually replied. Still trying to regain some pattern of breathing after the fit of crying. 'Ok, you eat later then,' he decided, reminding me of my Auntie Norma in Bradford who would always want to make sure that I was fed when I would visit. Like it had been the sole purpose of her entire being that she saw me with food in my mouth that she had personally prepared.

As he spoke to me. The other one, Jorge, freakishly had seemingly read my mind. Walking over to the corner of the room where the "entertainment system" was sat and pulled the table and everything on top of it over towards the middle of the room and closer to my chair.

'We are going out for a while so are you sure you don't wan't food?' the man, whose name I'd not heard spoken yet, in the Lacoste polo shirt asked. I didn't quite know what to make of the news that they were both going to be leaving again. They'd went to the trouble of specifically targeting me in that Irish bar which I assumed had meant that they'd already been watching me for a period of time. Go to all that trouble to get me out to this house. Then the minute they get me there the two of them appeared to be fahking off again?!

The question alone that he was asking me was farcical in itself. No doubt, the two of them looked like they were experienced in that whole kidnapping thing but yet I'd have thought that asking a girl if she wanted something to eat while she's not got any fahking hands to eat with would have appeared slightly obvious as being flawed?

'Well, okay, yeah I probably *will* want something later on to eat but....' I motioned my head from side to side in an obvious display of my hands being tied on either side behind me.

'Mierda, I am very sorry. Of course, the handcuffs!' He said with an embarrassed look on his face that they had made such a basic mistake. By the time the two of them left the house I had been fully equipped for a survival guide to being held hostage.

With one hand I was handcuffed through the gap on a bracket that was fixed to one of the windows. The window themselves obscured by some kind series of black bars running from top to bottom on the outside. I had a couple of ham and cheese baguettes made up for me. A two litre bottle of Fanta and the TV close enough for me to see the film, Top Gun, that was playing. Even if I couldn't understand the Spanish lingo that had been dubbed over top of the original sound. They'd even been so kind as to put two and two together and know that if they were giving me two litres worth of soft drinks then they would need to provide at least an equivalent sized receptacle accordingly.

They indeed, left me a large bucket along with a roll of toilet paper, even some hand sanitiser. They really had thought of everything. It would have been a lie if I was to say that I had foreseen my last night in Ibiza pissing into a bucket but for what it was worth. I was grateful for the humanity they'd shown, regardless of what the two of them had planned for me.

Sensing that the two of them were going to be gone for a while. Weirdly, despite the fact that they had just kidnapped me. I'd been left with the impression that the both of them were leaving me there alone and going, specifically, for a night out in Ibiza. I could even smell the aftershave that one of them had sprayed through in another room as they, in good spirits, laughed and joked about something in Spanish.

'Ok, you have everything, si?' The nameless kidnapper asked one last time. He had changed into a different colour and design of shirt. He had clearly reapplied some product to his hair. Those bastards WERE fahking going out! 'Who does that?' I reflected in disbelief.

'Ok, we will be back, don't wait up' he said jokingly to me as they got themselves together for leaving. Through the way that he had spoken to me. He, out the two of them, looked like the one to place your chips on being the one that would have been capable of displaying empathy. He was the one out of the duo that I felt like I could say something to, even if only a couple of words, and it still manage to remain civil.

'Why am I here, what do you want with me?' I pleaded. Preferring to sit on the side of sincerity in the hope that he would give me an answer. 'Well, it is like this,' he replied before taking a moment out to pause before he would speak again. 'Con rapidez, Gilberto' Jorge said, standing by the doorway to the room I was in and barging in on the conversation while tapping at his watch.

"Gilberto," wearing a weary look on his face which appeared to show evidence that working with this other guy wasn't always the easiest of tasks at times. Rolled his eyes in exasperation while still with his back to his colleague he then changed tact. 'I will explain all tomorrow to you' He left it at that in what looked like a clear attempt at appeasing both Jorge and myself.

'Bb b bbbbbut I fly home tomorrow to London.' I pleaded. More in hope than through any kind of actual confidence. This being something that Jorge, who looked like he was so itching to get out of the house so much that he was resembling a cat on a hot tin roof, found a piece of comedy genius.

'Yes, that is not going to be happening,' he laughed. Looking at Gilberto as if there was an in joke that existed between the pair of them. My heart sank at the news. So many things ran through my mind. Elle having to travel home alone. Well, if she'd decided to go back on her own? The reaction of my family and friends when I didn't return on schedule and stupidly (in the scheme of things) how much additional money I was now going to have to shell out to get myself back to Blighty. Of course, how much money British bleeding Airways were going to squeeze out of me was nothing other than redundant while I found myself handcuffed to a fahking window. Ironically, one that had vertical metal bars covering the glass. I was a prisoner in every sense of the word.

The both of them left soon after. Hearing the door closed followed by the two sets of footsteps walking on the gravel up to the car. It was only when the engine started with the vehicle rapidly driving off that it dawned on me that I hadn't heard any other cars since I'd been sat inside the room. Actually there hadn't been any noises from outside, at all. I sat listening to the car gradually become less audible as the two of them headed off to wherever their nightly plans were going to involve.

For the first time since I'd nipped away to the bathroom for a cheeky little pick me up inside Molly O'Hagen's. I now had an opportunity to take stock and try to come to terms with this new reality that I had been literally dragged kicking and screaming into.

Tom Cruise and Kelly McGillis were about to have a bit of a moment there on the screen which sent me into a compendium of thoughts relating to Stevie. How would he have been left feeling when the penny dropped that I hadn't turned up while knowing that it was the last time he was going to see me on my trip? Would he have been left annoyed or worried? He would try to call me, that I'm sure of but it wouldn't have exactly got him anywhere since Jorge had taken my phone from me back inside the car when we were in San Antonio. If indeed we were now in a completely different town?

I kept trying to tell myself that this was a time for priorities and that Stevie would have finally understood when all was explained to him. Of course he would. If we ever were to see each other again that was.

Alone with my thoughts which themselves felt like a prison cell. Mercifully I dropped off to sleep while still sat there on the chair. Only grasping that I had when I was rudely awoken by my kidnappers coming back into the room. Upon opening my eyes I could tell that it was now daylight outside. 'How long have they been out? The whole night?' I deliberated before it dawned that for me to question anyone else's evening behaviour in Ibiza would have been the height of hypocrisy.

Jorge, who had without question been hitting the liquor hard, made a beeline for me with a lecherous look on his face while Gilberto stood there squinting, trying to focus on a small piece of paper that he was holding in his hand. His mobile phone in the other.

'Did you miss me, babeee?' The less palatable out of them asked me with a leery look to him. Clearly taking some form of enjoyment out of the fact that I was as disgusted with him as I was frightened.

'Piss off you pervy cahnt.' I replied through bravado and nothing much more than that. I shouldn't have done. To do so would've only encouraged him and that was something that didn't exactly appeal much to me. He just laughed before moving close enough to kiss me on the cheek while purposely placing a hand on one of my breasts.

Taking his thumb and gently rubbing it over my nipple. 'FAHK OFFFFFF AND LEAVE ME ALONE!!' I screamed, catching the other's attention.

'JORGE! DETENER, FUCKING MALPARIDO,' the shout from Gilberto enough to have the creepy bastard back off again. From the short time that I had been around them. I'd been left with the impression that neither was really the "boss" as such in their partnership. If anything, Gilberto appeared to be the one who was the more likely to be the voice of reason. The one who would need to be responsible for keeping Jorge on a tight lead. It *did* worry me of the potential for what could happen if only Jorge and I were left alone. Somehow I hoped that Gilberto also had those same concerns and would already have known to plan accordingly for such.

Jorge stormed out of the room with a couple of choice words in Spanish for his partner as he walked past him. This left the two of us remaining in the room as Gilberto lifted the phone to his ear apparently in the process of making a call. It only took the opening sentence from Gilberto for me to sit a bit more upright in my seat. The call was evidently in connection with me.

I didn't know who he was speaking to but regardless of that, my hopes were sent soaring. I wasn't left with much time to contemplate further before Gilberto was handing me the phone and telling me that it was my boyfriend.

With no plan on what I was going to say I opened my mouth and the words spilled out. For all of two seconds before he moved the phone away from the side of my face. I could hear Stevie's shouts through the phone even from the widening gap that was being placed between the receiver and my ear. It made me want to break down in tears hearing the seriousness and desperation in his voice. How frightened he sounded and that it was me who was putting him through all of this.

I sat there carefully trying to listen while Gilberto took care of the rest of the phone call with Stevie. It all fell into place without any need for that explanation that I had been promised by my captor the night before. I was sitting there, for a few seconds at least, wracked with guilt over what Stevie had been dragged into. By the time Gilberto had ended the call I'd then found that it wasn't Stevie who had been hauled into this by me but in actual fact the exact opposite of. Being fair though, Stevie was nothing other than guilty by association of being the son of his father.

That was when it hit me that these two were more likely to be from Colombia than they were Ibiza. That alone, based purely on the notoriety that South American drug cartels enjoyed, scared me more than anything else that I had went through over the eighteen hours or so since "departing" Molly O'Hagen's the previous evening.

The call ended with Stevie being handed some kind of ultimatum. The crux of it being, if he wanted to see me again he was going to have to give them things in return. The main take away being that he was going to hand over his father. That gave me the fear. It was an unenviable position for someone to be placed in and I quickly put myself into his shoes. Left with what was undeniably the equivalent of that movie, Sophie's Choice.

Would I have given up my father in return for a boy I'd only known for weeks? The terrifying thing about it was that deep down in my heart of hearts. I knew that the answer would've been no, I wouldn't have. Stevie was an absolute fahking darling. Without question the best man I had ever met and yeah I very much had been intent on him and I picking things up with each other once we were both back in Britain.

To not have done would have been nothing less than a waste of a gift that had been thrown my way. You meet someone like Stevie and feel the depth of connection and chemistry that you have together. You find yourself with the willingness to grab hold of that person and never let go. To give up my father in the process? To grass him up to a couple of Colombian gangsters who, I assumed, had only bad intentions in store for him. I'm afraid that it would not have been something that I would've been able to do. You only get one dad and he had been my fahking world. The best father that anyone could wish for so to even think about having to betray him in any way was laughable, so unlikely it was.

I was still mulling it all over and facing up to the fact that if this was all going to come down to Stevie handing his father over to the Colombians then my chances of surviving were slimmer than a Rizla. That was when Gilberto and Jorge came back into the room. Changed, and by the sounds of the internal pipes in the house, having showered and out of the clothes from the night before.

'Do not worry, he will make the correct choice. His father is not a good man, your boyfriend will already know this. As you heard, I have given him until tomorrow to decide. Until then, you wait here. Tomorrow you will go home,' Gilberto said as he counted out a stack of peseta notes that would've choked a Hippopotamus.

'I wish I shared your confidence.' I tearfully replied, sniffing at my runny nose between words. Already trying to come to terms with the very real certitude that this didn't look good for me and no amount of hollow sentiments from the person who might well end up being the one who would kill me was going to persuade me of anything other than that.

'We are going out, you are good for everything you need until evening.' Gilberto told me. Safe in the knowledge of having personally seen to it that I had enough food for the three of us combined in addition to making sure I had a cleaned out bucket ready and waiting for another day of potty training.

With him mentioning about my provisions lasting until evening. That, at least, confirmed that I was going to have the house to myself for the day. 'Hmmmm what shall I do with the opportunity?' I pondered. Shall I maybe go outside and enjoy the sun's rays? Go for a swim or maybe even a nice walk to check out my new surroundings. The gallows humour in me rose to the top as I accepted that I was going to be spending the foreseeable chained to a window sat enduring a horribly sticky humid heat while watching TV shows and films that I couldn't fahking understand.

All the while, sitting slowly going out of my mind while wondering if by that point of the next day I would even be alive. The mind, at the end of an Ibiza trip, is hardly what could ever be described as mint and fresh. If your mind had legs then by the time your trip comes to an end it would be accurate to describe it as being on its last ones. Asking me to take on anything else to try and think about, especially as serious as being abducted. It really was too much for me to handle.

In amongst all of the me me me stuff though I managed to think (and appreciate) about the other side of the coin with Stevie and what he was going through. Having taken that call an hour before. Obviously he'd been playing at Space and for all I knew. Hadn't even been to bed yet when Gilberto had called him. The poor bastard could well have been out of his beautiful little mind on pingers and suddenly getting a call from kidnappers hitting him with the mother of all choices to have to make.

From the Stevie that I had met and got to know, though. I just knew that he would've been in complete turmoil over it. Whether he'd only known me three days, three weeks or three decades. He was one of the good guys, you know? Yeah, from what I could see. He had a colourful past and didn't look like he was ever going to be a pipe and slippers lets go to the museum at the weekend type of boyfriend but then again who the fahk was looking for one of them anyway?

He was warm, friendly, infectious, fun, loving, sincere and completely down to earth. Being down to earth while being a DJ at Space was a minor miracle in itself. He even played it down more than up. Was self depreciating about it all by always reminding me that he only played the earlier part of the night. When the place wasn't full to capacity but I'm sure we both knew that there were thousands of deejays across the world that would have been willing to do things to get that spot at the club that would not have left them with their dignity, intact.

You could tell though that he was excited about it (and so he should have been) with that little gleam he got in his eye when he would speak when on the subject of Space. It got me pondering over what that last set was like that he'd planned in my honour. Or so he had teased me about. What tracks he'd put in there for me knowing that I would completely go off the second I heard them? Obviously there were more pressing matters that I had to be getting on with thinking about but the thoughts of what he would have planned for me, knowing him, and how it could well have been the best night of my life, had I actually made it to take part in.

The day, left there in the house full of all kinds of understandable dark thoughts and regrets. All that I never got to do. The things I had wanted to say to people but always assumed that I'd get around to another day. How I had so much of my life still to lead and that it was going to be prematurely snatched away just because I met the wrong guy at the wrong time when, ironically, thinking I had met the right guy at the right time.

When the two of them arrived back later on in the evening. The whole kidnapping as it were took on a fahking Groundhog Day vibe which saw them coming back. Getting themselves ready with the showers, change of clothes and bite to eat. Gilberto making sure I was provided with food and sanitation while Jorge, true to form, was an unsettling cahnt. Then they left again.

I hadn't enjoyed the same level of sleep I'd had the night before when I had passed out. I sat there thinking about Stevie and how his mental state was at. I just wished that I could have been able to talk to him for a while. To tell him that I understood his reasons for choosing his dad over me and that he shouldn't let it haunt him over the rest of his life. I always had been a big believer in fate and that whole - everything is already written before it happens way of thinking. If that stuff *was* real then I'd been dealt an absolute shite hand by the looks of things, no mistake. A good portion of the night I was imagining the moment when these psychos would kill me and how they'd do it. I wanted to think of practically anything BUT my impending murder. That wasn't so easy however.

I wasn't sure what time I'd passed out but I was still awake when the sun began to come up in the morning. Regardless, I was sleeping when the Colombians eventually returned. It was them coming back that I was the most scared of because of what was going to follow as a result.

They entered the room with purpose and zero pleasantries as far as their houseguest was concerned. Gilberto took one look at me and without speaking, left the room again. Jorge? He stayed. Unsteadily on his feet. He staggered his way towards me. Had they already spoken with Zico and this was it?

There was just something "different" about the two of them than before. This fahking Jorge? Well yeah he was just the same as I'd always seen since being abducted by them but the way he walked towards me and the look that he had all over his face. It just felt that nothing good was going to follow. There were no sleazy subtle as a brick to the face comments from him. There *was* the creepy smile but his eyes were dead. Staring back at me, as if his mind was elsewhere.

'Now, we play, babeeee, si?' He said raising his hand towards my face and roughly taking a grip of my cheeks. Taking a hard grip of them and squeezing them tight which, apart from being painful as fahk, prevented me from telling him that actually NO we weren't fahking playing.

Then again, it didn't look like I was going to have much of a say in the matter. As he gripped my face he then took his other hand and slipped it up and inside my short dress (that had been saved for my last night on the island) up my leg, grabbing me. Roughly lifting me up for a second so that he could slip his hand underneath and grab at one of my arse cheeks really hard.

With my free arm I tried to fight him off but he was too fahking strong. I managed to get his hand off my face which allowed me to start screaming out. It was the most vulnerable I'd ever felt in my life. So defenceless. Wherever I put my hand to stop him he would just put his hand somewhere else. Then he brought out the gun and I just froze.

'Ahhhh, now you behave.' He said with such a smugness it was hard to stomach. 'Now you do every little thing that I say up until I put all of my bullets into your beautiful little head, si?' He said stroking the barrel of the gun up and down the side of my face. With the room already well on its way to warming up for the day. I couldn't help but notice the stark coldness from the steel of the gun against my cheek.

While still holding the gun close to my face, too scared to move a muscle. I noticed out of the corner of my eye him going for his belt and undoing it with one hand. I wanted him to just give me the six bullets that he had spoken about the night before when, before leaving for the night, told me that if I didn't behave he had that exact amount of bullets for me. I just wanted it all to be over. He seemed to have a little trouble with the top button in the jeans that he was wearing but empowered by the effect that the gun had instantly had on me. He wasn't for putting it down to help loosen the button. He was just in the process of it popping out of its hole when Gilberto burst into the room, talking on the phone.

Moving straight towards me. Jorge quickly dodged to the side, making for the button on his jeans. Looking as if he was trying to hide from Gilberto what he had been about to do with me. Gilberto pushed the phone towards me. He remained stoney faced as he did so. It all felt, off.

I couldn't even remember most of what I had shouted down the line to Stevie when I'd had the phone put to my mouth from the moment that it had spilled out of me. Mainly I was still dealing with the shock of what Jorge had been doing to me and it all came out when presented with the chance. I didn't even get the opportunity of hearing Stevie's voice one last time. Gilberto ended the call after only a few seconds.

Then came the arguments.

'We should have killed the girl yesterday, Gilly. The boy was never going to give up his papa.' Jorge said nonchalantly as if the price of my life had been worth not even a peseta to him. 'You waste our time, man. I don't know why you have to play the good guy?' He kept pressing Gilberto.

'Oh, maybe I am this way because I am not the type of person who just kills young girls because they have a fucking hangover? Maybe I like to keep the people alive that should remain living and make sure that the ones who are meant to be dead end up that way. It is not fucking brain surgery.' Gilberto hit back at his partner over what was undoubtedly some previous between them.

It hadn't been hard to notice that tucked away inside their exchange was the confirmation that I'd been anxiously hoping I wouldn't get. Zico had given them his decision. Despite already being in a sitting position I felt dizzy at the news. I knew it was coming but that didn't make it any easier to learn or stomach when it arrived.

I sat trying to take it all in whilst the both of them stood bitching back and forward. 'Maybe I'd get lucky and they'd shoot each other?' I sickly laughed to myself as things began to get dangerously heated between the pair of them. The mood having turned progressively nasty.

'Ok, ok, let's do this. I have a migraine and your trash talking is going to make me sick, Jugador' Gilberto finally appeared to back down although it seemed to be more because Jorge had been wearing him down than it was through any kind of fear. I could have well imagined Gilberto having no problems whatsoever turning into killing machine mode when the need arose despite the charm that he had to his personality. In that moment though I could see the other side of him.

Knowing that it was coming. I started screaming and wouldn't stop. I couldn't stop. It was like I'd lost all control. It stopped the two of them in their tracks mid argument as they both turned to look at me. The roll of tape soon fixed things for them, if not me.

Then followed the most sadistic of conversations, with me in a ringside seat, where the two of them debated how I was going to be killed. Jorge, who had all along, stated that he wanted to make it nice and quick and put some bullets into me. This saw Gilberto reminding Jorge that they had only rented the villa and couldn't leave any mess as there could not be a risk of anything leading back to Bogota.

The alternative, and much less messy on their part, was for them to suffocate me with a carrier bag. I couldn't believe what I was hearing. The psychological aspects of not only having to wait to be murdered but to sit and listen to the debate over what was going to be done to you was immeasurable. In your mind, visualising the atrocities happening to you right there as they discussed them was enough to send a person over the edge.

In a rare show of having something closely resembling a human side Jorge disagreed with his partner on this.

'She doesn't deserve to die that way. That is for a real rata to die. She is just unfortunate that she met us and deserves a quick death.' Jorge said in my defence. Like busses I had never agreed with him on anything since we had met yet I found myself agreeing with every single word that he had said towards Gilberto.

'Jorge? What do you think would happen if we made a mistake in another country, one that has not been bought and paid for by the brothers. A mistake that follows us back to Bogota and then on to Eddy and German? We have no protection from a Guardia Civil or Interpol. No bribing agents to make everything go away like back in Colombia' Gilberto bit back with an authority that must've resonated with Jorge. His partner standing there silent with no counter argument to speak of.

'I'll get the bag,' Gilberto said as he left the room. I had seen nothing of the hospitable and charming side of him since he'd come back into the house that morning. They were complex characters, the two of them, and no mistake. Unable to make any noise due to the tape. I sat there crying my eyes out. The tears running down my cheeks and then onto the electrical tape that was covering my mouth and then, eventually down onto my chin.

The panic and the fear that had consumed me. Jorge to my side remained silent, finally doing up his belt from earlier. Gilberto came back into the room with a Pryca Supermarket carrier bag and without looking at me once, handed it to Jorge. Telling him to make it quick for me before he then left the room again.

This was it then. I know that everyone is meant to think of all their loved ones and their most cherished of memories when they're about to die but I assure you. When you categorically know that you're about to be suffocated by a plastic carrier bag. The only thing that you can really think about is... that you're about to be suffocated by a plastic fahking carrier bag.

'I did not want this for you but Gilberto? It would not be good for him and I if we argue more. The Cartel comes before all but I would not expect you to understand. This is Locombia business, señora.' He said as he began to open up the bag and spread it as wide as he could. Seeing him do so sent me into a frantic panic attack, knowing what was about to come. THEN I started screaming, even if no one was going to hear it. Jorge would have heard a muffled version but I would have bet my life, ironic pun intended, on him having heard someone scream before he killed them many times so did not think that any of my actions were going to faze him in that present moment.

'I hope the afterlife is better for you than this one,' he offered, which was quite poignant for a cold blooded killer, I guess. Skilfully and unmercifully throwing the bag over my head and managing to tighten it with one hand while firmly holding my hand that was free of a handcuff with the other. I tried to thrash around but his strength kept me restricted. Having my mouth taped, it wasn't as if I'd previously been enjoying optimum options with regards to breathing before the bag went over my head. Through this I'd found that breathing only through my nose was an instant challenge. I tried to move my head violently from side to side but he never loosened his grip enough for it to make any kind of a difference. With the strength that he possessed he was effortlessly able to hold me in the one position.

I had never felt just so deliriously frightened in my life. The sense of panic inside me was of such levels I had never come close to experiencing before. The knee jerk reaction that your mind and body goes through when it susses out just what is happening. A survival instinct that you didn't even know you had and the pact that they make together to fight together literally for your life. Acceptance to your fate not an option in those all important seconds.

I wasn't sure how long he'd been holding it over me for due to the mass panic that was going on inside the bag but through sheer common sense I knew that it could only be a matter of seconds more before it started to have an effect on me. That was when, through the bag, I swore I could see the figure of someone. Fuck, maybe it was who was waiting on me after passing away, I thought it a possibility due to the whole brightness that surrounded the angelic like figure.

Suddenly it felt like Jorge had let go of the bag. I sensed this when I had jerked my head to the side randomly to shake him off and his hand appeared to have loosened it's grip. I then started to feel some air coming up into the bag. I breathed it in through my only available avenue. In one swift move I then had the bag pulled back up from over my head. Finding Gilberto standing there in front of me and Jorge to the side still holding onto the bag. I'd mistaken the dark figure of

Gilberto for an angel due to the Pryca bag being white which had given him such a surrounding glow. Fahking idiot that I am!

Gilberto stood there looking at me as he spoke on the phone. Whoever he was speaking to he was definitely looking at me in connection to the call. His smile and general personality that had been previously on show now restored to him.

The tape was ripped from my face which really fucking smarted. I know, I'd just had a bag over my head and taken so very close to brain damage central so you would have thought some tape being ripped off your face would've been a walk in Hyde Park but fahking hell, it hurt.

The phone was shoved in my face for such a short time I think I managed to get Stevie's name out before it was taken away again. Not that it stopped me from shouting and screaming, free of the tape over my mouth. I heard Gilberto say Stevie's second name though, straight after taking the phone away from me.

Gilberto appeared to be a happy man. I was still alive, all be that it almost came down to a photo finish and something that I feared would go on to relive for the rest of my life. Such a mentally damaging experience that it was, and then there was the fact that Zico was on the other end of the phone.

Something had happened, but what?

Chapter 33

Zico

How really though, with absolutely ride all in the way of prior experience, do you prepare yourself for going through with a "trade of goods" with Colombian cartel operatives? That was the question that I'd been asking myself from the moment I'd ended that life saving phone call. Talking to a man, who rather than share his name with me, appeared to revel in the nickname that he went by. Given to me like it had been some badge of honour.

In truth, I had no idea other than not to meet them somewhere that wasn't in public. That was just common sense and you didn't need to be versed in the ways of kidnap negotiation to know that. The more people the better. La Cobra and I had agreed to meet and do the exchange for later that day. Despite being a few steps away from being a basket case. I'd had to unscramble my head big fucking time to enter into discussions about kidnapped girls, mysterious fucking computer discs and killers sent from far away lands. I did take a lot comfort from the fact however that I never really had a fucking choice.

'Now, La Cobra, I'm not going to fucking lie to you here. I haven't got a fucking clue what I'm doing here but I suspect that you already know this. I don't come from a world where kidnap negotiations are as simple as selling a car in the newspaper like you lot. I don't know you but don't trust you, obviously I don't fucking trust you! Now while I haven't ruled out the fact that you're going to still try and kill the girl and me THEN take the disc. That still doesn't get you my dad so I'm hoping that you're going to do the decent thing and keep to your part of the bargain.' I stopped for a breath but was in no way finished. He was happy to let me continue.

'You don't need to worry about "tying up loose ends" and all of that. Mate? You seriously think I'm going to fucking say anything about this to the police after it's over? Do that and spend the rest of my life looking over my shoulder? No bueno, Senor eh?! I just want Selina back and you can then go and do whatever it is you're planning to do. So the only way that I'm meeting you to give you the disc is somewhere in public? You cool with that?' I was brutally honest with him while also showing that I wasn't naive about the possibilities of what could happen or that either I was going to get pushed around in all of it. I'm not even sure where the fuck the inner strength came from. I guessed part of it was down to the feeling that I had failed Flo that first time around and was hell bent on making sure that I made up for it now that I'd been given the second chance.

'Oh, brother. You need not worry, I am not here to cause problems,' he attempted to assure me.

'You've literally got my girlfriend gagged and, apparently, was a few seconds away from killing her. You're not here to cause problems, aye ok then, mate?' I kind of laughed at him sarcastically which had him laughing back. 'Oh, that?' Well no problems now, Mister DJ, you give me what you say you will and you and her will be sipping cocktails by tonight.' He assured me.

We arranged, as suggested by me, to meet at Cafe Mambo at six in the evening. Understandably I wanted Flo back as soon as possible but wanted to buy myself a couple of hours, if possible, to try and come up with some kind of plan. This was preferable to just going in there blind. Never more in my life had I needed Si than that afternoon. Knee deep in his own shite on the island. I had woken him up when I called early into the afternoon. Didn't take him long to get himself up to speed, mind. All he needed to hear was that Flo was alive and I was going to get her back which equalled WE were going to get her back.

I didn't need Si to fight my own battles. Fuck, I'd done that enough times over the years and no question but even to have him there as eyes and ears at Cafe Mambo during the exchange would've been invaluable, I felt.

I assumed that there would be two, possibly three of them there or there about when I got Flo so it would've been a wise move to at least try and even up the score. If you can call two ex Dundee Utility hoolies going up against two or three Colombian sicarios a fair fight, that is? I suppose if anything, what we lacked in marksman like shooting skills we made up for in chair throwing and hand gestures.

The cobra boy and I had agreed that when we met up I would exchange the disc for Flo and, while I would wait there with him, as collateral of sorts. I would part with my father's address *only* after I knew Flo was already in a taxi and as far away from Cafe Mambo as possible. He'd been cool with this suggestion. Maybe he had already assumed that because of him dealing with a clear novice in moi. He was the one that was always going to be firmly in control of the trade, wherever it would take place. I wasn't really giving a flying fuck who was in control as long as I got Flo back.

It was a tense car ride to Cafe Mambo. Well, tense on my part, anyway. Si had hoovered up a couple of healthy looking lines before we'd left my pad. Tense was not something my best mate could have been accused of. I'd declined the offer from him to get involved. Any other time (during the hours of a set, excepted) then aye but I wanted to be straight for this. I didn't want any fateful misunderstanding on my part because of me being full of Ching myself and therefore full of shit.

'It'll be fucking sound, Zeec.' Si said with extreme confidence as he focussed on the road ahead. 'You have something that they want and they have something that you want, a simple business transaction, my man. That's all it is.' He said, almost sounding like he was comparing it to me as if going into a shop and buying a bottle of Irn Bru.

'Little bit more to it than that though, mate, eh?' I said, aiming for diplomacy but not sure if I had pulled it off or not. The cracks were beginning to appear on my side. I knew that heading there, I was throwing up the potential for all kinds of unpredictable events to take place. Maybe they'd just swap what we both had and then go our separate ways like proper gentlemen?

Maybe they'd appear without Flo, take me AND the disc and then kill the pair of us anyway? I had no idea of what I was dealing with other than the premise that if these boys really did work for a Colombian cartel then there would have been no limits to the pain and suffering that they would have been capable of causing someone if in their way to doing whatever job had been assigned. The permutations of what might or might not happen were many and they hurt the head when they started to run around my mind.

'Let's face it, Si. We don't know what these Colombian cunts have in mind? When you're at the kidnapping level of the underworld and are recruited to get your hands on computer discs and stuff. You not think that suggests that these cunts are heavy duty?' I asked, trying to break through Si's Cocaine wall, built purely from bricks made from his own synthetic self assurance. 'It's not like they're just going to pull guns out in the middle of fucking Cafe Mambo, is it?' He smirked back at me in dismissal.

'Fucking Scarface, eh?....The Diaz Brothers sent their men EXACTLY to a fucking club to get Montana. What makes you think Ibiza and Cafe Mambo would be off limits? It's in their blood, man. They're fucking radge, mate' I replied, instantly regretting that I had held up a fucking film script as evidence in my argument against him.

'That's where this wee baby comes in.' Si said confidently as, while still driving, reached over to open the glove compartment that was in front of me. The door falling open and the gun that was sat inside it. 'What? What are you doing to do with that?' It didn't take any Ching to have me then in dismissal mode.

'Listen, Zico, their guns come out then so does mine.' He was fucking serious as well, that was the thing. He hadn't even fired it in anger since it had been given it to him. Yet here he was. The man that would provide my safe package in and out of Cafe Mambo, apparently.

'And what are you going to do, Jesse fucking James?' I mocked but he wasn't for hearing it. 'That all depends on which move these cunts want to try and make first,' the reply. 'I'll be ready with a response.' He said with a serious look on his face that made me want to tell him to turn the car around and let me get a taxi there instead.

Fucking hell, I had enough to worry about with all that lay ahead at the end of the short drive. I really could've done without the additional worries over the "gunman" in the drivers seat beside me. As we drove along the road, I wondered if they had already arrived there. Possibly they'd adopt a - watch us from a distance approach - to ensure that there was nothing suspicious enough to have them frosty about things.

While Si had already exchanged a few words with the two Colombians inside Space. It was only just that, a few words inside a busy nightclub. As far as him and I were aware. Si, at Cafe Mambo, would just be another face in the crowd of clubbers all hanging around drinking, enjoying the beats and waiting for the sun going down. We decided that he would go in first and carry out some reconnaissance on the place.

I remained in the car around fifty metres down the street from the entrance while he had a nose around to see what he could find inside there. Only after I got the call from him would I then leave the car to go in myself. I sat there mentally preparing myself for what I was about to go through with. At the same time, trying not to think about the potential for just how tits up it could've possibly went. I toked away on that much required joint. The one that I had brought out of the house with me but in all the commotion during the ride had completely forgotten that it had been away tucked behind my ear. Each drag I took on it long enough to make it count while I closed my eyes and eagerly shut myself out from the reality outside world.

That's when "Missing" by Everything but the Girl come onto the set that Si had playing on the CD inside the car. It was enough for me to open my eyes again and bring me back. It's funny how the world can seem to openly mock you with "coincidences" like that song coming on right at that moment. That kind of stuff absolutely fries my brain when I think about it too much. The song hadn't even finished before my phone rang.

'Right, mate. I've had a good look around the place. Flo is sat with another guy at one of the tables towards the beach area. He's wearing what looks like a red Ralphie polo and has black slick backed hair' Si passed on the information, giving me an idea of what I should've been looking out for once inside.

'His mate is sat at the bar, obviously they're trying to pretend that they're not with each other, like. Here's what we're going to do, Zeec. I'll be sat at the bar beside the boy with the moustache and the Barcelona top. I'll keep my eye on him while you're sorting out Flo. If he tries to make a move on you or Flo at any point, he won't even see me coming.' He asserted without any hint of nerves. I'd have been much more at ease had he been speaking in this way through some kind of experience in the whole arena of kidnapping negotiations. Not because he was fuelled by some Peruvian bad boy.

While it remained to be seen just what Si would do if and when required. It had definitely been a good idea for him to go in ahead of me and see what he could find. While it, in no way, eased any kind of nerves which were only ever building inside me and at a rapid rate. It helped me, at least, to be able to visualise what it was that I was walking in to. Where to look, knowing I was sitting down with just the two of them but with the added knowledge that there was more to things than just that.

'So are you ready then, Zeec?' He asked, me having not yet answered back. Instead, carefully measuring every one of his words. 'Of course I'm not fucking ready! Fuck it, let's go and get Flo back.' I replied with honesty but while also showing how "game" I was to go and get it done. That fitba casuals spirit never does quite leave you, eh?! I got out the car and took a slow walk down the street. Ensuring that I was able to smoke the maximum amount of the spliff before flicking it directly into one of the iron drains outside of the entrance to Cafe Mambo.

The place was completely rammed. Exactly as I'd hoped when I'd suggested it as the meeting place. The busier the better though so it was a comforting sight to see the crowd that were already in there. Drinks in hand dancing to the, uncharacteristic for that time of the evening, hi tempo beats. I'd already done my homework. Bob Sinclair, the French DJ, was in town, playing a special extended set there at the cafe to take the patrons right up until sun down. As expected. Word across the island had evidently gotten around.

As I made my way through the crowd, eager for that very first glimpse of Flo. I couldn't help but feel that this was so very much at odds with my image for one of these exchanges. In my mind it always seemed to involve some well dressed businessman type, flanked by a couple of his own men, carrying a briefcase to exchange for the goods. Generally in some deserted warehouse or equivalent. Alternatively, I was turning up to a busy bar in a pair of battered Adidas Wiens, white Edberg tennis shorts that I had been freshly sick over hours before and a (strategically chosen) Colombian national team shirt from the Ninety

Four World Cup in America that my dad had sent me the summer that the tournament was being held.

Briefcase? Such was the exact professionalism on show from myself. I'd almost broken the all important computer disc when it had slipped out of my pocket in the car and I'd found myself sitting on the fucking thing. Almost snapped it in two.

Then, through the gap between two girls that were drinking cocktails and dancing. I saw her sat there with him. Looking every inch someone who had been held prisoner for days and all the psychological baggage that would've brought. In the same clothes (I'd assumed) for the third day running. Any hint of make up that she might've had on, now a distant memory. Her hair up on top of her head in a bun. It wasn't just the material aesthetics like dirty clothes and zero make up that was worth commenting on. The major thing that struck me about her, while I'd been given the opportunity to clock her in a one way sense. It was that she was missing her shine. That cheeky and irresistible smile of hers. For the first time since of knowing her, that was gone. She looked, scared. There couldn't have been anyone who could have judged her on that.

She'd have probably given me a bit of that adorable sharp tongue of hers had she known I'd been thinking it but she looked like absolute shit. She looked like shit yet seeing her through the gap between those two girls as I approached. She looked the most beautiful sight that I had ever seen in my life.

Walking in-between the two girls dancing was enough for me to make my presence known to Flo and La Cobra (?) who must've both been on the look out for me, for their own private reasons. The two of them seeming to spot me at the very same time. Both sets of eyes instantly fixed on my direction. Weirdly, they both smiled yet the warmer of the two smiles came from the man, not Flo. While she'd smiled at me it had appeared to be one of tentative relief than anything else. The man's smile was one that more resembled his mate joining him for a couple of drinks that they had arranged.

They sat there with a couple of bottles of Corona and lime on the table alongside a closed laptop that was sat there in front of the man. When

I got to the table my instinct was to lurch towards Flo to give her a huge hug and to let her know that it was all going to be ok. She looked ready to meet me with that until, with both arms, he scooped one around her to hold her back while reaching out and pushing his hand into my chest. Motioning with his head for me to sit down on one of the chairs facing them.

As I sat down I had a quick glimpse around me towards the bar. Taking an "innocent" look at Si and the man that he was sitting next to. It took me all of a few seconds of seeing him to give me the shivers when it came to Flo being held captive by someone of that description. He looked a wrong un. The one with Flo on the other hand? He must've been in his forties but if I was to look as good as that when I was that age then I wouldn't be complaining.

'You ok, darling? They better not have touched a hair on your head, babe.' I said looking across the table at Flo. She was fighting back tears as she sat there looking back trying to reassure me that she was fine. It wasn't exactly what you would've described as believable though.

There was so much that I wanted to say to this cunt sat there in the red Ralph Lauren shirt. Every bone in my body was pushing me towards just letting rip at him for taking Flo. I had to play the game though and nobody needed to remind me of that. This was about her and nothing more and if, through my own fault, the situation was to go wrong then I would have been right back to that initial stomach scraping feeling I'd had earlier that day when Flo had been handed down her death sentence.

Through the levels of noise inside Mambo I could already tell that for the best part, this transaction was going to have to rely on some good old international sign language to reach a satisfactory conclusion. Looking at me, dropping his smile for a moment. He asked me if I had the disc. I couldn't hear exactly what it was that he had said but his action of outstretching his hand and then swiftly pulling all fingers back more than made up for the lack of word based communication.

I pulled out the disc and his face lit up. All I wanted to do was sit and look at Flo. A face that I'd assumed I would never set eyes on again. There would be all the time in the world for her and I, once him and I were done. While still holding the disc in my hand, I glimpsed at her and for the first time. I had seen even a smidges worth of a resemblance to her real smile.

As I held onto it he moved himself over the table up close to me and, speaking loud enough for me to hear but leaving no one else around a chance of picking it up thanks to Sinclair on the decks. He told me that if this was not the right disc and that I was trying to fuck him. Flo and I would not make it outside Mambo before being killed by his partner and him. Assessing the threat handed down to me. I had barely even noticed that while speaking to me he had plucked the disc from out of my hand before sitting back down again beside Flo.

He flipped open his laptop and plunged us all into a period of silence and nerve shredding anticipation. In amongst all of the random and varied scenarios that I'd imagined up ahead of the meet. The one thing that I hadn't actually thought of was that he would have had a fucking computer along with him to check the authenticity of the disc. Obviously this made good business sense to do so but with me being barely computer illiterate. I wasn't from the kind of world where people carried laptops around with them.

That's when I began fearing. What if this *wasn't* the disc? I had obviously assumed that it had been the it but what if it being stealthily hidden in my kitchen drawer had been fuck all to do with my dad and that I had just acted out of a hunch and was wrong? This really wasn't the time for me to find out that the disc was full of porn that some cunt had downloaded from the internet and wanted to keep hidden from his other half when they stayed there at the villa before me.

He inserted the disc into the side of the machine and from then, as far as he was concerned, the only thing that existed was whatever he was seeing in front of him on the screen of the laptop. As I waited there, praying that it was, indeed, the disc that was apparently worth killing for. I heard Bob Sinclair begin to drop "French Kiss" into his set and in what was a highly inappropriate moment all things considered. Flo and I exchanged a small cheeky smile at each other upon hearing the song. We'd only spoken about it the week before due to the infamous orgasm sample contained in the track. It was no time for cheeky smiles though.

Sitting there I was surveying his face for some kind of sign, preferably a good one. That was when that big smile appeared on his face. Leaving the relief washing over more than just my coupon. Seeing that face of his lift left me with the feeling of a huge wave crashing into me and washing off any apprehension that I'd been coated in.

'Bueno.' I managed to pick up from reading his lips as he nodded his head before launching himself back over the table to me. 'You are a man of your word, I respect that,' he said grabbing hold of one of my shoulders and giving it a friendly but painful squeeze.

'Now let her go and I will give you the address.' I said back to him while he was still hovering over on my side of the table. He remained still and stared back at me. I couldn't read him. Now that he had the disc, if there was any intentions to double cross me in any shape or form then this was most likely going to be the time.

'Of course! I too am a man of my word. What? You thought I was going to fuck you?!' He laughed at the mere suggestion that he could do such a thing. 'No of course not, you're just the type of person who would kidnap a girl and threaten to kill her while engaging in a spot of casual blackmail.' I laughed back at him without any hint of nastiness or aggression. 'A good and proper man of honour by the sounds, Senor.'

He did not take the joke in the way that it had been intended. Instead of laughing along with me over what had been nothing other than a piece of (fucking stupid) sarcasm. He sat there with an expressionless look on his face, staring straight into me in a way that sucked any cheek and sarcasm straight out of me. I sat silently staring back at him. Scared to open my mouth through fear of making matters worse.

Eventually he broke from our staring competition and looked to his side towards Flo. He then said a couple of words into her ear. Whatever it was that he'd said to her. It had her standing up to walk away from the table. I reached over to grab her hand and pulled her closer to me so I could speak to her. 'Walk right outside and get into the first taxi you see and ask the driver to take you to here.' I thrust a piece of paper into her hand which had the name of the hotel, The Balearic Park, that I'd arranged for us written on it. Given how resourceful the Colombians had already shown themselves to be. I'd assumed that they would have known where I had been staying. Through this, I felt that sending her back to mines might not have been the smartest of decisions. I wasn't even sure if I would go back myself until all of this shit was over and done with.

'Now go, babe. I'll meet you there in a while. Tell reception your name when you get there,' I urged her. Sensing the importance of my words. She nodded back with a tentative smile and walked off through the crowd of clubbers. It was hard not to notice as I watched her disappear from view that the sounds of that woman having the orgasm on "French Kiss" was belting out of the Cafe Mambo speakers. It was possibly a pretty accurate metaphor for how Flo (and I) were feeling right about then. Once she'd disappeared I immediately averted my gaze over towards the bar hoping that I was going to see both Si and the Colombian still sitting there. Any of them missing would not have represented good news with Flo now off on her own and vulnerable.

They were both still sitting there. Si, still flying and sat with a bottle of Bud in his hand. Appearing to actually be speaking to the other guy but it didn't appear too clear if it was an active two way conversation between them. You wouldn't have ruled out it being a ploy from Si. Acting the friendly drunk party goer in an attempt to distract the cartel boy.

I turned back around to *my* Colombian to get the rest of it over and done with. Despite the fact that my dad had lied to me, used me, stored sensitive information in my house like that disc, which he swore he knew nothing of. EVEN when he knew that it could save Flo's life. Me left with the knowledge that he could hide it in my place while knowing that it could lead cartel figures to my door looking for it.

Despite how flippantly he seemed to view the whole father and son dynamic between us. It still left me feeling like the worst piece of shit to be handing over the details to these killers that would see them darkening his door. Every word of the address that he typed into his laptop I felt my dad and Eva were being taken closer to their fate. Once he had the full address typed in he quickly gave it the once over before slamming the screen down towards the keyboard and closing it all together.

I'd played this moment out in my mind so many times leading up to the meet but I could never have planned for just how anti-climatic it was in reality. Grabbing his laptop and stopping to neck what was left of his bottle of cerveza. He slammed the empty bottle back down onto the table. 'After today, you will have no problems with me or anyone from Bogota. This ends with your father. Oh, nice touch with the Colombia shirt, I like it.' He slapped my face gently and then walked off. Leaving me sat frozen to the spot. Hoping to fucking god that there would be no more last minute twists to all of this as he walked away behind me. There was.

I was just about to turn around see the what the Si situation was like when I felt the hand on my shoulder. He'd returned, my guts dropped. 'Oh I almost forgot, I need your phone, Mister DJ. We would not want anyone tipping off Señor Duncan about any visitors would we?' THAT was a problem. Despite the fact that my dad had brought all of this onto himself. I still could not consciously play such a major part in it without trying to do something about it.

Then there was Eva. She most definitely didn't deserve what was heading her way in the shape of those two Colombians inside Cafe Mambo. I knew that it would have been a major risk to take and that it may have come back to haunt me very fucking quickly but I had always planned to call my dad. Try and warn him the moment that the cartel boys left the bar. I'd, at least, wanted to ensure that him and Eva would manage some kind of a head start. I had actually tried earlier in the day, more than once but could not get him to answer. I'd guessed that this may well have been a product over how our last phone call had went. If so, this really had not been the best day for my father to choose to screen calls from his son.

Taking my phone from me was the equivalent of removing my arms and legs and asking me to dance while juggling. It wasn't as if I was going to find Peter Duncan's name in the local phone book was I?

Reluctantly I handed it over to him. 'Fucking hell, Carl Cox's number was in there,' I despaired before I then pragmatically accepted that by losing my phone there and then. It would bring about more serious consequences than me having the phone number of someone that I was always going to be too fucking scared to use in any case.

'Bueno, bueno. Adios, Amigo' He said tucking my phone into his pocket as he walked off in the direction of the bar. This time I kept my eyes fixed on him. He joined his mate, they exchanged a few words between each other before leaving a few minutes later. Si, who had locked eyes with me while the two Colombians were talking, stayed sat there at the bar until they had gone before then rushing over to join me.

'It's all fucked man' I sat with a feeling not unlike a whitey that any toker across the world will have no choice but to admit having at least once in their life. 'What do you mean, man? Flo's long gone, safe and sound. So are you. Just give Pedro a quick bell and job done.' He mapped it out as if it was child's play. Which it would've been had "La Cobra" not just relieved me of my Motorola.

'Aye, that's the problem, he took my phone from me to STOP me from calling my dad.' I despaired, empathising words all over the place. 'Not a problem my man,' he replied with that Ching driven look of confidence, taking a swig of his beer. 'Call him from my phone then,' He advised, sliding his Nokia over the table towards me.

It made no sense why Si had my father's number in his contacts. It wasn't like they were mates or fuck all. Maybe it had been a gear thing while he was on the island? Whatever the reason it was the godsend that was at least going to give my dad and Eva a fighting chance of keeping their heads above ground, for a little while longer at least.

I ended up having to hand the phone back to Si to get him to make the call for me. The keys were set up in a completely different way to my one and I hadn't a fucking scoob what I was doing. It wasn't like this wasn't life or death urgency when it came to time or anything, either!. He handed the phone back to me with the call now ringing. My dad answered after a few rings. The call itself lasting marginally more than the connecting rings had.

'Simon' He said on answering, as if he hadn't a care in the world.

'It's not Si, it's Zico and by the fucking way. If you're lucky enough to live through the next twenty four hours. You and I are sitting down and having proper words once all of this blows over but for now. You and Eva need to get your stuff and go. Where, that's up to you but they're on their way right now.' I said in a confused mix of rage, disgust and concern.

'You disappoint me, son.' The solitary four words he replied back to me with before the line went dead.

Chapter 34

Eva

Peter and I were just about to start tucking into a garlic and chilli shrimp cocktail that I had freshly prepared for us. He was in the process of pouring the wine when his phone began ringing. Normally when we'd eat, we operated a no mobile phone policy. This had been introduced, mainly to stop him from answering the incessant calls that he would be receive morning noon and night.

It appeared to be his "friend" Si on the other end, Peter smiling as he answered. Then the smile gradually started to drop until it was gone completely.

'You disappoint me, son' Was all he said before ending the call almost as quickly as he'd answered it. He left the dining room straight after, to go outside the villa. Returning around five minutes later to rejoin me to have our dinner.

'Everything ok?' I asked, which was really nothing more than going through the motions. He wasn't going to tell me anyway. 'All fine, darling,' he lied as he took a big swig from his glass of Sauvignon Blanc. It had almost been a three hundred and sixty degree turn for me. Back in a secluded villa in the middle of nowhere. The only difference being that Peter was around a lot more than he was back in Bogota although whilst he was there he wasn't really "there."

Reverting to type. He effortlessly found a way to change the subject and steer things away from whatever potential problems that were mounting up for him, and by proxy, I. He began speaking about the fact that we weren't going to be in Ibiza for too much longer and where we should be looking to settle. It took me by surprise for him to be springing such a life changing topic of conversation on me. 'Just nowhere that is cold,' I laughed. 'You can take the girl out of Bogota but you can't take her need for the Bogota heat out of her.'

'I was thinking the same thing, there are some Caribbean islands that seem perfect for us that I was looking into. I just need the paperwork to be completed before we can get ourselves out of Spain.' he continued. 'Yeah, what's the hold up with that? It was only meant to take a couple of days?' I asked. I didn't know anywhere near to the ins and the outs of it all. How much money Peter actually *had* was anyone's guess. Where it was all being held and in which countries. Again I was blissfully unaware.

'It should be any day soon, we'll get our arse's back over to Barcelona. I'll sign all of the documents and we'll be off riding into the sunset.' He said to me as if he was laying out some simple plans for us to go to Asda and then B&Q on the way home.

We were still discussing future plans well into dessert. It felt nice, like a chat that a couple would do with major life changes, exciting changes lying ahead. It felt like we had the chance to wipe the slate clean of everything. There had been so much that I had been angry about with Peter over recent times but I was still willing to forgive and forget. I knew that I wasn't marrying a saint in him so I could hardly have acted higher than mighty when a part of his life came biting him on the behind.

I was just about to put a spoonful of Chimney Cake and ice cream into my mouth when I heard the front door opening. No knocking in advance, simply the door opening and a pair footsteps walking across the wooden floor of the hall leading into the kitchen. I was startled, Peter, instead, calmly took another sip of his wine while the footsteps, very slowly, began to get louder.

'Pedrrrrrrrrrrito, Pedrrrrrrrrrrito' came the voice from down the hall. I looked at Peter who was seemingly unfazed by the fact that we had some intruders in our house. Two strange men soon finding their way into the dining area with us still sat there at the table. 'Ahhhh there you are!' Said one of them. A tanned man with oily black slick backed hair in a red shirt. I was more alerted to, and alarmed over the fact that he was holding a gun in his hand.

'I spy with my leedle eye something beginning with RRRRRRR, for rrrrrrata.' He continued which left the other one, this greasy looking unkempt man in a football top, laughing at his comment. 'Gilberto, so glad you could stop by. Jorge, como esta?' Peter said, as if he was meeting up with two old friends. I couldn't also help but notice just how calm he was over the fact that the two of them had marched their way into our house with guns in their hand looking for him.

'You have been a difficult man to track down, Pedro.' The red shirted man continued while him and his partner stood there with their guns firmly trained on the two of us. 'Although, I guess that I have you and your wife to thank for such a nice trip away from Colombia. Jorge has managed to visit the Nou Camp and I have eaten the best paella in the world so it has not been all full of frustrations.'

While it was a scary situation to be finding yourself in sat at the dinner table I had been given a bit of hope in the sense that this man appeared to be a talker. If they had come here to kill Peter, and I, they would have possibly done it as soon as they'd caught sight of us. The pair of them looked like they were in no rush to be putting some bullets into us.

'You must've known though that we would find you, no? If you didn't then you really did not pay as much attention back in Bogota than you should have done.' The man said which appeared as much for to massage his ego and remind Peter of the reputation that he carried than anything else.

'I wasn't in as much of a panic to avoid you, Gilly because I hadn't done anything.' Peter sat and put across in the most cool of ways. 'I see, I see what you mean, Pedrito. Apart from the whole stealing of the computer disc that, alone, would be worth fifty million dollars easily to any of the other cartels. The disc that would put the brothers out of business and in jail if sat in the wrong hands. Apart from stealing that I guess that you really haven't done much wrong, actually' He sneered back at my husband.

This disc? I'd heard talk of a disc during one of Peter's calls but had no idea what it pertained to. Peter certainly wasn't the type to be needing anything computer related. I had to set the alarm on his watch for him. That's how much of a technophobe he was. I'd heard him flat out deny in a phone call that he had the disc and yet here in our kitchen stood two men who had flown all the way from South America to get it from him.

'So anyway I guess the holiday is at an end for Jorge and I. The party is over, certainly for you and your bitch wife.' He spat, his mood dropping like a stone. This was when I began to see the true intentions of the visit from the pair of them. They *were* here to kill us.

'No no no no' I started to repeat again and again to him while Peter remained freakishly still. This was looking very suspiciously like this guy had earlier just delivered some kind of a pre planned monologue but was now starting to wrap things up.

'Awwww come on Gilberto, we can talk this over. I can make you a very rich,' Peter attempted to talk the hitman round via a subject that even I knew was popular in Colombia, bribery. 'SHUT UP, you know what would happen if you were to ever turn on the Ramirez brothers.' The Colombian, raising his gun up further and with more intent, interrupted Peter. He'd appeared visibly irked at the suggestion that he would even be seen as open to taking a bribe. Worryingly, Peter was smiling as he was trying to talk to the guy. We were seconds away from being shot and killed by hitmen and he was sitting there drinking wine and actually smiling? The red shirted Colombian's partner mimicked him. Raising his pistol up and pointing it at me.

It was only when the red dot appeared on one of their heads and then the other, from through separate windows inside the spacious dining area. It was only then that I realised just exactly why Peter had been so cavalier about the whole seriousness of the situation.

The two Colombians looked at each other in dismay. Seeing matching dots on each others heads. Now knowing that their job had just become a lot more complicated. 'Hijo de puta,' cried the greasy looking one with the moustache in resignation. It didn't take a few years of living in South America to know that particular insult. Peter sat there laughing back at them. It was a Peter that I had never witnessed before and regardless of him being responsible for saving us from being shot. I didn't like what I was seeing.

The level of shithousery that he was capable of and the lies. The kind of world that he existed in that he was comfortable in having hitmen coming to our home to kill us. The very same world that I wasn't comfortable being a part of. 'That's it for me, enough,' I decided. While this situation appeared to be far from played out, I was done. Yeah, there were red dots fixed to the two of them but that did not mean that they had lowered their guns however.

That factor was soon changed when I heard the sound of the front door opening once more. New footsteps running down the hall. In came, Finnan. One of the Scousers who had, completely without warning, started to hang around the villa not long after we had moved in. They mainly stayed outside in the grounds and I'd barely had any contact with any of them other then making the occasional cup of tea for them. Peter had said that I was just to think of them as security and that I'd barely even know that they were there.

'I'll take these, boys.' Finnan said in that unmistakable Liverpudlian accent. The two hitmen giving up their weapons without any real resistance. They appeared to know that they were beaten. Finnan, collected both handguns and exited the dining room again. Leaving the four of us alone once more.

'Me underestimate you? Gilberto? I think that you may have underestimated me, brother.' Peter said before picking up a piece of the Chimney Cake and shoving it in his mouth. 'Pedrito, I have the disc, I can return back to Bogota and say that I killed the two of you. The brothers will never know otherwise. Please spare me and Jorge here. It could be, what is the phrase? Happy medium?' "Gilberto" pleaded. His earlier cocky and arrogant demeanour unmistakably now gone.

'Awww come on now, Gilly, we both know that you and El Jugador, if only for to maintain your reputation, would chase Eva and I until the sun burns out and the earth along with it. I do have one question for you though. The disc? Where is it?' Peter, completely in control and knowing it, sat holding court.

'That would not be part of the deal, Pedrito. I know you know that I could not return to Bogota without it,' he tried to reason back.

'CNN breaking news, Gilly. You're not in any position to set any parameters with regards to making deals. Meh I didn't think you'd tell me anyway.' Peter replied dismissively, not appearing exactly impacted by the mans unwillingness to play ball with him.

'We did not think that your son would give us your address either but he still did,' spat the other one whose name I caught as Spanish for player. He seemed to have went past his colleague's strategy of trying to talk his way out of things. It looked like he had already decided that he was going to go out on his terms.

'Yes, he stabbed me in the back, we'll talk soon about it.' Peter replied calmly without any emotion to his face. 'Oh and actually, Jorge that reminds me, I had a question that I had always wanted to ask you?' my husband continued. 'Oh si? what is that then' he replied to Peter who, before answering the Colombian back, picked up his glass of wine and raised it into the air. Almost like he was toasting the pair of them. I was still wondering what he was doing right about the time that both Colombians realised *exactly* what he was doing. They both tried to move out of the way but were never going to be faster than the bullets that Peter had summoned with one raise of a wine glass.

Jorge, who had taken some shots to the head was killed instantly. His blood and brains spraying the kitchen wall behind him. Gilberto, "luckily" had avoided any head shots but was lying in a crumpled up bloody mess on the floor. Having taken some shots to the chest. The sound of his wheezing, not exactly leaving his chances of survival sitting too high. That was the point though, he wasn't meant to survive.

I sat there in shock for the best part. When those bullets came flying into the room I had almost jumped out of my skin, letting out a scream. Peter had quickly grabbed me and thrust my head low down towards the table. It was only when we looked up and surveyed the damage that I found one dead and one as good as. Peter got up from the dining room table and walked over towards the one called Gilberto and stood over him.

'You know, Gilly, I always liked you. Weirdly it didn't matter to me how many people that you'd killed. You always were a good guy. The opposite of that now piece of shit deceased buddy of yours. If it wasn't you it would've been someone else doing the job though so, I get it. Nothing personal taken. Now, amigo, I'll make it quick for you if you tell me where the disc is?' I was in disbelief. Sitting there watching my husband, although I had now decided that it was going to be a case of husband for how much longer? Negotiating with someone over what kind of a death they would be given.

'Fuck you, maricon,' he said with what appeared to be all of his strength by turning to the side to look up at Peter while spitting at him in some kind of feeble attempt at show of defiance.

'Eva, come here and search his pockets,' Peter shouted over to me while he took his foot and placed it over the mans throat. Pinning him down. 'NO' I screamed back at him. It wasn't like there was any threat that a defenceless and dying man was going to pose me but that wasn't really my issue. I wanted no part in rifling through the pockets of a man who was close to death. There was just so many wrongs attached to taking part in something like that.

'EVA get your fucking arse over here and search him,' he ordered back at me with a foreign kind of authority that I'd never heard from him. Strangely I complied. With only the usual items such as money, keys and a phone in his pockets there was nothing of any particular interest to Peter. Neither was the result of the searching of his dead partner's pockets.

'No luck amigo, you'll never find the disc. You think that we would be stupid enough to carry something so valuable around with us?!' Spitting blood, he lay there on the floor taunting Peter. 'Well, here's the thing. I neglected to mention earlier that I was already told that you had my address and, knowing you both. I figured you would come straight here. Now what would be the chances that you were to have found out my location round about the same time as you recovered the disc? Would you have been so stupid to come straight here without having safely stored it somewhere … *that* is more the question.'

Fuck, it was such a different side to Peter. I might have almost found him hot and sexy through just how commanding he was were it not for him, instead, repulsing me through how much of a disregard he had when it really came down to anyone else other than himself. I fully appreciated the fact that the two of them had came with the sole aim of murdering us but it was the effortless way that Peter had dealt with it.

What he had evidently planned out following that phone call he took just before we started dinner. It was a little unsettling to see someone that you think you know completely and that you had already seen all sides to them that they had. This was a side that you would never, ever wish to see in your partner. Anyone in your friends or family circle, period.

'FUCK YOUUUUU' Gilberto shouted back as Peter, grabbing the keys that had been recovered from Gilberto's pocket, left the kitchen and walked down the hall and left the house. He must've been gone a good ten plus awkward as hell minutes which left me still sitting in the dining room along with a wheezing and cursing Colombian gangster.

'He will get you killed, your husband.' He shouted, unable to see me but sensing that I was still there in the room along with him. I chose to ignore him even though I genuinely felt like the man had a point in what he was saying.

What would come next. Now that these two men had been killed, or as good as. Would more Colombians follow us to wherever our next destination would be? I wanted no part of it. I was sitting there contemplating just admitting defeat. Saying that it had been a wild ride and that there would be no shame in returning to Manchester. That was when Peter came dancing back into the kitchen holding a computer disc in his hand. From the look on his face it was *the* disc.

'BINGO!' He laughed down at Gilberto. Waving it back and forward. 'Ok, I'll give you a while to lay there with your guts hanging out of you and think about all the things that you've done and what you never got the chance to do, you know? Standard stuff like that. My wife and I will be departing soon so before we go. You and I will talk then about putting you out of your misery.' By doing so, Peter letting me know in a second hand way that it looked like we were on the move, again.

'Eva, grab your stuff, darling. We've got a plane to catch, we're getting out of Ibiza.' He shouted in a jovial mood that really did not match up to the events that had just taken place. It was notable just how much of a spring to his step he had returned back inside the kitchen while clutching the disc.

We were ready to leave within fifteen minutes. Whereabouts we were flying to, that was between Peter and whatever airline or private jet company that he had hired.

As we left, he told me to go on ahead and out to the car while he "grabbed something." Instead of fully continuing on my way. I hung around in the hallway to see if I could hear anything from the kitchen. Peter surely speaking to Gilberto, who was still alive lying there on the floor. I couldn't make out any dialog being exchanged between them but when I heard the gun go off. I knew that Peter had killed him, and our marriage in the process.

I hurried out to the car with Peter joining me soon after. Before getting into the car he issued a couple of orders to one of the Scousers outside the villa. Making sure that they would get rid of the two bodies, clean the blood up from inside the kitchen and then, just as he was about to jump into the drivers seat. Telling him to thank "Danny and Carl" and to tell them that they had made a good friend and that he would be in touch.

With that we were pulling away from the villa on route to the airport and out of Ibiza within hours.

Chapter 35

Zico

It took until the next day before the whole picture started to become a whole lot clearer and, as fucking always when it came to my life. Thing's hadn't all entirely been as they'd appeared when Flo and I had passed out through sheer exhaustion there in our room at The Balearic Park. Personally, after, the most draining and mentally taxing day of my life.

When I woke, Flo was still sleeping. I lay there looking at her. Ready to pinch myself to make sure that it wasn't some dream and that I was soon going to wake up in my own place. Forced again to deal with the reality of me, the day before, having this girl lying there beside me killed in favour of that disingenuous and duplicitous father of mines.

As she gently snored there beside me, possibly enjoying a nice dream to herself judging by the small smile that was on her face. It all started coming back to me. The disc, the meeting at Cafe Mambo, those highly questionable and hypocritical four words that my dad had said to me before hanging up, the last words that, as it was going to turn out, he would ever say to me.

The talking until the sun was almost ready to come up with Flo where she had filled me in on everything that had taken place while I shared my side of the story. I almost passed out when she told me about the bag over her head and how close my phone call had actually been. I knew that La Cobra had said I'd been close but I thought that was just brinksmanship on his part. I had been dreading the part where I had to tell her about choosing my dad over her although with her telling me about being suffocated by a carrier bag. That alone obviously meant that it was hardly going to be a spoiler for her when I told her *why* the bag had went over her. I had clearly not delivered what it had been they'd asked me for.

Lying there replaying the day. That's when I remembered that I didn't have a phone. Something I was going to need pronto. So as not to wake her unnecessarily. I kind of slithered like a snake out of the bed. We'd already found out how creaky it had been the night before so any major movements from me would surely have woken her. I threw on some shorts and nothing more. Quickly writing out a note for her on some hotel stationery in case she woke before I returned and walked down to reception to use one of the internet terminals that they had for their guests.

I had to get the young girl from behind reception to get it all set up for me. Last time I'd used it I'm sure that I had started it all off by going to a place called "Lycos" and then you typed into there whatever it was that you wanted to find. I couldn't get it to work though but after thirty seconds she had it on another page called Yahoo and I was off and running.

The only real place I needed to look for was Lee's agency so that I could get hold of his number. Didn't know if he even had a fucking website or not but I figured that there would be at least his details on there somewhere. Cunts that are on the internet all the time are never done telling you that you can find anything you want on there. I'm not sure if anyone really does know that to be true or not though considering most go right onto the porn and then don't get any further forward after that.

After typing the name of the agency into the search bar. The top match took you straight to the official Ragamuffin Talent website. It was too mad seeing myself on there inside the list of artists that were available for booking from the agency. I'm sure Lee had told me about the website but I hadn't been paying attention because it was all computer stuff which I'd always found boring. Once I'd gotten hold of Lee's contact details I called his mobile straight away from reception. It gave me a chance to hear him answer the phone to someone that he, as far as he was concerned, doesn't know. His professional voice, if you will. Complete knob that he is, was almost local radio station worthy the cheese like patter when he answered.

Very unlike Lee, he remained silent while I took him through all of what had happened since I'd left him that voicemail to say I needed out of playing my set right up until leaving Cafe Mambo the night before.

'Jesus fahking christ, Steven. Ah'm fahking speechless, mate,' he responded to me in astonishment. 'So look, aye, it's all been a bit mental but I really need your help. With me having to give up my phone I'm kind of lifeless without one here, can you help with one? You've always got one spare so you were the first person I thought of. 'Say no more, fella. I'll get one couriered over to you. Where is it that you and Flo are at just now?' He asked, agreeing to help. Exactly like I knew he would.

'Well that depends on if you're going to tell two Colombian hitmen who are currently holding guns at your head right now.' I laughed only to be hit with a fit of paranoia over just how easy and plausible that scenario was. Lee laughed along with me. Adding that I should stop being a silly bollocks and to just to spill the address and there would be a phone sent over to me within the hour. Si had agreed to call me at the number of the hotel the next day when I was getting into my own taxi outside Cafe Mambo to follow after Flo. Before I headed back up to the hotel room I'd checked with reception to see if there had been any messages for me but was told nada.

I got back up to the room to find Flo now awake. Lying there in bed with a big smile on her face when she saw the door open and me walk back through it. I looked at her, barely unable to understand how she could even smile. Even after she'd left Mambo and arrived back to the hotel her ordeal hadn't exactly really been entirely over. By the time I'd caught up with her back at the hotel. She had spoken to Elle to let her know that she was safe. In doing so she was able to establish just exactly what had all gone on with Elle after she had been snatched. The night that had been spent looking for her then up to Space to see if she was there. The next morning was when the two of them were meant to be flying home. That had left Elle in a horrible position.

Like any self respecting Ibiza party goer. Elle had reached the end of her holiday with not even enough money to buy a can of Coke. She had desperately tried to have some extra funds sent to her from back home but had come up with zilch. Miss the flight home and Elle was effectively penniless with no money for food or means for a flight home. She returned to England, vowing to get the money together for a flight and would effectively turn around and fly right back out again if there had been no contact from Flo.

Before she left. She had notified the police as her best mate missing. All of Flo's belongings were handed to the hotel and then onto the Guardia Civil for safekeeping until they could officially begin the search. This only coming when she had been missing for the designated amount of hours for a person to be confirmed as "missing." Elle had been in the process of looking for more flights when she had received the phone call from Ibiza.

All of this meant an unwanted trip to the local police station with Flo having to put in some kind of Meryl Streep Academy Award winning performance for the officers. Obviously, she had nothing to hide. She was the victim in this after all. Even so, before her and I went to visit the police we had agreed that she'd leave all talk of Colombian hitmen off the table. Too many questions would follow after that, too many people that would have been brought into it but the primary, and fully justifiable to both Flo and I, reason was that we saw no reason to potentially bring any trouble on the Colombians and in doing so bring it right back to us. The Bogotá boys simply hadn't happened as far as Flo and I were concerned.

As a cover story we agreed that she would say that a couple of men snatched her from the pub, having drugged her. They had then held her inside a house blindfolded and through the state that the drugs had left her in. She could not remember what had taken place while there. No recollections of being raped, not much in the way of flashbacks at all due to being drugged over various intervals.

When the police inevitably tested Flo for drugs they would have had no problems in finding traces of more than one type of narcotic. She'd easily taken care of that during her three weeks in the sun. The police were fully sympathetic to her and did not appear to question any of the story that she'd told them. They had only really begun to launch the investigation a couple of hours earlier when she had still not turned up and been reported as safe.

She was handed back her suitcase along with her passport. The woman police officer out of the two that had questioned her was even so helpful as to suggest to Flo that with this being a serious crime that she had been the victim of. She should call her airline and explain why she was not able to make her original flight. Advising that most airlines operated a policy to ensure that their customers managed to make it home in such unusual circumstances. Before we'd even left the station we'd ended up getting Flo booked on a British Airways flight back home in a couple of days time for nothing other than an insignificant ten pounds "goodwill gesture processing fee."

With all of that arranged. Flo could enjoy her last day in Ibiza with no hassles lying ahead. Apart from some much needed relaxing together while nervously waiting on any forms of blowback from what had taken place the day before. The only things that were on the cards for the day was watching the two Euro Ninety Six semi finals and then, and I would revert back to the whole waiting to see if there were any repercussions to supplying the location of where Peter and Eva were. If things had appeared settled, I would be playing my set on the terrace. Flo getting herself a second bite at the cherry when it came to her farewell set that I'd put together.

Being honest I didn't think that she would have been ready to go out so soon to a night like Space. I wouldn't have blamed her if, for a wee spell at least, she'd have wanted to stay inside a house with triple locks on the front door. I'd said that I would have made sure that Si went with us and didn't take his eye off her for one single second during my set. She just laughed at me and asked if I'd forgotten about how tough she was herself.

Having survived a couple of days with two cartel sicarios Her toughness was never going to be something about her that I would ever doubt.

We were in the middle of choosing what we wanted sent up for breakfast from room service when the room phone started to ring. I answered it straight away figuring that my phone had arrived and was downstairs waiting on being collected.

'Telefono, senor,' said the male's voice and without any form of telephone handling skills. Transferred the call straight through without me having even said a word in return. 'Zeec, that you, mate?' came the next voice. It was Si. 'Alright Si, I'll have a new phone soon by the way so I'll bell you when I've got it,' I said while looking over to the table where the beermat from Mambo with Si's number scribbled on it sat.

'Aye, cool cool, no worries, mate, but listen.' He replied. 'Yesterday was fucking mental all that happened, Zeec.' He followed up, stating the obvious. No one needed to tell me just how out of the ordinary a day that it had been. 'Aye you can say that again,' I laughed in agreement.

'No, shut up for a moment, listen to me. Yesterday was fucking mental, as in last night what took place *after* we all left Cafe Mambo,' he insisted, trying to get through to me so that I would stop and listen. 'Fuck, what happened to you?' I asked, not too sure whether I wanted to know or not. I'd woken that morning, Flo beside me in bed and it had appeared that the nightmare was over. Yet here was Si with more. Why is there always, more? 'It isn't about what happened to me, Zeec.' He tried to explain.

As he started to speak, Flo could see from my face that something was up. Grabbing and pulling at my arm in desperation to know what was going on. 'Shhhhh, I'll tell you in a second,' I assured her. By the time Si was done speaking I'd been given enough material to have Flo sitting in silence for hours as I brought her up to speed.

Where the fuck did I even begin? The fact that Eva had called Si an hour before from Barcelona. That her and Peter were alive and that the two Colombians were not? The revelation that days before. Si and Peter had come up with a plan to ensure the safety of my dad and stepmum. A plan that Si, unselfishly put his own safety at risk to push through. That my dad was already in a position to protect himself from the sicarios and had STILL allowed me to leave Flo in such a dangerous position.

According to Si. Peter, having knowledge about what kind of work that he'd been doing while in Ibiza, had asked if Ivan Camacho's outfit was one that would have been willing to offer any kind of protection that Peter could pay for. Nothing too big, just two or three men to be around the villa as insurance against any unwanted visitors. Si had asked Camacho if this was something that he was in the market to provide but with the ongoing troubles with the O'Hallorans. He'd told Zico that he couldn't spare any of his men.

When Si had went back to my dad and told him that if it hadn't been for the Scousers then Ivan Camacho would have been willing to help out. 'Well let's go to the O'Hallorans then,' had been my fathers reply. Apparently my dad had heard of Danny and Carl O'Halloran and knew how top level they were. That they were in fact already involved in protection.

Then again, what weren't those Scousers into? Understandably Si wasn't exactly in favour of going looking for the brothers given how his last visit to them had gone but my dad can be ultra persuasive when he puts his mind to it. He'd told Si that it literally would be a life and death situation if he could not get protection for him and Eva from the Colombians, who by that time were already in Spain and on the trail.

Si, ending up as the middle man between my dad and the two brothers in a deal that made the Scouser's an obscene amount of money inside an extremely short amount of time. This, along with promises from my father to hook them up with contacts in South America who would help expand their narcotics enterprise that they had going on in England and Spain.

The "security" coming in handy when, as my dad knew they would and had even been given confirmation by me, the men from Bogota came calling. According to Eva, in the scrambled call she'd made to Si after not getting an answer from the phone that I no longer owned. The hitmen had came into their house with guns and were about to kill both her and Peter only for the Scousers to deal with the South Americans.

According to Si. All he had done had been make the introduction between them all. I certainly hadn't been surprised over the news that Peter had manipulated Si into believing that I should be kept out of the loop over it. My father putting it across to Si that with the Colombians already having been caught sniffing around Space looking for me. The less I knew about everything going on. The more his and Flo's life would be protected.

I couldn't have said that I was unhappy at the news of the two sicario's deaths. That was one major thing less to be worrying about. Peter Duncan had played a blinder there, you had to hand him that. It was the way, when it all started to come out, though that he had went about it. The half truths and down right lies that he told to everyone while receiving fuck all but help in return. The amount of times that he had a chance to step in and save Flo from being executed and didn't. The sly move he had pulled with the disc. The fact that he'd had the Bogota hitmen killed was neither here nor there. They were only killed when *he* needed them taken care of and not because Flo or I needed it to happen.

With him and Eva leaving Ibiza I wasn't even going to now get the chance to have that talk with him and given all of what had happened in Ibiza while him and Eva had been there. I wasn't entirely sure if the two of us would speak again, ever. Knowing just what he was capable of I could've easily went the rest of my life without seeing that face of his. I still owed it to myself though to have one final chat with him and hoped that I'd get the chance, whenever it may come.

Si and and I ended the call with arrangements for coming with Flo and I to Space at night as I launched my way into explaining all of the current events to the impatient looking girl lying on the bed beside me.

By the time I was through explaining to her. There was a definite feel of the nerves that were there between us. The ones that had been present in an elephant in the room kind of way, having entirely lifted. There was a feeling that maybe just maybe we were out of the woods in all kinds of ways.

The threat from Colombia was now gone, that much was so. With my dad having left Ibiza I was free of all the problems that he had brought. Fucking hell, by the next day, Flo would be gone too. Leaving Si and I back on our own again like none of it had even happened. Left there with around a month still left and ready for whatever that unpredictable crazy island wanted to throw at us next.

I'd never have imagined it but when I'd arrived for the summer and soon found myself moaning over the lack of sleep, too much drugs and crazy women. I didn't actually realise just how easy I actually had it. It was probably a good life lesson learned though for next time I'd find myself cursing the world for conspiring against me just because I was left with a sore head through too many Class A drugs and no sleep.

Completely drained by all of the recent day's events. Flo and I spent the afternoon lying in the hotel room smoking Hash and watching the earlier Semi Final from the Euros. The match, before the main event later that evening of England and Germany, between the French and the Czech Republic. Despite the fact that she hated the sport. Flo contently lay cuddling into me, occasionally smoking on her joint and watching along with me.

The referee blew the whistle after one hundred and twenty forgettable minutes of regulation and extra time to signal for penalties with the teams still goalless. Clearly not really having much clue what had been going on in the game and, only after hearing the commentator say that the sides were now heading for a penalty shoot out, Flo sparked into life.

'Ohhhhh penalties! That's the only exciting thing about football,' she said excitedly with a big smile on her face. 'Aye, you probably won't want to see them later on tonight though, babe.' I laughed back at her.

'Ze German's aren't too shabby at them, like.'

Printed in Great Britain
by Amazon